RACING HEARTS

What Reviewers Say About Dena Blake's Work

Where The Light Glows

"I'm still shocked this was Dena Blake's first novel. ...It was fantastic. ...It was written extremely well and more than once I wondered if this was a true account of someone close to the author because it was really raw and realistic. It seemed to flow very naturally and I am truly surprised that this is the authors first novel as it reads like a seasoned writer..."—*Les Reveur*

Unchained Memories

"This story had me cycling between lovely romantic scenes to white-knuckle gripping, on the edge of the seat (or in my case, the bed) scenarios. This story had me rooting for a sequel and I can certainly place my stamp of approval on this novel as a must read book."
—*The Lesbian Review*

"The pace and character development was perfect for such an involved story line, I couldn't help but turn each page. This book has so many wonderful plot twists that you will be in suspense with every chapter that follows."—*Les Reveur*

A Country Girl's Heart

"Dena Blake just goes from strength to strength."—*Les Reveur*

Visit us at www.boldstrokesbooks.com

By the Author

Where the Light Glows

Unchained Memories

A Country Girl's Heart

Racing Hearts

RACING HEARTS

by
Dena Blake

2018

RACING HEARTS

© 2018 By Dena Blake. All Rights Reserved.

ISBN 13: 978-1-63555-251-5

This Trade Paperback Original Is Published By
Bold Strokes Books, Inc.
P.O. Box 249
Valley Falls, NY 12185

First Edition: September 2018

CREDITS
Editor: Shelley Thrasher
Production Design: Susan Ramundo
Cover Design By Jeanine Henning

Acknowledgments

Thanks to the BSB team. It's a long journey from beginning to end, but you all make it seamless. Thank you to Len Barot and Sandy Lowe for being so awesome and giving me the opportunity to share my characters with the world. Seeing them in print will always be a thrill. Thanks to my editor extraordinaire, Shelley Thrasher, for teaching me something new with each book and always making me look so good.

Thanks to my friends Kris, Erin, and Lisa. The constant support you provide is a much needed light at the end of the tunnel. I'm forever grateful you're in my life.

Thanks to Kate for taking this ride with me and loving me through it all. You have my heart. To my kids for being my rocks and supporting me in every way. I will always love you the mostest. To my awesome family for being my biggest fans.

Thanks to Robyn for reading my books from the very beginning.

Last but certainly never least, thank you to all you readers out there. You give me reason to write.

Dedication

For all the NASCAR junkies out there.
The need for speed is strong in this one.

Chapter One

The shrilling screech of metal scraping pavement pierced Sam's head. "Shit! Not again!" She watched the number-thirteen car slam into the barrier and immediately took off toward the pit truck. Racing across the Sonoma Raceway track, she couldn't take her eyes off the crash. No way in hell would she lose her brother today.

"Don't blow!" she shouted, watching twisted metal rip from the mangled machine and fly across the roadway. The first high-speed impact. The car was moving at an incredible speed, and more collisions would come.

The packed stands cleared as the car shot across the track without slowing, smashing into the side barrier. After skidding across the asphalt again after the impact, the car finally stopped. The engine burst into flames—Sam's worst nightmare. Soon the whole car would be engulfed. Her heart hammered and her vision tunneled as she sprang into action, speeding to the mangled race car. Dead or alive, she wouldn't leave Tommy to burn.

Heat radiated through the windshield, the intensity of the blaze unreal. *Please don't die, please don't die.*

She jammed her foot down onto the brake and halted the truck. It bucked as she bolted from it.

Her father's voice screamed through her headset, "Damn it, Samantha, stay back! Let the emergency team get him!"

She searched the track for the fire truck. "Wait? Are you crazy? It's gonna blow." She refused to leave this to someone else. Tommy would be dead before they even got close. She ripped the headset from her head, her scalp stinging as a tangled wad of hair went with it.

Her eyes and nostrils burned as she ran toward the inferno, the scorching heat unbearable. She turned her head down track. The fire crew would never make it in time.

Sam had no choice but to act—*NOW*. She shut her eyes for an instant, steeling herself for what would come. Then, with no more hesitation, she reached through the window, groping for the harness release.

"Fuck!" She hissed a breath through her teeth. The searing hot metal of the buckle blistered her fingertips. Pain shot across her skin, nearly knocking her off her feet. Fumbling through her pockets, she took out a red bandanna, wrapped it around her hand, and reached back into the car. She popped the harness button and yanked the straps from Tommy's unresponsive body. She hauled him through the window with all her strength, and his weight took them both to the ground.

"Stay with me, Tommy. We're halfway there." Sam pulled herself up, dug in with her heels, and dragged him across the asphalt backward. An explosive pop blew her to the ground again. She knew that sound too well. The car would explode any second. Heaving Tommy to one side, she rolled on top of him to shield him from the blast.

Ow! Pain seared through her. She stared at her leg and panicked. *Fire!* She slapped the spreading flames, a useless tactic. Sam tugged at her racing-suit zipper but realized her mistake. Without the added protection, she'd be toast. She couldn't expose herself to the flames.

She fell to her knees and the car exploded again, blowing her to the ground headfirst. Sam raked her hand across her splitting head. Blurry eyed, she tried to see her fingers, barely able to focus. Covered in blood, her hand shook. No hope for them now.

Blinking, she saw the stream of suds spewing from the fire hose. Flames swallowed the foam flying silently through the air before it even touched the car.

She made out black boots in the distance. More firemen. Raising her arm, she shouted, "Over here." But they didn't turn. She shouted again. Still no response. Was her voice working? Only a deafening, high-pitched tone rang in her ears.

Looking over at her brother, Sam stared at his vacant face. She touched his cheek and shivered. It was cold. She was too late. She blinked again, trying to maintain focus. *Forgive me, Tommy.* Her vision faded and everything went black.

❖

A constant beep forced Sam to pull her weighted eyelids apart. The lingering stench of heated pavement slowly dissipated, replaced by an antiseptic smell. The new odor produced an overwhelming feeling of relief.

White walls, window, TV. Too much noise. She turned her head, following the annoying sound. *Heart monitor.* She was in the hospital.

"Where's Tommy?" Her words were muffled.

"Hang on there, little lady." Ray pulled the oxygen mask from her face.

"Tommy? Is he okay?" Her voice didn't sound right. It was low, and rough. Probably from the smoke.

"He's alive," he said, his upbeat tone contradicting his sober expression.

"What's wrong?"

"Nothin'." He still wasn't smiling.

Ray was her best friend—he wouldn't lie to her. Tommy must be alive, but something was definitely wrong.

"Ray, tell me straight. What's going on?"

Ray's eyes skittered anxiously. "His neck is broken."

"Oh my God."

"He's paralyzed."

"Permanently?"

"Not sure. The doc says they have to wait for the swelling to go down. See how bad the nerves were damaged."

Crazy thoughts flew through her mind. *Did I do this? Would Tommy have been okay if I hadn't pulled him out?* Her blood pressure spiked and the machine alarm whined.

"Settle down, Samantha." Her father's thunderous voice shot through her. She hadn't seen him until now. He must have been sitting in the corner chair.

"Where is he, Paddy?"

"A couple doors down." Ray turned slightly as Paddy stood. "Your dad's been up with him most of the night."

"What happened?"

"The crash probably caused the damage, but they can't say for certain." Paddy raked his hand down his red-freckled face. "Why'd you rush in there like that, Samantha? I told you to stay back." His voice rumbled. He wasn't holding his anger very well today.

"The car was on fire, Paddy." She held her tone steady, trying not to provoke him. "It was going to explode."

He grabbed the bed rail, twisting his hands around it. "You should've waited for the rescue crew."

"The fire trucks were nowhere in sight."

"I know you did the best you could, Samantha." His tone softened. "But—"

"But what, Paddy? I got him out of the car." She raised her voice, and his eyes narrowed.

"If you'd waited, he might not be paralyzed." The bed shook as he released the rail.

"I wasn't going to let my brother burn up in that car." The tortured moments in the fire scorched through her again.

"The boy can't walk, Samantha." He turned away muttering. "Force him to live like that for the rest of his life or…"

"Or what, Paddy? Let him die?

He let out a heavy breath. "I'm not sure this was the better choice."

"Tommy would want to live. Paralyzed or not." Sam couldn't believe what she was hearing. Would her father really have let him burn to death?

"One thing's for sure. He'll never be able to race again."

"That's an awful thing to say." She bolted up in the bed. Her backside burned, a rush of heat flooded her, and she thought she might throw up.

"Maybe we should come back later." Ray slipped something long and round into her hand. "The nurse said to push this button when the pain gets too much. It's morphine."

She sank back against the bed and immediately pushed it multiple times. "When can I go back to work?"

"Let's not worry about that," her father said. "Ray can handle things for now."

"How's the car?"

"Totaled. We need a new one."

"I have to get it ready." She tried to swing her legs to the side of the bed but couldn't. They felt like bricks.

"You're going to stay right here for the next few days," Paddy said.

"And Tommy?" Her words slurred. The medication was kicking in.

"I'm afraid he'll have a much longer stay." She saw the disappointment in Paddy's face. Had she done the wrong thing? Was it her fault Tommy was paralyzed? At the time she was so sure she was doing what had to be done.

Her mind faded into a haze, her eyelids heavy again.

The warmth was gone. She reached for the blanket. No blanket. She forced her eyes open. Large nurse, hovering above.

"Time to get you up and out of bed." The nurse took Sam's hands, gently pulling her into a sitting position. "Can you swing those legs off the bed for me?"

Nodding, Sam took in a deep breath and searched the bed for the morphine button to squelch the pain. No button. She followed the tube in her arm to the saline hanging from the pole. *No morphine.*

The irritating beep was gone, but Sam was still on edge. "What time is it?" She hauled her legs to the side, found them much lighter now.

"It's almost nine. You slept well last night."

After wrapping a light cotton robe around Sam's shoulders, the nurse prompted her to lift her dangling feet before sliding a pair of slippers on them.

"Can I see my brother?"

"I'm not sure that's a good idea." The nurse transferred the IV bag from the bed to a portable IV pole.

"Please. I need to see him." A young woman dressed in purple scrubs and a white lab coat slid the glass door aside and entered the room. Sam wasn't sure who she was, but this was overkill. "I can get out of bed myself."

"Go for it." The woman raised her eyebrows. "I'd *like* to see what you can do."

Sam eyeballed the nurse. "Nice attitude."

"This is Jade Barnes, our resident physical therapist."

Sam took a double take. The woman didn't look old enough to be out of high school.

"She wants to see her brother," the nurse said.

Feeling Jade's gaze rake across her, Sam shot her a demanding stare.

Jade gave her a subtle smile. "Maybe for just a minute."

Sam stretched her legs to the floor, and pain shot up her backside. Fighting to catch her breath, she stumbled forward, grabbing the IV pole.

"Take it easy." The nurse held her steady. "You need to do things a little slower for a while."

She sucked in a deep breath, letting it shudder out. "Which way?"

"I'll take you." Jade tried to grasp her arm, but Sam flinched.

"I don't need your help." As she pulled herself upright with the IV pole, her stomach roiled and lodged in her throat. "Just tell me where he is."

"Out the door and to the right." Jade offered her arm to steady her.

Sam ignored it, leaning on the IV pole instead.

"I heard you were a tough one."

Sam glared at her.

"It takes a lot of courage to pull someone out of a burning car." Jade's tone softened, the admiration in her voice sounding sincere.

"He's my brother."

"You saved his life, you know?"

"I paralyzed him."

"No, you didn't." Jade stepped in front of her. "His neck was broken in the crash."

"But I made it worse."

"You couldn't have done anything to prevent it."

"Do you know that for sure?"

"Ninety-nine percent certain," Jade said, moving to her side, continuing down the hallway.

Sam almost believed her. There was still that one percent.

Jade stopped before they reached the door. "You need to know a couple things before you go in."

"I'm all ears." Sam propped her shoulder against the wall for support. Walking wasn't as easy as she'd thought it would be.

"He's wearing what we call a halo vest. It's a little daunting at first sight, but it's not a permanent fixture. It's only there to keep him immobile."

"That's all you can do for him?"

"The only other option was to do surgery right away and fuse the broken bones with metal pins, wires, and bone grafts. He was in pretty bad shape when he came in. The doctor didn't want to risk surgery."

It was more serious than Sam thought. Her brother would probably never walk again.

"We're hoping he'll regain some upper-body movement by letting some of the nerves grow back together. In order to do that he has to stay perfectly still. Understood?" She raised her eyebrows, waiting for a response.

"Understood."

Rounding the corner, Sam saw her semi-conscious brother. No burns or scrapes. He appeared to be perfectly normal except for the rigid frame locked around his head, neck, and chest. Sharp spikes twisted through his scalp into his skull. It had to be painful.

"I sure did it this time, didn't I, Sammy?" Reality dampened her brother's usual playful tone. "I guess Lucky Thirteen's good fortune ran out."

She couldn't stop the tears. "I'm so sorry, Tommy."

"I'll be okay, sis." He gave her a loving smile. "But from now on, you're gonna have to do the driving."

"No driving for at least a month," Jade spouted, following Sam in with the rolling IV pole.

"Who are you, my mother?" Tommy asked, grinning.

"Worse. I'm your physical therapist." She gave him a don't-mess-with-me look before glancing over at Sam. "Are you okay?"

Sam nodded.

Without hesitation, Jade grabbed Sam's hand and placed it on the bed railing. "I'll be right back. You two visit for a few minutes."

"I'll be counting every second." Tommy shot her a wink.

"Hold that thought." Heading to the door, Jade smiled. "After a few days of therapy, you'll never want to see me again."

"Look at you. Flat on your back and still flirting." Sam took his hand and squeezed it. He didn't squeeze back. He couldn't feel her. She swallowed hard, fighting back the tears.

"What can I say? The girls love me."

"Has Erica been in to see you?" Sam didn't like his soon-to-be other half. She'd swooped in six months ago and dug her claws in deep. Now Sam was afraid Tommy would realize the woman was made of pure greed.

"She stopped by this morning. Didn't stay long."

"Not taking it well?" Pain shot through her leg. Sam let Tommy's hand drop and gripped the bed rail.

"Not taking it at all."

"I don't know what to say, Tommy." That wasn't true. For starters, she could say *I told you so*. The woman was a gold-digging bitch.

"You don't have to say anything. I'm not stupid, Sammy. I knew what kind of woman she was when we met." He gave her a wicked smile. "We both got what we wanted."

"Life goes on, I suppose."

"It sure does. Don't blink, or you might miss it." He clamped his lips together into a half-hearted smile. "Besides, I've got this pretty little physical therapist to spend my time with now."

Jade walked back into the room shaking her head. "You might not feel the same about me next week."

Sam took a good look at her. Even without heels, Sam towered over the woman. Considering Sam's five-foot-nine frame, that wasn't unusual. Jade brushed back her dark, shoulder-length hair, and Sam caught a glimpse of a small heart-shaped tattoo on her neck just behind her multi-pierced ear.

"You ready to go back to your room?"

"Yeah. My leg's hurting a little." That was a lie. The pain was throbbing up and down her entire backside. She could barely stand.

"Just a little?"

Grabbing hold of the IV pole, Sam clenched her jaw. "That's what I said."

When they reached the doorway, Jade stepped in front of her and held eye contact. "I'm your therapist too. You need to be truthful with me."

"It hurts like hell. Is that what you want to hear?" she whispered, trying not to let Tommy overhear. "Can you get me a wheelchair?"

"Coming right up." Jade slipped down the hall and came racing back with one. "I'll order something for the pain as soon as we get you back into bed."

"Why'd you take me off that machine?" Sam winced, lowering herself into the seat.

"I don't want you to be in pain, but you need to be coherent. We have a lot of work ahead of us if you want to get out of here sooner rather than later."

"The sooner the better."

On their way out the door, Jade glanced over her shoulder at Tommy. "After I take care of your sister, I'll be back to see you."

"That sounds promising."

Sam watched her cock her head as though she was going to give him a stinging retort, but instead she clamped her mouth shut.

"Your brother's some kind of Romeo, huh?"

"Take it easy on him. I think he lost his fiancée this morning."

"The blonde?"

Sam nodded.

"I'll save my banter for later in the week when he's just starting to hate me." She rounded the corner into the room. "So what do you think happened with the car? Steering-column failure?"

Sam glared up at her. That was an odd question coming from a therapist.

"I'm a fan. Cars are a hobby of mine."

She should have guessed. Jade was a track junkie gone straight. "I won't know until I get out of here and take a look at the car."

"I bet it was the steering column. It probably locked up."

"You said that, not me."

"You won't even hazard a guess?"

"That would be unprofessional."

"Come on. That's what you're going to check first, right?"

Sam narrowed her eyes. "You should really keep your mouth shut. Rumors get started that way."

Jade tried to help her into bed. Sam waved her off, slapping her hand accidentally. "Sorry. It's easier if I do it myself." After climbing in, she closed her eyes momentarily, trying to stifle the pain. "Can you get me that pain medication now?"

"Sure. Be right back."

The woman was asking questions more like a racing official than a physical therapist. She was trying to make Sam admit something she didn't know, but to admit something was mechanically wrong with the car would be professional suicide. She'd be blocked for the rest of her career. She would never admit anything like that to anyone, *under any circumstances*.

Chapter Two

Three months to the day after the accident, the halo vest Tommy had endured was finally removed, and he was being released from the hospital. It was a bittersweet moment for Sam. He'd regained feeling in his upper body, but the doctors told him his spinal-cord injury was permanent. He would never walk again.

Three months seemed like a lifetime. Three days of this place had been enough for Sam. After her release, she couldn't wait to get back to work. If nothing else, it kept her mind off Tommy.

Sam checked her watch. They weren't letting him go for a few more hours, but she wanted to watch his therapy session and talk to Jade before they left. As she approached Tommy's room, Sam heard laughter. Poking her head inside, she spotted Jade sitting on the foot of the bed, seeming pretty cozy with him.

"Hey, Sammy. You're early."

"I thought you might want some company, but it looks like you have plenty." The words came out harsher than she'd meant them.

"We were just discussing our mutual love for racing."

"I'm sure you were." Sam watched Jade slide her hand down Tommy's leg to his foot, and it gave her an uneasy feeling. It was Jade's job, and he couldn't feel it, but the movement seemed very intimate.

"Did you hear the good news?" Tommy asked.

"What news?"

"Jade's agreed to stay on as my personal therapist." He and Jade shared a warm smile, and Sam suddenly felt like an outsider.

She pinned Jade with her stare. "What about your work here?"

"Your brother convinced me to take a hiatus." After giving Tommy's toes a light squeeze, she pulled the blanket over his legs and slid off the bed. "I haven't seen you in a while."

"My schedule's a little off. I've been busy getting the new car ready."

Tommy's eyes lit up. "I can't wait to see it."

"I can take you by today, if you're up for it."

"I'd love it." He shifted his gaze to Jade. "You wanna come?"

"Sure." She glanced from Tommy to Sam. "If Sam doesn't mind."

"No. Of course not." A total lie. She'd been doing that a lot lately, and it was getting easier every day.

"How are your burns? Do you need them checked?" Jade pulled up the back of Sam's shirt before she could stop her.

"Thanks. I've got it." She spun around, pulling the fabric from Jade's hand. "I've gotten pretty good at taking care of them these days." Sam evaded her gaze.

She hated being mean to this woman, but she couldn't stop herself. She'd helped Sam with her burns and had done wonders with her brother's attitude. Something was suspicious about her. She was always asking questions, which made Sam uncomfortable.

"No problem. I'm spending most of my day with your brother anyway. I figured as long as you were coming to see him, I could take an hour out to dress your burns."

Sam could've asked her sister. But she hadn't seen her since the first day she was in the hospital. Faith's social calendar was much too busy to expect anything from her. She wouldn't be comfortable with Paddy, and Brad, her on-and-off again fiancé, would never have been able to stomach it.

"That's so sweet of you." Tommy didn't take his eyes off Jade. "Isn't it, Sammy?" She knew what that gleam flitting in her brother's eye meant. Another reason she didn't like Jade.

"Yeah." She headed for the door. "Jade, can I talk to you in the hall for a minute?"

"Sure." Jade patted Tommy on the leg. "I'll be right back, sweetie."

Sweetie? She took Jade's arm, rushing her into the hallway. "I thought I told you to be careful with him."

Jade shrugged. "What? We're friends. That's all."

"That's not what he thinks, and you know it."

Jade peeked through the door at Tommy and smiled. He was still watching her. "Would that be so bad?"

"You're no different than Erica."

"Except for one thing." Jade's smile faded into a scowl. "I'm still here."

"What happens when his therapy is done?" Sam's voice rose. "Are you going to follow him from track to track? Because you know he's not going to give it up. Whether he can drive or not, racing is his life. His place is with me. I'll take care of him."

"Can you?" Jade's brows rose in the same lofty fashion they had when Sam first met her. "His needs are different now. He requires twenty-four-seven care."

Sam didn't respond. She truly didn't know if she could tend to him.

"I didn't think so. I can give him that and possibly make him happy too."

"What's in it for you?"

"There's no prize here. I really like him. Does there have to be something more?"

"And when you get tired of his needs? What's going to happen then?" Sam didn't give her a chance to answer. "I'll tell you what's going to happen. You'll bolt, and I'll be left to pick up the pieces."

Jade took in a deep breath. "I don't know what's going to happen between us down the line. But good or bad, don't you think you owe it to Tommy to let him find out for himself?"

As Jade started toward Tommy's room, Sam grabbed her arm and swung her back around. She wasn't done yet. "So help me God, if you break his heart." She dug her fingers deep into Jade's arm.

"Believe me. I need him as much as he needs me." She tugged out of her grasp. "Tell him I'll be back in a few minutes." She headed behind the nurses' station and out of sight.

Sam didn't know what Jade meant by that, but her clouded eyes gave her away. She *did* need him for some reason.

❖

"You want me to do what?" Drew laughed at Captain Jacobs's request.

"I want you to back up Barnes at Sonoma Raceway." He was serious.

"Barnes doesn't want me for backup." Since the incident last year, no one wanted to partner with Drew. That was just as well. She didn't intend to get attached again.

"She'll just have to deal with it."

"I'm not a homicide detective. I want back in Narcotics."

"You think anybody there wants to work with you? You've alienated anyone who's tried to get close."

"I work better alone." The captain was right. She'd burned too many bridges.

"I need someone with racing experience." He took in a deep breath. "You're all I've got right now." Ignoring Drew's protest, the captain pulled a file and a flash drive from his drawer. Slapping it onto the desk he said, "No more arguments. As of now you're a driver for Freemont Oil."

Deciding that working Homicide was better than working paper behind a desk, Drew stuffed the flash drive into the pocket of her leather bomber jacket before picking up the file and thumbing through it.

"But Barnes is with Kelleher Motorsports."

"Putting you directly in would look suspicious. You're a smart girl, Thompson." He gave her a smirk. "I'm sure you can find a way."

After dropping the file onto the corner of the desk, Drew jammed her fingers into her jean pockets and paced the office. The captain knew she couldn't resist a challenge.

"How deep is she?"

"Haven't heard from her in weeks."

"She okay?"

"I don't know." The captain's forehead creased when he glanced up. "Like I said, she hasn't checked in."

"Is she staying at the motel by the raceway?"

"Supposed to be. The whole race team is there."

"I'll check it out and let you know what's going on in a few days."

Drew must have watched the recording fifty times and couldn't figure out who would risk their own life to pull an unconscious Tommy Kelleher out of that flaming race car. After she slapped the laptop closed, she rolled the question over and over in her mind.

Accidents in racing weren't unusual, but too many in a row on the same race team sent up a red neon flag. Flopping back onto the bed, Drew wondered how she'd gotten stuck here, in this low-budget hotel, working this dead-end case. She traced the small cracks across the white, plastered ceiling with her gaze. *What a dive.*

Why Captain Jacobs had given her the case, she didn't know. She guessed he'd thrown her a bone to make up for the bullet she'd taken in Narcotics. Something to take her mind off the event that still plagued her. Like that could ever happen. The reoccurring ache radiating in her shoulder would never let her forget.

A year of undercover work and the whole drug case had been blown in an instant. Her testimony had put the right people away, but her best friend and partner had been killed. The doctor said the post-traumatic-stress-disorder episodes she dealt with might fade eventually, but he couldn't guarantee it. The more she thought about it, the more her head hurt.

She opened her suitcase, took out a bottle of ibuprofen, and popped off the top. After shaking a few out into her hand, she slapped them into her mouth and washed them down with a fresh beer.

"New case, clean slate," she told herself, dropping the bottle back into the bag and flipping it closed.

She'd already scoped out the common areas and met a few of the drivers earlier. That had been easy. Drew knew her way around the track from the driver's seat. Getting in close with the mechanics wouldn't be so simple. Drew loved to race but hadn't paid much attention to the workings of an engine. This dude would have access to the garage.

Taking another swig of lukewarm beer, she grimaced and set it on the table. She'd have to pick up a cooler and a bag of ice tomorrow. Now it was time to hit the bar down the road. First introduction, Slick, crew chief for Kelleher Motorsports, and the best mechanic on the circuit.

❖

Most of the drivers made it a habit to hit the nearest bar after a long day at the track. The one closest to Sonoma Raceway was nicer than most and included a restaurant as well. In addition, it was just down the road from the motel most popular with the drivers and their crews.

Samantha Kelleher, aka Slick, had just pushed back her plate from dinner at the bar and was mid-sentence when the tall, dark-haired woman slipped in between her and Ray.

"Excuse me, sweetheart. Can I steal Slick away from you for a minute?" She motioned to the bartender for two shots of Jack Daniels.

Sweetheart! Boy, this chick has balls. Sam thumped her fingers on the polished wood finish, waiting for the stranger to turn and offer her one of the shots. She would politely refuse, of course. Even if the woman had forgotten her manners, Sam always remembered hers. Her father insisted on it. When the woman slid the shot over to Ray, Sam realized her mistake. *Big* mistake.

Undeniably tempted, Sam leaned up against the brass-metal-framed oak bar and circled her finger around the rim of her glass. The thought of pouring her drink over the brunette's head crossed her mind, and Sam seriously considered it. Besides the mistaken identity, she'd hardly given her a look, let alone an appropriate apology for the interruption.

Tossing the impulse aside, Sam raised the glass to her lips and let her gaze trip across the back of the woman's neck. The distinct white line left just below her dark-caramel hair made Sam shiver. She was a sucker for a clean-cut neckline.

"I hear you're a pretty good mechanic," the brunette said before downing her shot.

This chick is a driver. Even with her back to Sam, she heard the arrogance in her voice.

She shifted to see past Ms. Badmanners and gave Ray a wink. He grinned. Her old friend Ray knew when she was peeved. Right now, he was acutely aware of how close this jackass had come to being soaked.

"I think I can probably say that old Slick here is a great mechanic." Ray stared over the woman's shoulder at Sam and tipped his beer. "What can I do for you?"

"I need a little help with my engine." She offered Ray her hand. "Drew Thompson. I drive for Freemont Oil."

Setting his beer on the bar, Ray ignored her hand and picked up the shot. "Freemont, huh?" He hesitated until Sam nodded, prompting him to respond. "They've got a good rep. What's wrong with *your* crew chief?"

"Let's just say he and I don't see eye to eye."

"Where's it at?" Ray scratched his head, waiting again for a sign from Sam.

"The number-three garage."

Sam gnawed on her bottom lip for a minute before giving Ray another nod. The woman was an arrogant ass, but considering the best drivers often were, she'd captured Sam's interest.

"I'll come by and check it out in the morning."

"Thanks. I'd appreciate it." She gave Ray a pat on the shoulder and headed to the door.

Sam watched her as she crossed the room. Broad shoulders, nice ass, and a bad-girl swagger. It was probably a good thing the woman had ignored her, or *Sam* might be the one making the big mistake tonight.

Sam threw the door open and crossed the room quickly. After sliding onto the bar stool, she ordered a Crown and water and pressed her fingers to her forehead. She'd already popped enough ibuprofen to burn a hole in her stomach, but the incessant pounding in her head was still going strong. Today had been ridiculously long in the garage, and her argument with Brad this evening had thrown her day into the "sucked" category. Every time she saw him lately, their conversations morphed into raging battles. All the signs were there. He was having another affair.

The man had done everything in his power to get out of the bar early tonight and didn't ask her to come along. Brad was a master of seduction, but tonight it wouldn't be Sam in his bed. Maybe that was for the best, seeing as how she'd started the affair with him just to spite her father. Each passing day, they were drifting further apart. It would be more difficult to bridge the gap this time.

Working nonstop on the new car wasn't helping the situation. Not having Tommy around the last few months had turned out to be harder than she'd thought, and now that he was back, he was more of a distraction than a help.

Sam wanted to hit the circuit hard this year. She still had a lot of work to do before she would be satisfied with the car's performance. They had only two weeks left before the Dodge/Save Mart 350 at Sonoma Raceway, a road course touted as one of the most difficult on the circuit. The corners made even the most experienced drivers look like amateurs. Luckily, Sam had the advantage. Sonoma was her home track, so she knew it inside and out. This was one race she wanted to win, and to make that happen, her car had to be in tip-top condition.

Hearing a familiar voice, Sam glanced to the end of the bar, where she caught a peripheral glimpse of Drew Thompson, the arrogant driver who'd interrupted her conversation with Ray earlier. Sam should've given her a piece of her mind right then and there, but as her sister always pointed out, Sam had a major personality flaw. She wasn't good at being the bitch.

Veering her gaze back to the mirrors mounted behind the bar, she watched the woman's reflection as she spoke. Suddenly her voice deepened and she broke into laughter. Her lips spread into a crooked grin, revealing one front tooth overlapping the other just enough to make her undeniably sexy. *Damn! She caught me looking.* Sam let her gaze drop to the liquor bottles lining the shelf at the bottom of the mirrors and held it there. Considering the smile along with her square jaw, Sam was sure Drew wasn't turned away often. Nevertheless,

Sam continued to stare straight ahead, reciting each brand of liquor in her head as she studied the labels. Just how long would it take Drew to get the message? *Not interested!*

❖

As soon as Drew Thompson saw the woman parade into the room, her mind went to work branding her as high-maintenance. With fiery-red curls and a seductive stride, this woman oozed sensuality and confidence. She really didn't have the time or energy for any of that right now. But then again, she never could resist a challenge.

It took only a few minutes to catch the redhead watching her, so maybe it was worth a try. Sliding onto the bar stool next to her, Drew donned her sexiest smile and waited for the woman to turn her way. Judging by her reaction, or more specifically lack thereof, it seemed as though she was going to ignore her. If the woman thought she could get away with that, she had another think coming.

Reaching for the bowl of nuts, Drew purposely clipped the top of her glass and splattered her drink across the bar in front of them.

"Hey!" The redhead's arms flew up.

Drew grabbed a bar towel and sopped up the liquid. "Sorry about that. How 'bout I buy you a drink to make up for the mess?"

"Already have one, thanks." The woman raised her glass and then set it back down onto the bar in front of her.

Drew noticed the ring when she saw the woman's gaze fix on her finger. Even in the dim lighting, the diamond sparkled with her every move. In one swift motion, she flipped the jewel around to the inside of her finger, then picked up her drink and took a large gulp.

Noting the attitude and the ring, Drew stayed put, thinking she might get something out of this after all. She'd enjoyed benefiting from an angry, unhappy lady once or twice before.

"Waiting for someone?" she asked.

"No," the woman said, still not giving Drew her complete attention.

"It isn't often I see a pretty lady sitting alone at the bar," she said, observing how beautiful she was even with the sour disposition.

The redhead turned and narrowed her eyes. "Probably because there's always some Casanova around who can't stand to leave a woman alone."

"Ouch." She gave her a wounded pout and slid back off the stool.

"Wait." She touched her arm lightly. "I shouldn't have said that. I'm sorry."

Drew stopped, letting the warmth of her hand linger on her skin. She actually sounded sincere. Maybe she wasn't your average high-maintenance woman.

The woman blew out a breath. "I've had a really rough day, and I'm taking it out on you."

Drew dipped her chin in acknowledgment. "Apology accepted."

"Please, don't leave on my account." She gave her a soft smile. "I'll try to be more pleasant."

"Want to talk about it?"

"No. Not really." She turned, and Drew followed her gaze across the room to the dance floor, where the crowd had thinned measurably in the last few hours.

"Would you like to dance?"

Her eyes flashed back to Drew's, and the pensive emerald-green pools penetrated her instantly. She could see this was a woman who would surely leave a girl knowing she'd been kissed. Drew took her hand and led her across the room. Sensing no boundaries, Drew held her firmly against her and floated her around the dance floor. Feeling her hands cling to her shoulders, Drew wasn't surprised when they traveled to the back of her neck and her mouth slowly made its way to hers, softly touching, baiting, searching for some sort of comfort, she imagined. The kiss deepened, and Drew let her hand slide down the woman's sides, skimming her breasts with her thumbs, making it clear the interest was mutual.

Drew pulled back slightly, expecting a well-earned slap across the face. Instead she caught the come-and-get-me glimmer in the woman's eyes.

"Do you have a room?" she whispered.

"I'll meet you at the door." Drew turned to the bar and tossed a twenty across it. "Mine and the lady's."

Drew was in paradise as she indulged in the sweet taste and the simmering scent of the woman beneath her. Her flat belly yielded under her hot, pressing mouth, and the subtle resonance of moans spurred her on full force until the moans increasingly resembled cries of pain rather than pleasure. Drew pushed up onto her elbows and hovered, watching tears roll from the eyes of the half-naked woman on the bed. She couldn't even look at Drew. *Just my luck.* She let out a heavy breath and rolled to her side. Drew might be a little lacking in the morals department, but she certainly couldn't continue now. Helping an irresistibly hot body get back at her partner was one thing, but taking advantage of a distraught, weeping woman wasn't her style.

"Why can't this be as easy for me as it is for him?" Her sultry voice dropped to a faint whisper.

Drew took her hand and fingered the diamond ring. "Apparently you're a woman with a conscience."

"I shouldn't be here." She popped up, found her shirt, and jammed her arms into the sleeves.

"Maybe not, but you can't leave like this."

"I'm so sorry." Dropping back onto the bed, she clenched her arms across her chest and sobbed quietly.

"It's okay." Drew took the blanket from the bottom of the bed and covered them both. The little lady didn't know what she was missing. Drew considered herself, among other things, the best lover on the California Highway Patrol. Of course most of the others were assholes, and that was kind of a given when it came to satisfying a woman.

Encircling her waist with her arm, Drew pulled her close, then closed her eyes and focused on the case she was working instead of the soft, beautiful redhead lying in her arms.

CHAPTER THREE

Awakened by the small stream of sunlight bleeding through the curtains, Sam rolled over and found herself staring at the handsome stranger's face. Rugged and tanned, it had a definite masculine aura. She had an average nose, but it pulled to the left as though it had been broken once or twice. Expressionless now, the woman seemed perfectly content as she slept. From Sam's first impression at the bar, she would've never guessed her to be so forgiving.

Drew's hands had been working the buttons quickly, and Sam had let her blouse fall to the floor. In the heated frenzy, she'd quickly forgotten about the man whom she'd given up so much of herself to support. After tumbling together onto the bed, the handsome stranger had only hesitated long enough to pull the shirt over her head before letting her mouth trail back up Sam's neck to her lips. Her fingers had pushed the black silken straps from her shoulders, and her breath had caught at the thought of this strong, sexy woman wanting her.

Drew had slowly, methodically removed Sam's bra, and when she brushed her thumb across Sam's nipple, the sudden sensation had made her shiver. With no time to recover, the intensity had reversed, and heat had seared through her. Drew's mouth had trickled like a sweltering summer rain across her breast. She'd shuddered and leveraged herself to meet Drew's lips. Then she'd closed her eyes, and Brad's face flew through her mind. At that point, she'd cursed herself and gone limp onto the bed.

She hadn't known what else to say last night. The poor woman had to have whiplash. Sam had put the pedal to the metal, topping out her speedometer, and then without any warning, she'd slammed on the brakes. Closing her eyes and taking in a deep breath, she felt an odd, comforting scent fill her head. She ran her fingertips across Drew's chin as she remembered the feel of its smooth texture trailing across her skin. Then her lips, umm…soft, sensual lips streaming down her body.

Drew shifted slightly, and Sam snapped her eyes open. In the slight glow of sunlight, Sam watched her, waiting for some sign of consciousness. When she saw none, she swept the room with her gaze—clothes hanging out the side of a suitcase, an empty pizza box in the trash, and half a six-pack of beer on the table. Nothing personal here. She was no different from Brad. When the event was over, this woman would be gone with the race.

Sam felt empty and alone. She hadn't meant to drift off to sleep last night. Since her brother's accident, she hadn't been able to sleep for more than a few hours at a time. But she'd been here all night, feeling safe and somehow comforted by a woman she barely knew, a perfect stranger who had more compassion for her than her own family did. She had to get out of there. Now. Sliding out of the bed, she grabbed her shoes and slipped out the door.

Sam peeked around the corner and sprinted up the stairway. Luckily her benevolent stranger's room was on the opposite side of the hotel from her own. She'd already made a fool of herself once this morning and didn't want any messy confrontations with Brad. She thought she'd had it made, but halfway up the steps, she was startled from behind.

"Late night, huh?" Jade stood at the foot of the stairs, towel in hand, wearing a bikini and flip-flops.

"Actually, I was just going out for coffee." Dropping one shoe, Sam turned around abruptly. "Lost my shoe on the step." She picked it up and gave Jade an innocent smile. Slipping them both on, Sam hoped Jade hadn't picked up on her feeble attempt at deception. From the smile Jade gave her, she probably had.

Jade remained at the bottom of the stairs assessing Sam's appearance. Sam followed her gaze and hoped she hadn't taken note of what she'd worn last night.

Tight black pants, red silk blouse, uh-oh, she's staring. Sam's eyes darted to her blouse. Something was funny about the buttons.

Jade laughed loudly and Sam stiffened. "What?"

"Your shirt's on inside out."

Sam glanced down quickly, mortified to see she was right. Closing her eyes, she brushed the unruly curls from her face and sank onto the steps. She was in such a hurry to get out of there this morning, she hadn't bothered to check. *Damn!* She'd tried so hard to be careful, and now she'd been caught.

Jade took a few steps up, dropped her towel next to Sam, and sat down. "Don't worry. I won't tell anyone."

Sam let her head sink into her hands. "That would be a surprise."

"Why do you say that?"

"After the way I've treated you?" Sam said, raising her voice slightly.

"True. You haven't been very nice."

Sam tightened her lips and shook her head. *Haven't been very nice. That's a fucking understatement.* Since the day Jade had signed on as Tommy's physical therapist, Sam had made her life more difficult than finding a chameleon in a bag of Skittles.

"How are your burns?"

"They're fine."

"No problems with cracking skin?"

"I've been using the ointment you gave me." Sam felt really bad now. Jade had cleaned and debrided her burns daily for three weeks after the accident, and Sam still couldn't bring herself to like her. She supposed it was an unconscious effort to spare her brother another heartbreak.

After the accident, Tommy had been at his lowest. He not only had to deal with being paralyzed, but his fiancée had dumped him. Then, here came this black-haired, tattoo-ridden therapist swooping in to take advantage of him. Sam just knew the woman had piercings in places that would make her squirm. When Sam saw Jade getting close to her brother, she threw up all the roadblocks, but he fell for her anyway.

Jade caught Sam's evading eyes. "Tell you what. You promise to be a little nicer, and my lips are sealed."

Sam drew her brows together. "That's it?"

Jade shrugged. "That's it."

Sam heard a door shut upstairs and spotted Brad. Dressed in his usual jogging shorts and T-shirt, he was heading out for his morning run. She pressed herself flat against the steps and cursed.

Jade motioned down the steps. "Go. I'll take care of him."

Sam rushed down and ducked just out of sight under the stairs.

"You're up early," Brad said, starting down the steps.

"I'm going for a swim." Jade walked toward the pool, swinging her hips lazily. "You want to join me?" Flipping the towel over her shoulder, she glanced back. Sam knew the miserable cad's eyes were sufficiently glued to Jade's ass. In about five seconds, he would be in the pool with her, and Sam would have the green light to head up the stairs to her room.

Drew yanked open the side door to the garage, and a burst of cool air coated her face. Letting her eyes adjust to the lowered lighting, she appreciated the brief chilly sensation as the air mingled with the moisture on the back of her neck. She'd definitely needed a break from the scorching Northern California heat. She'd hoped to lower her body temperature a degree or two but saw no relief in sight from the unusual heat wave cursing the rolling hills of Sonoma County this summer.

After slipping inside, she swiped her sleeve across her forehead and scanned the huge, round-topped, hollow building. The earsplitting noise of a screaming guitar reverberated through the air, but no one appeared to be in the number-seven garage.

The metal door clanged against the frame as it swung closed, and the dank, musty odor made her mind scatter. She stopped, trying to make sense of it, but as usual the memory of her injury vanished as quickly as it came. Shrugging it off, she rounded the cherry-red, number-fifteen car, almost tripping over the steel-toed work boots sticking out from beneath it.

"Hey, Slick. I thought you were gonna come by and check out my car this morning?" She watched as a gloved hand reached out for the socket wrench lying on the concrete and pulled it back under the car.

Drew scanned the garage for the radio but couldn't locate it. She'd have to wait until the music broke to get his attention. She knelt down and picked up the open-end tool left close to where the socket wrench had been. Soon after, the hand reached out again and skimmed the floor, searching for it.

The music stopped, and the DJ's voice rang out. "You're listening to ninety-six point nine, San Francisco's number-one classic rock station."

Drew took the opportunity to break in. "You and I need to talk." She tapped the steel shaft of the wrench on the concrete.

The hand turned palm up, as if waiting patiently for it. She dropped it into the glove. Without flinching, the fingers twined around it before disappearing back under the engine compartment. After a few minutes of ratchet clinks, the person under the car slid out.

Drew shook her head and smiled as she stared at the grease-laden woman sprawled out on the roller board in front of her. With her red curls now neatly confined by a yellow bandanna, she was quite a vision. As she rolled off the board, Drew caught the gotcha smile she threw her and followed her to the refrigerator. She was definitely going to have her hands full with this one.

After lowering the volume on the radio, the fiery redhead took out a bottle of water, unscrewed the top, and flipped it into the recycle bin.

"And so we meet again," Sam said, locking her gaze.

"I didn't know you were a mechanic."

"Technician." She took a swig from the bottle before hiking herself up onto the workbench. Drew didn't like Sam in this position. It gave her the advantage of appearing just a little bit taller.

"What can I do for you, Ms...Thompson, is it?" Sam grabbed the edge of the bench and leaned forward, giving Drew a straight shot down her flannel shirt. "I don't think we've been properly introduced."

"You'd be correct." Drew took in the view before letting her gaze skitter up across her pouty lips and tiny nose to find the emerald-green eyes she'd already become intimately acquainted with the night before. "I'm thinkin' by now, maybe I should at least know your name."

"I'm Sam." She didn't offer Drew her hand. "For someone I don't know, I'm sure havin' trouble shakin' you." Bringing the bottle of water to her lips, she closed her eyes and took a long, slow gulp.

Drew put her hands on Sam's thighs and let her thumbs drag across the inside of her knees. She watched Sam's eyes dilate, and Drew tingled unexpectedly. *Damn, she's hot.* What exactly had she come here for? Drew shook her head. Time to back up now. "I'm looking for Slick."

She raised her hand in the air. "Also me." She reached for a clean shop towel, dribbled water across it, and blotted her face and neck. "Most people call me Sam."

"Wait a minute." Drew scratched her head. "The guy last night at the bar, who was that?"

"That was Ray."

"But he—"

"No, he didn't." Sam shook her head. "You made an assumption."

"My mistake." Drew let out a soft chuckle before resting her hands on Sam's knees and moving closer. "I didn't realize a mechanic..." Seeing the glare in Sam's eyes, she said, "I'm sorry, technician, could be so...engaging."

Sam quickly moved past her. "Your engine's gone."

"What do you mean gone?"

"I mean irreparable. Dead. Demolished."

"But it was just makin' a little noise."

"A little noise." Sam choked out a laugh. "I checked it this morning. It sounds like an old locomotive."

Drew raised her eyebrows. "But you can fix it, right?"

Sam frowned. "You threw a rod. Then you drove it around the track. The inside of your engine is spaghetti now."

"Damn!" Drew raked her hand across the back of her neck. The car was already dead before Drew got there, but she needed Sam to think she'd done it.

"The car talks to you. Listen more carefully next time." Sam picked up the wrench and pulled the socket off. "That is, if you can find someone to give you a next time."

"What the hell am I supposed to do now?"

"I suggest you find yourself a sponsor who can afford your sloppy driving habits." The drawer whirred as she slid it out, dropped the tools into their slots, and slid it closed again.

The side door swung open, and Brad strutted across the garage.

"Hey, babe." He slipped his arm around Sam, tugged her close, and kissed her hard on the mouth. "I waited up for you last night. Where'd you go?" His voice was low and demanding.

Sam glanced at Drew momentarily. "I stayed with my sister." She arched her back.

Drew watched as his grip seemed to tighten, suffocating her as though she were trapped in a hydraulic vise. He stared at her for a minute and then released her. "How is little sis?"

Her gaze darted back to Drew before she returned to the tools. "Ask her yourself. She should be here this afternoon."

"She's coming out today?"

"Yep. Said she wanted to check out the cars," Sam said, and Drew wondered if that was a lie as well.

"Good. I haven't seen her in a while." Brad turned to Drew as though he'd just noticed her. "Have we met before?"

"Drew Thompson. I drive for Freemont Oil."

Brad pressed a finger to his mouth. "Are you driving this race?"

"No." Sam smirked. "She killed her engine."

Jamming a hand into one pocket, Drew shifted her weight to one side before giving Sam a goofy smile. "I thought I was going to replace Gardner, but he decided to stick it out for a few more years."

"You know those old drivers. They never wanna let go."

"Yeah. Well, I'm not gonna be one of those old drivers. I want my chance now."

"Why don't you check with Paddy? He might have a slot for you. Behind me, that is," Brad said, slipping his arm around Sam. "Right, babe?"

"Right." Sam's voice deflated.

It seemed Brad didn't have Sam's back when it came to getting a driving slot. The egotistical jerk hadn't even thought of her.

Brad gave Drew the once-over before turning back to Sam. "Anyway, I have to get back out to the track, but I'll see you later."

Before heading to the door, Brad pressed his mouth to hers in what Drew took as a blatant show of possession.

"Don't forget about the welcome reception tonight," Sam said, squatting back down onto the roller board.

"I won't." The metal building rattled as he pulled the door open. "Dress pretty. I'll pick you up."

"Brad Wilkerson." Drew chuckled. "That's the guy you couldn't cheat on?" She'd seen him around many times, with many different women.

"He's the best driver on the circuit." She eased back against the board and pulled herself underneath the car.

"Whatever you say." Drew gave her a confident smile. Now that I'm here, that's going to change. "You just don't seem like his type."

"His type?" Reaching up into the engine compartment, she twisted sideways.

"Submissive. Wilkerson likes for his women to worship him." Drew stared at the long, slender legs protruding from beneath the car. Though they were now covered in dirty blue jeans, she remembered the skin hidden under them. "The man's an absolute ass." Her voice rang with unexpected hostility. "I can tell by that show of ownership he just put on."

She heard the wrench drop and saw Sam grab the frame. Sam and the roller board shot out from beneath the car, then jerked to a stop.

"What are you talking about?" Her brow rose curiously.

"The grab. The kiss. I couldn't help but notice you weren't responding."

Slipping off the board and onto the floor, Sam was visibly shaken by her accurate observation or maybe by her unwarranted annoyance. Drew didn't know which, but she could see it clearly.

"I'm not into public displays of affection," she said, scrambling to her feet.

"Was that visit with your sister before or after me?"

She swung around and stood with her arms glued across her chest. "What do you want from me, Ms. Thompson?"

That was a good question. For some unknown reason, right now she wanted to haul this stubborn redhead willingly into her arms, to protect her heart from the unfeeling bastard she was involved with. Drew loved the fact she could take care of herself, that she needed no one. Nevertheless, she stirred protective feelings in her that sooner or later would have to be resolved.

"Just a fair shot. That's all."

"A fair shot at what?"

"At you." Drew trailed her finger down across the hollow of Sam's neck, then her chest, stopping at the first fastened button of her shirt. Sam choked, and Drew could see she was caught off guard by her candor, and to be honest, she was a little stunned herself.

Sam shifted backward. Being this close to her benevolent stranger was unnerving. Drew smiled, revealing a pair of dangerously alluring dimples. All of a sudden the garage was unbearably hot. She was caught up in sensations she didn't know how to handle. Earlier, when Drew's thumbs had grazed the inside of her knees, her touch had produced a shudder in Sam she couldn't contain, and when she'd slid off the bench, her body had sizzled when she'd brushed up against her.

Get ahold of yourself, Sam! Steadying herself, she sucked in a deep breath to clear her head. But catching a whiff of the mysterious scent she recalled from the night before only made things worse. Nose to nose, her gaze met Drew's, and she froze. Sam had never met a woman who could fry her wiring with only one touch.

Sam fought the desire to fall into Drew's arms, but she had responsibilities that couldn't be ignored. One of them was making sure her driver was happy and focused. That meant her relationship status wasn't changing for the time being.

"If you haven't noticed, I'm already taken." The warmth stinging across her skin made Sam wish to God she wasn't.

"It didn't seem like it last night." Jamming a hand into one pocket, Drew shifted her weight to one side before giving her a slight smile, and Sam thought she was going to lose it right there.

"Last night was a mistake." She whipped around to the bench, chugged down the rest of the water, and tossed the bottle into the recycle bin. A *huge* mistake. It had to be. She could never be involved with a woman like Drew Thompson, one who could permeate her mind in only one night.

"You two have a don't-ask, don't-tell relationship?"

"Something like that." *On his part anyway.*

"Then it's forgotten." The animosity in Drew's voice disappeared, and her tone grew free and reassuring.

Sam hung a few tools on the wall before slowly turning back to her. "So you're not going to tell Brad?"

"What good would it do me?" Drew shrugged. "Now where can I find Paddy Kelleher?"

With wary eyes, she relaxed and leaned against the bench. "He should be at the track. If not, he'll be here this afternoon."

"You owe me." Drew smiled as she picked up a box wrench and reached past her to hang it on the wall. "But we'll talk about that later. Right now, I have to see a man about a driving slot." She touched Sam's cheek lightly, then turned and headed out the door.

Talk later? She didn't like the way that sounded. It wasn't necessarily her words but the slow, even way she'd spoken. Drew was assuming too much. As if she'd actually listen to anything she had to say.

Looking across the garage, she traced Drew's steps to the door, then whirled around and yanked open the fridge. Grabbing another bottle of water, she twisted the top off and took a quick, sloppy gulp. A trickle of water falling onto her chest made her shiver as she remembered the feel of Drew's fingers tracing her skin.

This is ridiculous. She up-ended the bottle and poured the remaining water over her head.

The woman had insulted her in the bar last night, practically assaulted her in her own shop this morning, and now she was after her driving slot. She tossed the bottle into the bin. So why did she have this incredible urge to follow her?

Sam smiled. Drew hadn't pushed her last night, that's why. Drew had wanted her as much as she'd wanted Drew, and she'd curbed her desire because Sam had lost it. She'd put Sam's feelings before hers, something Sam wasn't accustomed to in a partner. Brad was a very selfish lover.

Oh God, Brad! She tore out the door. She had to find Faith before he did.

Blocking the sunlight with her hand, Sam squinted and caught a glimpse of Faith's chestnut hair. It didn't take long for Sam to find her. All she had to do was follow the trail of men. Spotting Brad in the distance, Sam made a bee-line across the asphalt to her sister.

"Oh, my." Faith smiled and squeezed the strong, firm bicep of the man she'd been petting. "I don't believe I've ever had a man be quite so forward."

"Hey. I need to talk to you."

"Can't you see I'm busy with Mike right now?" Faith didn't take her attention from the driver she'd apparently set her sights on for the day.

"She'll be right back, Mike. This will just take a minute." Sam grabbed her arm and led her away.

"What are you doing?" Faith squealed, stumbling along after her.

"You give these guys way too much attention."

"I just give them what they want," she said, pulling her arm free.

"And what's that?"

"Plenty of loving with absolutely no strings." Faith lowered her chin, stared up through her thickened black lashes at Sam, and then turned and threw a wave back at Mike.

Sam let out a heavy breath and raked her gaze across the short shorts and tank top glued to Faith's refined features. The race-car circuit got very lonely, so how could a man resist?

"Some of these guys have wives waiting at home for them, you know."

"No need to worry about that. I'm not ready to settle down yet."

"You're impossible."

"No. Just realistic." Faith opened her clutch, took out a tube of gloss, and swiped it across her lips.

"Whatever." Sam shrugged and scanned a one-eighty behind Faith. "I need a favor."

"Okay." She let out a short breath and planted her hand on her hip. "Do I have to do it right now?"

"You don't have to *do* anything. But if anyone asks, just say I was with you last night."

Faith's eyes widened. "Does that mean big sis is getting a little action on the side?" Faith was eager to hear all of the juicy details, but she had loose lips, and Sam wasn't ready for this one to get out.

"Not exactly." Sam glimpsed Drew wandering around outside the garages searching for Paddy. "I just need you to cover for me this once."

"I don't know if that's going to fly, Sammy."

"Why not?"

"Because I was with someone, and I think he'd remember if we had a threesome."

"Damn it, Faith. Don't you ever sleep alone?" A shudder of panic rushed through Sam, and she spun around, taking a few steps.

"Not if I can help it." Faith glanced back at the driver she was cozying up to and threw him a sexy smile. "Are we finished here?"

Sam swiped her hand across the back of her neck. "Just hang on and let me think for a minute." After sucking in a deep breath, she let it out slowly. She had to stick with her original story. It would just be dumb luck if Brad found out. "Okay, this is what I need. Don't worry about anyone else, but if Brad asks, just remember I was with you."

"But—"

"No buts. Just do it, okay?"

"Okay." Faith whirled around. "Now, why don't you tell me a little more about those skills of yours?" she said, heading back to the driver.

CHAPTER FOUR

Y ou still haven't given me the invoice for that last order of tires?" Drew heard Paddy Kelleher's voice vibrate and chased it across the garage. She'd followed him from place to place all morning, but the man was slipperier than water on an oil slick. He kept getting away before Drew could approach him.

"It's right there on your desk." Sam's voice caught Drew's attention, and it shot an unnerving spark through her system. "I put it there yesterday," she said, and Drew watched her head into the office.

When Sam was completely out of sight, Drew made her move. "Hi, Mr. Kelleher. My name is Drew Thompson."

"What can I do for you, young lady?" Paddy said, shaking the hand Drew offered.

"I want to join your team."

"Check with Ray. He may need some help with cleanup." Paddy brushed past her, heading toward the two stacks of tires next to the far wall of the garage, and Drew followed.

"You don't understand, Mr. Kelleher. I want to be one of your drivers."

"You've driven before?" Paddy didn't turn as he examined the information on the tags stuck to the face of the tires.

"Yes, sir. For Freemont Oil."

"Drew Thompson," Paddy repeated thoughtfully. "That name sounds familiar, but I don't recall seeing it in racing."

"My father is Andrew Thompson."

"Andrew Thompson, the import-export mogul?" Paddy swung around abruptly, making Drew take a step back.

"That would be him."

Paddy's brows pulled together curiously. "You come from a wealthy family. Why don't they back you?"

"My mother doesn't particularly like her youngest daughter risking her life for fun."

"And your father?"

"He's okay with it, but he knows what'll happen if he opposes my mother." She let out a short chuckle. "He doesn't want to be left out in the cold, if you know what I mean."

"I know exactly what you mean." Paddy gave her a smile of acknowledgment. "We all try to deny it, but there's nothing like the love of a good woman."

"That's for sure." Drew thought about her former wife, Kimberly, and her stomach churned.

Paddy sat silently, surveying Drew for a few minutes. "Well, since we've been on this winning streak, just about everyone wants to be one of my drivers."

"I know that, sir. But if I may be blunt, they're not me." Drew held her tongue and waited.

Paddy raised an eyebrow and then shifted, giving her a stifling stare. "What kind of qualifications do you have that others don't?"

"I have instincts," she said, relieved that she didn't have to deal with the usual gender bias.

Paddy leaned back against the stack of tires and studied her carefully. Drew saw his close scrutiny. They were on the same page now. Paddy Kelleher was a racing legend, so the man had to know what Drew meant by instincts. Without them, Paddy couldn't possibly have been the driver he was in his day. Plenty of drivers out there had experience, but drivers with instincts can practically drive a track blindfolded. The track becomes part of them. They can feel the pavement deep inside. With all the technology these days, finding a driver with instincts was a rarity.

"Found it," Sam shouted, coming back out of the office. "It was buried underneath that pile of girlie magazines you call reading material." Spotting Drew with her father, she stopped. "Sorry. I didn't realize anyone else was here."

"Samantha, this is Drew Thompson."

"We've met," she said nonchalantly, handing him the invoice.

"Good, because she wants to drive for me."

"Really?" Her voice deepened with sarcasm.

"What do you think? The girl says she's got instincts."

"Instincts. I'll believe that when I see it." She let out a short breath. "Besides, I'm the next driver in line for this team, Paddy." She crossed her arms across her chest, and Drew knew she wouldn't be an easy sell. "Any car I fix, I drive."

"That's not going to happen, Samantha." Paddy's eyes grew narrow. "And don't think I won't replace you if I have to."

"Good luck finding another crew chief with my skills."

"Come now, Samantha. At least give the girl a shot." Paddy rubbed his hand across his face roughly.

"The *girl* is an absolute idiot." She let her arms drop, planting her hands on her hips. "What kind of a driver doesn't know when she's thrown a rod?"

"You said it. I'm a driver, not a mechanic," Drew shot back, forcing her gaze up Sam's long, curvy torso to meet her impenetrable stare.

"Any driver with half a brain can tell when something's wrong with her car."

"Then why didn't Tommy come in before Lucky Thirteen fell apart?" Drew could see the remark provoked an unexpected gut-wrenching reaction in Sam, and her sudden vulnerability made Drew shift uneasily. "I'm sorry, Mr. Kelleher. But with all due respect to you and your crew chief, I'm sure you know from your own experience, a driver doesn't always hear the subtle hints a race car produces before something goes wrong."

"A thrown rod is not a subtle hint. The damn thing sounds like a jackhammer." Sam regained her composure and gave Drew a heated glare. "You're supposed to handle an engine, not mangle it."

Drew clenched her jaw and matched Sam's stare. "If the valves had been adjusted correctly, it never would've happened."

Sam's brows rose, and her lips flattened as she threw up her hands. "Not my problem. I'm not your tech." She swung her gaze quickly back to Paddy. "I won't pit for this arrogant—"

"That's fine. Because I won't drive any machine you lay hands on."

Paddy clanged a wrench against an oil drum, sending an ear-piercing echo throughout the garage. "All right now. I've heard just about enough from the both of you." He pointed the wrench at Drew. "If you drive for me, Samantha will be your crew chief." He held up a hand as Sam started to protest. "And you, young lady, may be my daughter, but you are still in my employ. If you want to keep this job, you'll work on whichever car I decide."

"She's your daughter?" Drew darted her gaze back and forth between them, her mind in a spin. What the hell had she gotten herself into? She had no idea this bull-headed, beautiful woman was part of Paddy Kelleher's family. Sam was her prime suspect.

Paddy smiled slightly. "My oldest and most stubborn," he said, with a grumble.

Drew should've seen it. Red hair—tenacious—the resemblance was obvious now. She'd only thumbed through the case file, but she hadn't seen anything about Paddy's daughter being his crew chief. This would definitely complicate things.

"Right now my only open driving slot is for testing and backup," Paddy said.

"I don't want to be anyone's backup. I want to race." Drew glanced back over at Sam to make sure she was buying her act. She could see by the scowl on her face she was taking it in bigtime.

"That's all I've got right now. Take it or leave it."

Drew took in a deep breath and let it out slowly. Making it known that she'd blown up her last sponsor's car was a risk, but she had to make sure no one else out there would touch her. She had to be on the target team. Drew needed to be close to her suspect. She hadn't realized, the other night, that she'd already made it to the inside track.

"You'll give me a fair shot?"

"Aye." Paddy nodded. "You'll have to prove yourself, of course."

"You've got yourself a backup." Drew shook his hand and headed for the door before she took her phone and sent a Tweet to get the word out.

❖

Sam was fully aware Paddy could, and would, put another car on the track if he wanted. Instincts or not, he had too much money invested to unleash this hot-headed chick on the racetrack without seeing what she could do first. With the recent rash of accidents, Sam knew his threats to fire her were idle. Paddy wouldn't trust any other technician to work on his cars.

"You'll be gone in a week," Sam mumbled, giving Drew a smile of satisfaction when she glanced back at her. No respectable driver would settle for being backup.

"Don't look so smug," Paddy said, apparently catching Sam's expression. "If the young lady turns out to be as good as she says, I will put her in the race. In the meantime, you and she had better learn to get along. She's going to be testing every car you work on."

"What's the matter with you?" She threw up her arms. "You don't know anything about that girl, and you're willing to let her drive a two-hundred-thousand-dollar car?"

"I know more than you think, Samantha." He narrowed his eyes. "You'll just have to trust me on this one," he said, going into the office. "Now show Drew the bus, and see if you can find her a racing suit that fits."

This is just what I need! Seeing Drew around the track once in a while was one thing, but working with her on a daily basis would be a whole different story. Her phone chimed, and she took it out of her pocket just in time to see "Newest driver @kellehermotorsports #NASCAR #speed" scroll across the screen. She tapped the message and pulled up Drew's profile.

NASCAR Driver, likes it fast…on the track.

Un-fucking-believable. Another message scrolled across the screen. Brad had tweeted a response.

@drewthompson backup drivers never get track time #alwayslast.

Sam smiled. "Let the games begin."

Sam caught Drew just beyond the side door of the garage. "Hang on a minute. Paddy wants me to show you the bus."

"I thought you didn't want anything to do with me."

"I don't, but that won't prevent me from doing my job."

"So you're going to take one for the team, eh?"

She lifted her lips into a plastic smile. "Something like that."

"Lead the way." Drew motioned her in front.

"It's right over here." Sam pointed to the brightly colored custom racing bus parked a few yards away. "Paddy likes to keep it close." She unfastened the latch and tugged at the back door, but it didn't open.

"Here. Let me help you with that." Drew reached around and grabbed the knob. The door was open with one swift tug, and Sam was trapped between Drew's great-smelling body and the side of the bus.

Within seconds, Drew's mouth was on hers, and they were locked in a heated kiss. As Sam's mind spun out of control, she tried to think of a single reason why she didn't like her. But with every one of her nerve endings sizzling, she couldn't recall. She wrapped her arms around Drew's lean frame and swept her hands up her back. When Drew's hands crept up the inside of her shirt, she couldn't stop them, didn't want to. Before they met the hot skin of Sam's breasts, the loud roar of a race-car engine reminded Sam where she was. At the track. In broad daylight. Where everyone knew her.

Sam snapped her eyes open and shoved Drew away. "Stop. I told you, I'm not interested."

Drew's lips pulled into an irresistible smile. "That's not the impression I'm getting."

Sam swallowed hard and stared into her smoldering brown eyes. "I'm here right now only because Paddy has an eye for drivers. After seeing that engine you killed, if it were up to me, I wouldn't let you drive a Tonka Truck."

"Thank God for Paddy." Drew leaned in to kiss her again.

Sam closed her eyes and turned her head, trying to shake the unnerving feeling of surrender floating throughout her body. "I said stop!" Sam's voice faded into a desperate plea. If she wasn't careful, she'd fall right back into Drew's arms. "I'm begging you. Please don't."

Drew let out a heavy breath, backed up, and let her turn to speed up the steps. Sam glanced back over her shoulder to find Drew right on her heels. She'd let her go, but she wasn't letting up. She felt like sweet little Penelope Pussycat on the run from Pepe Le Pew, only not so unwilling. Soon enough Drew would have her cornered at the end of the bus, and she'd be back in her arms again. *Lockers.* She stopped, opened one of the lower cabinets to use as a barrier between them, and a shoe toppled out.

"That's strange. There shouldn't be anything but extra suits in here."

Drew picked up the shoe and raised her eyebrows, prompting Sam to continue.

"Sonoma is our home track. Most of the crew has family in the area. We don't use the bus for anything but storage when we're here. Paddy keeps this garage year round."

Drew fingered the limited wardrobe. "Looks like someone chose not to go home."

"Maybe." She plucked the shoe from her hand and tossed it back into the locker. "Or someone just forgot to clean out their locker."

"So where do you live?" Drew was using that hey-I'm-interested tone again.

"I pretty much live on the road."

"All the time?"

"Sometimes I stay with my sister."

"Doesn't leave much to come home to, does it?"

"The racing circuit is my home."

Drew's eyebrows popped up again. "No plans for the future? Spouse? Family?"

"I wouldn't be good wife material." She let the spring-loaded cabinet door clang shut. "The track really isn't the kind of place to raise a family." She let out a sigh. "Not a normal one, anyway."

"Are you speaking from experience?"

She glared at Drew. She was doing it again. Being too nice. Acting interested in things other than the race. Things she shouldn't be interested in.

"Let's get back to business, shall we?" Sam jerked open a drawer. It slammed straight into Drew's leg, and she grimaced. *That should dampen lover-girl's libido for a while.* "These are for tools. Parts are stored underneath the counters. Up the steps is a couch and TV, someplace to rest when we're at another track." Sam turned and brushed past her, heading back to the entrance to another set of lockers. "These are the crew lockers." She yanked open a door and tossed a racing suit at her. "Here. Try this one on."

"Right now?"

"Sure. Why not? You don't have anything I haven't seen before." Maybe if she saw her body again, she'd realize Drew wasn't all that great.

"Okay." Drew slipped off her jeans and then her shirt. Sam froze. Her pulse rang in her ears, and her cheeks heated. *Sports bra, abs, boxers. What the hell was she thinking?* She was much better than Sam remembered, and now Drew had caught her reaction.

Sam pulled open another locker. "The helmets are in here. Find yourself one that fits." She turned and flew back down the center aisle and out the exit.

CHAPTER FIVE

Jade kept her distance, watching Brad as he pulled Sam hard against him and covered her mouth with his. Not being much of a voyeur, Jade had already started to turn away when she realized something was different about the woman she'd been investigating and took a second glance. Same hair color, same build, but it wasn't Sam trapped in Brad's clutches. It was someone else. This was a new development. She discreetly followed them as they walked around the outside perimeter of the garage. He took the woman's hand and led her around the back of the building. Jade crept to the corner and peeked around, catching the woman settling into Brad's arms and kissing him again.

"Sam was out last night. She used her sister for an alibi." He looked irritated.

The woman backed up and locked her arms across her chest. "You're not actually jealous, are you?"

He slipped his arm around her waist and pulled her back to him. "Why would I be jealous when I've got a younger, prettier model right here?"

"That's a good question." She kept her arms locked in front of her as he worked on softening her up.

Jade knew from her research that Brad's digressions were plentiful, but hadn't witnessed any until now. It wasn't a secret that the man was promiscuous. Sam and Brad had frequent public arguments about his affairs. Their romance had been rocky and often volatile over the past few years.

Jade shivered. Watching Brad charm the woman made her skin crawl. Time to let them know their secret was no longer safe.

"Whoops," Jade said, rounding the corner. "Aren't you mauling the wrong woman?"

The woman waited for Brad to respond, then answered when he balked. "I was upset about something, and Brad was just helping me work through it."

"That's great. I mean, that you're here to comfort random groupies." Jade let out a short breath. The whole idea that Brad would comfort anyone was ridiculous.

"I think so." The woman brushed past her. "If you'll excuse me, I've got to get going. I have to pick up my dress for the sponsor party."

"From the cleaners?" Jade liked to make groupies squirm. She thought it was funny that a few tattoos and piercings had such an intimidating effect on other women.

"From the designer." The woman let her eyes sweep up to meet Jade's, and her lips squeezed into a pretentious smile. "It might be a stretch for you, but maybe I'll throw it your way when I'm done with it."

"Thanks." Jade smiled. "I'll have to have it taken in, of course." She didn't know how Brad attracted the rich ones.

He tried to slip by, but Jade flattened a hand on his chest. "Hang on a minute, hotshot."

"What?"

"You don't fool me one bit. I just can't believe you'd do that shit right here at the track."

He raised his hands in innocence. "I'm not doing anything. You heard her. She came to me for comfort."

"Comfort? Is that what you're calling it now?"

"Oh, I get it." He gave her a cocky smile. "We didn't get to finish our swim this morning." He backed her up against the metal building and whispered in her ear. "I'm free now."

"I'll never be that free." She slid her knee up the inside of his thigh and pressed it to his groin. "I suggest you back up."

He shrugged and pushed away from the building. "You still seeing Tommy?"

"Yep."

"Let me know when you're ready for a real man."

"He's twice the man you'll ever be."

"I don't think so." His smile faltered. "Never was, never will be."

She clenched her fists and trapped them by her sides. *Remember what the doctor said—verbalize. Put your feelings into words. Beating someone senseless doesn't help anything.* Only one problem—the words were there. They just wouldn't come out. Before she could respond to Brad, she heard the side door clang shut, and he walked to the corner to see who it was. She followed. Peering past Brad, she was surprised to see Drew Thompson strutting across the asphalt. *Damn! What the hell is she doing here?*

The door swung open again, and Sam flew out, chasing Drew. Jade couldn't hear what she was saying, but Drew stopped, they talked for a brief moment, and then Drew followed Sam to the racing bus.

"You may have some competition," Jade said, quickly slipping back into her fictitious persona.

"Who? Her? The girl's an amateur." Brad glanced at Jade, and his eyes narrowed. "She's got nothin' on me."

"Maybe." Jade smiled at Brad's obvious irritation and couldn't resist adding fuel to the fire. "But she's got Sam's attention."

❖

"Don't tell me you actually hired that amateur," Brad said as he paced the ten-by-twelve office.

Paddy stayed focused on his paperwork. "She's your backup. I expect you two to get along."

"What about testing?"

"She'll take the car out for that too."

"She blew up her last car."

"If Samantha has to ride with her and show her what to look for, she will." Paddy glanced up and caught Brad's scowl. "You have a problem with that, young man?"

"No problem as long as she keeps it professional." Brad clenched his jaw.

"Why wouldn't she keep it professional?"

"She's an opportunist. Gets what she wants and then gets out."

Paddy dropped his pen and pushed back in his chair. "And you're not?"

"We're not talking about me."

"If my little girl didn't like to stick thorns in my side, she wouldn't even be seeing you. Would she?"

"That may be the way it started. But…"

"But what, young man? I see how you treat her. Do you want to be getting into that now?" Even though Sam didn't think so, his attention spanned more than just the racetrack.

"No," Brad said.

"Then let's be rid of the whole conversation, shall we?"

"Yeah, whatever. I'd like to be rid of Drew Thompson." Brad pulled hard at the old wooden office door until it flew open, hit the wall, and bounced back at him.

As Paddy watched Brad storm across the garage, the tiny hairs on the back of Paddy's neck stiffened against his collar. If a killer was indeed on the loose, his first suspect would be the man that had just left his office—the driver who out of succession was now filling his number-one slot. Detective Drew Thompson might be an inconvenience, but Paddy wasn't about to let Samantha be the next victim in this bizarre series of so-called accidents.

The hot water felt good as Drew let it rain across her shoulders. She had just run the circuit of exercise machines in the gym located in the California Highway Patrol Office in San Francisco. She wanted to keep her body primed. Racing took a lot of strength and stamina. She hadn't had much time to recuperate from her last undercover assignment. She'd thought she was going to be a boxing trainer, but she'd gotten screwed again. The captain set her up as a sparring partner instead, and she was still recovering.

Keeping in shape was a plus because it gave her an advantage over the more seasoned detectives. But on the other hand, the old coots always gave her the tough assignments. That was her penance for trying to keep one step ahead of Mother Nature.

She kneaded her shoulder with her fingertips and thought about the beautiful redhead who'd used it for a pillow last night. *Samantha Kelleher, aka Slick.* She'd definitely earned her nickname. The after-effects of her kiss still lingered on Drew's lips. Her blood rushed south, and she reacted. Her response time was still good, another affirmation of her sexuality. She dialed the temperature to cold and doused herself until the throbbing pulse between her legs subsided. Flipping the knob back to hot, she closed her eyes and ran through the case in her head.

"Figured I'd find you here." Jade's voice interrupted her thoughts.

She felt the whoosh of cool air and opened her eyes, but didn't budge. "Checking me out again?"

"Nothing I'm interested in." Jade's gaze crept from head to toe and back again. "I want answers."

She ignored the scrutiny, squirted some shampoo into the palm of her hand, and lathered up. "Answers to what?"

Jade had been undercover for almost six months now, and Drew was sure she didn't like the fact the captain had sent her in after her. Besides the fact that Drew had let her partner get killed, she'd also been too involved with her job. She was nowhere to be found when Jade's sister had started to hemorrhage. If Drew had been there, her wife and baby might still be alive, a fact for which she would never forgive herself.

"What in the hell were you doing in Paddy Kelleher's garage today?"

"Captain Jacobs thought you might need some help."

"I figured she'd send someone in, but on one of the other racing teams."

"I need to be closer."

"I saw you today with Sam. You're already in closer than you should be."

"You can never be too close." Drew smiled and gave her a wink.

Drew had been pleasantly surprised to find that Paddy's top mechanic, Slick, was also his oldest daughter. Drew had her in with the Kellehers now.

"Listen, it's getting a little cold in here. Can we finish this in the captain's office?" She stuck her head under the stream and let the soapy water spray out at Jade.

Usually Drew would have a whole line of questions to fire at Jade, but she'd forgotten to take the case file with her after Captain Jacobs briefed her yesterday. She liked to fly by the seat of her pants, but if the captain knew she didn't have a handle on the investigation, he'd have her head.

Jade slid the shower curtain closed. "You'd better not skip out on me, Thompson."

"I'll be there in about ten minutes." She smiled to herself. She intended to devote her full attention to the investigation of Samantha Kelleher.

❖

After Drew left the gym, she rounded the corner and headed straight for the captain's office. The glass door rattled loudly when she closed it. "You didn't tell me Kelleher had another daughter."

"It's in the case file I gave you." The captain looked to the corner of his desk. "Which is still right here."

Jade picked it up and scrunched her nose. "Didn't you read it, Supercop?"

Drew grabbed it from her and dropped it back onto the desk. "No matter how much I don't like you, I would've never let you go in there like that."

"I could've used a heads-up too." Jade popped out of her chair and moved toward her. "Number one." She flipped her index finger up. "I didn't know when you were coming. You could've blown my whole cover." She flipped up another finger. "Number two. Do your job. How was I supposed to know you didn't know who she was?"

The two of them argued until Captain Jacobs stood up between them.

"How can I tell you anything when you don't check in?" he said, pointing at Jade. "And you, hotshot," he turned to Drew, "should've read the file before you went anywhere near that track."

"I thought I'd just wing it."

"Hopefully you didn't screw up too badly."

"She blew up Freemont's engine." Jade gave her a mocking smile. "That's gonna cost you."

"You did what?" The captain's face turned deep red.

"You told me to find a way in, and I did." Drew raised her arms, praising herself. "Standing before you is the new backup driver for Kelleher Motorsports."

"No way," Jade said.

The captain interrupted her. "I'm afraid she's right. I gave Paddy Kelleher a call after we spoke yesterday."

"So you got it because Paddy knew who you were." Jade's voice rang with satisfaction. "You blew up that engine for nothing."

Drew rolled her eyes. "The car was out of commission before I got there. Does Paddy know we're looking at his daughter for these accidents?"

The captain nodded. "He knows we're looking at everyone. He's adamant it's not her, but he's agreed to keep it to himself so as not to compromise the case and put anyone else in danger."

"So, partner, are we going to work together on this, or do I have to do it all myself?"

Jade picked up the manila folder and pinned it with her hand to Drew's chest. "Read the file. Then we'll talk."

"When?"

"After the party tonight?" She pulled open the door before turning back. "You do know about the welcome reception, don't you?"

"You bet." Drew wouldn't miss another chance to rattle Sam's cage.

Drew tossed her key onto the table before fishing her phone out of her pocket and pushing the voice-mail button. She hadn't been up to answering the call earlier. Jade's voice and attitude came through loud and clear.

FYI. The welcome reception is at the Eldorado. The party's small and informal, just something to let everyone get to know each other before the competition begins.

She smiled and dropped her phone on the nightstand. It was a refreshing change to know Jade's anger wasn't about the death of her sister. She knew the job, and, unlike her father, she'd stopped blaming Drew a long time ago.

Flopping sideways across the bed, she opened the case file and spread everything out in front of her. She thought she'd scanned through all of it when she was in the captain's office. But if she'd missed a daughter, she'd probably missed something else too. Sifting through the printed pages again, Drew remembered why she'd put it aside before. The file contained page after page of information on Faith Kelleher. She'd collected more race time with drivers than their cars. From the few pages she scanned, Drew surmised that Faith didn't have much interest in racing. She was more of a social, party girl. Not her kind of woman.

"Ah-ha," she said, her interest piqued. There it was, tucked all the way in the back. Two single-spaced pages on Samantha Kelleher. Pushing the file aside, she raked her arm across the bedspread to clear a spot and propped herself up against the headboard.

It seemed as though racing ran deep in her veins, just like her brother and father. She held up the file pictures and chuckled. She was definitely more attractive.

Flipping to the next page, she could see both Samantha and Tommy were stung with the passion for speed, something Drew understood all too well. The three Kelleher children had traveled with their father throughout his racing career. While Faith took only to the parties and the men, Samantha and Tommy had worked the circuit since they were teenagers.

Samantha had something on her brother, however. Over the years she'd developed into one of the best mechanics on the circuit. While Tommy raced, test-driving was the closest Sam ever got to the track. Apparently Paddy Kelleher had a soft spot for his little girls. He liked keeping them close. And safe.

Tommy, on the other hand, seemed to have an inbred ability for racing. The reflexes, the stamina, and the instincts—he had it all. Having a championship driver for a father didn't hurt.

Drew was an avid racing fan. She remembered seeing a magazine article once quoting Tommy, saying his goal in life was to win as many races as his father had during his career. He was halfway there when the last accident happened. Paralyzed from the waist down, Tommy Kelleher would never race again.

"Where's the mother?" She rummaged through the papers again but didn't find a single sheet of information on her. She let her head fall back against the headboard and groaned. She was going to have to deal with Jade whether she wanted to or not.

After sliding everything back into the file, she glanced at her watch, shot up, and shoved the file under the mattress. She had a party to crash.

❖

Sam tugged at Brad's arm one last time and let out a sigh. Getting him away from the usual group surrounding him wasn't going to happen tonight. She made her way to the bar and had just ordered a drink when someone took her hand and pulled her out onto the dance floor.

"You changed your mind?" Sam said, letting a deceptively sweet tone of enthusiasm ring in her voice. When she realized who it was whisking her around, a flurry of excitement rushed through her.

"I didn't get to tell you earlier how much I missed you this morning." Drew immersed her face in Sam's hair.

The sound of Drew taking in her scent gave Sam a strangely intimate feeling. She pushed back until Drew's arms put up a roadblock and wouldn't let her move any farther. "I thought it was best not to prolong your pain."

"Thanks for the concern, but I kinda liked it."

Sam stared at her curiously.

"It's been a while since I've had a woman in my bed for anything more than just good old primal sex." Drew's soft sensual lips pulled into a contented smile, producing those irresistible dimples dotting the tips.

Sam glanced around, hoping no one had overheard them.

"No need for alarm. I told you, your secret is safe." Drew gave her a subtle wink. "Now loosen up and dance with me."

Sam reluctantly relaxed into her arms. "When we met you didn't tell me you were a driver."

"As I recall, the subject of what either of us did never came up."

Sam caught her bottom lip between her teeth. "Thank you for last night," she said softly, stumbling for words. "Most people wouldn't have been so understanding."

"Not a problem." Drew gave her a slight smile. "By the way, I still have a very lovely black lace bra that I believe belongs to you."

Sam remembered the feel of Drew's fingers pushing the straps from her shoulders, and her breath caught. "I'll be needing that back."

"Anytime you want to come by and get it, just let me know."

Sam lowered her lashes and let her mouth curve into a smile. The woman had to know she was making headway, and Sam liked the attention she was giving her. But then she heard Brad laugh, and a twinge of guilt shot through her. It wasn't obvious, but she knew he was watching her. He was always watching.

"You wanna make him jealous?" Apparently, Drew saw it too.

"I don't think it would do any good." She stared across the room. Seeing Brad carry on with his usual pack of mindless track groupies didn't concern her anymore. Their gazes locked, and she gave him a thin-lipped smile before shifting her attention back to Drew.

The tempo slowed, and Drew pulled Sam to her. "Follow my lead," she whispered, hovering closely.

Drew's smooth cheek brushed softly against Sam's, and she was stung with desire all over again. She felt the warmth of Drew's breath in her ear, and every one of her nerve endings tingled in succession. Drew's lips crept back across her cheek, meeting Sam's, and she was sucked into a slow, arousing kiss.

Sam's body was stripped of all its strength, and Drew was part of her again. Clinging helplessly as Drew took her into this huge black hole of desire, all sense of right and wrong vanished. She gasped for air, sinking deeper into this magical pool of sensations flooding her system.

With a ragged breath, Drew pulled away slowly. "I can't believe that idiot would pass up a woman like you." Drew grabbed her hand as it rose, and grinned. "Don't. If you slap me, it'll have absolutely no effect on him."

Say something. Say something now! Or she'll know you enjoyed it. She'll know you want more. "Slap, hell. You're lucky I don't put a fist in your mouth," Sam shot back in feeble protest, waiting for the fire between her legs to subside. Still shaken, she remained close, using Drew for support, trying not to let her see the quick-burning impact she'd had on her.

"Come on. This will really piss him off." Drew pulled her off the dance floor and out the side door of the bar.

"Stop." Sam raised her voice, ending with a mixture of annoyance and laughter. "I don't want him to think I went to your room with you."

"Why not? You did last night." Drew shrugged, letting her hand drop.

Sam narrowed her eyes. "That was a mistake."

"Was it?" Drew closed in on her, backing her up against the building. "If I had known *he* was the reason you were so upset, I wouldn't have stopped."

"Yes, you would have." Sam tried to ignore Drew's fingers creeping up the sides of her rib cage.

"You're right. I prefer it when a woman wants me. Like you do right now."

"I don't—" Drew's mouth was on hers again, filling her with utter need. Responding urgently, she let the passion ignite between them. Drew's hands roamed the length of her torso, gently descending across the sides of her breasts and down to her waist.

Sam shivered. *This is a mistake.* There was just a certain kind of woman a girl kept her distance from—a woman whose touch made your skin sizzle. Drew was definitely that kind of woman.

"Just let me know when you want to pick up your bra," she whispered.

Sam's nerve endings were still burning hot. She should look away, but Drew's dusky brown eyes were magnetic. She couldn't budge if she'd wanted to. Not even an inch.

The door flew open, and Brad appeared. "Planning on taking my fiancée home, Thompson?"

Drew chuckled and backed up. "Not tonight." She flashed Sam a shot of her irresistible dimples. "She's not my type."

Still recovering from the kiss that had made her legs all but turn to jelly, Sam steadied herself against the building and watched Drew stroll across the parking lot. When she got into her Jeep, she glanced back over her shoulder at Sam, and suddenly her brain kicked back into gear.

"Your type, my ass!" she shouted.

The Jeep flew out of the parking lot, and she almost went after it. She wasn't doing a very good job of concealing what she and Drew had shared, and Brad didn't seem to like it.

"Dumpster-diving again?"

"As if you care." She pulled her key out of her pocket and took off to her car. "What happened to 'we're just having fun here'?"

"Of course I care," he shouted, running after her. "I don't like the idea of my woman giving it up to someone else on the circuit." He caught her hand and yanked her around.

As she pulled loose, her wrist tingled with pain. "That's what it's all about, isn't it?" She let out a disgusted sigh. "Your precious reputation. You could care less about me." She tugged the car door open and slid inside. Firing the ignition, she threw her sixty-seven Camaro into gear and punched the pedal. The engine roared and the car bolted.

"Damn it, Sam!" Brad jerked back out of the way as the car door slammed shut and she sped off.

Sam lost him at the first light. She was already up in her room, out of sight when she heard his car fly into the parking lot and screech to a stop. The metal stair railing rattled, and she knew he was on his way up. She watched the knob turn on the locked door and ignored his protests when she wouldn't let him in. She knew it would be quick and urgent. No foreplay, no tenderness, just get-right-down-to-it sex. A single physical act with no emotional attachment on either part. Worlds away from what Sam really wanted.

As she lay awake, all Sam could think of was the penetrating heated kiss from Drew Thompson, a woman she barely knew. It had been a long time since she'd felt need like that.

She rolled to her side, and her mind drifted to Brad. He wasn't a compassionate man by any means. He was demanding and controlling, not only of her, but of everyone around him. On the racetrack it was about winning. When he was with *her*, it was about fulfilling his needs.

Sex to him was a release, not a pleasure. It was something to keep his mind clear. Sam knew he would never be completely hers. Their relationship had become a disappointing substitute for the kind of loving connection she longed for.

Chapter Six

It was almost midnight when Drew found the door to the number-seven garage unlocked. She slowly pushed it open, slipped inside, and snuck around the perimeter. Hiding in the shadows, she watched someone re-assemble what looked like an injector on the workbench. When she moved in for further investigation, the person swung around, and Drew dropped to the floor.

The sweat trickled across her forehead. The cold dampness was creeping into her bones, and the scar under her armpit ached.

It was happening all over again. She stared across the concrete floor, and all she could see were the hollow eyes of her dying partner staring back at her. It had been almost a year now since it happened, and Drew had gone over it a million times in her head. She still couldn't move.

The unbroken silence was deafening. Then it came, the simple echo of a chillingly familiar sound. Drew raised her head and found herself staring into the barrel of a Glock nine-millimeter pistol.

Jade lowered her weapon and slid it back into her ankle holster. "What the hell are you doing here, Drew?"

She smiled smugly. "You've gotten better."

"I had a good teacher." Jade headed back across the garage.

Drew laughed abruptly. "I never thought I'd hear you say that." She jumped to her feet, following her. Jade was her first rookie partner. Fresh off patrol, she was good, but still had a lot to learn back then.

"Don't count on hearing it again." The venom in Jade's voice wasn't surprising.

"You got any aspirin around this place?" Her head was splitting, just as it did every time she thought of that fateful night.

"Memory nagging at you again?"

She nodded.

"Check over there in the lockers. You might find some there."

She pulled open the first of five gray-metal painted lockers. Finding nothing, she slammed it closed and went to the next and then the next. She spotted a bottle of aspirin, along with some deodorant and cologne in the third. As she took it off the shelf, a small newspaper clipping floated to the ground. Drew picked it up and turned it over. The name McNamara caught her eye. She reached up, slid her hand across the top shelf, and found more clippings.

"Whose locker is this?"

"Nobody uses those lockers anymore. All the suits are stored in the bus."

"Come here and look at these."

"Look at what?" Jade asked, heading her way.

"These articles on racing accidents."

Jade frowned. "Really? How many?" Her voice took an alarming dip.

"One, two, three—there's got to be at least five of them here."

"There *have* been a lot of crashes on the circuit this past year. Someone's probably just keeping track."

Jade took a few from her. "Or maybe someone here has a bizarre notion of keepsakes." She rummaged through the contents of the locker. "The only thing I can tell from this stuff is that it probably belongs to a man."

"Either that or someone else put it here to distract us."

Jade studied the articles for a minute before snapping pictures of them with her phone and handing them to Drew. "Leave them exactly where you found them, and I'll keep an eye on the locker, see if anyone comes for them."

Drew slid the clippings onto the shelf next to the deodorant. Popping the top off the aspirin bottle, she let a few tablets roll into her hand before placing it back onto the shelf and slamming the locker closed. She grabbed a cupped-handful of water from the sink to wash the pills down before following Jade to the bench.

"You want me to help you out with some of this stuff?" She picked up an open tube of grease and sniffed it.

Jade took the tube from her, screwed on the lid, and lobbed it up onto the shelf. "You're a driver. Drivers are like hotshot detectives. They don't clean up the messes they leave."

"And you're supposed to be a physical therapist. What are you doing here?"

"Helping out in the garage keeps me informed." The metal building rattled, and Jade glanced over her shoulder. "Now, why don't you get out of here? I don't need you hanging around, screwing things up."

"What'd I do to piss you off now?" She reached up and pushed the teetering cylinder of grease farther onto the shelf.

"I saw you tonight on the dance floor with Sam."

"Yeah. So what?"

"So did everyone else."

"Good show, huh?" Drew had watched Sam from the corner of the bar. She could see her tugging at Brad's arm, motioning toward the dance floor. The sight of her long, lean legs formed out in tight, faded blue jeans made her pulse bounce. And the shimmering black sweater clinging to the rest of her had sent her heart into a double dribble. Anyone would have to be a fool to turn her away, yet Brad did. He'd dismissed her without so much as a smile.

"Pissed that jerk, Wilkerson, off." She gave her a satisfied smile before taking the race schedule from the hook on the wall.

"I think you pissed Sam off pretty good too."

"Maybe so." After leaving the party, Drew had waited and watched by the pool. When Sam took off to her room, Drew had toyed with the idea of going up after her. But that would've been tempting fate. Sam was madder than a declawed alley cat, and Brad had shown up within minutes, following her to her room. Drew had to leave. She couldn't stand the thought of Brad touching Sam. Now she was here, trying to use her sleepless night for something more productive.

"I thought you were going to cool it."

"I didn't take her back to my room." She wished she had.

"But that kiss you gave her was scorching." Jade raised her eyebrows.

"All in a day's work." She tried to shut Sam out of her mind, but knowing that Brad was still running thick in her system affected her more than it should.

"As long as that's all it is."

"Of course it is." She relaxed back against the bench. She could feel Jade watching her, studying her every move, trying to read her. She'd turned out to be a good cop after all.

"How're you going to get her to trust you?"

"By simply letting her get to know the real me." She threw her hands out in front of herself and grinned.

Jade widened her eyes. "Oh yeah. *That'll* do the trick." Her voice was thick with sarcasm.

"Oh, and thanks for watching me make a fool out of myself the other night in the bar."

"Goes to character." Jade chuckled as she dropped a few tools into the chest. "You can't know everything, or you'll seem too perfect."

"What do you mean?"

"I mean, if you want to make any headway with this woman, you have to be real. Real women have flaws." Jade turned, letting her gaze sweep Drew's body. "Lots of them."

"Just try not to make me look like too much of an ass, all right?"

"Don't worry. I won't leave you swinging again. Whether I like it or not, we're partners." Jade offered her a hand and she shook it. When Jade let go, Drew turned her hand and stared at the sticky black grease in her palm.

"You're definitely a driver." Jade chuckled and pointed across the garage. "The sink's over there."

Drew squirted some hand cleaner into her palm and rubbed her hands together before rinsing them under the faucet. "I see you're making headway with her brother." She pulled a few paper towels out of the dispenser and dried her hands. "Six months undercover is a long time. Gets pretty lonely."

"I really like him." A flit of excitement flew across her face and vanished as quickly as it came. "He's a nice guy."

"He doesn't seem like your type." Drew had seen Jade's eyes sparkle like that before and knew it meant she was involved. But how deep?

"My type?"

"Men who can perform," she added, pushing to see if she'd read Jade's reaction right.

"You want to work together or not?" She slammed the tool drawer shut. Drew had hit a nerve.

"Just seeing how far in you are."

"If you'd worried about yourself as much as you worry about me, you'd still have a wife."

"Maybe so." Drew had been crushed when she'd lost Kimberly. If she'd been home with her, maybe she and the baby would have made it. But she was undercover, only home for a few days at a time, and Kimberly hadn't told her about the spotting. By the time she'd found her, she was unconscious and had already lost too much blood.

Drew gave her anything and everything she'd wanted, except her time. A side effect of the job. Kimberly knew Drew couldn't change and accepted that fact. Losing her hurt more than anyone could fathom. Drew had decided right then she would never make herself that vulnerable again. She'd put up an emotional wall. Invisible as it was, no one could breach it. Being involved was just too painful for her to endure again.

"I'm sorry. That was uncalled for."

"No. You're spot on." She raked her fingers roughly through her hair. "And that's my cue." She headed for the door.

Jade trailed after her. "I miss her too, you know."

"I know you do." She shook her head. "No one will ever understand me the way she did."

"Same here. But who knows? Maybe someone else out there understands a twisted soul like you." Jade reached for a shop rag to wipe her hands. "But I can guarantee you won't find her in this garage."

"Just hoping for a little fun." She half smiled and gave Jade a wink. "You know, something to pass the time."

"Sam likes the rebels. But I'd advise you to mix a little compassion in with the macho. That boyfriend of hers is a real jerk."

Drew raised her eyebrows. "Aren't you getting a little too personally involved?"

"It's hard not to with these people." Jade flipped her hair back and slid her hand onto her hip. "They're so…embracing."

"I know better than to get involved, and so do you."

"At one time I did," Jade said softly. "I guess I just got tired of being alone all the time."

"Alone is good." She continued to the door. "No responsibilities. No complications."

She'd worked hard to stay connected to Kimberly, but that had ended tragically. She wasn't ready to settle down again. The picket fence, the family just wasn't in the cards for her. How could she even think about having another one? She was an undercover cop, for God's sake. Her life would never be stable.

Sam cursed from the side of the track as the number-fifteen car swerved toward the inside wall. The front tire hit the edge of the pit curb, catching the tire, pulling the front end up and over the barrier. Realignment, balancing, new exhaust seals. Another day's work shot to hell. She rubbed her forehead wearily and trudged back to the garage.

Drew pulled into the garage and stopped. The engine made a loud, rhythmic, popping sound as it idled.

"Shut it off and get out," Sam shouted over the engine.

Drew unfastened the restraints and pulled herself up onto the door. "What the hell was that noise?"

Sam rolled her eyes. "Mechanics 101. You blew an exhaust manifold gasket when you jumped the curb."

Drew took her helmet off and set it on top of the car before swinging her legs out and sliding down the door. "The rear end was pretty loose. I was having trouble controlling it."

"I was hoping the cloud cover would cool the track down some today, but it's still pretty hot outside. The suspension isn't adjusted quite right."

"Can you fix it?" Drew asked cautiously, one eyebrow up, the other down, and her lower lip puffed out into a funny grimace.

Sam covered her mouth, trying to suppress her laughter, but it came out in a low, throaty burst. "Do you think you'll ever learn anything about these cars?"

Drew embraced Sam quickly, trapping her arms against her sides. "Why would I do that when I have such a beautiful technician to fix them for me?" Picking her up, Drew swung Sam around until she was dizzy with laughter.

"Stop." Her feet dangled just above the floor as she tried to regain her composure, but the longer Drew held her, the more she laughed.

"Not until you promise to fix this one." Drew jammed her face into the crook of Sam's neck and blew.

"I'll fix it," she said in a breathless squeal. "Now stop!"

Drew stopped taunting her, yet she lingered, her face immersed in Sam's hair. She slowly let her slide down her body to the floor. "That wasn't so hard, now was it?"

"No." She stared into her eyes. *This is the hard part.* Drew's mouth just inches away from Sam's, her breath warmed her face. The beat of her heart raced in such a thunderous rhythm, it created a huge crater in her chest. When Drew's gaze fixed on hers, a sudden sense of immediacy emerged, and torrid feelings of desire swept through Sam. Snaking her arms around Drew's neck, she let her mouth meld onto hers. Sam's heart pounded wildly, making it hard to breathe. Nerve endings suddenly spiked, and her body sizzled. *This is too much—she's too much.* With her hands pressed hard against Drew's chest, Sam pushed, creating some much-needed space between them.

"Sorry," she choked out. Shoving her hands into her back pockets, Sam sent her gaze immediately to the floor. "I shouldn't have done that."

"No need to be sorry." Drew cupped her face in her hands and planted her lips on Sam's again. Sam let out a slight moan and quickly yielded to Drew's mouth once again.

She felt no trace of opposition this time. Sam melted into Drew's arms, surrendering completely, reveling in the new blaze of sensations she was igniting.

Sam heard the door swing open and immediately broke free. Physically shaken, she quickly slipped into the office and flung the door closed behind her. The hollow wooden door banged against the frame and slammed back open without latching. Heading straight into the bathroom, she flipped on the water and stared into the mirror. Her hands shook as she splashed cold water onto her heated face until the warmth in her cheeks subsided. She reached for the gold chain hanging on the hook next to the mirror and pulled it over her head.

What the hell am I doing? Her hormones were raging like she was a teenager in heat. She tugged the towel off the rack, sank onto the toilet seat, and patted her face dry. She had to get herself together before she went back out there.

Drew pushed the office door open without knocking. "Brad's trying to find you."

Sam jerked her head up, panicked.

"I sent him into the supply room. Thought I'd give you a little time to recover."

"Thanks." She bolted up.

Drew rounded the desk. "Don't worry about me. I won't tell." She skimmed her hand down Sam's arm.

Don't, Sam told herself, but she had to take just one last glance. Drew's penetrating eyes entranced her, and goose bumps emerged on her entire body instantly, sending a tingle of excitement through her. She was too close. Again.

She heard the supply door swing shut, and in less than a minute Brad was coming through the office doorway.

"I've been looking for you," he said, brushing past Drew.

"I heard." She peered up at him. "I was on my way out." She straightened a stack of papers on the desk.

"Is everything all right?" His gaze darted from her to Drew and back again.

Shit! He can see it. He had to know something was going on. Her cheeks were pink, and he must have seen the stare between her and Drew when he came in.

"The car blew an exhaust gasket. I have to change it."

"That shouldn't take long, should it?"

"No. I was debating whether to get all greasy again before the sponsor party."

"Do it tomorrow." Brad took her freshly cleaned hands, and she couldn't hide their unusual warmth. "Where's your ring?"

Staring at her bare finger, she hesitated before reaching inside the collar of her shirt. "I don't wear it in the shop." She pulled out the gold chain with the ring dangling on the end of it. "I put it on the chain and hang it in the office when I'm working in the garage."

"Why?"

She drew her brows together. "Because I've become quite fond of all my fingers. I'd hate to get my ring caught on something and have one ripped off."

"Oh. I never thought about that." Slipping his arm around her waist, he pulled her to him. With Brad's mouth pressed firmly to hers, she closed her eyes and waited for the tingle. But it didn't come. Nothing. No passion, no fire, not even a spark. Through slitted eyes, she caught Drew watching. Sam opened her eyes fully and made contact, Drew's gaze didn't falter, and the unnerving sting returned.

As they parted, she let her gaze drift back to Brad. "Will I see you at the party tonight?"

"Wouldn't miss it."

"Maybe I could go with you now." She shot him a sexy smile. "We could just skip the party." She didn't think she could stand another night being thrown together with Drew.

"Gotta be there, babe. I'm the star." He kissed her on the cheek. "Without me there is no party." He slapped Drew on the shoulder before swinging back around, pointing a single finger at Sam. "I'll see you there."

"We're not going together?" Sam hated walking into parties alone.

He swung back around as he walked. "I've got a few things to do this afternoon, but I won't be too late. Dress pretty," he shouted without turning.

"Dress pretty," she mumbled, whirling around and slamming the tool drawer shut. She'd put on this ridiculously obvious display of public affection just to show Drew she was happy, and then Brad had to treat her like she was some kind of trophy.

"Will I see you tonight?" Drew asked.

Out of the corner of her eye, she caught Drew's smile as she crept up behind her.

"I didn't realize you were still here," she said nonchalantly.

"Caught the whole show." Drew touched Sam's shoulder and she jerked away. "It *was* for me, wasn't it?"

"Boy, you've really got a big ego."

"That's beside the point." Drew took her hand and moved closer.

Sam's skin sizzled, and she glanced at her hand. She yanked it away. "Stop!"

"All right." Drew's hands flew up in surrender. "But you didn't answer my question."

She turned and went back to the tools. "I don't know." She clanged a wrench into the drawer and, with a resigning sigh, swung back around. "Parties like that are more my sister's forte."

Drew swept her finger down Sam's nose and pinched her chin. "I don't have any interest in your sister."

She hesitated and peered through her lashes at Drew. "Maybe you should be. She's younger, and more importantly, she's single."

"But I bet she can't get my motor running like you can." Drew's lip pulled to one side, into a smile.

Sam closed her eyes and stood perfectly still, waiting for the burn of Drew's lips on hers once again. Instead, she heard footsteps crossing the garage. She opened her eyes and watched Drew go out the door. If she went to the party tonight to see anyone, it would be her.

Drew sat alone in the corner booth reading the case file. She tore the top off two packets of sugar and dumped them into her coffee. Without stirring, she took a big gulp and suffered the slow burn across her tongue.

Flipping through the information on Brad, she knew the man regarded her as a threat. And rightly so. Drew liked spinning his lady's world.

The door swung open, and Jade shouted a takeout order of burgers and fries to the waitress behind the counter before sliding into the booth. They'd agreed to meet at this out-of-the-way diner about twenty miles from the track. "What's up? I can't stay long. Tommy's out in the van." She pulled the file around in front of her. "I see you found the info on Sam."

"I got tired of reading all that crap on her sister."

"A lot of interesting stuff, huh?"

"What's your take on her?"

"Faith? She's got quite a resume."

"If you're auditioning for men." She smiled, recalling some of the wild adventures listed in the file.

"She does like them." Jade took a piece of paper out of her pocket and slid it across the table to her. "I made a list of all the guys."

"In date or performance order?" She chuckled.

"If you didn't pick it up from the case file, some of the names are the same." She pointed to three different ones on the list. "She's got a thing for drivers."

"What about Wilkerson?"

"No. He's doing someone else."

"Seriously?" She didn't understand why. Sam was ridiculously hot.

She nodded. "I caught the two them the other day behind the garage."

"Son of a bitch."

"He's hit on me a few times, too."

"Does Sam know?"

"Not sure." Jade picked up Drew's cup, took a sip, and winced. "She probably knows about the fooling around, but not sure about the most recent."

"What a jackass. She's way too good for him." She shook her head

"You'd better watch yourself, hotshot. Messing around with the boss's daughter could be dangerous."

She knew that, but watching Sam toss tools and slam drawers this afternoon had been an entertaining sight. The woman was hot when she was angry and even more gorgeous when flustered.

She hitched her lip up to one side and winked. "That's my kind of danger."

The waitress brought Jade's order to the table, bagged and ready to go.

"What happened to the mother? I don't see anything in the file on her."

"Mom was killed by a drunk driver when Sam was ten." Jade grabbed the bag and hollered to the waitress, "Put the burgers on her bill." She gave Drew a quick wink and headed for the door.

She shot up out of her seat. "Hey, wait a minute."

"Can't. Gotta go."

"Drunk driver. Why the hell did you have to tell me that?" Sliding back into her seat, Drew jammed the papers back into the folder and slapped it closed.

CHAPTER SEVEN

After arriving late to the sponsor party, Sam and Faith found the coat-check and slid their coats across the counter to the young lady.

"I hate these parties." Sam tugged at her snug-fitting, black velvet dress.

Faith's eyes swept the tall, dark stranger standing in the doorway. "Really? I love them."

"Kissing up to all these snooty people?"

Paddy appeared from behind them, took the coat-check ticket, and slipped it into his jacket pocket before giving Sam a parental glare.

"They're called sponsors, Samantha." His words rolled deeply, the *r*s ringing with the thick brogue still imbedded from his Irish homeland.

"Sponsors. Right." She rolled her eyes. "More like silver-spoon-fed snobs."

"The more silver, the better," Faith quipped, still eyeing the stranger, who was now reciprocating.

"If it weren't for them, we wouldn't be where we are today."

With the girls flanking him, Paddy put a hand on the back of each one of them and guided them into the main room. "Now put on those beautiful smiles and keep us in business."

"But Daddy, I thought I'd get a drink first," Faith said.

Paddy eyeballed the stranger she'd set her sights on. "They're mine for now, young man. Go find yourself a drink elsewhere," he said, waving him off. It was common knowledge that when it came to parties, Faith had a bad habit of over-indulging.

❖

Sam sipped her champagne and smiled each time Paddy introduced her to someone new. Being ushered from sponsor to sponsor was just part of the game, and she was required to play along. Faith had managed to break away for a bit to hook up with the stranger at the bar, but Sam had been stuck with Paddy since she'd arrived.

"Ah, here's another one of our gracious hosts, now." He reached out and offered a large burly man his hand. "Samantha, this is John Weston from Weston Meats."

Sam offered her hand. "Nice to meet you."

"My pleasure." He took it gently and raised it to his lips. "Such soft hands for a technician."

Sam smiled. "This is a lovely party, Mr. Weston."

"John, please."

"John." She smiled as she dropped her chin. "Thank you so much for your support." Sam didn't like schmoozing with the sponsors, but she was very good at it.

John stopped one of the waiters as they went by and took a toothpick-skewered smoked sausage off of the tray. "Have you tried our new crispy critters?"

"Not yet." She feigned a smile. "I'm not very hungry."

"Oh, come on. Just try one. They're good little things, if I do say so myself." He held it up with the toothpick, staring at it as if it were a prized child.

She politely took it and bit a small piece off the end.

"Pop the whole thing in." He guided her hand to her mouth. "That's the best way."

Reluctantly opening her mouth, she smiled, letting her teeth clamp around the toothpick as she slid it out. She immediately exchanged her empty glass of champagne for a full one from a passing tray and washed the vile taste from her mouth. First it was meatballs, then beef tips, and now pork sausage. Being a pesco-vegetarian by choice, she'd managed to keep the red meat to a minimum, but her stomach had already begun doing flip-flops at all the foreign foods she'd introduced to it tonight. Business was business, and Paddy would have a fit if she turned her nose up at any sponsor's product.

"Is that your new backup driver over there?" John motioned to Drew on the other side of the dance floor.

Sam's interest was piqued, but she didn't turn.

His smile broadened. "She sure seems to know what side her bread is buttered on."

Sam couldn't resist turning slightly to see what John was talking about. When she saw he was referring to the beautiful tall blonde Drew was dancing with, an unexpected wave of jealousy whipped through her.

"For the moment anyway." Sam glanced back at Paddy and could see he'd caught the fire in her eyes.

"She's got good taste. You have to give her that," John said, giving the blonde the once-over.

"Maybe too good for her own welfare." Paddy chuckled.

"Excuse me, gentlemen. I need to go freshen up." Shaken by the surge of adrenaline rising inside, Sam took off across the room.

After passing Drew and her mystery date, Sam peeked over her shoulder. She stumbled when she ran smack-dab into the man in front of her.

"I'm so sorry," she said, quickly wiping the droplets of champagne from his lapel.

"It's okay, Sam," he said, giving her a huge smile.

Seeing his round, friendly face, she forgot her embarrassment. "Ray." Her voice squeaked with a mixture of surprise and relief. "I didn't know you were here." She smiled, peering around him. "Where's Jenna?"

"She couldn't make it." His eyes swept the floor, revealing the usual timid fashion he embodied. "Not feeling good tonight."

"Oh. I'm sorry." She leaned in to regain eye contact. "I hope it's nothing serious."

"No." He smiled. "Just a little touch of the flu."

"Give her my best, will you?"

"Sure thing."

She glanced back over her shoulder to see Drew's dance partner heading toward the ladies' room. "Will you excuse me a minute? I was on my way to freshen up."

"If you ask me, you're as fresh as they come."

"Well, thank you, Ray. You're a sweetheart." She instinctively straightened his cockeyed tie before smoothing it inside his jacket. "Is this new?" she asked, noting the elegant feel of the silken tie and cashmere jacket.

"Yeah. You like it?"

"I love it. Save me a dance?" She kissed him on the cheek, then moved around him and headed to the ladies' room. She slipped through the door just behind the blonde. Trying to find some way to detain her, Sam patiently waited for the two women reapplying their lipstick to exit. She picked up the hand cream, then the tissues. *Nothing.* Dropping them back onto the gaudy metal tray on the basin, she got an idea.

Sam had accomplished her task and was on her way to the bar when Drew caught her by the arm.

"I knew you'd come." Drew said, pulling her onto the dance floor. Dancing fast and fluidly, she glided Sam around the floor gracefully until the tempo slowed. Then in one smooth step, Drew had her trapped in her arms, pressed firmly against her. The woman was good at just about everything. "I'm glad you finally snuck away from your father."

"The ladies' room is always a good out."

Drew let her fingers trail down Sam's spine. "You seem tense."

Sam avoided eye contact, fighting to suppress the same crazy feelings she'd tried desperately to ignore for the past few days.

"More tense than usual." Drew smiled and ventured closer, pressing her cheek to the side of Sam's head, immersing herself in the untamed curls surrounding it.

Sam kept her body stiff and unyielding, trying to maintain her distance. "I don't like this game you're playing with me." She didn't smile as she stared into Drew's eyes, letting her know she was dead serious.

"No more games. I promise."

Sam relaxed and let her body meld to Drew's. She took in a deep breath, and her head filled with the light, simple scent she emitted. The same scent she remembered from the night they met. *Baby powder.* No loud, overpowering cologne like most of her suitors. She smelled soft and comfortable, and the aroma excited her, in an odd sort of way. It was getting harder to be near Drew each day.

Drew's hand roamed the small of her back, drifting lightly across the top of her ass, and Sam's breath caught. She had to get away from her before things spun out of control again.

"Why don't we sit this one out?" She tried to pry herself away.

"We're just getting started." Drew held on tight, moving her to the music.

Out of the corner of her eye, she glimpsed the fuming blonde she'd locked in the bathroom. Burying her face in the crook of Drew's neck, she settled back into her and watched the blonde cross the dance floor.

Jade sat next to Tommy, moving to the slow, jazzy beat. Watching Sam cling to Drew on the dance floor made her stomach twist. She knew her sister's death wasn't Drew's fault, but seeing her with another woman wasn't natural.

A tall, dark-haired man crossed Jade's field of vision, stopped in front of her, and blocked her view. Still concentrating on Drew, she shifted her gaze around him.

"You want to dance?"

"No thanks," she said without looking up.

"You can if you want," Tommy said.

She glanced at the man with the dark features and chiseled chin. "I said, no thanks."

Tommy slid his palm across her bare shoulder and down her back until she felt him slip his thumb just under the edge of her red halter dress. "Are you sure? I don't mind."

"I'm fine right where I am."

"How about Ray?" He motioned across the room with his hand. "I'm sure he'd be happy to take you for a spin."

Jade drew her brows together as she twisted around to face Tommy. "Trying to get rid of me?" She raised her eyebrows.

"Just thought you might like to dance."

She leaned in and whispered in his ear, "If I wanted to dance, I'd take you back to the hotel room and do it just for you."

Tommy's cheeks flushed, and his smile widened as he glared up at the stranger. "Take off, buddy. She's with me."

"How about me? Would it be all right if I stole a dance?" a deep familiar voice asked.

Dad? Jade hopped up quickly

"What are you doing here?" She scanned the room for a sign of more police presence. "Are you working?" she asked, lowering her voice.

He whisked her out onto the dance floor. "Nope. Tonight I'm an invited guest."

"You got an invitation to this party?"

"I finagled an invitation. I saw they put Thompson on your case and thought I'd check in on you to make sure everything is all right."

"Everything's fine, Dad. You know I can take care of myself."

"I do know that." He glanced at Drew, and she saw his jaw clench.

"It wasn't her fault, Dad."

"She should have been there with your sister."

"She's still fighting her own demons about that."

"I hope so." His voice was strained.

"You need to let it go."

"I just don't trust her."

Jade tilted her head. "You never did tell me what happened the night Drew got shot."

"I don't know. I wasn't there."

"But you were on the case, weren't you?"

"Yes, but she chose not to wait for me that night. They went in alone, and her partner died because Drew was too cocky for her own good."

She got the feeling her father was keeping something from her. "How do you know Ship didn't make the call?" Craig Shipley was a senior officer and had been Drew's partner for the better part of ten years. Jade knew if they went in without backup, Ship was probably the one who gave the order.

"I just know." Jade saw something in her father's eyes she didn't like, something that looked like satisfaction. Was he glad Drew had been hurt?

Since her father's transfer to Internal Affairs, communication between them had been sparse. Jade knew Internal Affairs was investigating Drew for drug trafficking before the shooting. Being under suspicion is just part of the job when you work in narcotics. When they'd questioned her, she hadn't given them any information they didn't already have, but her father thought she should've cooperated more.

Jade had followed the code. When Drew denied being involved, Jade backed her up. But one question still nagged at her. What else had happened that night? Something had. She could feel it in her gut, but Drew maintained she'd told her everything.

"Listen. I didn't come here to talk about Thompson."

"What did you come for?"

"You haven't been home for six months. Your mother's been worried."

"Seriously?" She smiled. No matter what story he made up, her father would never tell her mom she'd been out of touch for six months.

"Okay. I was worried," he said, giving someone across the room a nod.

Jade turned to see who it was. Catching Ray in her line of sight, he raised his glass and smiled. "You know Ray?"

"No. Just fending off a tasteless stare."

"From Ray? Are you sure it's me that has his interest and not the redhead in the velvet dress?"

"That guy's had his eyes glued to you since you got up."

Glancing back at Ray, she noted his gaze was nowhere close to her.

"Well, I'd better get back to my date," she said as the music trailed to an end.

"You going to introduce me?"

"That's probably not a good idea. I mean, with the case and all. Seeing as you're a cop, I've been avoiding the parent subject." That had just become harder to do. Tommy would definitely have some questions for her now.

He squeezed her shoulder. "Come by and see me sometime. Let me know how things are going."

She nodded and then headed back to Tommy, already regretting the lie she'd planned to tell him.

❖

By the time Sam saw Brad arrive, she was tucked tightly in Drew's arms on the dance floor. The funny thing was she didn't care if Brad was watching her every move, but this spot in Drew's warm gentle grasp was getting way too comfortable.

She felt a hand on her shoulder and turned, welcoming the interruption. It was Paddy, who'd brought her another sponsor to charm. She glanced over at the bar and saw Brad already downing a string of shots. That wasn't the kind of impression he needed to make at this particular party. Managing to set Paddy's focus on Drew, Sam snuck away to get Brad under control.

She caught his eye as the bartender poured him another shot of whiskey, Brad's usual poison. He downed it and slid the glass back to the bartender. She heard him order another as she moved down the bar to join him.

"Don't you think you've had enough?"

He cocked his head but didn't smile. "Having a good time?"

"Not really. You know I don't like these things." She smiled at the bartender. "Water, please."

"So you were just suffering out there on the dance floor?" His tone matched his hardened stare.

"She asked, and I accepted." Her response was as blunt as the question. "Is that a problem?" She caught him glancing across the room at Drew. "Don't tell me you're jealous." Catching her tongue between her teeth, she let out a short breath. The man had never shown any sign of it before.

Brad's stare darted back to hers. "You're free to dance with track-trash, if you want."

"*Me* and track-trash?" she blurted before clamping her mouth shut. This wasn't the time or the place to discuss either one of their choices in bed partners.

He picked up his glass and sucked down another shot of amber liquid. "Well, I'd better make the rounds." He twirled his glass across the bar.

She grabbed his wrist, his eyes narrowed, and she released it immediately. "Will I see you later?"

"Nope."

❖

Drew turned and Sam was gone. Weaving through the crowd, she spotted her at the bar with Brad and rounded the dance floor. From the way she took off, it didn't seem like they were having a friendly conversation.

"Hey. What happened? You left me all alone with Paddy and that chatterbox. Man, he can talk." She cupped Sam's shoulder and let her hand glide down, enjoying the soft silkiness of Sam's skin.

"All that dancing made me thirsty." She held up her glass as if trying to justify her trip to the bar. "I needed some water."

"Deserter."

Sam plucked Drew's hand from her arm. "Besides, you should get back to your date."

She smiled, amused by Sam's obvious jealousy. "And you, yours." She motioned to Brad, who was mingling with a small group of women.

"Actually," Sam said, giving her a big smile, "I've suddenly become dateless."

"Well, in that case, I'd like you to meet someone." Drew glanced over her shoulder, trying to spot Liza. "There she is." She raised her hand and waved her over.

Sam's eyes widened when she saw the blonde approaching, and then her brows pulled together in irritation. "You're going to introduce me to your date?"

She nodded. "My sister, Liza."

Drew saw the color drain from Sam's face as she rushed past her. "You'll have to excuse me for a minute. I think Paddy needs me."

"What?" She spotted Paddy in the crowd. "He's not even looking this way." She glanced back, only to catch Sam's backside as she headed across the room in the opposite direction.

The woman was a complete mystery. One minute the connection between them was as obvious as the finish line. The next it was clouded with exhaust.

Sam's black velvet dress was clinging to her hips as Drew watched her slip away in a slow, sexy motion. One thing was clear. No matter how blurred things seemed, she was hot.

"I could have used some help back there," Liza grumbled, straightening her dress. "Some woman just locked me in the bathroom."

"Locked you in?"

"Yeah. She jammed something in the stall door. They had to call maintenance to remove it."

Drew turned around quickly, just in time to catch Sam biting her bottom lip as she watched them. Her body tingled. It had been a long time since a woman had flattered her so indirectly.

Drew turned back to Liza. "You could've just crawled under."

"Are you crazy?" She ran her hands down her body, continuing to adjust her dress. "This is a Versace original." Collecting herself, she scanned the crowd.

"Description?"

"Redhead in a black dress. I only caught a glimpse of her as she held the door when I went in, but I'd know that designer knockoff anywhere." She put her hand to her head. "She totally blindsided me. How's my hair?"

Drew laughed, listening to her sister babble on at the speed of light. The woman could get more information out in a matter of minutes than Drew could absorb in an hour.

Her eyes flared. "There she is," Liza squealed, trying to push past her. "I'm going to wring her neck!"

Drew curled her arm around Liza's waist and pulled her back.

"Let me go. She's getting away."

"Remember what Mom said about causing scenes." Liza was a bit high-strung, and although she never looked for trouble, it seemed to follow her. "Besides, she may have mistaken you for someone else."

"You know her?" Liza's finely arched brows rose.

"Intimately," she said with a grin.

A slow smile crept across her face. "She thought you and I..."

"Apparently." Drew smiled, thoroughly pleased that she'd gotten under Sam's skin enough for her to do something so outrageously immature.

Liza frowned. "I guess I'll have to let this one go, then."

"I don't know about that. A little backlash couldn't hurt."

"You are a very bad girl, Drew."

"That's what the woman wants." Drew watched Sam at the coat-check. Their gazes met again, and she gave her a scorching smile. Slipping her coat on, Sam pulled her gorgeous red hair from her collar, then turned and took off out the door.

"Aren't you going after her?"

"Nope. I'm going to get another drink." Weaving through the crowd to the bar, Drew knew this would be continued later.

❖

Sam entered the hotel bar and found Drew exactly where she thought she'd be. The familiar shiver of excitement surged through her. She'd done a terrible thing earlier, but in her own defense, Drew had never said anything about having a sister. She strolled across the room and dropped her bag onto the bar. "Dance, stranger?"

Drew swung around, slid off the stool, and followed her to the dance floor.

Feeling the slow burn of Drew's fingers trailing down her back, Sam shivered before turning and melting into her arms. "Sorry about the party. I didn't know she was your sister."

Drew smiled, and those damn dashing dimples appeared. "It would've been okay if she wasn't?"

"You know what they say. All's fair in—" What was she saying? She couldn't be in love with Drew. She'd known her less than a week. "Well, anyway. I am sorry." She let herself relax.

She so enjoyed the touch of this woman holding her, and the way she made her feel about herself was incredible. Sam actually felt like a woman again. Staring into Drew's soft brown eyes, Sam wasn't confused anymore. She was sure she was treading in dangerous waters. She closed her eyes and let her mouth fuse with Drew's in a soft, searching kiss.

Drew groaned. "It seems like we've been here before."

"I think we have." Pressing herself against her, Sam could feel Drew's heart pounding. "You want to try again?" Gazing up at her through long, darkened lashes, Sam felt a vulnerability she hadn't before. What if Drew rejected her?

"Are you sure?"

She nodded before sucking Drew's bottom lip between hers and letting her teeth drag across it. Without another word, Drew took her hand and pulled her along behind her.

Once they made it to Drew's room, they tumbled onto the bed. Sam was enjoying Drew's warm hands roaming her body when suddenly she was clammy. *Oh God, not now.* Her stomach churned, and bam. It was in her throat.

"Stop." She shoved Drew to the side and ran to the bathroom. All the bits of food she'd managed to choke down at the party were coming back to haunt her.

"Are you all right?" Drew's muffled voice came through the door.

She heard her grip the doorknob, and she scrambled to twist the lock before Drew could open the door.

"I'll be okay in a few minutes," she managed before retching again.

"Sam, open the door, so I can help."

"Please, just give me a minute." No way was she going to open that door. Throwing up in front of any woman was bad enough, but being in the process of making love to her when it happened was absolutely horrifying.

The rattling of the doorknob stopped. She must have given up. Sam pulled herself into the corner and let her head rest on the edge of the cold, porcelain tub. Squeezing her eyes shut, she begged for this to be a dream. A burst of air whisked across her face, and she opened her eyes. Drew was standing at the sink, dousing a washcloth with water.

"Something you ate?" She sat down next to her and slid the cool, wet cloth around Sam's neck.

"Apparently." She groaned and leaned against her.

After a few minutes of silence, Drew nudged her and got up. "Come on. Let's get you to bed."

Sam reached for her hand, and she pulled her unexpectedly weak body up. Stopping at the sink to rinse her mouth, she stared at the ragged woman in the reflection. Totally drained and embarrassed, she followed Drew out and crawled into bed.

"I'm so sorry." She couldn't believe this was happening.

"It's all right," Drew said, pressing her lips to Sam's forehead. "There's no hurry."

"Right." She nestled neatly into the crook of Drew's shoulder. "No hurry." She shouldn't be here, and she knew it. This was a sign, some sort of confirmation. After all, she wasn't actually a free woman.

Chapter Eight

S am fired the engine and let it run for a time before turning it off again. "Ray, check out this injector." It wasn't obvious, but Sam could see fuel.

"I don't see any cracks." He looked over her shoulder, then reached down and swiped the bottom of it with his finger. "It's a leaky injector. Must be the sensor."

"Over-worked and underpaid. Must be something wired wrong inside. Just like us," she said with a chuckle. "Do we have a new one?"

"Yeah. There's one in the bus. Want me to get it?"

"Hey, speaking of the bus. I found some clothes in one of the lockers. You know anything about them?"

"I must have forgotten to clear them out after the last road trip."

Sam knew that wasn't true. She'd cleaned out the bus herself.

"I'll get that pump," Ray said, and headed for the door.

"Ray?"

"Yeah." He swung back around, continuing to walk backward.

"How's Jenna?" She'd realized he hadn't said much about his wife lately.

"She's good." He stopped walking. "Anything else?"

Sam smiled. "Just one more question."

"Shoot."

"Have you heard anything about Drew Thompson?" That was a loaded question. "I mean anything I need to know about her driving?"

"Word around the track is she's a little crazy but has the skills." He hedged, scratching at the small amount of hair left from his flattop haircut. "I hear her family's got money."

Sam cocked her head. "Money?"

"Yeah. Lots of it."

"Really? I wonder why she doesn't buy her own racing team."

"Don't know. Maybe you should ask her to pitch in and sponsor us."

"Oh, shoot." She touched her forehead. "I almost forgot. I have to meet with some guy from a local winery. Do you think you can get started on that sensor for me?"

"Sure. Go ahead. I'll take care of it."

Drew's hair flew freely around her head. The air was crisp and the temperature an exhilarating sixty-five degrees. A welcome contrast from the past few weeks of constant heat. It would've been a perfect morning if she hadn't woken up in an empty bed.

She went through the evening again in her head. She'd told Sam it was all right, but that wasn't totally true. She'd never wanted anything or anyone as much before. Last night, she'd curbed her desire, held Sam in her arms, and thoroughly enjoyed it. One way or another, she'd had to feel her warmth.

Drew slowed, flashed her pass, and continued through gate number one, down into the main paddock. With qualifying runs set to begin this afternoon, the track was busy with race teams from all over the country. She whipped into her usual parking spot and hopped out of the Jeep. After checking her reflection in the side mirror, she raked her fingers through the mass of dark hair and headed to the garage.

Drew grinned, watching Sam as she snapped up the maintenance chart and flipped the pages. She was thoroughly amused at her own string of bad luck. Twice now, she'd had Sam right where she wanted her and was unable to complete the task at hand—a task she'd originally been reluctant to undertake but now was determined to accomplish, even though it would shatter every rule she'd ever made for herself.

❖

"Ray, throw all those winery stickers away," Sam shouted, letting the door fling open and bang hard against the building.

Propositioned again. If that idiot thinks I'm going to sleep with him for a few measly thousand dollars, he's got another think coming. It didn't happen all that often, but when it did, the jerk was usually pretty sorry he'd ever made the mistake by the time Sam finished with him.

"Did you get that injector replaced?" Sam pushed the office door open. "Ray, you in here?"

After dropping the sponsor papers on the desk, she headed into the bathroom. She ripped open a package of antihistamines she took from the cabinet, popped one into her mouth, and chased it down with a gulp of cough medicine. Something in the air was sure making her sinuses go crazy. If she didn't nip it in the bud, she'd have a full-blown sinus infection by race day.

She picked up the thick black marker on the desk and wrote *RAT* across the sponsor sheet. Paddy would know what she meant.

Backing up, Sam felt a warm body against her back and stiffened.

"I keep having this same dream." Drew's voice was slow and mysterious. "This beautiful woman keeps showing up in it."

There they were again. Sam let the usual string of sensations Drew triggered zap through her. She didn't move until Drew took her shoulders and gently nudged her around to face her. The scrappy style of her naturally blown-dry locks made Sam's heart flutter. She was unbelievably sexy this morning. In a move of pure self-preservation, she backed up to create some much-needed distance between them.

Drew moved closer as Sam retreated. "Last night she was in a slinky black dress." She was good at this game, definitely an experienced player.

"A dream?" she said as she cocked her head.

"It had to be." Drew shrugged. "She was gone when I woke up this morning." She trailed her thumb across Sam's cheek and cupped her face in her hand. "Slick." She smiled. "The name fits. You *are* a slippery one."

Sam hesitated a moment before reaching up, curling her fingers around Drew's wrist, and moving her hand. "Maybe that's where you should keep her…in your dreams." Sam wasn't much for wearing her feelings on her sleeve or rehashing embarrassing moments.

"You're probably right about that." Drew reluctantly agreed and backed up. "So, what's on the agenda for today?"

"After I finish replacing this injector, you'll need to take me out on a test run."

"Do I have time to grab something to eat?"

"Sure. Go ahead. I'm gonna be a few more minutes here, anyway."

"You want something? Eggs? Sausage? Bacon?"

"No thanks." She went to the sink, filled a plastic cup with cold water, and took a large gulp. "And don't bring any of that into my garage," she shouted after her.

Her stomach rumbled as she rounded the car. It didn't have anything in it besides the herbal tea she'd drunk this morning and the medicine she'd just taken, but the thought of food made it threaten to spew.

After about thirty adjustments and as many laps around the track, Sam was still stumped as to what was causing the flat spot in acceleration. Whenever the engine hit ninety-five miles per hour, the car felt like it might stall. She'd thought it was the sensor, but she'd changed that this morning, along with all the gaskets and seals that went with it. Still she detected a flat spot. It had to be some kind of compression leak, but damned if she could find it.

Frustrated, she was losing her focus. The heat, the stress, everything was getting to her. Having Drew peer over her shoulder was also taking its toll. Questions, questions, and more questions. Finding the problem was hard enough without having to explain everything to her. Plus, she smelled so damn good. Drew was a distraction she didn't need.

Sam slid into the car and turned the ignition over. "Keep an eye on the sensor." Punching the pedal, she revved the engine hard. No miss at first, but the longer it ran, the more the engine began to falter. "Is the PSI somewhere between four and six?" she screamed over the engine's roar.

"It's just below four, and I hear a hissing sound," Drew shouted back.

She turned the ignition off and the garage was silent. "Damn. I just changed that." Dropping her head back onto the window frame, Sam let out a low grumble. She didn't know what the hell was going on. Something was heating up, expanding, or shrinking.

Slapping her hands to the roof, Sam pulled herself up out of the driver's seat and sat on the door. *Think, Sam. This can't be that hard to figure out.*

Paddy came through the side door and let out a suffocating cough. "Smells like fuel in here."

"Bad injector sensor."

"Turn those fans on and get this car out of here now," he said.

The crew scrambled to push it outside, and Paddy ducked his head under the hood. "What the hell is going on here, Samantha? There's fuel visible here."

"I don't know." She threw up her arms and followed him back inside. "I just changed that sensor an hour ago."

The pages rustled as Paddy checked the maintenance chart before tossing it to Sam. "Right after Ray changed it. Damn it, Samantha! What's the matter with you?"

"That's impossible." She flipped through the pages quickly, stopping cold when she saw the single page with Ray's handwriting on it. "This entry wasn't here earlier. I know I checked it."

"Plain as day, Samantha." Paddy shook his head. "Plain as day."

Drew took the clipboard from her. "I know you're not feeling good. Maybe you just overlooked it."

"No. It wasn't there." She went to the bench and picked up the empty carton. "It was still in the box," she whispered, her mind working, trying to figure out how she could have missed the entry.

Paddy followed her to the bench. "What's wrong with you, Samantha?"

"She had a little bout with the stomach flu last night," Drew answered for her.

"Well, why didn't you say so? Go back to the hotel. Lie down for a while. Ray can take care of this." He glanced around. "Where is Ray?"

"I don't know, but I screwed it up, so I'll fix it."

"Suit yourself."

Even with Drew continuing to hover over her shoulder, Sam had the bad sensor off and the new one bolted on within fifteen minutes. Her small fingers worked quickly, sliding the female electrical connections onto the male leads. Just a few more little wires and hoses and she'd be done.

"Doesn't that hose go on the bigger of the two nipples?" Drew asked, leaning in behind her.

Sam turned her head slightly, and Drew edged closer. This was a very dangerous position to be in.

"That's the one you removed it from, right?" Drew's voice was slow and guarded.

Inspecting the two hoses, Sam saw she was right. She snatched the hose off the smaller nipple and pushed it onto the bigger one.

"I was stretching the hose. It goes on easier that way."

"Oh, I see. Sorry. I was just trying to help."

"You know what would be a big help?" Sam popped up quickly, hitting her head on the hood. "Damn!" She closed her eyes to absorb the shooting pain.

"Are you okay?" Drew moved closer.

"Stop!" Sam put her hand up between them. "Would you just back off and let me get this done?" She dropped her shoulders and let out a heavy breath. "Listen. I'm sorry, but don't you want to go help Paddy or something?"

Right at this moment, what Drew wanted was to wrap her fingers around Sam's sweet little neck and pull her in for, what she knew would be, a phenomenal kiss. Instead, she turned and went to the sink to give them a cleaning. Flattening the crease on the maintenance chart, she could see someone had deliberately folded the page up to hide Ray's entry. And now, purposely, or not, Sam had almost connected the hoses incorrectly. Drew might not be a car whiz, but she was trained to remember detail. Was it sabotage or human error? That was the question lurking in her mind.

"Maybe when you're done, we can get out of here for a while," Drew said as she observed the small container on the shelf above the sink, then picked up the tube sitting next to it. "Which one of these do I use?" She unscrewed the top and gave it a sniff.

"Use the stuff in the metal can." Tilting her head back, Sam took in a deep breath and blew it out as she moved her head from side to side, stretching her neck.

Drew stared at her beautiful red tresses flowing down her back. Remembering their smell, their silky texture, their weight lying across her chest last night, she was wet immediately.

"I guess I could use a little time out of the garage." Sam reached down and finished connecting the last of the hoses. "I just need to make sure this sensor works."

"You want me to fire it up?"

"Would you? Please?"

Drew hit the ignition, and the engine roared as it slowly accelerated. "How's it look?"

"No leak. Everything's tight this time." Sam squeezed her fingers together and swung them in front of her throat. "Cut it."

Drew shut off the engine. "Okay. Now let's get out of here for a while." Drew pulled herself up and swung her legs out easily.

"Where to?" Sam dipped her hands into the cleaning goop and wiped them off before washing them.

Smiling lightly, Drew wiped a black smudge from Sam's cheek. Mean as a snake and covered with grease, and Drew still found her absolutely irresistible.

"You'll see." It was time she got Sam on her own turf.

CHAPTER NINE

Planting her hands firmly on her hips, Sam stood directly in front of Drew, blocking her shot. "I thought you said you weren't going to play games with me anymore." It might only be miniature golf, but Drew was winning, and Sam didn't like it.

Drew stretched out an arm and nudged her to the side before hitting the red golf ball around the obstacles and into the hole. "What's wrong? Can't take a little competition?" She crossed her arms and raised an eyebrow.

"I can take it, all right." She swung the putter hard against the little yellow ball. "Damn," she said, watching it hit a bump, fly past the hole, over the concrete border, and onto the next putting green.

Drew frowned. "You're putting too much power in your shot."

She flattened her lips and pulled her brows together. "What?"

"Here. Let me show you." Drew wrapped her body around Sam's and covered her hands with her own on the putter shaft.

Feeling the warmth of Drew's breath on her neck, Sam nervously bumped up against her, and a charge of excitement shook her. Drew shifted closer, slid her chin onto Sam's shoulder, and took in a long, slow breath. Sam got the message loud and clear, and her body betrayed her again.

"Let the putter do the work," Drew whispered, then lifted it slightly and let it swing back down to connect. The putter sent the ball rolling easily into the hole.

"Yessss!" Sam swung around and let her gaze dart from Drew's soft, sensuous lips to her steamy brown eyes. *Zing!* There it was again, that overwhelming need to kiss her. Flying around this familiar slippery track made Sam's heart race. In an instant her mouth was on Drew's, and her tongue was roaming through her lips, feeling, tasting, wanting the victory she'd forbidden herself just a few hours before.

This felt right. It was like she was meant to be linked with Drew. She tingled with the excitement of a first date, yet the kiss rang with the familiarity of old lovers. She'd touched her intimately, felt her long, lean body on hers, twice now, and hadn't been able to complete the task she craved.

"Hey, do you think you guys could do that somewhere else? Or at least let us play through?" A voice from behind them broke through the fog she'd been immersed in, urging Sam to break away.

"Sure," Drew mumbled. "We're done here." Moving a strand of hair from Sam's face, she didn't break eye contact. "Aren't we?"

"Uh-huh," Sam managed to say. Still reeling from her own indecision, she took Drew's hand and let her lead her off the course.

"What do you want to do now?" Drew asked, moving in to kiss her again.

She was caught. Boxed in. Snared in a trap of her own making. Sam knew exactly what she wanted, but Drew was so much different than anyone she'd ever known, and Sam might very well lose her heart. What was she going to do now? The wind shifted, and she caught a whiff of exhaust.

"Go-carts!" Sam grabbed Drew's hand and pulled her around the corner. "Come on. I know they're here somewhere." Spotting the track, she let Drew's hand go and raced to the first open cart. "Now, *I'm* going to show *you* how it's done." She lifted her eyebrows and gave her a smile as she slid into the seat and fastened the safety harness.

"Bring it on, baby," Drew said, taking the challenge and sliding into the cart behind her.

Weaving in and out between the other carts, Sam gave herself a substantial lead, but Drew was gaining. As she took the curve, Sam thought she saw Brad at the end of the track. She jerked forward as her cart bumped the cart in front of her. When she looked up again, he was gone. *I must be out of my mind. Brad can't be here.*

She turned to see where Drew was but couldn't spot her. By the time she circled the track, the drivers had slowed, and the attendant was directing everyone back into starting position.

A surge of panic shot through her. What if that was Brad? He and Drew could be getting into it right now. She didn't need that conflict. She weaved through the slowing cars, pulled the go-cart into the lane, and screeched to a halt. She popped out of the car and searched the track, relieved when she spotted Drew sitting on the side of the track next to a little girl. Brad was nowhere in sight.

"What happened?" Sam asked the attendant.

"Someone threw this rock onto the track, sending the little girl into the curb." She handed her a boulder the size of a baseball.

"Jeez—is she okay?"

He nodded, hopping on the back of a go-cart. "She's just a little shook up." He gave the starter rope a tug, but the cart didn't fire.

"Who would've done something like that?" Sam tossed the rock into the grass.

"Probably some teenager. Their parents bring them here and just let them loose."

Sam frowned. "She seems okay now."

"Yeah. Your girlfriend got her calmed down for me."

"She's not my girlfriend," she said, then moved close enough to hear Drew soothing the girl with her calming voice.

"Whatever," the attendant said, yanking the rope harder. The engine fired, and he raced it around the track.

"She's just a…" She started to protest but realized it didn't make any difference what the attendant thought.

Watching Drew gently wipe the tears from the little girl's cheeks made a rush of warmth hit Sam. She was so attentive, so loving. Paddy would've yanked her up by the arm and made her get back in the cart. She would have given anything for that kind of attention from her father when she was young. Hell, she'd give it now.

"Is she all right?" Sam said, kneeling down on the grass next to Drew.

"Yep. She's a tough one." Drew took the little girl's hand and helped her up. "How about some pizza?" she asked, leading her to the track exit.

"Pepperoni?" the girl asked, staring up at her with innocent puppy-dog eyes.

Drew scrunched her nose and smiled. "The only kind."

"Where are her parents?" Sam whispered as they walked.

"Apparently, she's here with her older brother and his girlfriend."

"Where are they?" She took a quick sweep of the area.

"Don't know."

Sam snapped her head back to Drew immediately, widening her eyes. "They left her here to ride this alone?"

"Looks like it." Drew scratched the back of her head. "I told the kid manning the ride, if he comes after her, we'll be inside." She stopped, seeming to second-guess herself. "Is that okay with you?"

"Of course." Sam nodded, surprised Drew thought she had to ask.

"Here." Drew handed a few tokens to the little girl. "Why don't you go play a couple of games while we order the pizza?"

"Thanks." She grabbed the coins and raced across the room to the arcade games.

"You like pepperoni?"

"I'll just have a salad."

Sam stood behind Drew, watching the little girl play a video game. It seemed the big, bad racecar driver had a soft spot for kids. Suddenly Sam found herself wanting to wrap her arms around Drew and never let go. Suppressing the urge, she took in a deep breath and touched her lightly on the back instead.

Drew turned slightly. "Everything okay?" Her hand brushed around Sam's waist, and she melted into her.

Sam nodded. "Everything's good."

Seeing Drew soothing the little girl until her tears had subsided made Sam's heart twinge. Sam was gradually learning that behind the thick crust of arrogance was a sweet, gentle woman, which made Sam want her even more.

"One pepperoni pizza coming up." Drew took the plates from the counter and handed her one. "Salad bar for you, my dear."

Sam stared into Drew's warm chocolate eyes and felt herself sinking again. "That was awfully nice of you. Helping her like that." Why did she have to be so blasted nice, and funny, and cute?

"Nothing more than I would expect from any average person in the same situation."

Drew didn't realize Sam saw her as much more than average and found herself hoping for things in the future that would never happen between them.

"So how about we find a table?" Drew handed her a soda. "It's root beer," she said before Sam asked.

Sam gave her a soft smile. Drew must have noted her drinking habits. She didn't order soda very often, but when she did it was always caffeine-free. "I'll be right back," she said, setting her drink on the first empty table.

Lettuce, tomatoes, cucumbers—not the best salad bar in town, but it would satisfy her appetite. After filling her plate, Sam returned to find that Drew had moved them to a booth by the window.

"What was wrong with that table?"

She stood up and motioned to the arcade games. "I thought it might be a little quieter over here." Drew offered her the seat next to her, but Sam opted for the other side of the table, sliding in just far enough to force Drew to remain in the seat across from her.

Visibly amused at her need for distance, Drew slid in facing her and sat staring at her.

After slipping the wrapper off her straw and plunging it into her soda, Sam shifted uncomfortably. "Stop it."

Drew grinned. "Stop what?"

"Staring at me like that."

"The pizza isn't here yet. What should I do instead?"

"Talk or something."

"All right. Tell me how you got the nickname Slick?"

"What do you think?"

Drew closed her eyes as though she were deep in thought. "Because you like to get naked, pour Slick Fifty motor oil all over your body, and slide around on the garage floor?"

"No." Rolling her eyes, she shook her head. The woman was impossible.

She reached over and rubbed a strand of Sam's hair between her finger and thumb. "Hair's clean, you probably wash it daily, so it couldn't be that." Letting her finger trail down her jawline, she pinched Sam's chin softly between her thumb and forefinger. "Maybe it's because you're so slick, no one can catch you."

She was doing it again. Sam cursed herself for letting Drew affect her this way. She cleared her throat. "None of the above."

"Then, how?"

"I'm not sure I want to tell you after all that." Sam gazed at her through long, lowered lashes. "It's going to ruin my mystique."

Drew took her hand and swept her thumb across the back of it. "At this point, I don't think anything could ruin that."

The touch unnerved her. She sucked in a deep breath to calm herself before speaking. "I wouldn't be so sure about that. Samantha Louise Kelleher. Initials SLK. Aka—Slick."

The vinyl crackled as Drew shifted in her seat. "Not so mysterious after all."

"When I was a kid, Paddy always put Slick on the entry form instead of Samantha. Some races weren't gender friendly. It wasn't officially in the rules, but 'no girls allowed' was a common bias. Sometimes they would find ways to exclude me. After a while they caught on and accepted the fact that Paddy was going to enter me, whether they liked it or not. We didn't have to pretend anymore, but the nickname stuck."

Drew raised an eyebrow, and her gaze swept down to her breasts. "Couldn't they see you were a girl?"

Sam followed her gaze and smiled back. "I was a late bloomer. I didn't get these until I was about seventeen."

"Why aren't you driving now?" Drew's brows pulled together. "I can't be the only reason." She leaned forward, plucked a cherry tomato from Sam's plate, and popped it into her mouth.

"You're only part of it. Since Tommy's accident, Paddy is suddenly acutely aware of the dangers of racing."

"From what I saw today, I think you can handle it."

Drew stretched her arms across the top of the booth, and her shirt tugged up. Sam couldn't help but notice the flat belly and defined abs. Her gaze fixed and she couldn't move. Damn, she was trying so hard to be cool, but all Drew had to do was stretch a little, and her hormones topped out.

"One large pepperoni." The waiter slid the pizza onto the table between them.

Her eyes darted to the pizza, then to Drew. Saved, she thought, catching a glimpse of her smile.

"Bobbie." Drew waved the little girl over. "Pizza's here."

"My name's Barbara," she shouted, hurrying across the room to the table.

"Didn't you tell me Bobbie is your nickname?"

She scowled. "I did, but I don't like it. Bobbie's a boy's name, and I don't want to look like a boy."

Drew let out a chuckle. "You're not going to look like a boy if you don't want to." She smiled broadly at the ten-year-old, who hadn't even begun to develop into her true beauty. "Take Samantha, here. She's gorgeous." Drew reached across the table, curling a strand of Sam's red hair around her fingertip. "And *everyone* calls her Sam."

Bobbie perked up quickly. "They do?"

"Yep." Sam nodded, unwinding the strand of hair from Drew's finger before forcing her hand to the table beneath her own.

"Wow. Then Bobbie might not be bad. It's not as much a boy's name as Sam." She grabbed a slice of pizza and stuffed the end into her mouth.

Drew chuckled. "I'm sure you'll be even prettier than Sam."

"I'm going to be beautiful," she said, her eyes gleaming with excitement. She took another bite of pizza, dropped it onto the plate, and ran back to the video games.

"Beautiful. Where did she get that?" Sam laughed.

Drew let her gaze flash back to Sam and could see she was serious. She had no idea how many heads turned when she passed.

"My God, woman. Don't you know how sexy you are?" Matted, windblown hair, and all, that fact was undeniable.

"Not me." She seemed surprised. "I'm just an average technician trying to make a living."

"Just watching you eat that salad would send any woman reeling." She had methodically separated out the vegetables and cut each one into equal parts.

"What do you mean?"

"I've never seen anyone eat with such structure." Drew grinned. "I mean, one piece at a time."

"Each one of these has its own unique flavor." She set her fork down, picked up a piece of lettuce, and tore it in half. "Open your mouth." She put half into Drew's mouth and then half into her own. "Lettuce can be leafy and flavorful, depending on the kind you choose." She took a slice of cucumber and bit a piece off before feeding Drew the rest. "Crunchy, yet somewhat bland." She lifted an eyebrow. "Am I right?"

"Absolutely. And the tomato?" Drew asked curiously.

"The tomato," she took the knife and cut the petite, shiny-red globe in half, "is the kicker." She slid half into Drew's mouth, then held her half up in front of her. "On the outside you have the smooth skin to glide around in your mouth." She slid it down her tongue. "And on the inside you have all these different shapes and textures to explore." She turned it upside down and raked it across her teeth, capturing the pulp just inside her mouth. "If you mixed all these things together, you'd never get to experience all that." She smiled mischievously and chewed the remaining piece of tomato.

"Are you sure you're just a technician?" Drew relaxed, letting herself feel everything she'd just heard. She smiled, strangely contented to sit across from this woman who could totally turn her on with one look, and who might also be a cold-blooded killer.

Bobbie came running back to the table. "I got three hundred thousand on Space Invaders."

"Wow! That's great," Sam said. "Why don't you sit down and have some more pizza." She scooted over, letting her slide into the booth next to her.

"There you are." A straggly-looking teenager approached the table. "I've been searching all over for you."

"You just went off and left me. I could've been killed. Wait 'til I tell Mom." Bobbie squeezed her lips together tightly.

Drew noted the sudden flash of panic on the boy's face. He wasn't sure if it was because his sister could've been hurt or because she was going to make sure he got in deep trouble when he got home. "We had a little accident on the go-carts, but she's fine now."

"I only left for a minute," the boy grumbled, his voice filling with concern.

Drew frowned. "She's ten. You shouldn't have left her at all."

He dropped his shoulders. "My girlfriend wanted a soda."

Drew held her temper. "Next time take her with you."

"I know, I should've, but my girl doesn't like having her tag along."

"Where is the old crab anyway?" Bobbie spoke up before jamming another slice of pizza into her mouth.

He glanced back over his shoulder. "She got mad and took off with some friends."

Drew's demeanor softened. "Want some pizza?"

"Sure." He sat down, grabbed a plate, and pulled half the pizza onto it.

Sam slid back in her seat, and Drew could see her watching as she gave the teenager a lengthy lecture on the responsibilities of being an older brother. The boy nodded and continued to wolf down piece after piece of pizza, staring mindlessly at her through the gel-stiffened strands of hair hanging across his eyes.

After finishing off the pizza, Sam and Bobbie hit the ladies' room before they all walked to the parking lot. Bobbie's brother pulled opened the car door and slid into the driver's seat. "Thanks for taking care of my sister," he said, glancing up at Drew.

"No problem." Drew pushed the car door closed. "Just remember what I said."

Bobbie rolled her window down and waved wildly as they drove off.

"The boy looks pitiful." Sam threw her arm up, returning her wave with just as much enthusiasm. "What did you say to him?"

"I told him he would have many girlfriends, but only one sister." She spoke in a rhythm as though she were Confucius.

"Ah, the philosophic racer."

"That's me." Drew took her hand and pulled her toward the Jeep. "Come on. Let's get out of here."

Sam glanced over her shoulder. "The kid can't be too bad. He drives a sixty-nine Chevelle."

"I'm sure when it comes to women, he'll make his mistakes just like every other teenager." Or adult, Drew thought as she tugged Sam close, slipping her arm around her waist.

Sam seemed to hesitate, then let her arm curl around Drew's waist. This reaction, coming from any other woman, might lead Drew to believe she didn't want to be this close. And she shouldn't. *Drew* shouldn't, but God help her, she wanted it. She wanted it more than anything else she'd ever wanted before, and something about the way Sam touched her told Drew she wanted it too.

When they reached the Jeep, Drew caught the steamy, impassioned glint in Sam's eyes and tingled, and she urgently wanted to explore it. Drew hadn't been with a woman who could make her want to do that in a very long time.

"Where are we going—" A fleeting touch of Drew's lips to her mouth interrupted Sam's question.

Drew opened the Jeep door for her. "To get some real food. I'm starving."

Sam hopped up onto the seat. "You should've stolen that last slice before that malnourished teen got it."

"Malnourished." Drew let out a short grunt and slammed the door. "Bottomless pit is more like it," she said, rounding the Jeep to the other side.

Chapter Ten

I'll have the New York strip, medium-rare, baked potato, and a side of mushrooms." Drew handed the leather-bound menu back to the waitress before glancing over at Sam "Aren't you going to have something?"

"No. I enjoyed my salad earlier."

"You certainly did."

"Anything to drink?" the waitress asked.

"Wine?" Drew glanced back to Sam.

"Red, please."

"Two glasses of the house red."

Sam tore off a piece of sourdough bread and jabbed at a pad of butter with her knife.

"I thought you weren't hungry?"

"I'm a sucker for fresh-baked sourdough." She popped a piece into her mouth before ripping off another. "Word around the track is you come from a pretty wealthy family?"

"I guess you could say that."

"So why don't you have your own racing team?"

"Someday I will." Drew smiled. "But I'm going to do it on my own terms."

"If my father was willing to give me a team, I'd take it in a minute."

"No, you wouldn't." Drew shook her head. "Too many strings."

"I wish there were more strings. Paddy's given me plenty of," she raised her fingers in air quotes, "stuff. It'd be nice to get a little of his time instead." Sam shifted uncomfortably. "I guess it just goes to show that every family's different."

The waitress appeared with the wine and disappeared again in silence.

"Aren't you with him at the track all the time?"

"Me and twenty or thirty other people."

"I didn't realize."

"Of course you didn't. Things aren't always as they seem." She tapped the table nervously with the butter knife.

Drew reached for her hand, and Sam picked up her glass and took a long, slow drink of wine. Definitely time to change the subject.

The waitress reappeared and slid a plate of food in front of Drew. Sam watched her jab at the steak, cut a piece off, and stuff it into her mouth.

"The wine's good. How's the steak?"

"Great. Want a bite?"

"No, thanks. But I will take a mushroom." Sam speared one with her fork.

Drew picked up the bowl and let a few tumble out onto her steak, then set the rest in front of her. "Help yourself."

"Yesterday in the garage, I noticed you and Jade seemed pretty friendly. Do you know her?" Sam swirled the wine in her glass, then watched the fingers of liquid slowly trickle back into the small pool at the bottom. "I mean from somewhere else." It was none of her business, but she had to ask.

Drew hesitated, put down her fork, and picked up her wine. "I married her sister."

"Married?" *I almost went to bed with you.*

"I lost her a few years ago." She took a drink of wine.

Sam thought for a minute. A few years. Was that long enough to have found someone else? "She couldn't take life in the fast lane?"

"She died."

Sam's heart dropped. She hadn't expected those words and didn't know what to say. She sank back into her chair as her mind spun with questions she shouldn't ask.

Drew flattened her lips, and Sam knew her reaction had been obvious.

"What happened?" *Did I actually ask that?*

Drew pulled her brows together and cocked her head.

"I'm sorry. That's none of my business. I shouldn't have asked."

"No. It's okay. She was pregnant and started hemorrhaging."

"The baby?"

Drew shook her head slowly.

"Oh, God, Drew. I'm so sorry."

"Thank you." She smiled slightly.

"How long were you married?"

"Five years. I met her at a fund-raising event." Drew smiled as though remembering the moment. "We both ended up outside, avoiding the crowd. We talked all night and into the early morning hours."

"Sounds like a fairy-tale meeting." Something Sam had always wanted.

"Yeah. I guess so." Drew rolled her lips together. "I've never been able to talk to another woman about her before."

"It's hard to get over something like that." She was speaking from her own experience now. "And getting involved again—have you done that? I mean, is that even possible for you?" It wasn't easy for Sam.

Drew smiled. "Not until you."

Sam rolled her eyes. "We're not involved."

Drew let out a deep, rolling chuckle. "Oh, but I think we are." She grinned, flashing those gorgeous dimples. "Dangerously involved."

Drew was obviously avoiding what had to be a painful subject, but she couldn't hold her laughter. The bouncing eyebrows, humorous tone, and looming stare hit her right in the heart. Now her cheeks were heated and she was embarrassed. As they say, timing is everything, and Drew seemed to be an expert at it.

"Stop it," Sam said, shaking her head.

Drew pushed her plate to the side, then took Sam's hand and thumbed her naked ring finger. "How 'bout you? Are you involved with anyone, besides me?"

She pulled her hand from Drew's and pressed it to her chest, searching for the ring that hung on the chain around her neck. "You know I am." Her voice was low and soft. She didn't feel like laughing now.

"You can't honestly tell me you're serious about that jackass Wilkerson."

"He wasn't always an ass," she mumbled, and gave her a thin smile. "He was my first love."

"Was?"

Sam stared at table and let her finger follow the weave of the white, cotton tablecloth back and forth in front of her.

"Things between us have changed over the years." She blew out the words in a sigh. "His ambition has replaced any affection he ever had for me." Glancing up into Drew's soft brown eyes, she hesitated.

Of all people, why was she telling this woman her innermost secrets? A woman from whom she should be keeping her distance. She was desperately trying to stay aloof, but after what Drew had just told her about her wife and seeing her today with Bobbie, Sam's resolve was weakening. Drew had punched a huge hole in her guardrail and quickly slipped through it. With no effort of her own, the perfectly defined road Sam had paved for herself seemed to be crumbling right in front of her, and she had no idea where it was leading.

She shrugged and picked up her glass. "But you really don't want to hear about my deprived love life, do you?"

"First loves are always special, but sometimes you have to let them go for your own good."

Sam wondered if Drew's wife was her first love. "It's not a perfect relationship." Sam sipped her wine. "We stray from time to time, but somehow we always seem to end up back together."

"I've heard." Drew threw her arm up for the check.

"What do you mean, you've heard?"

"I'm not one for rumors, but there's been talk around the track about you and Frank—"

"Frank MacNamara?" She felt the blood drain from her face. The pain seared through her as though it had happened only yesterday.

She'd loved Frank, at least she'd thought so. When he was killed, Sam didn't think she could go on. She'd never expected it, but Brad was there to help her through the loss.

"Whatever happened between Frank and me is my business." Sam could hardly speak. Drew was way out of bounds.

"I'm sorry. I shouldn't have brought it up." Drew reached for her hand, and Sam moved it back into her lap.

"No, you shouldn't have." With tears threatening to spill out at any moment, she slid out of the booth and stood up. "I'd like to go back to the hotel now."

❖

Sam didn't speak on the ride back and barely mumbled a short good-night when Drew walked her to the door. She didn't know what was worse, almost blowing the case or having Sam hate her for being such an unfeeling bitch.

Drew hadn't intended to hurt her, but she'd needed a reaction. She had to know if Sam was a woman with deep, dark secrets, a woman with an improbable but not impossible past, a woman with a temper hot enough to kill. Sam had a temper all right, but her reaction wasn't what Drew had expected. Her face had paled when she'd mentioned MacNamara. The happy glimmer in her eyes had suddenly vanished into a murky pool of sadness.

The question had flown out of Drew's mouth before she'd known what she was saying. She'd been so wrapped up in Sam, she'd forgotten she was working. And then, for lack of a better story, she'd lied to cover her ass. Drew hadn't heard anything around the track about them. Everything she'd learned was from the case file.

The mere mention of Frank's name had seemed to flatten Sam like a freight train. When Drew heard the torment in her voice, it had thrown her off her game because she'd seen pain like that before. On more than one occasion, she'd told victims' families of their premature deaths. With strangers it wasn't as difficult to put up a wall, to ignore what they were feeling, but she'd never understood the full extent of their pain until she'd lost Kimberly. Sam was a strong woman, but Drew could see the anguish clearly in her eyes.

Drew opened the door and tossed her keys onto the small, round table in front of the window. *If Sam killed him, why would she be so upset? Maybe she didn't mean to. Maybe she was just trying to prevent him from racing.* But why? Drew couldn't figure her out. Sam was getting in her head big-time, and her cover was on the verge of being blown.

Drew had hoped Sam wouldn't pick up on her familiarity with Jade, but she should've known better. The woman didn't miss much. She hadn't meant to go into the particulars of Kimberly's death. Sam didn't need to hear her sad stories any more than Drew needed to hear hers. Sam's relationship with Brad reminded Drew too much of her own life, of how she'd neglected Kimberly. Her determination to show everyone that the rich kid could actually work for a living had left Kimberly alone and vulnerable. Drew had realized too late what she'd had, and now she was gone.

She flopped down onto the bed and opened the case file. Tapping her pen on each piece of her full name, she recited the initials out loud. "S.L.K." Why hadn't she noticed that? *She calls her father by his first name. Is that out of convenience or disrespect?* She jotted down a few notes. Maybe it was just plain self-preservation. Everyone Sam got involved with seemed to have their own agenda. The woman had absolutely no support in her life, romantically or otherwise.

Drew raked her hand down her face. That should have been her first clue. She was missing a lot lately. Too much. She moved her head from side to side, listening to the joints in her neck crack, before leaning back against the headboard and closing her eyes.

Who was she trying to kid? She knew what the problem was or, more specifically, who it was. She had fiery red curls, beautiful emerald-green eyes, and a boldness that made Drew's insides burn. Not to mention, when they'd first met, Sam had impressed her with a heated kiss that had lingered on her lips for hours. Drew opened her eyes and bolted off the bed in a panic. This had to stop.

CHAPTER ELEVEN

"Jade, stop it."

"Why?" She continued nipping at Tommy's lower lip.

He grabbed her shoulders and held her at arm's length. "I mean it. Stop!"

With her legs tucked beside his thighs in the wheelchair, she sat back onto his knees, facing him. "What's wrong?"

"Why are you here?" His voice was strong but rang with a tinge of insecurity. "With me."

"What kind of a crazy question is that?"

He let out a heavy breath. "I mean, with all the other men around here, why would you want to stay with a man who can't," he let his gaze drop, "even dance with you, for God's sake?" She could see he was serious. "There are certain things I'll never be able to do."

"Don't you think I know that?" She blew out a short breath. She couldn't believe what he was saying. "Have I ever made you feel like you were any less of a man?"

"No, but—"

She pressed her fingers to his mouth. "Have I ever led you to believe you haven't satisfied my every need?"

He closed his eyes and shook his head as if clearing the visions from his mind. "I see how other men look at you, and I know you see it too."

She let out an irritated breath and pushed herself up, out of his lap. "I'm with you, dummy! Not them!"

"For now." His voice was filled with an odd sound of acceptance.

Jade grabbed her sweatshirt and let out a loud growl. "I'm getting really tired of having this same conversation, Tommy." She stopped just short of the door and turned slightly. "Just because a man has a working penis doesn't make him whole."

After pulling the door closed behind her, Jade threw herself up against the wall and slapped her open palm against the pale-blue stucco. Sure, she knew other men found her attractive, but she'd had her fill of those jerks long before she'd met Tommy. She'd been with plenty of men that were lacking in other areas—areas of the heart, areas Jade found she couldn't live without, didn't want to. Finding a man who loved her, not just for her body, was a never-ending search. Then she'd come across Tommy, a kind, loving man who shared long conversations and actually seemed interested in what she had to say. Now he was trying to push her away. Job or not, this was where she belonged, and she wasn't about to give him up.

Feeling the chill of the night air, she pulled her sweatshirt over her head and headed to the pool. She kicked one of the metal chairs as she passed, winced, grabbed her foot, and flopped down into one of the lounge chairs.

❖

"Sam, you in here?" Brad gave the door a light knock as he pushed it open.

"I was just coming to find you." She mustered an energetic smile, hoping he wouldn't ask where she'd been all day.

He brushed past her. "Have you seen my belt?"

"It's over there." She pointed to the chair. "Where are you going?"

"To the bar."

"Oh." She noted his neat appearance, laced with heavily scented cologne. "I was hoping maybe we could just hang out here tonight." She pressed herself against him and began to unbutton his shirt. "You know. Have some nice, quiet alone time."

He moved her hands and refastened the buttons. "I'm meeting some of the guys. We're going out."

After the thoughts she'd been having about Drew, she deserved his infidelity, but it still hurt.

"Fine." She shrugged, letting her hands drop. "Go do what you want, but don't come back here half-lit expecting me to entertain you." She whirled around and took off out the open door. Sprinting across the balcony and down the stairs, she slowed before hitting the pool area, flopping down into the lounge chair next to Jade.

"Hey," Jade said.

"Hey." Sam noticed she was holding her foot. "What'd you do?"

"Fucking chair got in my way." She held her toe momentarily, as if waiting for the pain to subside.

Sam relaxed back into the chaise and stared up at the stars. "What are you doing up this late?"

"Can't sleep. There's a jackass in my bed."

"Mine's going out."

Jade's face twisted. "I just don't understand it."

"Understand what?"

"You're beautiful," she blurted, producing a momentary flash of awkwardness in Sam. "Why don't you find yourself someone who treats you better?"

Sam took in a deep breath and let it out slowly. "I'm not good with commitment." She stared up at the second floor and watched Brad come out of her room, go a couple of doors down and into his.

"Then why does it bother you?"

"I don't know." Untrue. She knew what it was. She couldn't stand the fact that she wasn't enough.

"You're not in love with him."

"No." She shook her head.

"Then get out of it."

"It's not that easy."

"Sure it is. You have to look out for number one, Sam."

They watched as Brad came out of his room and slipped on a black leather jacket.

"Where's he going?" Jade asked.

"Bar hopping."

"You're way too nice," Jade said. "And your brother, what's up his ass today?" Her voice rose. "I just want to hang out with him, and he keeps pushing me away. I'm so tired of dealing with men who only think what's on the outside is important." She popped up and swung her legs to the side of the chair. "You must have to deal with your own challenges."

Sam immediately thought of the hurdles she was constantly jumping to earn the respect of the male drivers.

Jade glanced down at Sam's ample cleavage. "Like getting someone to see beyond the rack."

"Jade." Sam shook her head. "Just because you work with these guys doesn't mean you have to talk like them."

"Sorry." Her tone dropped to a whisper. "But you know what I mean."

"I do. I can also understand where Tommy's coming from." This wasn't a discussion she wanted to have, but she'd promised Tommy she'd give Jade a fair shot, and she had to be honest.

"You can?" Jade pulled her brows together. "Then would you please explain it to me?"

"You know that Tommy was engaged at the time of his accident, right?"

Jade nodded.

"Has he told you anything about her?"

"No. He doesn't like to talk about her."

"She didn't handle it well." Sam shook her head. "She came to see him only a few times in the hospital, and within six weeks she was gone."

"Why?"

"I don't know." Sam shrugged. "I think she liked the idea of being with a famous racecar driver." She smiled and let out a short breath. "And then, of course, there was the sex issue."

"Are you kidding me? I've never had a kinder, gentler lover in my life." Her voice sounded deflated. "I mean, I don't think there's anything he won't do to please me."

Whoa! Too much information. Discussing her brother's sex life wasn't on the top of Sam's to-do list. Sam smiled and glanced away briefly, trying to avoid Jade's searching eyes.

"You have to believe me. He—"

Sam raised a hand to stop the next string of intimate details set to spill out of Jade's mouth. Apparently, she wasn't giving up, so Sam shifted sideways in her chair to face her.

"Listen, Jade. I really do like you, but if you're not planning to stay around, you need to leave before he falls in love with you."

Jade rolled her eyes and let out a heavy breath. "What about me?" Her voice rose quickly. "Doesn't anybody care that *I* may have already fallen in love with *him*?"

"Have you?" Sam asked pointedly. Jade hadn't been around long enough for the thought to enter Sam's mind, but she could see Jade was dead serious. It was never about the hair, the tattoos, or even the piercings. Sam's only concern was her brother.

"I don't know." She let her face drop into her hands and rubbed her eyes. "He's so funny and kind...and...so many other things." She hesitated. "But he just won't open up to me." She let out a low rumbling growl. "He's so frustrating sometimes."

"I think he's afraid you won't always be satisfied with him."

"You know there's a lot more involved in loving someone besides fucking. I've been with a few men in my life. Some good, some bad. Tommy's different." Her eyes softened. "I connect with him in a way I never have with anyone before."

Sam smiled at her conviction. She wished she had such passion in her life.

"Sex is more than an action. It's a state of mind, a reaction to someone who brings out the best in you," Jade added.

Sam was just now beginning to realize that fact since she'd met Drew. Her attention strayed as she thought about the night they met. She'd offered herself freely to Drew, and then even after having second thoughts, Drew hadn't taken advantage of the situation. She'd been gentle and understanding. Nothing at all like Brad. He would've continued without the smallest thought or concern for her.

"I know you're just playing the good sister, but I'm not going anywhere." Jade reached over and shook the chair. "All I want is to make him as happy as he makes me."

The jiggle of the chair snapped Sam's attention back to the conversation. "I'm sorry, Jade. I think I may have misjudged you."

She gave her hand a firm squeeze. "You're not like every other woman out there."

Jade's eyes began to well. "You must think I'm a babbling idiot." She swiped at her face, drying the moisture from her eyes.

"Not at all."

"Hello, ladies," Drew said, standing behind them curling her fingers around the top bar on each of their lounge chairs.

They both stared over their shoulders at her. Sam flushed before she darted her gaze back to Jade. She could see the lightbulb flashing in Jade's head. The woman surely knew now whose room she was coming from the morning she'd run into her on the steps.

"Guess we're not the only night owls around here," Jade mumbled.

"Mind if I join you?" The metal scraped against the concrete as Drew pulled a chair over.

"Hotel pool. You're a guest. Can't do much about that," Sam said, letting her less-than-eager tone show through. The woman was becoming an absolute pain in the ass. Showing up everywhere Sam went. Flashing that smug, egotistical grin at her. Making her react in ways she didn't want. Making Sam have a good time in spite of herself.

Drew smiled amusingly and turned to Jade. "Any objections?"

Jade gave Sam a curious look. "By all means. Have a seat."

"Where's that Neanderthal boyfriend of yours?" Drew flopped down into the chair.

None of your business. Sam wasn't in the mood for twenty questions again.

"He went out," Jade said when Sam didn't answer.

"Without you?" Drew rolled his eyes. "The man's a fucking idiot. I wouldn't leave you alone for a minute." Drew was using that playful tone again, but this time Sam refused to let her guard down.

"Funny." Jade smiled at Sam. "We were just talking about that."

Traitor. The compassion Sam had felt for Jade a few moments ago vanished.

Jade shrugged and gave Sam an innocent smile before she caught her bottom lip between her teeth and jumped up. "Well, on that note, I think I'm going to hit the sack." She feigned a yawn. "I'm sure

Tommy's wondering where I wandered off to by now." She put her hand on Sam's shoulder and gave it a light squeeze. "You two have fun."

Jade glanced back at Sam and winked. She would make her pay for this later.

Drew chuckled, and Sam peered up into her dark-chocolate eyes. Her stomach flip-flopped. Maybe the penalty wouldn't be too stiff.

"Guess she didn't like my company after all."

"Imagine that," Sam mumbled.

"You want to go do something?"

"It's a little late for miniature golf, isn't it?"

"Yes, but alas, I can think of other things to do in the moonlight." Drew leaned forward, engaging Sam in an eye-scorching stare.

"Like?" she whispered uncomfortably, expecting Drew's mouth to impact hers at any moment.

"Come on," she said, grabbing Sam's hand and catapulting her out of the chaise.

"Wait a minute!" Sam pulled free. "I can't just take off in the middle of the night."

Drew raised her brows. "You have someone to answer to?"

Sam thought about her earlier encounter with Brad. By now he was off seducing one of his little track groupies. She pulled her hand across the back of her neck before turning her attention to Drew. "Where are we going?"

"You'll see." Drew smiled, taking her hand and towing her along beside her.

This was turning into a bad habit—letting Drew take her on these little adventures, giving her the impression she would go anytime, anywhere she wanted. Sam was asking for trouble.

Drew drove across the peninsula to Marin County and took the Lucas Valley exit. After taking the winding road into a heavily wooded area, she veered off the main road onto a well-driven dirt path. Even with the high beams on, all Sam could see were huge redwoods surrounding them. As they drove deeper into the darkness, she wondered what she'd gotten herself into. Then she saw the lights illuminating from within the forest.

"What the hell is that?" A chill ran down her spine and she leaned closer, grabbing Drew's arm as random thoughts swirled in her head. Was she going to be abducted, whisked away in a spaceship, never to be heard from again?

A sneaky smile crept across Drew's face. "Mud racing. I hope you don't mind getting a little dirty."

Sam widened her eyes with excitement. "Are you kidding me? I'd love it."

As they pulled in, people clad in all colors of racing leather quickly surrounded the Jeep.

"Drew," a tall, curly-blond-haired man shouted. "Haven't seen you here in a while."

"Been a little busy lately, Joe." Drew hopped out, walked around to the back of the Jeep, and took out a couple of helmets. "I brought some new competition," she said, tossing one to Sam.

Joe gave her the once-over and smiled. "Not bad."

"Does she know the rules?" a knockout brunette asked, slipping in next to him.

"Don't worry, Kate. I'll fill her in."

"Rules? I thought these races didn't have any." Sam said.

"It's not really a rule. It's just something between Joe and me. I'll explain after we get going." Drew walked around to the other side of the Jeep.

Kate eyed Sam suspiciously. "You don't seem like her type."

"And what type would that be?" She raised an eyebrow at the petite woman dressed in tight, black leather.

Kate's thick, full lips curved into a smile. "That would be me."

"Oh." Sam's tone was low and even. "I'll keep that in mind," she said flatly, amused that the woman thought she was competing with her in any fashion other than the race.

"You do that." Kate's voice rang with irritation.

Sam caught up with Drew and Joe as they were coming back from the makeshift entry booth set up in the back of an SUV. "Who are we racing?" she asked as she surveyed the variety of people and vehicles lining up. She saw everything from sixteen-year-old boys in Honda Civics to women in their fifties driving Baha Bugs.

"Kate and Joe," Drew said, reaching into the Jeep and pulling the custom-installed shoulder straps from behind the passenger seat.

"Imagine that." Sam looked up and smiled as Kate threw her a two-fingered wave.

"We never lose," Joe said.

Sam shivered. The way he'd said it, along with his stare creeping up her body, made her skin crawl.

"There's a first for everything." Sam climbed into the Jeep and pulled the straps free on the driver's side.

"I like a woman with fire." Joe tilted his head slightly. "She's driving, right?"

"Yep."

He swiped his hand across the fender. "She'll be a pretty trophy." Joe's smile broadened. "Definitely the prettiest one yet."

"I wouldn't get too confident if I were you." Drew chuckled and stuck his hand out. "Good luck."

"You too, buddy." Joe slapped his hand to Drew's.

"Sounds like your friends are pretty good." Sam watched them walk back to their Jeep. "Or at least think they are." She climbed out of the Jeep and headed Drew's way. "Did I hear something about a trophy?"

"It's more of a status symbol than a trophy." Drew met her at the back of the Jeep. "Wrong side." She motioned. "You're driving."

"Me first?" Slipping the helmet over her ears, Sam suspected there was something more involved in this race.

"You can do it. Go-carts, race cars, mud cars—the basics are all the same."

"But this is going to be a lot more fun." Sam smiled, pushing her curls back out of her face before tucking them up into the sides of the helmet. Sliding into the driver's seat, she fastened the shoulder harness and started the engine.

"See those two big stumps." Drew pointed just ahead. "That's the start."

"What's my first turn, right or left?"

"The track goes up and to the right, then zigzags through the trees and back around to the left."

"How long is it?"

"Only about three-quarters of a mile, so we take two laps."

"Why two people in the Jeep? Wouldn't it go faster with less weight?"

"Yes, it would, but you wouldn't want to drive this track alone."

Joe pulled up next to them, giving Sam a wink before sliding across to the passenger seat. Kate climbed into the driver's seat, looked over at Drew, and blew her a kiss.

"What's that about?" With her foot flexing hard against the accelerator, Sam quickly shifted her attention from Kate to Drew as the engine raced.

"History. Oh yeah," Drew shouted over the engine. "I forgot to tell you that one rule." She gave her a sly grin as she grabbed the roll bar, bracing herself for a quick start. "If you lose she gets my Jeep."

The flag went down, and Joe let out a screaming howl as Kate took off like a bat out of hell.

"What?" Sam shouted, popping the clutch.

"You heard me. Now get moving."

Jamming her foot to the gas, Sam gripped the steering wheel. They flew over the first hill and around the turn with ease, but the zigzag through the trees was a little more difficult to maneuver. Mud spattered up into the Jeep, they were trailing, and it was almost impossible for Sam to see through the windshield. Drew turned on the wipers and pressed the washer-fluid button. The mud swished back and forth across the windshield in front of her.

"I can't see!"

"Hang on. I'm gettin' it." Drew pulled a jug of water from the back and poured it over the top of the glass, clearing a small, murky area for her to see through. Now she understood why she needed a passenger. No way in hell was she taking her hands off the wheel.

As she took the inside line around the curve, the rear of the Jeep in front of them slid across the mud. Sam took the opportunity to move ahead. Downshifting, she heard Drew let out a wail as she bumped her way past them and shot out in front as the second lap began. Going into the zigzag in the lead gave her a definite advantage.

At the last curve, the Jeep slid out, coming close enough for Drew to touch the massive redwood timbers. Bracing for impact, Drew grabbed at the roll bar. Sam pulled it back to the inside track and made it out of the trees without a scrape.

Sam gripped the steering wheel, trying to keep in tight around the last curve. She maneuvered the Jeep skillfully, holding the rear just in front of Kate. When she hit the straightaway, Sam double-clutched, threw it into fourth gear, and they flew across the finish line.

"Wow!" she squealed, letting the mud-ridden machine slide sideways to a stop. "What a rush!"

Sam tugged her helmet off and dropped it into her lap. She grabbed Drew's face in her hands and gave her a long, hard kiss. She was on fire and suddenly wished there weren't so many people around. She pulled back and stared into Drew's piercing, dark eyes as the small, screaming crowd approaching.

"I guess you've still got it, Thompson." Holding up his pink slip, Joe sounded disappointed.

"That's hers," Drew said, motioning to Sam.

"Keep it." She smiled.

"You sure?"

"I'd hate to take away your pride and joy."

"I owe you one." He kissed Sam lightly on the cheek. "I'll look forward to next time."

Drew smiled widely. "It's a good thing you won. I told him if they won, you'd go out with him."

"Maybe I still will." She tilted her head, watching Joe as he walked away.

"You can't go out with him." Drew snorted out a laugh.

"Why not?

Drew's lip curled into a sexy grin. "Cause you're totally into me." She pulled out her phone and took a selfie with her. Then quickly tagged her in a Tweet.

@samkelleher awesome on and off the track.

"You are so full of yourself." She bumped her shoulder playfully. "How could you enter a race with rules like that? You could've lost your Jeep."

Drew shot her a goofy grin. "I knew you'd win."

Sam wiped a glob of mud off her sleeve and threw it at her. "You're damn lucky I did."

Moving closer, Drew stared deep into her eyes. "No luck involved, remember? It's all skill." Another glob of mud fell from the roll bar onto Drew's head, and Sam laughed.

"You are absolutely covered." Sam smiled, brushing the mud from her head before dragging her fingers down Drew's neck and across her shoulder.

The electricity zapped through her, and Sam wanted to kiss her again. She dismissed the urge quickly and focused on Drew's shoulder, scraping the mud from it and tossing it into the darkness.

"Is there a car wash around here?" Sam asked, laughing uneasily as she sank back in her seat. "We'd better stop and get wet, or by the time we get back to the hotel you're going to be stiff as a board."

Drew smiled and pulled her lip between her teeth.

"Sorry. Bad choice of words." After that kiss, Sam was already soaked, with absolutely no relief in sight. She would make sure of it.

CHAPTER TWELVE

A fter driving the short distance from the wooded area to the paved road, it wasn't long before Drew pulled into a gated drive. She killed the engine and lights before getting out of the Jeep. Sam slid out and watched her squeeze between the overgrown boxwood shrubs to scale a six-foot stone wall.

"Come on," Drew said as she sat on the wall and waved her over.

Sam stayed put on the other side of the shrubs and planted her hands on her hips. "Do you know these people?"

"The house belongs to a friend of mine."

Sam glanced at Drew, then at the shrubs.

"Just raise your arms and squeeze through."

Sam did as she said. Grabbing Drew's hands, she let her tug her up onto the wall. Hanging halfway over, she blinked at the tropical paradise in front of her.

"Your friend doesn't mind you showing up in the middle of the night like this?" she asked, and swung her legs up and over, dangling them on the other side of the stone wall.

"He's out of town. I check on the place for him while he's gone."

"Then why are we climbing over the wall?"

"Left the key in my other pants."

"Your friend must do pretty well." Sliding off the wall onto the slick grass, Sam let out a squeal when her legs went out from under her. She ignored the sting shooting up her spine and scrambled to her feet.

"Let's just say he's made a few wise investments." Drew grabbed her hand and pulled her along. "There's an outdoor shower next to the cabana."

"There's a cabana?" Sam said, rubbing her tailbone.

"We can probably find some dry clothes in there."

Drew pulled her around the edge of the pool and into a huge stone enclosure. After turning the water on and waiting until it warmed, Drew ducked under the vast waterfall and rinsed the mud from her head.

Sam squeezed her eyes shut and followed her in, going face-first under the massive stream of water. The rushing surge felt amazing flowing through her hair and down her body. Warmth soothed her mud-stiffened skin as the water washed the dried muck away. She wiped the moisture from her eyes and caught Drew surveying her. Sam glanced down at her sheer-white, clinging, cotton shirt. She was getting a clear shot.

She gave a slight smile at the thought of how Drew had begun to explore her the last time they were together. The night had ended badly, a complete disaster. A miserable train wreck at best. Drew had been teasing her for days, but now it seemed she was back in the driver's seat. Time to give Drew a taste of her own medicine.

"You wanna help me get these clothes off?" she asked, and Drew's gaze flew back to hers. She gave Sam an unreadable stare, and Sam shuddered when she thought Drew was actually going to take her up on it.

Drew gave her an easy smile and pointed to the water lever. "Just turn it right or left to control the temp," she said, clearing the raspy lump in her throat and stepping out. "I'll see if I can find some dry clothes."

"Thanks." Sam pulled her soaked T-shirt over her head and tossed it over the top of the stone enclosure. She peeked out just in time to see Drew balk when it sailed past her, landing on the concrete in front of her.

Drew stopped just inside the door of the cabana and opened the electrical box. "Gate lock, landscape lights, pool light." She sounded them off as she flipped the switches one at a time. "That should do it." She rummaged through the drawers in the rustic Polynesian-crafted dresser and took a few things before heading back outside.

Noting the absence of the sound of rushing of water, Drew glanced over at the shower and let her gaze follow the trail of clothes leading to the pool before fixing on the body swimming just below the rippling water. *Damn! The pool light was a bad idea.* She dropped the clothes onto the chair and waited for Sam to surface. She didn't dare go any closer.

"How about a moonlight swim?" Sam asked, emerging from the water in front of her.

"I have to wash down the Jeep." She turned and headed for the gate. "I set some clothes out for you."

Letting her mind flash back to Sam in that scant T-shirt, Drew smiled at the grin she'd given her. She wasn't embarrassed or uncomfortable. She seemed entertained by her reaction. She glanced over her shoulder before going out the gate. Intentionally or not, she'd given her another glimpse of just what she was missing, and the impact had been completely arousing.

"Get your mind back on track," Drew mumbled to herself, tugging the hose free from the spindle. Earlier Sam had kissed her hard and deliberately, erotic enough to produce an arousal in her she hadn't expected. When Sam's sultry green eyes met hers, she'd almost lost control.

She heard a splash and peeked back through the slats of the wrought-iron gate. Naked woman? Muddy Jeep? Normally there would be no contest, but considering the circumstances, Drew knew this was the right choice tonight.

After spending the better part of an hour washing the thick coat of hardened mud off the undercarriage of the Jeep, Drew had her hormones back in check. She picked up the helmet Sam had worn and plucked a stray red hair from the foam padding inside. Not much had survived the last accident at the track, but the two previous crashes had left the cars partially intact, and Forensics had been able to collect a small amount of DNA evidence. She popped open the glove box, reached inside, and took out a plastic bag. Hopefully, this sample would rule Sam out as a suspect, but it might firm up the case against her.

Drew dug deeper in the glove box, searching for the slick plastic cover of her cell phone. She punched in a number and pressed it to her ear. "Hey, Boss. I've got a DNA sample for you, but she's not giving up much information."

"Have you gotten close yet?"

She peeked through the gate again. "I've been pretty close tonight."

"Get closer."

She caught a glimpse of Sam swimming laps up and down the pool, and her pulse quickened. She spun around and paced down the driveway. "You *want* me to sleep with her?"

"I don't care what you do. Just get me some evidence. Find out who's causing those accidents."

Drew pulled the phone from her ear and stared at the screen. Had she really heard what she'd thought she had? Did the captain just give her the green light to sleep with her suspect? That was totally against protocol.

Drew paced back up the driveway to the Jeep, tossed the phone back into the glove box, and slammed it shut. She wasn't sure what to do. It would be easy to let things run their course, right here, right now. Sam had let Drew know more than once she was willing. Maybe she should go ahead and do it. Then she'd be rid of all these feelings mixing her up inside. Or would she? Drew actually liked Sam. She couldn't picture her blowing up the cars she'd put so much effort into creating. And her reaction earlier at dinner wasn't typical of a cold-blooded killer.

She reached in the backseat for a towel and swiped it across the rear quarter-panel of the driver's side. Not a scratch on it. Sam was an excellent driver. During the race, Drew had thought they might make contact with the trees on more than one occasion, but Sam had kept it under control. She was impressed. That didn't happen very often.

Drew gave the Jeep a good drying before checking her watch. An hour and a half. Surely she'd given Sam enough time to be out of the pool and dressed. She pulled the gate open and peeked around the stone wall. Damn, she was still in there.

Watching her swim slow, fluid laps sent a thrill through her. Her nakedness blurred just enough by the rolling motion of the water was a total turn-on. Everything seemed perfect—the setting, the mood, the woman. But she had to resist.

Drew snuck through the gate and headed for the shower.

"You coming in?" Sam said.

"I'm gonna to hit the shower." She kept her distance from the pool. Another glimpse of Sam would put an end to her resolve.

"Come on, jump in. The water's great."

"No. I'm good." That was a laugh. She was far from good. Drew knew where this was going, and she had to do something to stop it. Fast.

❖

Sam kept her face half-submerged in the water. She was spending an awful lot of time teasing this woman. She wasn't even sure what she'd do if Drew actually called her bluff. She wanted Drew, but that didn't mean her conscience wouldn't get in the way again.

And what about Drew? Would she go through with it? Her wife had died…during childbirth. Divorce she could handle, but the memory of a perfect wife. How could she compete with that?

She waited a few minutes and then climbed out of the pool, went to the shower, and peered inside. She watched the water rush across Drew's shoulders and the taut muscles of her back. She gazed lower, stopping at the distinct tan line at her waist before probing the virgin-white skin of her butt. Then Drew turned and…*Wow!* The visual was incredible.

Sam bolted, throwing herself against the outside of the stone-wall enclosure. Her heart, ready to rocket through her chest, pounded wildly as she thought about the exquisite creature on the other side of the wall. She took a deep breath and started in, but then her hand brushed against her thigh and she felt it. The roughness of the scars left from the accident.

She dropped back against the wall and struggled with the paralyzing memory. The heat-searing pain—then the sudden but brief relief as everything went numb. That was all she could recall, but it was enough to throw her into uncontrollable sweats.

Kneading the pink, uneven skin with her fingertips, Sam cursed. How could she have forgotten about them? They were horrible, ugly scars that Brad couldn't look at, let alone touch. She could never let Drew see them.

In a panic, she rushed over to the clothes Drew had laid out and pulled them on. The navy-blue T-shirt and sweatpants were baggy enough to cover everything she wanted to hide.

After settling into the oversized hammock that hung between two of the miniature coconut trees, Sam closed her eyes. She'd teased Drew enough for one night.

Sam was almost there, to that dazed state between semi-conscious and completely relaxed, when Drew's muddled voice broke through the dreamy-darkness in her head.

"You ready to go?"

Sam sighed, opened her eyes, and stared up into the stars. "It's so beautiful here. I hate to leave."

"We should get back. We've got a big day tomorrow."

"I was just settling in. Can't we stay a little while longer?" She shifted to make room for Drew in the hammock. "Sit with me?"

Drew sank down onto the grass next to her instead.

Letting out a soft chuckle, Sam propped herself up on one elbow. "You know, I'm beginning to think you're all show and no go."

"Oh, believe me." Drew brushed Sam's lips with hers. "When I'm finished with the show, I'll be ready to go."

"I can't wait for that," Sam said, leaning closer for more. The hammock turned, and Sam tumbled out on top of Drew. *Zing!* There was that feeling again. She stared into Drew's chestnut eyes and forged ahead. Her mouth met Drew's in a soft, slow frenzy as she immersed herself fully in the kiss. God, her lips were soft, simply perfect for her own.

Drew broke away and moved swiftly out from under Sam, letting her slip off onto the ground. "It's getting pretty late."

Totally confused, Sam remained motionless on the soft bed of grass. Here she was all fired up and ready to go. Did Drew want her or not? That was a stupid question. Of course she wanted her. Sam knew when a woman was interested.

"We'd better get going." Drew offered her hand, Sam took it, and she pulled her up. Her soft body pressing against Drew's once again, their eyes connected instantly, and she could see that it was difficult for Drew to resist. Drew released her, and she followed her back to the Jeep. Drew wanted her all right. She wanted her so much she'd lost her usual cocky banter.

Without turning on the light, Sam snuck into her room. And after she let her eyes adjust to the darkness, she saw that the bed was empty. Brad had heeded her warning and slept in his own room, or more likely someone else's. Either way she was relieved he wasn't there.

Sam removed the golden chain from around her neck, let the half-carat diamond ring slide into her hand, and dropped it just inside the night-stand drawer. She needed to be free of him, if only for one night. The ring was no longer a symbol of love but a symbol of never-ending captivity.

She glanced at the clock—after three. Tomorrow would be another day with him, but tonight would be hers and hers alone. She took out her phone and viewed the Tweet Drew had sent.

@samkelleher best date I've had in a long time.

Was it a date? She contemplated the picture. They were certainly a mud-covered duo. Maybe it was. She smiled and tweeted in return.

@drewthompson it was definitely an adventure.

Even covered in mud, Drew's boyish grin was absolutely charming. With little left of the night to sleep, she would have dreams filled with visions of Drew, the intimate stranger who seemed to fill her world with happiness.

CHAPTER THIRTEEN

Sam swigged down the last drop of coffee and slid the cup onto the workbench. She'd abandoned her usual cup of herbal tea because she needed caffeine more than purity this morning. Sleep had evaded her last night, and she'd broken yet another of her self-motivated dietary rules to help her get through the day.

She picked up a can of carburetor cleaner and pressed the top with her finger. It sputtered a few drops of liquid before air hissed through the nozzle. After tossing it into the trash, she stretched to rummage through the various cans on the shelf above the bench but couldn't locate a new one.

"Ray, could you check the supply room for another can of carburetor cleaner? I thought there was one up here but can't find it." She wiped down a piston and slid it into one of the shafts. "I know it's a mess in there. As soon as I get these seated, I'll be in to clean up," she said, reaching for another piston.

"No problem." He pulled the metal door open and let it slam shut behind him.

She heard the clang of the metal door again. "You found it already? For the life of me I couldn't locate it earlier."

"I don't know what you're missing, but I found what I need." The sound of Drew's voice set off the usual buzz within her.

Sam glanced back over her shoulder and shook her head. "What is it with you? Why do you keep coming back?"

"I think you know the answer to that," Drew said nonchalantly, assessing her appearance.

She let out a quick breath and whirled around to face her. "Is it because you really want me?" she asked, lifting her left eyebrow suspiciously. "Or because you can't have me?"

"I'm not really sure." Drew smiled hesitantly. "But if last night was any indication, I was thinkin' your position on that might have changed." Drew took Sam's free hand and slowly raised it to her lips.

"About that." Sam smiled subtly. "I really should apologize." Turning slightly, she set the piston down on the clean cloth she'd laid out on the bench. "I had a great time at the race, but I shouldn't have baited you like that."

Drew widened her eyes and let her jaw drop. "Am I to be left feeling like a woman scorned?" she said, her voice rising in satirical melody.

Sam laughed. "I guess so." Planting her elbows on the bench, she leaned back against it. "It was fun but inappropriate." She closed her eyes and let the tingle she'd felt wash over her again. "Yes, definitely inappropriate."

"But I was really hoping to do it again soon." Drew took her hands and backed her up against the bench. After lacing their fingers together, she locked them behind Sam and held them firmly against her ass. "Why don't we start over," Drew whispered, brushing Sam's lips with hers.

The warmth of Drew's tongue penetrated her mouth and sent Sam's mind spiraling into no-man's land again. She couldn't remember the last time she'd been kissed so thoroughly and with such passion or how long since she'd kissed someone back with such intensity. With her heart pounding wildly, she pulled her hands free and slid them to the back of Drew's neck, then into her short hair, sweeping through it as Drew pulled her closer. The sound of labored breaths followed by soft, sensual sighs echoed in the hollowness of the metal garage as Drew's hands roamed the curves of her body.

"Do you have any idea what you're doing to me?" Sam's breath was low and thick.

"I want to do so much more." One by one, Drew unfastened the buttons of Sam's shirt.

"Someone might…" Drew's thumb slid across her nipple, and Sam couldn't stop the throaty moan that passed through her lips.

"I threw the bolt," Drew said against her cheek as she continued to trail her lips down to her neck.

"Oh my God." Sam's voice lowered, wants and needs exploding inside her. Letting her head fall back, she opened the pathway down her neck, begging Drew to travel farther. She tugged blindly at Drew's pants, but she shifted just out of reach. She diverted her hands quickly up her shirt to Drew's smooth abs.

Drew's mouth was scorching as she explored Sam's breasts, which were unbelievably sensitive. It took only one flick of Drew's tongue to make her incredibly wet. She unzipped the fly of Sam's jeans and slipped a hand inside. Sam shuddered when Drew stroked a finger through her drenched folds. Sucking in a ragged breath, Sam tried to slow the rush taking her.

She shouldn't do this, it was wrong, but every inch of her wanted it. Drew's mouth and hands were like heaven. Sam hadn't been this turned on in…forever. She caught Drew's hand firmly between her legs and opened her eyes wide, meeting her gaze. She had to know what Drew was thinking before she let the orgasm capture her.

Pure pleasure, that's what she saw in her scorching brown eyes. Sam pressed into her hand, Drew continued until the orgasm took over, and Sam held on tight, launching into a frenzy of mind-shattering sensations. Drew had catapulted her into the moment, and she came in a fast and hard fury she hadn't experienced in years. She climaxed wishing they were somewhere else where she could share the intense heat she now knew they could produce.

Sam sank against her and sucked in a deep breath. "You *are* a bad girl, Drew Thompson."

"You're amazing, Samantha Kelleher." She pressed her mouth to Sam's, giving her one more heated kiss before she turned and headed out of the garage. "Someday, you *are* going to come and get that bra of yours." She didn't look back. "But until then, I'll see ya 'round, sweetheart."

Sweetheart. She smiled. The first time Drew had called her that, she'd hated it. Now it was the best sound in the world.

Hair tousled and cheeks warm, Sam zipped her pants and buttoned her shirt, thinking of the woman whose taste was still lingering on her tongue. She'd clearly given Drew the red light, and she'd blown right through it. She'd committed a moving violation, and Sam hadn't stopped her. Instead, she'd enjoyed it. No, she'd reveled in it. Drew was in hot pursuit, and the rush of the chase was outweighing Sam's conscience.

She heard the metal door click open. "Did you forget something?" Fastening the last of her buttons, she turned from the bench.

"I just got here," Brad said.

She turned back to the bench in panic. "Oh. I thought you were Ray."

"How about a quick lunch?" he asked.

"I'm not hungry." She reached for one of the pistons she'd been cleaning, hoping he wouldn't notice the heat she was still feeling in her cheeks.

"Okay then, how about a quickie lunch?" He pressed himself against her back and nipped at her neck roughly.

"Brad, stop. I've still got a lot of work to do on this engine." She twisted around, shrugging him off.

He spun her back around and pushed her against the bench. "What happened to that wanton woman from last night?" He slid his hands down her arms before reaching around to unbutton her jeans. Feeling him pressed hard against her, Sam knew she didn't want this kind of love anymore. She spun around, put her hands on his chest, and shoved.

He held up his hands. "Whoa. All you have to do is say no."

"I thought I just did."

"Okay." He backed away and took off out the door.

Tears soaking her cheeks, Sam closed her eyes and struggled for breath. She couldn't let him see her tears. She sank down against the tool chest. She couldn't remember the last time Brad took the time to satisfy any of her needs. Each day she was with him, she felt more used. She couldn't stay with him any longer. She had to end it.

A few minutes later Sam heard the metal door to the supply room click open. She swiped her sleeve across her face and hopped up.

Ray held up an aerosol can as he crossed the garage. "It took some searching, but I finally found it."

Panic surged through her. She'd forgotten all about sending him to get it. "I'm sorry, Ray. I got kind of busy out here." Searching his face for any reaction, Sam wiped the rest of the moisture from her cheek. She hoped he hadn't seen what had just happened. If he had, he would clearly think she was some kind of shameless tramp. In fact, Sam was beginning to wonder who she was herself.

"You okay?"

"Yeah. I'm fine, Ray. Just a little stressed."

"I straightened up while I was in there."

"Thanks." She threw her arms around his shoulders and held on tight. He seemed to be the only man in her life who didn't expect anything from her. "I don't know what I'd do without you." His arms lingered, and Sam surrendered to the unexpected comfort she felt. "How about you, Ray? Are you okay?" She patted him on the shoulders before letting her hands slide down his arms into his.

He dropped his chin, avoiding eye contact. "Yeah. I just need this job, and with the new driver and all…"

"Ray," she said softly, leaning in to get his attention. "I need you here, and as long as I'm crew chief, you don't have anything to worry about. Okay?"

He smiled. "Okay."

She gave his hands a light squeeze before releasing them. "Now let's get this car put back together. Drew has to qualify this afternoon."

"What about you?"

"It's not my turn, Ray."

"That isn't right, Sam, and you know it."

"Paddy handles the drivers, and what he says goes. Whether I like it or not."

"Damn drivers think they can come in and take whatever they want." His heated posture had Sam thinking maybe he *had* seen what just happened.

"Come on, Ray. It's not that bad. I'll get to race someday."

"Well, it's not fair, that's all."

She turned and searched the bench. "I had a box of antihistamines around here somewhere. Do you know what happened to them?"

"I thought they were Paddy's. I put them in the desk."

She headed into the office. "Thanks."

"You sick?"

"I think it's allergies. Something must be blooming."

Chapter Fourteen

When Drew left the garage, she didn't dare look back. She'd had to get out of there fast. Wanting to make love to Sam was a natural response, but these feelings were pushing her over the edge. Sam's hands had probed her with such urgency, Drew had lost every sensible thought in her head. At that moment, nothing was more important than satisfying her.

Her mind filled with Sam's taste, and Drew fought to shift it elsewhere. Clearing her head had never been this much of a chore. Sam's wandering hands and writhing body had done things to her she fully expected but couldn't seem to shake.

"What are you in such a hurry for, hotshot?" Jade caught up with Drew, taking two steps to every one of Drew's.

"Lunch." That would do, but she really needed a little fresh air and a lot of distance from Sam.

"Get any info last night?"

"Not much on the case."

"But I bet you learned a whole lot more about our suspect."

Drew stopped to protest but couldn't. Jade was right. She'd learned that Samantha Kelleher could turn her inside out with one glance.

"Anything we can use?"

"I got a hair sample. Dropped it off at the lab this morning." She walked a few steps before stopping again. "Hey, what's with your dad?"

"My dad?"

"Yeah, since when is Internal Affairs interested in an ordinary homicide? He caught me in the hall this morning and started quizzing me about the case."

"I don't know." Jade shrugged. "Maybe he's gonna recommend you for transfer back to Narcotics."

Drew flattened her lips. "I doubt it. You forget he had me transferred out before I was released from the hospital."

"And then *he* transferred to IA." Jade's voice dropped momentarily, as though she were getting something Drew didn't. "Are you sure that wasn't because of Kim?"

"Are you sure something else isn't going on?" Drew skirted the issue. She wouldn't even have met Kimberly if her father hadn't introduced them.

"I don't know, Drew. Maybe he just doesn't want us working together again."

Drew leaned up against the counter at the snack shack and shouted inside, "Two dogs, mustard, and relish." She glanced back at Jade. "You want one?"

"Sure. No relish."

"Make that three. One, no relish."

Drew handed one to Jade and jammed one into her mouth.

Jade took a napkin and wiped a glob of mustard from Drew's chin. "Sorry. Old habits." Jade handed the napkin to her. "You know, I never could figure out why my dad let you marry Kim."

"You talk like he could've stopped it."

"He knew you were my partner and that I kinda had a thing for you."

Drew arched her eyebrows. "A thing?" It all made sense now. Right after she and Kimberly started seeing each other, Jade had transferred to homicide. They'd been trying to get her for months, but she wouldn't budge. Then all of a sudden she gave Drew some line about career opportunities and took the transfer.

"That swagger of yours is a real turn-on, but when you hooked up with my sister, I got over it real quick." Jade smiled and shook her head. "I should've never invited you to that party."

"Your father invited me, remember?"

"Yeah. I guess he did."

Drew watched her gaze follow Tommy as he raced his wheelchair to the van. He rolled onto the lift and closed the doors.

Her gaze snapped back to Drew. "It worked out for the best."

"You really love him, huh?"

"I do." She grinned when Tommy waved her over.

Drew walked with her. "What are you going to do if he turns out to be our culprit?"

Jade gave Drew a blistering stare. "Same thing you're going to do if it turns out to be Sam."

What exactly that was, Drew didn't know. All she knew for sure was the feeling in her gut told her it wasn't Sam.

While Drew stopped to talk to Tommy, Jade rounded the front of the van and hopped into the passenger seat. "Where you going?"

"Parts."

"Need any help?"

"Nope. I got it. You qualifying this afternoon?"

"As soon as Sam gets the car ready." Drew slapped the top of the door with her palm. "See you later."

Drew watched Sam from across the garage. Dressed in a plaid flannel shirt and blue jeans, she seemed such a contrast from the posh woman she'd held in her arms just a few short nights before. She was just as beautiful with grease streaked across her face as she was the first night Drew saw her in the bar. By the scowl on her face, Drew could see she was having a heated discussion with Brad. After waiting and watching, she decided to interrupt before it got out of hand.

"Got her all fixed up?" she shouted across the garage.

Sam held up a finger and glanced over, but didn't smile. "Don't take it out yet. I want to show you what I did."

Anxious for her turn in the qualifying heats today, Drew leaned up against the number-fifteen car and waited for her stomach to settle. Nerves, envy, jealousy, she didn't know what it was, but watching Sam interact with Brad had her lunch on the verge of coming up.

Jade reached into the car, took the helmet from the seat, and tossed it at her. "I sure hope she's not the one."

"Why?" That was a stupid question.

"Let's face it, Drew. Like it or not, I know you pretty well, and I can see you've got it bad."

"She's a suspect, nothing more." She was lying.

"That's bull. The two of you can't keep your eyes off each other."

Catching Sam's glance, Drew smiled.

"I remember that glint in your eye from when you and Kim first got together."

"Let it alone, Jade." Drew pulled her helmet on and slid into the car.

"You better watch yourself, or you're going to get us both killed."

Drew narrowed her eyes, then fired the engine and raced out of the garage to the track.

Sam was waiting, body rigid and arms crossed, when Drew pulled back into the garage. Pressing her foot hard on the brake, Drew came to a screeching stop. She could see Sam's face in heated movement but could only imagine the fury in her voice echoing in the metal building.

"What the hell are you doing?"

"Racing." Giving her a huge smile, Drew hoisted herself out of the car and slid down the side onto the concrete floor.

The anger flared in Sam's eyes. "Don't take the car out again before I tell you what I've done to it." She reached in, popped the hood, and then went around to the front of car. "You could have blown everything I just fixed."

"I qualified." Drew's grin spread widely. "This girl is starting at number nine."

Sam lifted the hood and ducked under it. "What you did out there today was not only dangerous and reckless, but you also showed no regard for any other life on that track. If you think everyone else doesn't see that, you're deluding yourself."

Drew just stared. She'd expected Sam to be happy she qualified. "Is everything all right?" That was a loaded question. "With the car?" Drew's voice was low and strong. She was going to hold her ground on this one.

"Damn it." Sam slammed the hood down and bolted toward her. She was coming in hot, so Drew braced herself for a battle.

Sam took Drew's face in her hands and growled as she kissed her hard. She pulled back momentarily to look into Drew's eyes. "I have no idea how you do it, but watching you drive does something crazy to me." Sam sucked her tongue against her teeth, producing an indescribable sound, one that aroused Drew even more than the kiss. "And you did qualify." Sam grinned. "That's what's important," she said as she jumped into Drew's arms, wrapped her legs around her waist, and kissed her again.

This time Sam's mouth was soft and sweet, inviting Drew in deeper. She held Sam tight against her, taking in the reward she offered, the taste of the woman who dominated all her thoughts, the taste of victory. Drew immersed herself in all things Sam, her enthusiasm, her taste, her scent. She was lost in her. Sam was rapidly sucking her into this notorious world of fast cars and even faster women.

Voices just outside the garage seeped through their hazy entanglement, and Sam immediately dropped to her feet and shoved her away. "Sorry," she whispered, sucking in a ragged breath. "Again, that was inappropriate." Tracing her lips with her fingers, Sam's hand shook as she peered up at Drew through her thick auburn lashes.

"Definitely inappropriate," Drew said, trying to calm her desire as she stared into her shimmering emerald-green eyes.

"But well deserved." Sam caught her lip between her teeth, and her gaze darted away before she swiped her palms on her blue jeans and went to meet Paddy as he entered.

Many congratulations were being given, with plenty more to come, but all Drew could think about was the beautiful woman she'd just held in her arms. From day one, she'd known this assignment would be a struggle. She had two lifelong devotions—her job and her passion for racing. Now a third factor had entered the equation—Samantha Kelleher, killer or victim. She'd left Drew smoldering, legs shaking and aching for more. Even from across the room she could see Sam was feeling the impact as well.

CHAPTER FIFTEEN

The door was unlocked when Sam got back to her room. Pushing it open slowly, she peeked in and saw a beautiful black silk dress lying on the bed. She rushed in, picked it up, and held it against her. The thought of an extravagant night out completely washed away all her problems for the day. Brad had acted in typical fashion this afternoon, selfish and indifferent. This was his typical way of making it up to her.

Lying on the dresser was a beautiful drop-pendant necklace and a note reading, "Seven sharp." Maybe a night out was exactly what she needed to get Drew out of her head. Sam glanced at the time on her phone, then back at her reflection in the mirror. It was already after six, and she needed a shower desperately. On top of that, it would take her the better part of an hour to tame her terminal mass of curls. Luckily, she had her routine down. After many years of working in the garage, smells and smudges were challenges she'd learned to conquer.

Sam pulled the slinky black dress over her head, letting it slide down her body. The silk fabric cooled her warm, freshly cleansed skin, and she shivered with excitement. She backed out into the room and glanced at her phone again. Happy to see she'd made it through her routine in record time, she sucked in a deep breath and assessed herself in the full-length mirror hanging on the closet door. Strapless and stretched to the seams, it fit like a glove, a very tight glove. Surveying herself, she turned sideways and let her hand drift down across her stomach. The curves and swells were still in all the right places. She felt like a woman again, which didn't happen very often. Considering her occupation, most of her wardrobe consisted of jeans and T-shirts.

It was almost seven, so she slipped into the bathroom to check her makeup one last time. While her hair was still damp, she'd pinned it up elegantly, letting just a few curly strands hang down on each side. It felt a little stuffy for her, but it was a good style with the dress. She stared at the woman transformed in the mirror. Something was missing. Lipstick. She needed some color. As she rummaged through her makeup bag, she heard the faint knock on the door.

"Door's open. I'll be right out," she shouted. After swiping the wine-tinted stick across her lips, she wound it down into the tube and slipped it into her clutch, then headed out to see her date. "This dress is beautiful. A little tight but beautiful..." When she saw Drew all decked out in a black suit, black shirt, and gray silk tie, her stomach vaulted into a full gymnastics routine. She was absolutely the most handsome woman Sam had ever seen. Hair tamed and spiked, Drew flashed her a smile. Sam's heart sputtered, and her knees went weak. For a brief moment, she thought she might liquefy and ooze right down to the floor.

Drew's gaze followed Sam's curves from top to bottom as if savoring every inch. "Appears to be a perfect fit."

Sam let a slow smile spread across her face. "I wasn't expecting...such a dashing escort." No sense in telling her whom she was expecting. She turned to the dresser, popped a few vitamins into her mouth, and washed them down with a swallow of bottled water.

Drew was apparently happy with the compliment, because she smiled, and her dimples set deeper into her cheeks. As Sam reached for her clutch, she saw her engagement ring on the basin. She picked it up and instantly made what could turn out to be the worst decision of her life. She took it across the room to the nightstand and dropped it into the top drawer.

She took a deep breath. "What's the occasion?"

"My parents are having a little get-together."

"Did you say your parents?" Sam twisted to face her. "You want me to meet your parents?" No one had ever taken her to do that.

"Of course," Drew said matter-of-factly. "They would think it rude not to bring my number-one mechanic home to meet them."

She smiled as the gymnastics meet in her stomach progressed. "Number-one mechanic, huh." She still preferred technician, but it was useless to correct Drew. She picked up the drop pendant and held it out.

"Among other things." Drew's tone was low and seductive as she took the necklace and let her fingers drag slowly across Sam's shoulders before fastening it around her neck. Her hot breath seeped into Sam's ear, and she closed her eyes, fighting the urge to turn and push her onto the bed. She wanted to touch every inch of her, to plunge her tongue deep into her mouth, to beg her to touch every part of her. When Drew traced her earlobe with the tip of her tongue, the dress, the hair, the makeup didn't matter anymore. She swung around and smothered Drew's mouth with hers. Slipping her arms in under her jacket, Sam grasped her shoulders and slid her leg between Drew's. The groan Drew let out as she rocked against her sent Sam reeling.

Drew broke away. "We'd better go."

"What?" Sam said in shallow breaths.

"My parents," Drew mumbled, ignoring Sam's tongue sweeping across her lips.

"Your parents. Right."

"They expect me to be prompt."

She pressed her thigh firmly between her legs. "I like prompt."

Drew smiled and backed up. "If I don't put some distance between us right now, I'm going to be premature." Pulling Sam along behind her, Drew let out what Sam knew was a growl of frustration and yanked the door open.

Sam didn't realize it until after the valet took the Jeep that the porch rose to reveal a hidden stairway leading directly down into a ballroom. She glanced at Drew, then at the mansion. What had she gotten herself in to? This was really old money. Why in the world was Drew bringing her racecar technician home to meet it?

Sam descended the steps and waited for Drew at the entrance to the elegant ballroom. She stood staring in awe, gazing at the lines of the distinctly etched molding joining each wall to the next. She admired the beautiful landscape murals painted between the long luxurious curtains flanking the false windows. She was way out of her league.

The woman is dynasty offspring. My God, there's the governor! She had to get out of here. Sam swung around and sprinted back up the steps. *Meet her parents! What was I thinking? I must have been out of my mind.*

Drew met her halfway up and blocked her path. "Not so fast." She must have seen the panic in Sam's eyes.

"I can't do this." She couldn't make any commitments to this woman. Meeting her parents was a pledge, an unspoken promise of something more.

"Sure you can. They're just like you and me. They've just got a little more money, that's all."

Sam widened her eyes in sarcasm. "Enough money to buy their own country."

Drew let out a chuckle. "Maybe a small one."

"Where are your parents?"

Drew pointed across the room. "Dad's talking to the governor, and Mom appears to be assisting one of the staff."

Sam glanced over to see a gorgeous blond woman who seemed to be showing one of the waiters how to hold a tray of champagne glasses.

"What's she doing?"

"Mom's a soft touch. She's always taking in strays and trying to make them better." Drew smiled. "I think she'll like you."

What was that? Some kind of a crack about her lifestyle? She might not have an actual permanent address, but she wasn't a stray.

"Come on. Let's go see her before she gets hung up with someone else." Drew let her hand slip into Sam's and led her across the room.

She tried to free her hand. "I'm not ready to meet her yet."

Drew held tight, continuing to pull her along behind her. "Let's get it over with, shall we? Then we can enjoy the rest of the evening."

She stopped short. "Or would you rather wait until she's visiting with the first lady?"

"No!" The word came out louder than Sam expected, and she jerked her hand to her mouth. Catching Drew's smile and a few guarded stares from other guests, Sam could see she was enjoying her unease. Drew turned and quickly closed the gap between them and her mother.

"Hey, Mom," Drew said, creeping up behind her.

She turned, and Sam could see her mother's eyes fill with elation. That was something to come home to. She'd never seen that kind of reaction in her father's eyes.

"Drew, darling. I'm so glad you came tonight."

Sam wasn't surprised when Drew dropped her hand and put her arms around her mother for a long, blissful hug.

"Mom, this is Samantha Kelleher."

"Nice to meet you, dear." She gave her a warm smile.

"The pleasure's mine, Mrs. Thompson."

"Please, call me Johanna."

"Johanna." Sam nodded.

Drew located the bar across the room. "I'll get us a drink." She cocked her head, silently soliciting her order.

"Crown and water, double," she said, narrowing her eyes.

"Mom?"

"No thank you, sweetie. I've already had a glass of champagne."

"I'll be right back." Drew smiled and moved through the crowded room to the bar.

"That's a lovely dress, Samantha."

"Thank you. I just came across it today." Sam's gaze darted to Drew at the bar and then back again. A rush of heat flooded her. Earlier, when she'd found Drew in her room, her body had betrayed her and was progressing to high treason as the night went on.

"If you don't mind my asking, where did you two meet?"

"At Sonoma Raceway."

"Yes. The raceway." Johanna lowered her voice and took in a deep breath. "Hopefully she'll give up that hobby. It's too dangerous."

"It's not a hobby, Mom." Drew handed Sam a glass. "I hope it isn't too strong."

Couldn't be. Right now, she'd drink it straight. She took a large gulp and let it burn down the back of her throat. "Perfect."

"I don't know why you chose not to be a lawyer like your brother," Johanna said to Drew before turning back to Sam. "Do you know how dangerous racing is?"

"I do." Sam smiled, raising her glass to her lips again.

Johanna looped her arm with Sam's. "Maybe you can convince her to stop."

"That's unlikely, Mom. Sam's my team technician."

Now she was a technician. Sam rolled her eyes, knowing Drew had said it just so she'd have to explain to her mother.

"Technician? Does that have something to do with computers?"

Drew stood back and smiled, leaving this one for Sam.

"It's a fancy name for mechanic."

"Really?" Johanna's voice rose as she backed up and, without any discretion, swept her gaze up and down Sam. "Well, at least now I understand why Drew likes racing so much." She darted her gaze across the room. "Will you excuse me, dear. I see your father is being cornered by that old windbag, Marlin. If I don't interrupt, he'll monopolize him all night."

Sam caught her bottom lip between her teeth before letting it curve into a half smile. "Was that supposed to be a compliment?"

"I believe so." Drew looked over her glass at her. "She's really not all that bad once you get to know her."

"I'm sure she's absolutely delightful, dahling," Sam said, batting her eyelashes.

Drew laughed. "All right. She *is* a little stuffy."

"They seem happy." Sam glanced back, watching Johanna cling to her husband's arm, staring at him as though she were totally in love.

Drew's gaze followed hers. "I think they actually are. They have their moments, but they have fun together." She glanced down at the swirling liquid in her glass before returning her attention to Sam. "Someday, I hope to have that very same thing." She drank down the last of her drink. "Along with a few kids."

Sam choked on her drink. *Kids?* Would there be kids? The thought had never entered her mind.

Drew smiled as she took Sam's glass and set it on the table along with hers. "Dance with me."

She rested her arm along Drew's shoulder, while Drew held the other close to her chest as she whisked her around the dance floor. Sam closed her eyes and felt the subtle rhythm of Drew's heart against the back of her hand. The smooth softness of her face warmed Sam's cheek. She took in a slow, deep breath, and her subtle, powdery scent filled her head. Sam's world was spinning. She couldn't speak—she didn't want to. She would be happy to remain captured in Drew's arms for the rest of the night.

"Are you having a good time?" Drew asked. When she didn't answer, Drew kept her hand pressed firmly to the small of Sam's back and lowered her chin to meet Sam's gaze. She knew her eyes would give her away.

"You okay?" Drew asked in a whisper.

Sam nodded and let out a soft, contented sigh. She was more than okay. For once in her life, she felt completely safe. "We should find a seat. I didn't eat much today, and that drink seems to have gone straight to my head."

Drew frowned and took her hand. "Come on. Let's get some food in you." Pulling her through an elevated corridor, she weaved around a few waiters and pushed through a door into the kitchen. "Sodas are in the fridge." She pointed to the massive Sub-Zero in the wall. "Grab a couple."

Sam tugged the door open and took out a soda and a bottle of water.

After grabbing a box of crackers from the pantry, Drew picked up a tray of cheese and headed up the back steps.

"Where are we going?"

"To what used to be my room." Drew noticed her hesitation and gave her a suggestive smile. "I *could* show you the wine cellar if you prefer."

The door flew open and a waiter shuffled through.

Sam shook her head. "I think I'd like to see your room." It might give her some much-needed insight. Was she a suitor, or just an incorrigible bachelor, looking for a good time?

Drew led her up the winding staircase and stopped at the top. "My parents' room is that way." She pointed to the left. "And mine is down here." She headed in the opposite direction and didn't stop until they reached the end of the hall.

Her room was filled with a ridiculous amount of memorabilia. Sports trophies covered the shelves, and academic awards hung on the walls. Sam was surprised at how sparsely the room was furnished with only a small computer desk, a dresser, and a queen-size bed. Finished in dark-oak wood molding, the room was three times as large as her hotel room.

Drew set the food on the bottom of the bed and pulled the desk chair over to sit. That left the majority of the bed for Sam. She sat on the edge with her legs crossed, wondering if Drew had planned it that way. She didn't seem to leave much to chance.

She handed Sam a few crackers and motioned to the tray. "Have some cheese. It'll make you feel better." She opened a soda, which hissed before she took a swig.

"You were quite the over-achiever in school."

Drew popped a piece of cheese into her mouth and squinted. "Still am."

Sam tilted her head. "Really? I hadn't noticed." She ripped a slice of cheese in half and dropped it into her mouth.

"I don't like to lose."

"Already noted." She smiled as she surveyed the room. "You actually grew up here, in this room?"

"Yeah." Drew blew out the word and made a funny face. "I know it isn't much, but it served its purpose."

Pulling her legs up onto the bed behind her, Sam propped herself up on one elbow and raised an eyebrow. "You had your own private wing. Pretty convenient during high school, I bet."

"In college too." Drew moved the tray of cheese to the nightstand and stretched out next to her. "In fact, I'm kinda hopin' it's gonna work for me right now." She pulled the clip from Sam's hair. "That's much better." Tangling her hand in the curls, Drew cupped the back of Sam's neck and stroked the edge of her jaw with her thumb.

Sam closed her eyes and melted into her, letting herself feel the heat of Drew's mouth drag slowly across her cheek. Her warm breath whispered in her ear, and her breasts ached. She felt Drew smile before she moved slowly down to the sensitive spot at the base of Sam's neck. She let out a whimper and fell back onto the bed.

Sam heard a low throaty moan, Drew's, or maybe hers, she didn't know, but the sound made her wet with desire. The sleek sensation of Drew's tongue captured Sam's mouth, sweeping gently across the inside of her lip before diving inside, mingling with hers, touching, baiting, and making her want her all the more. Sam didn't think it possible at this point, but Drew was slowly and methodically proving her wrong about her own sensuality.

Drew's hand swept up Sam's thigh, leisurely making its way up her dress. "It's been a long time since I've had a woman up here."

Drew's hand stopped, she groaned, and Sam knew she was now fully aware there were no panties to be shed. Drew slid her fingers through the slick wetness, and Sam shuddered. Her nipples, hard and ready to be sucked, scraped against the inside of her dress. She was speeding full-throttle past the limits she'd set for herself.

"Drew. Are you up here?" The voice echoed through the hallway, and the door pushed open. "I was going to introduce you…Whoops." The woman jerked back into the hallway.

"Oh my God." Sam's face threatened to pale, but the heat was still sizzling in her cheeks. "Was that your mother?"

"Sister."

She let her head drop back onto the bed. "The one I locked in the bathroom?"

"The only one I have."

She shoved Drew to her side and sat up at the end of the bed. "Did she see me?"

"Just your feet."

She hopped up, raced to the mirror, and clipped her hair up. "Do you think she knew it was me?"

"No." Drew's voice held a hint of irritation. "But she'll see that later when I introduce you."

"We have to go back downstairs." Drew made no effort to move. "Now."

"Are you kidding? I can barely walk."

"Drew, please," she begged. "This isn't the way I want your family to know me." Sam wasn't sure why she cared. They were both consenting adults. She wasn't a high-society woman by any means, but this wasn't the kind of impression she wanted to make.

Drew growled and fell back onto the bed. "Just give me a minute."

"Thank you." Sam reached to touch her, but Drew waved her off.

"You'd better stay back, or you'll have to finish what we started."

They entered the ballroom, unnoticed, the same way they'd left through the kitchen. Drew searched the crowd for her sister. "There she is." She raised her hand, motioning her over.

The back of Sam's neck tingled, and her palms suddenly felt damp. "If you don't mind, I need to freshen up."

"You could have done that upstairs," Drew said, pressing her lips together.

Sam glanced at Liza, then back to Drew. "I'll be right back. I promise."

Drew smiled and brushed her lips against Sam's. "Take your time."

She needed a minute to figure out just what to say to the woman she'd locked in a bathroom stall. Now the same women had caught her getting it on in her parents' house with her sister. *I knew this was a mistake. I should've never agreed to come.* If she had any brains at all, she'd hightail it out the back door and catch a cab back to the hotel.

Drew watched Sam's hips swing as she walked the perimeter of the room. Sam glanced back over her shoulder and gave Drew an alluring stare that made her whole body heat. This woman was doing all the right things. She was everything Drew ever wanted and still her prime suspect.

Roaming hands, seeking mouth, thrusting thigh. She'd been so ready to come upstairs when Liza stepped into the room. Sam had blushed like a schoolgirl, which made Drew want her even more. How could a woman be so amazingly sexy yet seem so pure and innocent?

"Is that your newest?" Liza asked.

Drew turned and gave her sister a light kiss on the cheek. "Sorry I didn't introduce you earlier."

She lifted an eyebrow. "You were otherwise engaged." She peeked around her. "Where is the little tart?"

"Liza." Drew narrowed her eyes. "Be nice to this one, please."

Liza studied her face. "Okay. If you insist."

Drew saw Sam emerging from behind a small group of people. "Here she is, now," she said as she slipped her arm around Sam's waist, moving her in tight against her. Sam gave her a soft smile and her stomach dipped.

Liza's gaze swept quickly down to her shoes and back up again before offering her hand. "Nice to see you...standing up."

Sam shifted uneasily, and there was that blush again. "I think you two have met before, at the sponsor party." Sam slipped her hand up the back of Drew's suit coat and gave her a pinch that made Drew jump.

Liza pulled her eyebrows together and darted her gaze back to Sam. "I don't think so."

"*That's* right. I forgot." She pressed a finger to her lips and chuckled. "You didn't actually meet. Sam's the one who locked you in the bathroom."

Liza's powder-blue eyes grew dark. "You did that?" her voice rose.

"I'm so sorry. If I had known you were Drew's sister, I would have never—"

Liza laughed abruptly and her smile returned. "A woman with fortitude. I like that." She looped her arm with Sam's. "Come on. Let's you and I have a drink. We can get to know each other a little better."

Drew pulled her brows together. "Don't tell her all my secrets."

"Drew, sweetheart, you know me better than that. I'll only divulge enough to keep her interested. It might frighten her a tad, but I promise I'll leave her begging for more." Liza gave Drew a wink and shuffled Sam off toward the bar.

❖

Without turning on the light, Sam closed the door to her room and leaned back against it. Meeting Drew's family had turned out to be quite an adventure. Her sister had chatted her up for at least an hour with wild stories of Drew's youth before Drew had pulled her away to dance. Although they never did make it back upstairs to finish what they'd started, she'd had a wonderful time.

She would've let Drew stay the night, if she'd asked, but Sam had told her she had an early day tomorrow, and she didn't press. Had she finally found someone who cared as much about her needs and responsibilities as their own?

"Have a nice time?" The voice was low and flat.

She jumped at the sound. "Brad?"

Her hand searched the wall until she caught the light switch and flipped it up. As her eyes adjusted to the brightness, she saw him sitting in the chair holding a near-empty bottle of scotch.

"How long have you been here?"

"Long enough to see you throw yourself at your girlfriend." He slapped the bottle to the table.

She tossed her clutch on the bed. "Why do you care? You've had your share of women."

"In the public eye, you're still my fiancée." He stood up and blocked her path.

She brushed past him toward the bathroom. "We both know how loosely we use that term. It certainly doesn't give you the right to spy on me."

"What right does it give me?" He yanked her back and pushed her up against the wall. "The right to have you anytime I want?" He forced his mouth onto hers.

The stench of alcohol permeated her nostrils, and the foul taste of his mouth made her stomach lurch.

She tried to wedge her arms between them. "Brad, stop. I don't want this."

"Since when? You never complained before." He tried to kiss her again, and his beard scraped her skin, making it burn with pain.

"Stop!" She squirmed out of his grip. "Don't you want more than this?"

"This is all I ever wanted from you."

She slapped him hard across the face. If he wanted to hurt her, he'd certainly done it now.

His eyes darkened, and he came after her again.

She threw her hand up in front of her. "Don't you dare."

"Whatcha gonna do? Go running back to Daddy?" He slurred his words. "Don't you think he knows about all the women I've been with?" He picked up the bottle and sucked down what was left of the scotch. "What makes you think he's going to care about a bruise here and there?" He tossed the empty bottle onto the bed. "The old man needs me. He's not going to cut me loose just because of his precious little girl. Who else is going to drive that car for him?"

"I will."

"That's a laugh. You're a great mechanic, Sam, and I hear you're pretty good at driving go-carts too. But you and I both know you could never compete on the big track."

"I knew that was you."

"Just keeping an eye on the goods, sweetheart."

"Did you throw that rock onto the track?"

"What if I did?"

"You hurt that little girl."

"Wasn't trying to." She didn't budge when he moved closer and lifted the pendant from her chest. "Something new?" He ripped it from her neck and threw it to the floor.

She slapped her hand to the back of her neck to squelch the stinging pain. "Damn it, Brad." She crossed the room to the sink and dampened a washcloth. She stared at the cold, dark silhouette reflecting in the mirror and cursed herself. She hated the woman she became when she was with him. ""I'm not trying to hurt you, but I want more. I *need* a connection with someone." Placing the cold rag on her neck, she winced and turned back to face him. "Maybe actually get married someday, even have a family." Her voice faltered. "You and I both know that's never going to happen with us."

"You think you can have that with *her*?"

She shook her head. "I don't know." And she didn't, but she wanted to find out.

"So you're going to kick me to the curb."

"Brad." Her voice softened, filling with emptiness. "If you really loved me, you wouldn't have had any other women." Kneading her forehead with her fingertips, she paced the room. "I've already put up with a lot more than I should've. I'm tired of being humiliated."

"Come on now." He stepped in front of her and brushed the hair from her face. "Don't you think I know every time you feel a little neglected you cross that fine fidelity line you've drawn? I'm not the only one breaking the rules here."

A short wave of shock flashed through her. She didn't think he'd ever taken the time to notice anything she did. "That's not true. I may have straddled it, but I've never crossed it when we were officially together."

"You always come back." He turned to the door. "When things don't work out with Thompson, you know where I'll be," he said as he went out the door.

Sam dropped the washcloth on the basin and stared at her reflection. *The pendant.* She spun around and fell to her knees, raking her fingers across the carpet until she found it. The clasp was broken. She fell back against the side of the bed and pressed it to her chest. She *had* crossed the line. Not intentionally, but she definitely had. She'd let Drew do intimate things to her, and she wanted her to do them again.

Chapter Sixteen

When Drew pulled into her usual spot next to the garage, she saw Jade rushing over.

"What'd ya do to the little princess last night? She's in an awful mood this morning."

"Really?" Drew shrugged and hopped out of her Jeep. "I took her to a party?"

"That political thing your parents hosted?"

She nodded.

"What the fuck, Drew?" Jade grabbed her arm.

Drew turned her head slowly, fixing her gaze on Jade's hand. She let go, and Drew continued on her way. "You took her home? To meet your folks?" Jade sprinted alongside her.

"Rich-kid driver. That's my cover, remember?"

"You're *way* too involved."

"I'll get the job done." Drew spotted Sam at the snack shack buying a bottle of orange juice and found it impossible not to stop and watch her.

"Damn it, Drew." Jade shook her head. "You'd better make sure nobody gets hurt."

Without a word, Drew headed toward the snack shack to see Sam.

"Drew!" Jade shouted. "Are you listening to me?"

"Gotcha." She threw up a hand and gave her a wave.

"Hey, Slick. How's it lookin' this morning?"

Stifling a cough, Sam leaned her head back and stared up at the gray clouds looming above.

"It's lookin' like rain."

"Where's Goldilocks?" Drew had consistently called Brad the first derogatory nickname that came to mind from the first day they met.

"He should be here in a little while," Sam said without need of clarification.

"You want some breakfast with that juice?"

"No thanks. I need to get back to work." Not giving Drew a second glance, or a first for that matter, Sam headed off toward the garage.

"I'm going to get some food. I'll be there in a minute."

"Take your time," she said without turning back.

Sam was unusually distant today. Maybe the rain was putting her in a foul mood. Nonstop with no end in sight didn't make for a productive day.

She seemed preoccupied with the car, but Drew sensed something else was bothering her. Maybe last night was too much. The party, her family, the bedroom. Drew smiled. No. That wasn't it. She'd been too willing, too wanting, too wet. Something else was wrong, maybe something that didn't concern her at all. Giving Sam a little space was probably best for both of them. Sooner or later it would pass, or most likely, she'd blow and let her have it.

Brad came into the garage, and Drew could see he was the problem. At the sound of his voice, Sam tensed immediately. The obvious wall between them was becoming thicker. He advanced and she retreated. It was clear Brad knew something was going on between her and Drew, and he didn't like it.

He was showering her with kindness. *That's why she always goes back to him. He sees her begin to stray and smothers her with attention, yanking her back into his grasp just until the competition is gone.* Or in the recent case—dead. The selfish bastard liked keeping Sam on a leash.

Observing the interaction between them, Drew didn't know if guilt, want, or passion kept her going back. She turned to the bench, examining the various engine parts. Could Brad be involved in the accidents? She picked up a piston and pulled open a tool drawer. If Drew wanted to sabotage the car, she could do it, and Brad could too. She heard the metal door clang shut and turned. She and Sam were alone again.

"Where's he going?"

Sam glanced up from the engine. "He won't drive in this weather." She grabbed the top of the hood and slammed it closed. "We can't afford to lose another day because of this damn rain."

"I'll take it out," Drew said without hesitation.

"Are you serious?" Sam's lips tipped up into the first smile she'd seen all day.

"I'm game." Drew was surprised at how grateful she was. Sam did something to her, something new, something fresh. Whatever it was, she didn't quite understand, and she didn't want it to stop.

Sam slid through the window, positioning herself on top of the fire extinguisher, where the passenger seat would normally be.

"You can't go out there with me."

"Nobody else will be on the track in this weather. Just take me for a short run. No one will know."

"You don't even have a seat, let alone safety restraints."

"I'll be all right. You won't be driving that fast."

Drew slid in and fastened the harness.

"Put your helmet on." Sam handed it to her. "You have to at least appear normal. If we get caught, we're out. And remember. Don't take the speed up too high. I don't want to blow anything. Oh, and watch the corners. They'll be slick."

Drew smiled at her constant attempt to remain in control.

As they raced around the track, the rain slapped like bullets against the windshield

"Did you hear that?" Sam asked.

"What?"

"I thought I heard a slight hiss when you down-shifted."

"I can't hear a damn thing over this rain."

❖

Sam stuck her head out into the downpour. The rain was cold and hard as it pelted her face, but the smell of a heated track splashed with a gush of nature's juice was incredible. "Take the speed up a little, then down-shift again around the next corner."

"What the hell are you doing? Are you crazy?"

She glanced back to see Drew giving her ass a double-take and smiled. Driving with this kind of view could get a woman killed.

"Get back in here." Drew curled her fingers beneath the waistband of Sam's jeans and tugged.

Sam closed her eyes and let the warmth of Drew's touch subdue the cold rain before swiping her hand across the small of her back. She thought for sure she'd find a flaming match, but nothing was there except the lingering heat left from Drew's fingers. Shaking it off, she slid back into the car. "Sounds like a compression leak. Take us in."

As soon as Drew stopped the car, Sam was out, pulling the hood open. She adjusted a few wires and then stood back with her hands on her hips, staring at the engine.

"I don't get it. I just replaced these pistons."

"Maybe you have a defective batch."

"Or I've got bigger problems."

"What now?"

"I'll have to pop the head and find the bad one." She wrapped a towel around her shoulders, then gathered up her thick curls and squeezed the excess water out onto it. "You might want to find something else to do. This could take a while."

"I'll stay if you don't mind," Drew said, ignoring the brush-off.

"Suit yourself." She tossed the towel onto a stool and started to work under the hood.

"Don't you think you should change out of that wet shirt?" Drew said, creeping up behind her and taking her by the shoulders.

Sam stopped cold, and goose bumps popped up in all kinds of places. *There's that damn flame again. Put it out! Quick!* The heat of Drew's breath on her neck made Sam shiver, and her body spiked with desire.

"Please," Sam begged, melting back into her. This was absolute torture. "I can't play this game with you today. I *have* to get this car running."

"Is that the only reason?" She nudged Sam around to face her.

Taking Drew's face in her hands, Sam gave her a long, slow, tender kiss and then slid her cheek against Drew's. "That's all I can give you right now." It took everything she had to prevent what seemed to be the most natural thing in the world, fusing with the woman who seemed to anticipate her every need. If she continued staring into those sweet brown eyes, she'd be hypnotized, and her mind would be jumbled again. She wouldn't be able to work at all.

"You'd better get changed." Drew let her arms fall to her sides. "I've got an extra shirt in the office." She moved to get it, and Sam put up a hand.

"You stay there. I'll be right back." Drew would try to distract her again, and she couldn't afford that. Not today. She had way too much work to do.

"It's hanging on the back of the door."

Pushing the door open slightly, she began to unbutton her drenched flannel shirt and reached around for Drew's dry one. She jumped when she heard the squeak of the wooden chair roll back from behind the desk.

"Paddy." She slapped her hand to chest and sank back against the wall. "You scared me."

"I can see that." He leaned back and threw a leg up onto the corner of the desk. "Tell me, darlin', how'd you come to get so wet on the top of ya and nothing on the bottom?"

"I went out on a test drive with Drew."

"Did you say you went out with her?"

She nodded, waiting for him to blast her.

"Anyone see you?"

"Nope."

"Umm." He raised his eyebrows. "So, you've relented and actually decided to work with her?"

"Brad wouldn't take it out."

Paddy's brows drew together. "Well, I'll be havin' a chat with the boy about that." He got up, closed the office door, and nudged her into the bathroom. "Get yourself changed, and then you and I can have a little talk."

When Sam came out of the bathroom, Paddy was behind his desk digging through the papers scattered across it. Her father's filing system never failed to amaze her. His desk was always a mess, but he always seemed to know where everything was.

He glanced up momentarily. "How's the car running?"

"Honestly?" She pulled the desk drawer open and took out the packet of antihistamines she'd been dosing herself with for the past few days. "I think I've got a compression leak. It shouldn't take long, maybe a few hours."

"Are you sick?"

"My allergies are just acting up." Ignoring the mild heat radiating through her body, she went to the water cooler, filled a paper cup, and downed a couple of pills. Rubbing her face wearily, she slid down into the chair. "I think you should consider putting another car in the race, just in case."

"And who would you be wantin' me to let drive it?"

Sam gripped the arms of the chair and did her best to hold her temper. "You can let the man in the moon drive it for all I care, Paddy. But you need to have someone else in that race besides Brad."

"And if that one out there turns out to be the man in the moon?" He pointed at Drew through the window.

She paused for a moment, peeking over her shoulder. "Then, so be it." Sam had done all she could to let Paddy know she was ready. The next move was his.

"Is there something going on with Brad I should know about?"

"I don't think he has the best interests of the team in mind anymore." She hesitated. "He and I aren't going to be seeing each other personally in the future."

He sprang up from his chair. "Has he done something to hurt you?"

"Are you serious?" Paddy wasn't usually concerned about the minor details of her life.

"Tell me if he has, Samantha, and I'll take care of it."

He was serious. Could her father actually be that clueless? Never seeing the endless barrage of woman accompanying Brad in her absence? Not to mention the countless number he'd chosen to take to bed in her stead.

"No. Not this time." She shook her head and smiled in irony. "This time it was all me."

Paddy dropped back down into his chair and went back to his papers. "I'll consider it. Now you best get back to work."

She gripped the chair again and let out a heavy breath. That's it? No more questions? He didn't even make eye contact. As always, going any further with the conversation would be too personal for him. Too much like a real father.

❖

Drew stood out in the drizzling rain across from the garage, waiting for Sam to leave. The rain she could do without, but the lowering temperature was a welcome change from the constant heat they'd been stricken with the past few weeks. She took out her phone and posted another Tweet.

Awesome test drive today! @kellehermotorsports #NASCAR #notwilkerson.

She wanted to get as much exposure as she could, and if she pissed off Wilkerson in the process, all the better.

The rain hadn't fazed Sam at all, who was drenched to her shoulders, ringlets of red clinging to her face, and tiny droplets of water threatening to leap off the tip of her narrow nose. Drew needed to be near this woman, near enough to touch her, have her touch her in return. But when Drew had hauled her into her arms, she'd felt her body stiffen, straining to keep her distance. She'd wanted to shake her, to ask her if she'd felt nothing the night before. Maybe Sam *was* a cold, calculating killer.

The better part of an hour passed before Sam left the garage. Drew wiped the moisture from her face and sprinted in to see Paddy. She had to make it quick. Sam would be back soon.

Drew pushed open the office door, and Paddy shifted his gaze up from his paperwork.

"Are you going to let her drive?"

"I'm thinkin' on it."

"It's one sure way of ruling her out as a suspect. If you wait until the morning to spring it on her, she won't have time to fix whatever she's tampered with, if that's the case."

Paddy scowled. "I don't want her hurt."

Drew pressed her hands to the desk and leaned forward into Paddy's space. "If she did something to the car, she won't race."

"But if I'm right, she could get hurt." Paddy matched Drew's stare. "I can't very well offer her a chance and then snatch it back away."

"No, you can't." Drew pushed back off the desk. "But then at least you'll know one way or the other."

"What do you think I should do?"

"I think you should let her drive." Drew turned to leave, but stopping just short of the door, she slapped at the doorframe. "It's not an easy decision, but other people are in danger here. Two drivers are already dead, and your own son is paralyzed."

CHAPTER SEVENTEEN

When Sam entered the garage the next morning, she seemed pleased to see both Brad and Drew dressed and ready to drive.

The office door swung open, and Paddy stood in the doorway. "Samantha, you're late."

"With the new car coming in last night, I didn't get finished checking it out until after midnight."

New car? Drew didn't know anything about a new car. She should've stuck around last night, but she'd done what Sam asked and given her some space.

"Are you feeling all right?" Paddy gave her the once-over. "You look a little flushed."

"I'm fine," she said.

"Is the car ready?"

"Yep. I checked it out last night."

"Well then, go get suited up. You'll have to qualify."

"Me?" Her eyes lit in frenzied enthusiasm. Rushing to her father, Sam threw her arms around him.

Drew couldn't tell if the flash in her eyes was fear or excitement.

"Ray should have her back from inspection any minute." Paddy spun her around and pointed her toward the door.

She pumped her fist into the air before darting her gaze from Drew to Brad and back again. Drew didn't see any fear in her eyes, only pure excitement.

"She's a beauty." Brad's tone was less than enthusiastic.

It was obvious he wasn't thrilled that Paddy had bumped him this morning to let Sam qualify. And Drew wasn't thrilled he'd brought in a new car for her to drive. It was very unlikely someone could've tampered with a brand-new car. Paddy was a smart man. Suspect or not, he wasn't taking any chances with his daughter.

"You heard the man. Get moving." Drew gave her a shove. "You're in the fourth heat."

"Yessss." She hissed, catching a glimpse of the new car coming through the garage entrance. On her way to the bus, Sam made Ray stop the car and gave him a hurried kiss on the cheek.

"What's she so excited about?" Ray asked, pulling himself out of the car.

Drew swiped her hand across the midnight-blue finish of the number forty-four hood. "She's driving this baby today."

Ray spun around to Paddy. "I thought Brad was taking it out first."

"Change of plan."

"Are you sure she's ready?" Ray's forehead creased.

"Don't worry, Ray. She's more than ready," he said, heading across the garage.

"At least let me check it one more time before she takes it out."

"Did it pass inspection?" he shouted over his shoulder.

"With flying colors."

"Then leave it be." Paddy threw up a back-handed wave and disappeared into the office.

Drew caught Brad's scowl. "What's up with you?"

"She shouldn't be on that track."

"Why not?"

"Racing isn't a place for her."

"She can fix your car and warm your bed, but she can't drive a race car? That's a little archaic, isn't it?

Brad gave Drew a look she'd seen before. If she didn't know him, she might be afraid. But Brad didn't have the stones to challenge her. He was a shell of a man who had a nasty habit of preying on vulnerable women.

"You afraid she'll be better than you?"

Brad's eyes narrowed. "Mind your own business, Thompson," he said, rushing out of the garage.

"Sam is my business," Drew shouted after him as she followed. She wanted to be there waiting when Sam qualified. She glanced up at the sky as she sprinted to the pit. The massive cloud cover would keep it cool today, but if a storm developed, the trials would be postponed for yet another day. Hopefully the rain would hold off until tonight.

When Drew reached the pit, she watched Brad lean into the car and pull on the straps. He seemed to be making sure the restraints were fitted tightly across Sam's torso. Sam was listening to him intently but revealing no facial expression to indicate what he was saying. He was probably spewing a slew of passive-aggressive words laced with jealous intimidation in an effort to crush her spirit.

Drew couldn't stand the suspense. She had to know what the hell he was telling her. Bouncing around nervously, she popped Ray in the shoulder with her palm. "You got an extra headset around here somewhere?"

Ray pulled one off the fence and threw it to her. "No mic, but you can listen. Make sure it's set to channel nine."

"Thanks." She pulled the headset on and listened to the low whisper of Brad's voice.

"Just take a deep breath. You probably won't qualify, but make a good effort for Paddy."

Drew's heart pounded in her ears. This was Sam's only desire in life, and he was trying to convince her she couldn't do it. "What an ass," she said, rushing around the barrier.

Paddy reached across the fence and grabbed her by the sleeve, pulling her back. "You can't go out there. She's ready to roll."

Drew heard the engine roar, and the car raced out onto the track.

"Did you hear what he said to her?"

Paddy didn't bother to cover his microphone. "I heard it." His voice was firm and deep. "Samantha knows what she can do. Don't ya, honey?"

"Sure do, Paddy." Her voice was smiling, but Drew knew she was holding herself somewhere between the calm and the storm, waiting until just the right moment to let her adrenaline take over.

"Now get out there and stay in this race."

"You got it."

"I thought you weren't gonna let her on the track?"

Paddy flipped his microphone up away from his mouth, hauled in a deep breath, and let it out slowly. "She's got it in her mind to drive, and she won't give up 'til I let her." His voice was slow and deep.

"She might surprise you."

Paddy gave her a pat on the back. "That one always does."

Excitement tore through Sam, and her heart pounded wildly. Gripping the steering wheel, her hands trembled as she waited for the green flag. This was it. She was exactly where she wanted to be—driving a machine that could go from zero to one hundred miles per hour in under sixty seconds. Sam couldn't resist this rush. The flag was down and she went flying.

The race was on, but she was having trouble making it to the head of the pack. "I can't get between these guys." She waited for Brad to tell her where and when to shoot the gap, but he didn't.

"Aren't you going to help her?" She heard Drew's faint voice through the speakers in her helmet.

"She wanted to drive. I'm gonna let her."

"What the hell's wrong with you? Doesn't she mean anything to you?"

"When she's on that track, she's a driver. She should know what to do."

"I do know what to do," Sam said.

She heard flesh hitting flesh, then scuffling. *Jesus Christ, are they fighting?* "Hey! The race is only so long, guys."

"Tell her what to do," Drew shouted.

She heard Brad suck in a gasp of air and adjust his microphone. "Up your speed around the turns."

She'd already tried that once and felt the rear end start to slide. "I'm gonna spin."

"No, you won't. Just ease into the turn and then accelerate out slowly."

She came out of turn number four and hit the gas. Pulling inside she flew through the chute before easing off for the next turn. Adrenaline flooded her. She did it. She was running with the big guys now.

"That was good. Now remember, the fastest part of the track is after turn ten, but you'll have to slow up for turn eleven. After you get around eleven, punch it to the finish. That'll shave a couple seconds off your time."

"Got it."

Coming around turn eleven, she hit the gas and rocketed across the finish line, screaming in triumph. The adrenaline surge was so overwhelming, she was shaking. She wanted to fly around the track a thousand times more. The crowd was just a blur in her peripheral vision now. She'd never forget this mind-blowing sensation.

She eased off on the gas, but the car didn't slow. Her pulse raced faster. *Shit. What do I do now?* She couldn't breathe. *Calm down, Sam!*

"Whoooeee! Seventy-nine, point eight seconds," Paddy howled. " She's gonna do it!"

"Damn right she is." She heard Drew's voice, and her pulse steadied and pulled her back.

"You can slow down now, sweetheart. You're in," Brad said.

"Can't. The throttle is stuck." She jammed her foot to the brake—nothing.

"Flip the ignition," Brad said.

She reached for it but stopped. *I can't do that.* Her thoughts scattered. *What should I do? Think, Sam, think.*

"What the hell are you trying to do, kill her?" Drew's voice was faint.

"What?"

"Don't do it, baby." Drew's voice echoed in her ears. "Take it out of gear and punch the pedal. Remember? You told me that yourself. Mechanics 101."

"Go ahead, hotshot. You take care of her."

"Give me that." Brad's voice was gone, and the speaker crackled. "It's not working!"

"Kick it harder!" Ray ordered.

Sam couldn't do it. She was frozen.

❖

Drew listened for a change in engine tone. It didn't happen. "Damn it, Sam! You heard him! Kick it harder!" Drew shouted into the mic.

She heard the engine spike and then bump down to an idle. The car slowed, and Sam let it glide around the track. On the outside no one could tell there was a problem. Her voice was steady as stone, but Drew was quite familiar with the fear Sam was feeling. She had to be rattled.

Brad barreled into Drew, throwing her against the fence. "If she'd turned it off, the throttle would have reset."

"If you kill the engine, you lose all power. Without steering and brakes, she wouldn't have been able to control the car at that speed. She's not strong enough." Drew shoved him off.

"That's why you turn it back on."

"And what if it didn't start?" Drew was in Brad's face now. "I wasn't about to take that chance."

Paddy got between them. "What the hell happened out there?"

"You heard her. The throttle stuck." Drew didn't hide her concern.

"And?" he added, impatiently waiting for an answer.

"And it scared the hell out of her." Drew couldn't believe the man was so insensitive. That was his daughter out there. He had to know she was shaken.

Paddy turned to Ray. "What's happened with that car? It's brand-new."

Sam pulled herself through the window opening and yanked off her helmet. The crowd that had gone wild as she went speeding around the track cheered as she took off.

❖

When the race started, Sam had gotten lost in the euphoric feeling that flooded her. She'd been tempted to close her eyes and fly with the car, imagining she was on the fastest roller coaster ever built.

But it was no roller coaster. It was so much better. She was in control, with no one else there to throw a switch and make the car come to a screeching stop. It was all her.

When she'd eased her foot off the gas and the car continued to excel, her positive energy had thinned into pure adrenaline. It never occurred to her that something could happen to take the car out of her control. She wasn't ready to die, and if Drew hadn't been there, she might very well have done just that.

By the time she brought the car into the pit, she could barely breathe. She'd told herself to suck in air, but she couldn't get enough. With her heart thumping fitfully against her ribs, she thought it might explode any minute. She had to get away. She couldn't let anyone see her like this.

All her senses were completely full. The burnt rubber lingering on the track flooded her nose, the rumble of the engine still rolled in her ears, and her body ached. The force of the high speed had strained every muscle. Sam was physically fried.

"Sam, stop." Drew shouted after her, but she continued her rapid pace until she caught up to her at the curve. "Sam, come on. Let's get back to the pit. They're gonna start another heat in a minute."

Her voice shook. "I can't go back yet. Not like this." Sam stared down at her fingers, still purple and numb from gripping the steering wheel.

"Here. Take my jacket." Drew wrapped it around Sam's shoulders. "I'm sorry about yelling the way I did."

As she stared out onto the empty racetrack, the memory of the fiery crash that paralyzed her brother flashed through her mind, and she shuddered. "I didn't know what to do. I couldn't think. I couldn't focus."

"That's because when you're out on that track, you're a driver, not a mechanic."

"I can't drive. I can't work on engines. I can't function at all anymore. I don't know why Paddy trusts me with his cars."

Drew took her by the shoulders. "Because you're damn good at what you do."

"I could have killed myself and taken a lot of innocent people with me." Her tone was still and sober.

"Half-a-dozen other drivers would've driven that car straight through the tires and into the wall." Sam tried to turn away, but Drew took her face in her hands, demanding her attention. "You didn't. You stayed calm and got it under control."

"Yesterday I put in a faulty part, and today this happens." She struggled to hold back the tears welling in her eyes. "Stupid, amateur mistakes."

"It's okay."

Sam shook her head. "No, it's not. Don't you understand? I almost killed my own brother, and now he's paralyzed because of me." Her eyes were wide and searching. "I can't be responsible for hurting anyone like that ever again." She sobbed, burying her head in Drew's shoulder.

Drew pressed her lips to Sam's head. "You didn't paralyze Tommy. It was an accident."

She tried to pull away, but Drew held her firmly in her arms. This was uncharted territory for Sam. In the Kelleher camp no hugging was allowed. Her father always picked her up, swatted her on the butt, and encouraged her to go on. But he offered no comfort, no emotional support. Ever.

"The front axle was cracked. I should have caught it."

"When Tommy went out on that track, it was a hairline crack at most. That frame came apart because of his reckless driving, not because you didn't see it."

"He wasn't any more reckless than the rest of these drivers. The car should've been able to take it. I should have seen it."

"You know damn well Tommy felt that car shaking when it began to crack."

"I don't know that."

"Damn it, Sam. You would've. For God's sake, even I would've." Drew growled in exasperation. "If Tommy had pitted when he felt it, he wouldn't be in that damned wheelchair today. You would have found the crack and pulled the car."

"He should have come in," Sam whispered, staring, searching Drew's eyes for some glimmer of understanding.

"Yes, he should have, but like every other driver out there, he wanted to win." Drew's mouth hovered close. "We all want to win, Sam."

"I couldn't stand losing you." Sam covered Drew's mouth with soft, urgent kisses.

Drew swept her into her arms and buried her face in her matted locks, inhaling the heady mixture of hot oil and exhaust surrounding her. Even with the vague tinge of gasoline on her hands and exhaust in her hair, Drew couldn't resist her. Finally, Sam had given her a clue as to what was going on in that beautiful head of hers, a semblance of how she felt about her.

At this moment, holding her in her arms, the thought of jeopardizing her job was the farthest thing from Drew's mind. If she continued down this path, she'd have a guaranteed spot in the unemployment line when this assignment was finished. Possibly even before. But Drew knew only one thing for sure. She would never let Sam get in that car again. No way was she going to lose another woman she cared about.

"Come on," Drew said as she wrapped her arm around Sam's shoulder. "You need to get away from here for a while."

"No. I have to fix that throttle." Her voice cracked, and she trailed into a coughing fit.

"Look at you." Drew pressed the back of her hand to Sam's forehead, then her cheek. "Popping pills by the handful, drinking cough medicine from the bottle. You're sick. You need a break."

"Most of those pills are vitamins."

"They're not going to do any good if you don't get some rest."

Sam sank into her, and Drew knew she was too exhausted to fight.

CHAPTER EIGHTEEN

After tossing her bag into the back of the Jeep, Sam slid into the passenger seat and fastened her seat belt. She didn't pack much, only a day's change of clothes. One night away would be enough to get her back on track.

As they headed onto the highway, she gazed at the California countryside, still ablaze with the vibrant hues of early summer. It wouldn't last much longer. Hotter days were fast approaching, and the green-grass-covered hills were already beginning to turn brown and brittle with the heat.

She strained to keep her eyes open, enjoying the beautiful landscape. But the soothing warmth of the sun on her face made her lose the battle quickly, and her mind shut down.

"We're here." Drew nudged her lightly.

Sam fought to pull her lids apart and focus on Drew's face. "Already?" she mumbled, shifting sideways in the seat and letting her eyes slide closed again. She was having a hard time getting her body to budge. Apparently, she'd slept most of the way there.

"Come on, honey. Let's get you to the room, and then you can sack out again."

Honey. The endearment made her feel all giddy inside. "I'm fine right here."

"I guess I could call the bellman, and he could take you to the room on his cart."

Her head popped up. "Bellman? Where are we?" She slid out of the seat, blinking rapidly while her eyes adjusted to the sunlight.

"Goose Creek Inn."

She twisted her head around, taking in the lavish surroundings. "I can't afford this place."

"It's my treat." Drew took their bags out of the back, tossed the keys to the valet, and headed up the steps for check-in. Sam lagged back, admiring the white wood and Italianate accents of the early nineteen-hundreds building.

"Can I help you?" The man behind the registration desk was dressed in a white collared shirt and black vest.

"Hang on a minute." Drew hesitated, turning to Sam as she strolled across the marble floor. "Two rooms?"

She was leaving it up to her. Sam stared into Drew's chocolate-brown eyes, encouraged by her unassuming nature. Did she really want something to happen between them? She ached at the thought.

She smiled lightly. "One room should do." Something had changed between them this afternoon. Sam had done something she was never able to do before with anyone. She'd let Drew comfort her.

Drew's smile broadened in animated victory as she spun back around to the desk. "We need a suite for the night, please."

"Certainly. Can I interest you in any of the spa options?"

"Yes. I'd like a massage for each of us and an herbal sauna." Lifting an eyebrow, Sam tugged at Drew's arm. "In the privacy of the suite, of course." Tossing a credit card onto the counter, Drew paid no attention to Sam's protest.

"Of course." The man at the desk smiled and slid the credit card through the reader.

The Goose Creek Inn was somewhat of a landmark in Northern California. It was noted for discretion. At hiring, all employees were required to sign a privacy contract, guaranteeing their silence regarding all previous and future guests, no matter who they were or how famous they might be.

"Room thirty-two, miss. I'll have the bellman bring up your bags."

"I'll take them. Get the masseuse up there as soon as possible, please. We've had a long day."

"You've been here before?" Sam asked, her curiosity getting the best of her.

"I come here on occasion when I need to relax." Drew shoved the key folder into her back pocket, picked up the two small duffel bags, and headed across the lobby before abruptly turning back to the desk, catching the clerk's attention. "The room isn't near the elevator, is it?

The clerk shook his head. "You're at the east end of the floor, overlooking the garden."

"Great." She smiled at Sam. "Sunrise behind the hills. That'll be a treat in the morning."

Drew held the elevator door open, letting Sam step out first.

"This is it." She stopped at room number thirty-two and waited.

"Yes, it is." Drew dropped the bags and swept her into her arms, locking them around her waist. Sam snaked her arms around Drew's neck and kissed her completely. Every other time Drew was this close, Sam had been unsure and had forced herself to stop. Drew understood her, and it was time to let Drew know she was ready to let the boundaries go.

"Why don't we go inside?" Sam whispered.

"Okay." Drew picked up the bags and waited.

She stuck her hand out. "Key?"

"Oh." She shifted the bags and reached back to her pocket. Drew dropped the key on the floor and then fumbled for it. Yes, it was definitely time.

Within minutes of entering the room, Sam's mouth was back on Drew's, and she was responding in turn. Then they heard a knock on the door.

"Wow. These people are really on top of things," Sam whispered, her mouth still hovering closely to Drew's.

"That's why I like it here. Although I wouldn't have held it against them if they'd been really slow today."

Sam moved her hands up the back of Drew's shirt and scraped her nails across her shoulder blades. "Make them go away." Her voice was low and ragged.

"You'll like this."

When Drew pulled away, Sam grumbled and threw herself onto the couch. "I was liking *that*."

She pulled open the door, and a man and woman dressed in white entered, each carrying a bag in one hand and a padded massage table in the other.

"Go into the bedroom and take your clothes off."

Sam's eyes widened. If Drew thought she was going to strip and come back out naked in front of these people, she was sadly mistaken.

Drew chuckled, seeming to read her mind. "You'll find a robe in the bathroom."

Sam walked into it and closed the door. Now she felt like an idiot. But what was Drew expecting? She'd never been to a hotel like this before, a place where people flocked to satisfy your every whim and catered to you.

Pushing the vanity chair aside, she picked up a few of the fancy bottles from the elegantly tiled washbasin. Shampoo, conditioner, even hair spray. She turned to the tub and then hastily dropped the bottles back onto the basin. *Bath salts.* She tingled with excitement. It had been ages since she'd been able to enjoy a scented bath. She picked up the jar, opened it, and took a whiff. Roses. It smelled of pink roses in their fullest bloom. She closed her eyes and slid down into the chair. Paradise, that's what this was. Simply paradise.

She poked her head out through the bathroom door. "Do you mind if I take a bath first?" she asked, noting that Drew had already stripped and wrapped in a towel. Her arms and legs were tanned and well defined. She was absolutely gorgeous. Sam raised her gaze to Drew's, and the heat in her cheeks simmered. Judging by the smile on Drew's face, she saw it too.

"You take the bath last. Now change and get out here." Drew nudged her back inside the bathroom and pulled the door closed.

After Sam lay on the massage table for more than an hour, the masseuse had successfully worked her magic on the knotted muscles in Sam's neck. Her body had melted into pure Jell-O. Raspberry Jell-O, she thought, breathing in the fragrance of the scented oil.

"This feels amazing."

Drew sat up on the table, and her masseuse took a packet out of his bag before disappearing through the bedroom doorway.

"Where's he going?"

"To start the sauna."

She jerked her eyes open. "Sauna?"

"Yep. Whenever you're ready, it's right through the double doors next to the bathroom."

She closed her eyes again. "I don't even want to move right now." The words came out in a slow whisper. This was absolute heaven, and now that she'd been exposed to it, Sam didn't know how she'd live without it.

She watched Drew cross the room to the chair where her pants were tossed haphazardly over the top. Plucking her wallet out of the pocket, she slipped each of the massage therapists a generous tip.

"Can you pick up this table later?"

"No problem. Just set it outside the door, and housekeeping will get it."

Sam heard the door click shut. *Alone again.* The thought had her wet immediately.

"Come on. The herbs in the sauna will make you feel better."

"Do I have to?" She sucked in a long slow breath and held back a cough.

"Yes, you do," Drew said, lightly dragging her finger up Sam's leg, sending an erotic sizzle through her.

She rolled onto her side and covered herself with the luxurious terry-cloth towel draped across her back. "One might get the impression you've brought me here to seduce me."

Drew's fingers brushed softly against Sam's collarbone as she lifted the ring hanging from the chain around her neck. "That will come another time." She let it drop before pinching Sam's chin between her thumb and forefinger. "Right now my only interest is in getting you healthy." She took her hand and led her to the sauna.

Clasping the ring in her hand, Sam let out a sigh and closed her eyes. Brad's symbol of ownership. She'd forgotten about it, again. Sliding the ring to the top of the chain, she let it hang down her back. She didn't know why she kept putting it on. The golden charm had become a noose, strangling her every attempt at happiness.

"You go ahead. I'll be right in."

Drew's brows drew together.

Sam shot her a wild-eyed stare. "I have to *go*," she said, and headed into the bathroom.

"Oh, okay. I'll meet you in there."

Peeking out to see if Drew had left, Sam took the chain off and tucked it into the side pocket of her bag. She took in a deep breath as she entered the sauna and was actually able to let it out slowly. The constant nagging tickle in her throat was gone.

"It smells wonderful in here."

"It's a special blend of oregano oil, licorice root, and eucalyptus. A kind of homeopathic cure for the common cold."

Sam stopped in the doorway and stared. Although she'd been intimate with Drew more than once, their encounters had been far from exploratory on her part. It might have been only a fleeting moment when she'd caught a naked glimpse of Drew in the pool shower, but the image, still vivid in her mind, didn't compare to what was in front of her now. She glimmered with oil, a scant piece of white terry cloth tied loosely around her. This was an entirely different sight.

"It's getting pretty hot in here, huh?" In an attempt to disguise her sudden awkwardness, Sam blotted a towel across her forehead.

"The heat does seem to be rising a bit." Drew's mouth curved into an adorably sexy grin. "Take a seat and relax." She motioned to the bench. "You'll get used to it."

Sam sank onto the bench across from her and squeezed her eyes shut. She couldn't possibly relax with the full-color, three-dimensional, tanned, well-oiled body so near. Sam's imagination was shifting into overdrive. Her mind clouded with wild fantasies and desires she was aching to fulfill. Sam opened one eye slightly to capture a new picture of the main focus in her fantasy world. When she saw that Drew's eyes were closed, she got up quietly and ladled a spoonful of liquid onto the coals. Drew opened them momentarily at the hissing sound of the cool water hitting the blazing heat and closed them again as steam filled the room. Watching her relax against the wall with her legs outstretched, Sam wandered toward her in the mist. This woman was more than she'd bargained for, stirring wants and needs she hadn't realized existed. She let her towel drop to the floor.

Drew felt a subtle waft of air and opened her eyes. Sam was standing before her completely naked. Red curls, softened by the humidity, hung loosely on her shoulders. Skin glistening and cheeks pinked, she was an unbelievable vision. Drew was instantly wet as the sensation zapped through her, but more than just physical desire overwhelmed her.

Dark, sultry, and irresistibly wanting, Sam's shimmering green eyes peered down at her. "Shh," she said when Drew began to object. "Fourth time's the charm." Sam straddled Drew's lap and kissed her as she peeled the towel away. Their tongues mingled gently, in a soft, baiting dance before Sam slid her fingers into the wetness between Drew's legs.

A low growl erupted through Sam's lips as she broke away and stared into Drew's eyes. "Oh my god, you're so wet."

"Pretty much been that way since I met you."

Sam dipped her fingers into her mouth, closed her eyes, and let out an indescribable sound. Drew didn't think she could get more aroused, but she was wrong. She pulled Sam to her, and the steam from the sauna mingled between them. She could think of nothing more wonderful at that moment than feeling Sam's soft breast pressed to her own. Holding her tightly in her arms, Drew immersed herself in all that was Sam. This was worth waiting for. She was worth waiting for.

Drew trailed her mouth down Sam's neck, across the delicate ridge of her collarbone, while she let her hand roam down the soft sides of her breasts to her nipples, where she rolled one between her fingers. Sam hissed out a breath at the contact and arched her back. When she trailed her other hand lower and slipped a finger inside, Sam gasped and clung to Drew's shoulders as she began to move in a slow rhythm. Her lips pressed against the taut muscles of Drew's shoulder as she shifted and slipped another finger inside. Sam let out a tiny whimper when Drew stroked her clit with her thumb. Sam began to quake as her teeth scraped hard against her shoulder. Then without warning, her rhythm quickened as her moans rolled into high-pitched, labored breaths. She grasped Drew's head against her chest before she threw herself back, letting her weight pull Drew's fingers in deeper. Sam pumped against her until her orgasm peaked and she fell into her, tremors still rumbling through her.

Sam had concealed her urgency well. Drew hadn't thought she was even close, but with minimal warning, Sam had skyrocketed into orgasm. Drew wasn't prepared, and Sam's climax had very nearly sent her diving headfirst into her own heated pool of satisfaction.

"Snuck up on you, huh," she whispered, enjoying the achievement thoroughly.

❖

"Uh-huh," Sam mumbled, holding Drew tight and still enjoying the sporadic aftershocks. That was an understatement. Sam shifted, sucking in a quick breath as she continued to roll with wonderful sensations. She'd come so quickly and intensely, she'd been blindsided. She'd wanted to savor the moment, hold on to it as long as she could. She'd become an expert at giving pleasure, yet she was still quite inexperienced at receiving it.

When Drew's strong arms pulled her close, Sam grasped at her hair, tugging her head back to gain access to her neck. The taste of her still lingered on her tongue, and she wanted more. She slid off Drew's legs and knelt between them, taking in the sight of her. Strong shoulders, tight abs, small breasts, and gorgeous pebbled nipples. She sucked one into her mouth, and Drew arched against her as she teased it with her tongue. Drew tensed when she slipped a finger inside. Sam had to taste her again. She indulged in the sensation of the slick, wet crevice as she curled her fingers inside her. She made long, slow strokes with the flat of her tongue before taking Drew's clit and sucking it into her mouth. The groan that erupted deep within Drew drove Sam to move faster and harder until Drew trapped her between her thighs and flew into orgasm. Sam continued the pattern, reveling in the force of her release until Drew reached down and stopped her.

Sam straddled her again and trailed soft kisses up her neck to find Drew's mouth desperately seeking hers. The heat became suffocating.

"Ready for that bath now?" Drew asked softly, brushing her lips across Sam's shoulder.

"I want to stay right here." *Forever.* She kept her body glued to Drew.

"If I stay in here much longer, I'm going to pass out."

"Well, we don't want that now, do we?" She fluttered her lashes. "Wash my back?"

"Love to." Drew let out a low moan as Sam got up. "Nothing like being shoved out into the cold."

"You're the one who said we had to move." She stood, feeling wonderfully free and naked in front of Drew.

"Yes, I did," Drew said, taking her hand and leading her out. "I must be some kind of idiot."

Sam started the water and put a couple of towels on the basin. "Did you see all this stuff in here?" She picked up the bath salts and back brush.

"Use it. Comes with the room."

"Aren't you coming in?"

"No. You enjoy your bath. I'll rinse off in the shower and order some dinner."

"Oh, okay." She slid down into the water. "I won't be long." She rested her head back against the bath pillow and closed her eyes.

"Take your time," Drew said as she closed the door.

Drew smiled at the sight of her complete surrender. Over the past few days, she would've never thought a strong woman such as Sam could be rendered so completely helpless. She was surprised at how good it made her feel to see Sam so happy. Sam deserved places like this, and not just on special occasions, but all the time.

She pulled the door closed, then picked up the phone and called in an order to room service before getting into the shower. She'd probably ordered too much, but she was starving and imagined Sam was too.

Drew lathered up, washed all the remaining oils from her body, and let the heated water soothe her shoulders. She smiled, thinking about Sam's reaction when the masseuse started working on her. She'd simply closed her eyes and let out a soft moan. Sam might have seemed like a high-maintenance woman when she'd met her, but she seemed to have never experienced some pleasures in life before. She was completely aroused again. This power Sam had over her had to stop. She dialed the water lever to cold and shivered at the burst of icy water. She wasn't here for pleasure.

When Drew stepped out of the shower, she heard the faint knock on the door. Assuming it was room service, she dried off and wrapped a robe around herself before heading back into the main room. She let the waiter in and went back to get a tip from her wallet. When Drew got back to the room the young man had already transferred the food from his cart onto the table and was standing just outside the door waiting. Fingering through the bills, she pulled out a twenty and handed it to him.

Drew took a few steps toward the bedroom and then went out onto the balcony instead. The garden was empty except for a young couple huddling together on a blanket in the grass. Young love. She had only a vague recollection of it. She and Kimberly had been married just out of college.

She'd graduated with a degree in finance and could've worked for her father at a cushy job with an elaborate office in downtown San Francisco. Instead she had joined the highway patrol. Back then, she had something to prove to herself, her parents, and all the people who thought she grew up with a silver spoon in her mouth. By the time she realized that Kimberly had known all along she could make it on her own, it was too late.

She glanced over her shoulder into the room, wishing life could be that simple again. Yet she couldn't say whether she wouldn't have made the same stupid choices. She went into the bedroom, flopped down onto the cushy down comforter covering the bed, and closed her eyes.

Drew heard the click of the bathroom door and opened her eyes. Sam was radiant. Her face was slightly red, probably caused by a combination of the hot water and the low fever she'd been running for the past few days. Drew had purposely skipped the bath because she'd needed some distance. The thought of Sam's soft, freckle-flecked skin pressed against her made her weak. Not that she'd minded Sam clinging to her in the sauna. When she'd tried to shift Sam off her earlier, she wasn't budging. Drew knew that each moment she held her, Sam was becoming more attached.

Bringing Sam here wasn't a good idea. She'd told herself she'd brought her here to relax, but that was a lie. Drew wanted to spend every minute she could with her before she discovered who she was and why she was here. Soon enough, Sam would hate her, and Drew would hate herself when it happened.

Chapter Nineteen

Sam wasn't sure what Drew was thinking, and by the expression on her face it wasn't good. She'd indulged herself, taking an exceptionally long bath. She couldn't help it. Amenities like these were new to her. Maybe she'd given Drew too much time to think about what they were doing, about what she was doing here with Sam.

Drew swung her legs to the side of the bed and jumped to her feet. As she came closer, Sam closed her eyes and sucked in a deep breath, preparing for the letdown. When Drew's lips brushed hers, she could see in her warm brown eyes that everything was okay.

"I thought you might be hungry." Drew took her hand and led her into the main room of the suite. "I took the liberty of ordering a few things from room service." She pulled the chair out for Sam before lifting the top off the filet mignon. "I hope you don't mind."

She balked at the sight of beef. "Actually, I'm fine right now," she said, not wanting to ruin the gesture.

"Really?" Drew popped a mushroom into her mouth. "I'm starving." She lifted the lid from the plate of lobster. "I could eat both of these."

Sam tilted her head and smiled. "You knew all along."

"What? That you're a vegetarian?" Drew slid the chair under her as she sat. "A keen observer, I am."

"I see the philosopher is back." Sam laughed at the comedic accent she'd become strangely accustomed to hearing.

"The philosopher is always here." Drew pointed at her temple.

"It's a good thing, because I'm famished." Sam jabbed at the lobster tail with her fork and tore off a piece with her fingers. "Actually, I'm not a true vegetarian. I just try to stay away from red meat." She dipped the hunk of shellfish into the reservoir of butter before tilting her head back and dropping it into her mouth. "Umm," she said, letting out a muted moan. "This is wonderful."

Drew smiled at her indulgence. "So fish and chicken are okay?"

"I usually stick to fish." She popped another bite into her mouth. "You never know what they're pumping into farm-raised animals these days." She set her fork on the plate and reached for her glass. "For instance, do you have any idea what kind of steroids they've pumped into that filet?"

"Nope." Drew carved a slice and stuffed it into her mouth.

"It doesn't bother you that everything they've injected into that cow is now in you?" Spearing a piece of squash, her fork clanked loudly against the plate.

"No more than it bothers you to eat the pesticides sprayed on that rabbit food."

She dropped her eyes to her plate. "This isn't organic?"

Drew threw back in her chair and let out a burst of laughter. "Absolutely. I'm not taking any chances of you getting sick on me again."

"Please. Don't remind me. That wasn't my finest hour."

Drew lowered her chin and gazed up at Sam through her thick, black, splattered lashes. "I disagree."

Sam set her fork on the edge of her plate and watched Drew curiously as she opened the bottle of mineral water.

Drew poured them each a glass. "Nothing pleases me more than caring for a woman."

Picking up the newly filled glass, Sam didn't know how to respond. Was that a general statement? Or was that about the two of them? She knew how she felt. She thought so anyway, but having been hurt so many times before, she wasn't ready to put her feelings out there yet. She glanced back up at Drew briefly, catching her gaze. Quickly veering her attention to her plate, Sam decided she would concentrate on the gourmet meal in front of her for now.

A noticeable silence stretched between them.

"I've never met a woman who enjoys her food quite as much as you."

"I spend most of my time at the racetrack. I don't get this kind of luxury very often." She gave Drew a soft smile, thankful she'd been gracious enough to ease back on the intimacy, letting her off the hook for the time being.

Drew touched Sam's cheek with the back of her hand. "You deserve this every day."

Sam darted her gaze from Drew's. "This takes time and money, and I don't have enough of either for places like this."

"Soon, maybe you will."

Sam raised an eyebrow. Was this some kind of fairy tale? Was the woman going to whisk her off to some castle and take care of her for the rest of her life?

Drew trailed the last of the steak across the plate, catching the remainder of béarnaise sauce. "After we win the race."

Sam blew a short burst of air through her nose. She had a lot to learn about the payout in racing. "A lot of people have to be paid out of that prize money."

"You'll get a good chunk of it, won't you?" Drew set her fork down on the plate and picked up her glass.

"The driver gets the most."

Drew's brows pulled together as she dropped her napkin onto the table and leaned back in her chair. "And he doesn't share?"

"Not usually." Sam evaded Drew's stare, fixing her gaze on the ice bucket across the room next to the door. "Ooh, champagne," she cooed, in a feebly obvious attempt to change the subject.

"Compliments of the house."

"Let's open it."

"Maybe later. You really should rest now."

"I'll do it." Sam pushed back in her chair.

"Sit down. I'll take care of it," Drew said with a groan that quickly turned into a chuckle.

"What?" she asked, letting a whimsical smile take over her face.

Drew peeled the foil from the top of the champagne bottle and untwisted the wire securing the cork. "You've probably got pneumonia."

"Probably, but I've lived through worse," she said, flopping onto the bed.

"You never stop, do you?" The cork made a loud pop as Drew pulled it from the bottle. After filling the glasses, she dropped the bottle back into the ice bucket and carried them to the bed.

Sam took the glass she offered. "If I did, I might freeze up and never start again."

"To a victorious race," Drew said, clicking her glass against Sam's.

Sam took a sip and gazed over her glass at her. "And to another round in the sauna."

Drew flattened her lips. "That wasn't supposed to happen."

Was she disappointed? Wasn't it good for her? "Did you like it?" Sam asked reluctantly before taking another sip of champagne.

"Too much for my own good." Drew took Sam's glass from her and set it on the nightstand along with hers. "You should get some rest now."

She lowered her gaze. "I've never been with someone who was more concerned about pleasing me than number one."

"Some people just don't know what they're missing." Drew touched Sam's chin, prompting her gaze back to her. "Pleasing you is an absolutely phenomenal experience."

"I was hoping you'd say that." Sam nipped at Drew's bottom lip before their tongues mingled slowly. The taste of dry champagne became a sweet, irresistible nectar floating through her mouth.

Drew growled. "You really do need to get some rest."

"I couldn't possibly get any rest now," she said, her breath shallow and labored. "Make love to me, Drew." Her mouth went to Drew's again.

Drew sizzled all over. She was ready, willing, and eagerly able to do exactly as Sam asked. "You have to promise me something first."

"What?" Sam continued to nip at Drew's lip and then her chin.

"When we get back, you'll see the track doctor."

"I will."

"Promise?"

"Cross my heart." She took Drew's finger and swiped it leisurely across the flesh of her breast in the pattern of an X.

"One more question."

Sam's eyebrows rose in response.

"Can I drive this time?"

"I insist." Letting her hands drop to the bed, Sam invited Drew to explore wherever she chose.

The robe ties proved to be no barrier. Drew snaked them loose until they fell completely apart. Working her fingers under the robe, she felt Sam jump, her muscles tightening with her touch. She stopped, and Sam's burst of laughter told her it hadn't been a planned reaction.

"I'm sorry. I guess I'm a little…"

"A little what?" Drew mumbled, trailing the tip of her tongue up Sam's midsection. "Gorgeous?" She circled methodically around her nipple, then flicked it gently. "Irresistible." She slid across to the other. "Absolutely edible?" She sucked it deep into her mouth.

Sam's fingernails raked across Drew's shoulders and up her neck. "Ooh…yeah, edible, that's the one."

Her thigh pressed against the hot wetness between Sam's legs. Sam pressed back hard, begging for the erratic pool of sensations to be tamed into a long, slow-rolling boil.

Drew shifted and Sam moaned. Drew wanted inside now. Slipping two fingers deep into her, Drew savored the slow drag as Sam's muscles clamped down hard on them. Her body quivered involuntarily as she moved against Sam's thigh. With a groan, she pulled back abruptly, and Sam tugged at her waist.

"Come back."

"Not yet."

Drew's mouth replaced her fingers, and her tongue dipped inside, exploring at first, then stroking until Sam's hips rose hard against her, begging for more. She ventured farther, and Sam bucked. She continued the pace, Sam's writhing body shuddering with every stroke.

Eyes wide, Drew watched Sam's body rise and crumble beneath her over and over again. Her resolve weak, Drew let the climax take her. She wanted part of this magical place Sam was in. She wanted to be there, with her, now. Fully engulfed, she thrust harder and faster, unable to turn back, coming with her.

"Amazing." Her breathless speech only echoed in the midst of her rapidly beating heart.

Drew chuckled and rolled to her side. "You got that right." Today she felt like a kid playing Super Mario Cart, finding something better with each new level. "Now, can we rest?"

"Have I tired you out?"

"Sleep, I need sleep." Drew's voice came out in a low grumble.

"If you insist." Sam sighed. "I don't think I've ever had such an exhaustingly satisfying moment."

"I can't believe that." Drew's hand roamed down Sam's backside, and she flinched. "What's this?" She pulled the sheet back.

"Don't." Sam tugged at the sheet. "Please. They're ugly." Sam's eyes rose to meet Drew's gaze, searching for some sort of reassurance.

"They can't be." She kissed the tip of Sam's nose. "They're part of you." Pulling Sam onto her, Drew continued to sweep her fingers across the rough, uneven scar tissue covering Sam's ass. She remembered the explosion on the DVD, and a shiver rolled through her. It was Sam, not some heroic male who'd saved Tommy Kelleher. It was her body she saw engulfed in flames lying across her unconscious brother. Drew couldn't imagine the pain she'd suffered. "You saved Tommy." Drew's voice low, the words came out involuntarily.

Sam turned her head to the side, resting it on Drew's chest. "He would have done the same for me."

Drew took in a deep breath and pressed her lips to Sam's head. The faint scent of roses filled her head. "I believe he would have." She noted her sudden silence. "You okay?"

Sam raised her head, turned her gaze back to Drew's, and gave her a drowsy smile. "Just tired." Sliding into the crook of her arm, Sam closed her eyes and snuggled in tight. "Have you been with many women?"

That was a loaded question. "One or two." Drew had to know what was going on in her head. "I was just thinking." Sam touched her lips to Drew's chest. "I'm glad I got you seasoned."

I got you. Drew liked the way she said it, but she was still going to have to prove Sam wasn't causing the accidents before she could make it true.

Drew felt Sam's arms tighten around her and was overtaken by the feeling of contentment the simple action created. She'd just watched tremors roll through Sam and was completely in awe of her beauty. The vision of flushed cheeks, ruby-red lips, and glorious breasts popped into her head. Sam had glowed with desire, desire for her. Anyone would have to be an idiot not to cherish this woman.

What had she done? Drew was hanging on the edge, ready to fall onto a double-edged sword. She could feel it slicing through her as she held this beautiful, defenseless creature in her arms. She could very well be a merciless black widow, but Drew didn't care anymore. She would gladly take every drop of poison Sam was willing to give.

Sam's mind had splintered with light as she quaked over and over again with such force, Sam thought she might die of pure pleasure. When she'd opened her eyes, Drew had been hovering, staring at her blankly. She'd pulled Drew's mouth to hers, tasted herself on Drew's lips, and reveled in the pleasure this woman had just given her. She'd lifted her thigh between Drew's legs, felt the wetness, and been immediately aroused again. Drew shuddered, and she tingled, singed with a scorching flame when she'd soared into orgasm again. She'd thought she would shatter if it happened again. Drew moved slower and harder with every thrust, and she had quaked with pleasure, just the beginning of another long string of spasms. She'd bit her lip, trying to hold back the whimpering sighs, but she couldn't. The pleasure had proved to be too much. She'd let out a quick breath, shuddering uncontrollably as she pulled in the next gulp of air until the quakes slowed and she relaxed into a satisfied contentment.

The slow rhythm of Drew's heartbeat thumped in her ear, echoing to the same successive pattern as her own. It was hard to believe that only a few moments ago, her heart had been racing faster than she'd ever thought possible. She smiled as she drifted slowly off to dreamland, knowing she'd already been there once today. This had to be a dream—it was just too wonderful. *How did I get here, in this amazing place, with this amazing woman?*

Still holding Sam in her arms, Drew sucked in a deep breath and shifted her closer. Sam traced the line of her jaw with her finger and knew the answer to her question. That was the easy one. She'd never had anyone make love to her like that before. And for her to stay and hold her in her arms afterward, despite her horrible scars, gave Sam hope.

The warehouse was empty again. Air stagnant and hot, shots rang out, and the words reverberated in Drew's head. "I didn't want to do this, buddy, but you forced my hand. You turned out to be a better cop than I thought." Pain shot through Drew's side, the unwelcome reaction from the hard kick of a steel-toed boot. "Make sure they're both dead."

Drew heard the click of a trigger. She had only seconds before a bullet would pierce her skull. Adrenaline soaked her body. She scissored her legs around the gun-wielding thug, bringing him to the ground. The gun slid across the concrete floor out of reach. Drew searched for her ankle holster, her shoulder stinging as her would-be-assassin threw a punch into it. Her stomach lurched, and her sight faded momentarily. She slid her hand down her blood-soaked denim pant leg toward her backup gun. She didn't feel any pain there. Whose blood was it?

Got it. Drew felt the cold steel of her Taurus PT145. Her mind went blank. She saw two of them now. No, double vision—only one man. She fought to keep it together long enough to shoot. Finger on the trigger, she raised the gun and bolted up.

Where the hell am I? Drenched in sweat, Drew searched the room. Her hand trembled as she swept it across the cool, empty sheet. *Fuck!* She launched herself out of bed and into the bathroom. She couldn't let Sam see her like this. She turned on the shower and immersed herself until the shattered feeling from the persistent dream subsided. Someday she would be able to bury it.

Sam had been on the balcony watching the rain when Drew bolted up and rushed into the bathroom. Sam waited for her to come back out and handed her the fluffy white robe she'd worn the night before. Drew flashed her a relieved smile, and Sam thought she must have been worried she'd taken off again. Stepping back out onto the balcony, Sam couldn't imagine why a woman like Drew would worry about losing any girl. She'd checked her phone earlier and had seen the Tweet she'd posted on the way to the inn. It was a picture of Sam asleep in the passenger seat with the caption "sleeping beauty @ samkelleher." She certainly knew how to romance a woman.

Drew wrapped her arms around her waist. "It's pretty wet out here," she whispered. "You wanna go mud-racing again? Maybe I'll drive this time."

Sam leaned back against her and closed her eyes. "And if you lose?"

"I won't lose." She snuggled her face in behind Sam's ear. "You're going to have to stop leaving me like that."

"I'm right here."

Drew shook her head. "No, you're not."

Sam pulled out of Drew's arms, turned around, and kneaded the soft lapel of the terry-cloth robe between her fingertips. "I was just thinking about the race yesterday. After what happened, I don't know if I can do it again."

"Once you start feeling better, you'll get your focus back."

Sam leaned into her, letting her head rest against her shoulder. Being sick wasn't screwing up her focus. The woman holding her in her arms always caused that. Maybe the fever was making her so dependent, so pathetically weak. Sam was dangerously vulnerable, feeling even more defenseless than she had after Tommy's accident.

She took in a deep breath. Who was this woman, who not too long ago was a complete stranger? Sam didn't trust anyone, and she'd never allowed anyone this far into her life before. Drew was no longer a stranger. She was her lover now, someone she couldn't imagine living without.

CHAPTER TWENTY

Sam needed time to think about yesterday, last night, and this morning. She pulled herself under the car, slid the ratchet onto the oil plug, and mentally sank into her self-made sanctuary. She'd tried to resign herself to believing the fever had made her so vulnerable, not wanting to admit it could have possibly been anything different at this point. That's what it had to be. How else could she explain her constant euphoric state?

After several turns of the wrench the plug came loose, and oil oozed across her hands. She let the ratchet drop to the concrete floor and waited for the oil to drain. She squeezed her eyes closed and rethought the entire weekend chain of events. It wasn't the fever. No fever could possibly make anyone that deliriously happy.

Drew was everything she could ever want, but getting what she wanted could be dangerous. Brad would never let her go easily, and she couldn't deal with the conflict right now, not with only a few days left before race day.

Sam felt a strong, hard grip on her ankles. "Hey!" she yelled, grabbing at the frame of the car, trying to stop the force pulling her out.

Drew dropped down next to her and covered her mouth in a long, slow kiss. When Sam recognized her warm, familiar taste, she loosened her grip on the car, and put her oil-covered hands on the back of Drew's neck. Taking Sam's hands from her neck, Drew pressed them to her lips, then stuck her tongue out and scrunched her nose. Judging by her expression, Drew didn't appreciate the taste of aged oil as much as she did wine. She laughed, wiped a shop towel across her face, and gave Sam a sideways smile.

Drew sputtered and swiped her mouth across her sleeve again. "Did you see the doctor?"

Sam sat up and checked her watch. "It's lunchtime. Did you bring me something to eat?"

"Did you?" Drew raised an eyebrow and tilted her head.

She took the shop towel and wiped her hands. "Yes, but the track clinic is closed from eleven thirty to one for lunch."

Drew squatted and slid her knees on either side of the roller board. "I'll be happy to get you something for lunch. What would you like?"

She let out a low throaty chuckle. "I'm afraid what I want isn't on the menu." She let her fingers roam across Drew's sides before trailing them up her back.

With a groan, Drew pulled her in, subduing her with a long, heated kiss.

"You know, if you keep kissing me like that, you're going to get infected." Sam leaned in tighter, letting her gaze dart back and forth from Drew's mouth to her eyes.

"It's too late now. I've already got it bad." Drew dragged her thumb across Sam's cheek. "I'm going into the city to have dinner with my folks tonight. You want to come?"

"Dinner, with your folks?" *Absolutely not!* She wasn't about to put herself through that humiliation again. "I've got too much work to do. Besides, I'm sure your sister has filled your mother in on me by now."

"Yes, I'm sure she has, but I always find it best just to get your," her lip tugged up, "insatiable sexual appetite out in the open right from the get-go."

Sam slapped at Drew's shoulder. "Hey! That's not—" Drew crushed Sam's objection with her soft, seeking mouth. The battle lost, Sam let out a soft sigh as they parted. "Do you have to go?"

"Uh-huh, but I shouldn't be late." Drew popped up and reached for Sam's hand. "Now come on. By the time you get over to the clinic, it'll be open."

Sam dropped her shoulders and let out a heavy breath. "I'll go after I finish this."

Drew took Sam's hand and pulled her to her feet. "You'll go now." With her hands riveted to her hips, Sam prepared to spew out an ear-splintering protest, but something in Drew's deep, demanding tone made her balk.

"Please?" Drew said, before she could recover.

Drew was obviously truly concerned. "All right, but don't let anybody start this." She patted the hood of the car. "I still need to change the filter and put new oil in it."

Heading out into the stifling afternoon heat, Sam glanced back over her shoulder and saw Tommy heading into the garage. She turned to go back, only to see Drew giving her a back-handed wave, prompting her on her way.

Sam tugged at the clinic door. Locked. While rapping on the metal pane, she peered through the window. *Damn. He's not here.*

"What're you doin', Samantha?" Paddy's voice rumbled behind her.

"I need to see the doc." She gathered her hair together, pulling it into a handheld ponytail.

"What's wrong?"

"Just a little cold." She swiped the clammy skin of her neck dry. That wasn't true. This heat on top of the fever was killing her.

He frowned. "We need to talk about what happened on the track the other day."

Sam knew that expression. He was going to say something she didn't want to hear. "What about it?" She planted her hands on her hips.

"I'm going to put Brad in the new car."

"What? I qualified, didn't I?" She moved closer, invading his space. Sam wasn't sure she wanted to race after what happened, but she wasn't prepared for Paddy to yank the choice away.

"You did, but you were mighty shaken." He studied her, and his gaze didn't falter. "I need a driver who can handle a situation like that without panicking."

"I didn't panic. I brought the car back in one piece."

"I don't think you're ready to get back on the track just yet. Next time." Not waiting for a response, he turned, heading off toward the garage.

"If I wasn't your daughter, you wouldn't think twice about putting me back out there."

Paddy stopped and turned briefly. "But you are, aren't you?"

"That's not fair and you know it."

Ignoring her, he walked away.

She spun around, pressing her palm against the metal building. *Damn you, Paddy. This conversation isn't over yet.*

Drew waited until Sam was out of sight before going back into the garage to talk to Tommy. She hadn't had much time to do that since she'd arrived and wanted his take on the crash that put him in the wheelchair.

"Where's she off to?" Tommy asked.

"Clinic."

"She's finally going to have that cough checked out?"

"Yeah. I told her Paddy wouldn't let her drive if she didn't." Drew lied. It had become second nature.

"That true?"

"No, but it got her to go."

"She can be pretty stubborn."

"No kidding."

Tommy pulled open the fridge and took out a soda. "Want one?"

Drew threw up her hand and waited for Tommy to toss one over.

"I noticed you've been spending a lot of time with my sister." Tommy popped the tab, sucked down a big gulp, and let out a gasp.

It wasn't a question but was going to require a cautious response. Drew couldn't tell Tommy she was here to prove or disprove his sister had caused his and all the other accidents on the circuit this past year. And, by the way, somewhere along the line, she'd fallen in love with her.

Drew circled her finger around the rim of her soda. "We've spent some time together."

"What's Paddy got to say about it?"

"I don't think he knows."

"Why's that?"

"Just hasn't come up." Drew squeezed her soda can, making the aluminum pop. "What's with the third degree? It's not like I'm any worse for her than Wilkerson."

"No. You're not any worse, but are you any better?"

Drew got up, downed the rest of her soda, and tossed the can into the recycle bin. The aluminum clanged loudly against the inside of the metal barrel.

"Ask your sister," she said, heading for the door.

"Don't have to."

Drew slowed and turned around.

"I can see it every time she looks at you." Tommy slapped at the rubber rails on his wheelchair and rolled over to her. "I'm okay with it."

Drew shrugged. It wasn't like she needed his permission, but it felt kind of nice to know Tommy approved. Her cell phone rang, and Drew plucked it from her back pocket. She read the caller ID message "unknown caller" and glanced back at Tommy.

"Excuse me a sec." She hit the button and announced her last name as she walked across to the other side of the garage. Not that it would give her any privacy. You could hear the echo of a pin dropping in the huge metal structure.

"What's going on out there?" Captain Jacobs's voice came through loud and clear.

"Mom." She spoke just loud enough for Tommy to hear her. "How are you?"

"Don't give me that crap, Thompson. You'd better get your butt in here and give me an update, pronto."

"You bet. I'll be there for dinner tonight."

"ASAP," the captain barked.

"Love you too, Mom." She ended the call and slid the phone back into her pocket.

The last thing Drew wanted the captain to know was that she'd gotten attached to these people. Drew was always pretty good at profiling, but Sam was so scattered she was having a hard time pinning her down. At first glance all the signs were there. She had a neurotic, willful personality and didn't take crap from anybody. But Drew also found her to be a warm, compassionate woman. It was hard for her to believe she could hurt anyone.

Now it was time to go back to work. She was alone with Tommy. She could use this opportunity to gain some valuable information.

"Tommy, you mind if I ask you a couple questions?"

"About Sam?"

Drew nodded. "She was pretty upset about that throttle problem yesterday."

"Ever since my accident, she hasn't been the same. She tries to put on a brave face, but she's not like us."

Drew tilted her head in question. "What do you mean?"

"Even now," Tommy glanced down at his lifeless legs and gripped the arms of his wheelchair, "I'd go back out on that track today if I could. Sam says all she wants is to race, to be out on that track going a hundred miles an hour with no other goal than winning. I don't believe that's true. Fear's lurking in her head."

"You don't think she wants that?"

"She's my sister, Drew." His voice had a calm, compassionate tone. "I've seen her watch other women with babies. She wants kids someday."

Whack! It couldn't have been clearer if Tommy had reached out and popped her in the head with a lug wrench. Drew had been living in the moment for so long, she hadn't thought past tomorrow, let alone about starting a family again.

"She could've been killed pulling me out of that car. As it was, she got burned pretty badly."

"Wasn't she wearing her gear?"

"Sure, but even the highest-safety-rated suit can protect you from second-degree burns for only forty seconds. A minute-twenty max, *if* you're wearing racing underwear."

"Not a very long time, is it?"

"Not when you can't get out of a burning car." He hesitated, taking a gulp of soda. "Luckily Ray was there to take care of her afterward."

"Ray took care of her?"

"Came to the hospital every day. I think he spent more time with Sam than he did with me."

"Where was Wilkerson?"

Tommy flattened his lips. "He doesn't take the bad with the good. That's not his style."

"Tell me about the crash. I mean, if it doesn't bother you."

"I don't mind. The doctor says it's good to talk about it." He took another swig of his soda. "It was a perfect day for racing. Sixty-eight degrees, sunny, and not the slightest gust of wind. I took the first pace lap and increased my speed. Everything was fine, except I felt a little shudder as I rounded the corner."

"Did you pit?"

"No. I ignored it. It had rained earlier that day, so I figured the track was slick. The green flag was out and I took off. After that I didn't feel it again until I got to the last few laps."

Drew could see the sweat beading on Tommy's forehead. It was warm in the garage, but not that hot.

"You okay?"

"Sometimes it comes back like I'm still there." He grabbed a shop towel from the rack and blotted his face.

Drew knew that feeling all too well.

"I was in the last lap going down the first straightaway. I accelerated and felt the car shudder around the next turn."

Drew saw regret spread across Tommy's face. "I should've told Sam about it when I pitted."

"You knew."

He nodded. "But the car seemed fine, and by the time I felt it again, the race was almost over and I couldn't pit." He blew out a short breath. "I came around that last corner, took it faster than usual, guess I was getting antsy. We were neck and neck, and I wanted it so bad I could taste it." He paused. "Then the car pulled to the right so hard I couldn't hold it. I gave it everything I had and still went straight into the wall. I don't remember much after that. They tell me Sam pulled me out." He wheeled himself over to the tool bench, pulled open a drawer underneath, and took out a steering wheel.

"What's that?"

"A souvenir." He held it up and swiped his finger through the bolt hole. "See where it's bent?"

Drew could see where the pre-formed slot had been marred by the pressure. "Holy shit."

"I told you I tried. Ripped both my deltoid and triceps." He flexed his right arm and fingered the three-inch scar from the surgery on the inside of his arm.

"And your legs?"

"The G-force from the impact snapped my spine. The doctor said I was lucky to be alive."

"What about Sam? Why didn't she have her skin grafted?"

"I told her she should, but she wouldn't. She said I had to live with my scars every day, so she would too. She never wants to forget." He dropped the wheel back into the drawer. "That little hairline crack caused a lot of damage inside and out."

Drew nodded. "You aren't kiddin'." Tommy had no idea that crack had been caused by deliberately weakened steel.

The side door of the garage flew open, and they both turned.

"Hey, babe," Jade shouted, swinging the door closed behind her. "Paddy wants you to go with him to the inspection meeting." When she got closer, she pulled her eyebrows together. "You okay? You look a little flushed."

"Yeah. I'm fine." He scooted around her. "Is he already at the clubhouse?"

"Yep." She waited until Tommy was out of sight and then turned to Drew. "What's going on?"

"We were discussing the accident."

"His accident?" Jade's voice rose. "You should've talked to me about that. It's not good for him."

"It still bothers him?"

"Wouldn't it bother you if you were stuck in a burning car and couldn't get out?"

Drew pulled her brows together. "Sam pulled him out."

"But he doesn't remember that. When he thinks about it, his blood pressure skyrockets. He still wakes up in cold sweats during the night, trying to get away from the flames."

"Sorry. I won't bring it up again."

"Anything new on the case?"

"I have to go into the city."

"What for?" Jade snatched up all the dirty shop rags and tossed them into the linen service bin.

"The boss wants an update."

"Why's he riding you so hard on this one?"

"Don't know. Maybe because I screwed up the last one. I need to do some research on lover-boy Brad anyway."

"Oh. I thought you'd taken over that role."

Drew smiled as she headed out. "I'm workin' on it."

CHAPTER TWENTY-ONE

Sam glanced at her watch. Twelve thirty. She'd been waiting in Drew's room since eleven. Dinner with her parents shouldn't have taken this long. She should've gone with her, but she still had too much to do before the race. After her conversation with Paddy this afternoon, she wasn't feeling up to hobnobbing with the rich tonight.

Her head began to throb, and she scanned the room for an ibuprofen bottle. She spotted the suitcase on the chair and flipped it open. Rummaging through Drew's socks and T-shirts, she held up a pair of plaid boy-shorts and smiled. She dropped them back in and dug to the bottom of the bag. Nothing but clothes.

She closed the case and kneaded her forehead with her fingers. *The bathroom.* She went to the sink basin and found a bottle on the counter. She twisted the cap, but it didn't budge.

"Damn childproof bottles." She pushed, squeezed, and finally pulled the top off. After shaking out three tablets into her hand, she snapped the cap back on the bottle. After popping them into her mouth, she dipped her hand under the faucet and washed them down with a lukewarm swig of water before settling in on the bed.

She watched her stomach rise and fall with her breath. Closing her eyes, she imagined the heat of Drew's breath brushing across her. She didn't know how Drew had left such a mark on her so soon, but it was clear that she had. Sam yearned for her in every way. She was certainly not a virgin, but Drew sure made her feel like one. She smoothed her hand across her stomach, trying to purge the lingering feeling. When she felt the rough border of her jeans, she opened her eyes and hopped off the bed. After the way they'd made love last night, jeans and a T-shirt just wouldn't do.

Sam opened the door and peeked through it before stepping outside. The balcony was deserted, so she sprinted around to her room, opened the door, and squeezed through quickly.

She'd made it halfway. Now to find what she'd come for. She rushed to her suitcase, unzipped a small compartment inside, and held up a silk, emerald-green teddy. Her sister, Faith had convinced her to buy it not long ago when they'd been out shopping together, but she'd never had the urge to wear it until now.

She heard a thud against the door and spun around. Her excitement flattened. She'd wanted to surprise Drew. She heard another thud and her pulse raced. She tucked the silken piece of clothing back into her case, rushed to the door, and opened it. Brad fell into her.

"Omigod." Sam struggled to hold him up. "You smell like a brewery." In one swift motion he barreled through the door at her, and they tumbled onto the bed. She rolled him to the side and slid out from under him.

"How many drinks have you had?"

"Dunno." His words were slurred as he tried to catch the tail of her shirt when she stood up. "Come back."

"You're going to be out again tomorrow, aren't you?" She rubbed her face and paced to the window. "Paddy's going to replace you if you keep this up."

"He's not gonna replace me. I'm the best and he knows it."

"Then why don't you act like it?" She waited for his cocky response but didn't hear one. At the sound of a gurgling snort, she spun back around. "Oh, no—you can't stay here." She slapped at his face, but he didn't flinch.

Suddenly he grabbed the bed, lurched forward, and spewed all over both of them.

"Uh—Yuk!" Sam flew back, gagging. "Fuck!" She gave him a shove, and he flopped back onto the bed. She couldn't believe this was happening. She was supposed to be having a nice romantic evening with Drew, and instead she was covered in puke and dealing with a heaving drunk.

"Get up." She pulled his arm around her neck and led him into the bathroom. "Take your clothes off," she said, leaning him up against the wall and starting the shower.

He fumbled with the buttons on his shirt but had no luck. Sam held her breath as she unbuttoned the vomit-covered shirt and slid it from his shoulders. She pulled the button loose on his jeans, and the zipper went down with one swift tug.

"There. Now get in."

"You're not going to help me with the rest?"

"No." She picked up his clothes. *I am so done with you.*

"How'm I gonna get in there?"

"You figure it out." She turned and pulled the door closed behind her. She gagged and tried not to breathe as she dropped his shirt into the sink, then peeled off her own. After slipping on a clean shirt, she rinsed the clothes and hung them across the balcony railing. Her stomach turned as the stench of liquor and vomit hit her when she came back into the room. She dug a perfume bottle out of her cosmetic bag and squirted it a couple of times. A miserable end to a miserable night.

She heard Brad fumbling with the doorknob. "You okay in there?"

"Can't get the door open."

She pushed it open, and he was right where she'd left him, only now totally naked and dripping wet. She let her gaze sweep his length and didn't feel even a twinge of desire. Only regret. She pulled a towel from the rack and wrapped it around his waist.

"No takers tonight?" He slurred his words.

"Stop." She blotted his chest, then his hair. "Come on. Let's get you into bed." She wedged her shoulder under his arm and guided him out. Before she could pull the blanket back, he was on his way down. She let him drop onto the bed.

"Why couldn't you have just gone home with someone tonight?" She pressed her fingers against his neck and felt his pulse, slow but rhythmic, so he was still alive.

She pulled his legs around, then went to the other side of the bed, wedged her arms underneath him, and shifted him to one side. After glancing at her watch, she let out a heavy breath before flopping down onto the vacant side of the bed. It was close to two o'clock, and her romantic surprise for Drew would have to wait. It seemed as though Drew had stayed with her parents for the night. She clicked off the light, then crossed her arms and sank back onto the pillow.

Sam glanced over at the pathetic man lying beside her. How had she ever gotten involved with him? Charm, arrogance, and a handsome face, that was how. Sam never could resist a rebel, especially if they got a rise out of her father. She put her hand on his chest and felt his slow, erratic breaths. She had to make sure this one made it through the night, for Paddy's sake.

Chapter Twenty-two

S am rattled the doorknob to Drew's room, but it was locked. She gave the door a soft knock, and it whooshed open.

She pushed inside and closed the door. "I missed you last night."

"I got in pretty late."

She snaked her arms around Drew's neck. "I waited up for you, but then I figured you stayed over." Something wasn't right. Drew didn't kiss her and wouldn't make eye contact. "What's wrong?"

"I went to your room last night."

Panic flooded her. "He was drunk."

"That's your excuse for hopping back into bed with him?"

Sam dropped her arms from around Drew's neck. She couldn't believe she would think so little of her. She'd opened her heart to Drew, and now she was questioning her fidelity. "I didn't—"

Drew grabbed her shoulders roughly. "Didn't what? Think I would be back last night? I can't believe you slept with him."

Sam batted Drew's arms away and poked at her chest. "Since when do I have to answer to you? Did we say we were exclusive?"

"You're damn right we're exclusive. I thought we were going somewhere with this."

The sinking pain in her chest intensified. Her combative response had become so second nature, the words had spewed out involuntarily, and it was too late to take them back. *What am I doing? This is Drew.* She raked her hand across her face and fought to speak softly. "Do you have any idea how hard *this* is for me?"

"Hard for you?" Drew brushed by her. "One night you're in my bed. The next you're in his." Drew paced the room, dragging her hand roughly across her neck. "I've never shared a woman with anyone before." Hesitating in front of the door she yanked it open. "And I'm sure as hell not going to do it now."

"You really want me to leave?" Her voice came out in a whisper.

"Yes."

❖

Sam's beautiful green eyes drooped like a wounded puppy's, but Drew didn't cave. She couldn't get the vision out of her head. Last night, she'd knocked lightly before she'd pushed open the door to Sam's room. She'd given her eyes a minute to adjust to the darkness and then dropped back against the door. Sam had been tucked in tightly next to Brad, with her head on his shoulder and her arm across his naked chest. The night before she'd made love to her, and now she was back in bed with Brad.

She watched Sam walk out the door, slammed it behind her, and paced the room. *Fuck! That was stupid.* She'd tread on hot coals for Sam, and she'd just thrown her out. Drew didn't know when it had changed, but Sam was much more important to her than any job. She should've let her talk, but jealousy had consumed her. She jerked the door open and rushed out after her. She had to have a reasonable explanation.

Sam wasn't in her room, so she went straight to the garage. She spotted Sam by the number forty-four car, but Brad was MIA once again. That meant Drew was driving today, and she was going to have to make things right between them.

"How're we doin' here?" Drew asked.

"We?" Sam's eyebrows rose, but her face remained expressionless. "There is no *we* here." She seemed to have rolled from hurt to pissed.

Drew clenched her jaw. "The car. Is it ready?"

"Yeah, but my driver's not. He's hung over."

"I'll test it."

With one eyebrow still cocked, Sam stood back and crossed her arms. "Are you sure you want to share?"

Drew got her message loud and clear. Sam was angrier than she'd ever seen her, and Drew didn't like the fact that she'd made it happen. She should've trusted her. She stared into her eyes, gauging the fury in them. She wanted to take back everything she'd said but didn't know how to begin.

Sam broke contact to glance over Drew's shoulder. Drew turned and saw nothing. "What's up?"

"There was a guy in here earlier, said he was lost. I just saw him pass by again." She lifted her eyebrows. "Maybe I should invite him in for a drink. We can throw another person into this mess."

"I'm sorry." Taking note of her combative stance, Drew knew the wall wasn't coming down today. She climbed into the driver's seat and fastened her helmet. "Can we talk about this?" She slid the steering wheel onto the shaft and fired the engine.

Sam's scowl faded, and she blew out a short breath before glancing back at the rest of the guys. Besides the usual crew, the garage was full of stragglers today, and Drew knew she wasn't about to give them anything more to talk about.

"Not now." Her stance might have weakened, but her tone was still strong and demanding. "I rebuilt the clutch, so it's—hey!" she shouted as Drew threw the car into gear and took off. She'd waited just long enough for her angry green eyes to meet hers. Drew knew how to break in a clutch.

❖

Fuck! Drew had done it again, just took off without listening. Sam didn't care how angry Drew was with her. This was a dangerous business, and if she wanted to continue on this racing team, she had to listen to Sam, whether she wanted to or not.

"Damn it, Drew! Come back here!" She shouted as the crew hustled out to watch her test run.

"What's wrong, Sam?" Jade smiled widely, Tommy beside her. "Tommy told me you like a driver who can handle a tight clutch."

"Tommy said what?" Sam glared at him.

"Better be careful, sis. Word travels faster than cars around this track."

"You shouldn't believe everything you hear," Sam shot back, showing him a spark of anger she knew he'd recognize. Tommy had made a habit of testing both of his sisters' boundaries as a child. Faith had always ignored his taunting, but Sam had a wicked temper.

Tommy tilted his head. "So, it's not true?"

Sam narrowed her eyes in warning. He was waiting for her to blast him, but she held her temper. "You'd better stop, Tommy."

He smiled. "I'm proud of you, Sammy. You've grown up."

"It's about time you noticed," Jade said, giving Sam a wink.

Jade slid onto Tommy's lap, straddling him. Sam could see her gaze zoom in on his just before their lips met. Tommy seemed to have found true happiness. She envied her brother. It was obvious Jade loved him and not just for the benefits of being on the circuit. Jade filled his heart, but Sam still saw reluctance. Tommy apparently wasn't sure he did the same for her.

"You know, if I was Tarzan and you were Jane, there might never be a Cheetah." Tommy's tone was teasingly serious.

Jade laughed abruptly. "Cheetah was a monkey, silly."

"Oh." He hitched one of his eyebrows up into a cockeyed grin. "Whatever. My point is there may never be any kids for us."

"I'm not interested in kids, right now." She pressed her forehead to his and lowered her voice. "We'll worry about that when, or if, that time comes." She twisted around and sat forward on his lap. "Now I'm hungry, so put this thing into high gear and take me to lunch." She glanced back at Sam. "You want anything?"

"Bring me back a sandwich."

"Tuna or egg salad?"

"Whichever."

"Ray?" Jade solicited his order.

"No thanks." Ray watched as they rolled out of the garage. "She's an original."

Sam chuckled. "Oh yeah."

"You're worried about him." Ray's usual low-easy tone filled the garage.

"I'm a little overprotective after that last heartbreak."

"I never did like that one. Spoiled rotten."

"And this one?" Sam needed to know if her judgment was clouded by Jade's willingness to keep her secrets.

"She's good for him. Doesn't let him wallow in self-pity."

She turned to see them cruising around the corner. "I'm giving her a shot, Ray. Only because he seems to be happy at the moment."

"What about you, Sam?"

She snapped her gaze back to meet his.

"Are you happy?"

"Let's see now." She pressed her finger to her lips and glanced up at the hollow, rounded ceiling. "I'm twenty-eight, single, and surrounded by people all the time." She shrugged. "What more could a woman want?" Too bad saying it didn't make it real. Sam was good at putting up a front, but in truth she wanted more. A lot more.

Drew pulled the car back into the garage and came to her usual screeching stop. She'd had time to think it over and realized Sam was right about one thing. She shouldn't bring up their personal business in front of everyone else. For that matter, there really shouldn't be any personal business at all. She'd blurred the lines and lost sight of her mission.

"Don't take the car out again until I'm ready." Sam's tone was more harsh than usual.

"Okay." Drew held her tongue. It wasn't all her this time. Something else was bothering Sam.

"Okay?" Her brow rose quickly. "That's all you have to say?"

Drew looked sideways at Ray. "I'm sorry, Mom? I won't do it again?" Her voice thickened as she bobbed her head slightly.

Ray chuckled but seemed to see Sam's dead-serious expression and quickly stifled his laughter.

"You drivers are all alike. Stupid, self-absorbed—"

"Hey now! I may be a bit self-absorbed, but I'm not stupid."

"Then why don't you listen?"

Drew dropped her helmet onto the seat and headed out of the garage. "I've had enough of this conversation."

"Get your ass back here and fight with me, damn it!"

"You've got the wrong person for that," she shouted without breaking stride. "When you're ready to talk to me civilly, you know where to find me."

Brad strolled in through the side door with his usual smug manner. "Sounds like you and your girlfriend are having a little spat."

"Leave it alone, Brad." Sam tried to stifle her cough but failed. "I'm not in the mood for any of your crap either." Swiping the bottle of cough medicine from the bench, she swallowed a big gulp.

"At least I'm man enough to stand up to you."

"Is that what you call it?" She tugged open the refrigerator, took out a bottle of water, twisted the top off, and took a big gulp. "You're a real piece of work, you know that?" she said, her cough settling for the moment.

"Let me know when you've got the car ready for me."

"The car was ready an hour ago. Drew took it out. I don't need you now." She slapped the water bottle to the bench.

"Don't get used to that. Thompson isn't going to replace me."

"I wouldn't be so sure about that. At least she can perform."

He gave her a splintering stare and started toward her. Sam heard the clink of Tommy's wheelchair coming through the entrance, and Brad stopped.

"Watch out for your sister. She's in rare form today," he said, spinning around and whipping past Tommy.

"Why do you let him treat you that way?"

"Stay out of it."

"I know of at least one person around here that would treat you a whole lot better."

"I'll choose who I want to be with, Tommy. I'm not a victim."

"Victim." He let out a short breath. "That's your word, not mine. But if you're not, stop acting like one."

"Just leave me alone." She put her hand to her head and felt the fever radiating. "I'm not up for this right now." She felt dizzy, and everything went black.

❖

Sam tried to move, but everything hurt. Ignoring the pain, she pulled herself up in bed. *Where the hell am I?*

Drew sprang to her side. "Hang on there."

Sam studied her face. She seemed groggy. "Is this your room?"

Drew nodded. "I told Paddy I'd keep an eye on you while he's at the track."

"How did I get here?"

"You passed out in the garage." She brushed a curl from Sam's forehead. "You promised me you were going to take care of this. See the doctor."

She rubbed her forehead. "I went, but he wasn't there."

Drew shook her head. "I should've taken you myself."

Sam threw the covers back. "I don't have time for this. I've got a race to prepare for." Her vision faded, and she grabbed the corner of the nightstand to steady herself. "Whoa." She fell back against the pillow.

Drew lifted her legs onto the bed and pulled the blanket across them. "You're on the brink of pneumonia. The doctor gave you a shot. Now just lie back and rest."

She rubbed the tender spot on her hip. "That's what that is."

"You also took a good bonk to the head when you fell."

"How long?"

"At least a day, maybe two." Sam sat up again, and Drew smiled as she steadied her. "Your health is more important than any race, Sam. Ray can take care of the cars until you're up again."

Sam sank back down into the pillow. "Ray. Yeah. He can do it." She closed her eyes and everything faded again.

CHAPTER TWENTY-THREE

S am clanged the side door open and caught a glimpse of Ray. "Hey, sunshine, you're back," he said. "I missed you the past couple of days." She could see by his moist brow and grease-stained coveralls that he'd already been hard at work this morning.

"Sorry about that, Ray. I feel much better now." She threw her arm across his back and gave him a soft pat. "How are things coming?"

"Right on schedule."

"Thanks for picking up the slack. I don't know what I'd do without you."

"You know I'm always here for you, Sam."

Even though she'd heard that statement from him a million times before, Sam detected something different in his voice this time. "Is everything okay? How's Jenna? I haven't seen her around the track lately."

"Jenna's good. Remember, I told you she's got a new job and doesn't have much free time."

"Oh." She scrunched her nose. Sam didn't recall him telling her anything about Jenna and a new job, but then again, she hadn't been running on all cylinders lately. "Tell her I said hi."

"Sure thing."

She ducked her head under the hood. "Where are we at here?"

Sam heard Drew's voice echoing into the garage from just outside. She hoped she was only passing by, but could tell by the distinct pattern of her footsteps that she was headed inside.

They'd made their peace about the misunderstanding, and Drew had taken excellent care of her over the past few days, waiting on her as well as keeping her warm at night. Sam had been thrown back into the fire again. With constant thoughts of being locked together smoldering in her mind, she'd ached to feel Drew inside her again. Drew hadn't crossed that line again until last night when Sam had kissed her softly, touched her intimately, and begged her to make love to her. She'd done it, making her come repeatedly throughout the night. It was all Sam could think about. This mesmerizing state Drew kept her in had to cease, or she would never get any work done.

"Can you give us a minute, Ray?" Drew said.

Ray glanced at Sam and she gave him a nod. "Sure thing. Be back in ten."

Ducking her head back under the hood, Sam shook when Drew slid her hand up the back of her shirt. The feeling was so unnerving, she popped up and smacked her head hard against the hood.

"Damn." She winced, holding the back of her head as she waited for the pain to subside.

"You okay?" Drew moved forward and Sam backed up. "Sorry. I didn't mean to startle you."

She sucked in a deep breath, hoping the ringing in her ears would stop soon. "What's up?"

"You snuck out early this morning. I just wanted to come by and make sure you're okay."

"I'm fine."

Drew reached for her head. "Why don't you let me check that?" Sam pushed her hand away.

"I said, I'm fine."

Ignoring her protest, Drew slipped her arm around Sam's waist and tugged her close. "You know what the doctor said."

"Yeah. Well, I think he's in cahoots with the competition."

Drew pulled, Sam pushed, and with a fading smile, Drew released her. "What's wrong now?"

It was time to focus on the car. Over the last forty-eight hours she'd had a lot of time to think. Racing was the only concrete thing in her life, and she was screwing it up royally. Her health, her emotions, everything was out of control. Something had to give.

"I can't do this anymore."

Drew's full, dark brows pulled together. "Do what?"

"Him, you, me, us."

"I thought things were good between us."

"They are." She sighed, shifting uneasily. "But I can't live like this."

"What? Happy?"

If she was going to do this, it had to be now. She closed her eyes and blew out a deep breath. "Have you ever had that all-consuming feeling when you're with someone?" Drew smiled and touched her cheek. Sam put her hand immediately on Drew's and removed it. She had to do it. She had to bare all and then cut clean. "I can't think straight when you're around, and when you touch me like that, I can't function at all. I can't afford to be in this helpless state all the time."

Drew slipped her arms around her waist, and she reacted with a jolt. "You're sick, Sam. That's what's messing up your focus. You'll feel differently in a few days."

"No." She fixed her gaze on Drew's and pried her arms away. "I won't. I can't."

"You'd rather be miserable than be with me?"

She'd hurt her. Sam could see it clearly in her eyes. It made her stomach rumble, but she had to do it. "At least my heart would be safe."

"What about my heart?" Drew's expression was still and sober. She backed up and stared before turning around. "I'm going to suit up, and then I'm going to take the car out. If you're not here when I get back, I guess I'll see ya 'round."

She watched Drew walk out before picking up the wrench and clanking it down onto the air-filter cover. *No, I can't see you around. That's the problem.*

After numerous attempts to restart, the pit crew rolled out and pushed Drew and the number-fifteen car back into the garage. As Sam stood watching through the office window, a wave of relief whooshed through her. She could tell by the way Drew was slamming things around, she was pissed.

Drew gave the office door an open-palmed whack, and it bounced against the wall and back at her. Sam held her chuckle when it popped her in the face.

"What's the matter with it now, Samantha?" Paddy's tone was strong, demanding her attention.

"Same thing." She shrugged. "I've been fighting that flat spot since the beginning of the week."

"I thought you had that fixed." Drew gave her a dead-serious stare, making no attempt to hide her suspicion. "The car's been running smoothly for two days, and now all of a sudden this problem is back?"

Sam could see Drew thought she'd done something to the car, but she hadn't. It had been a fortunate coincidence. If there was no car to drive, Drew wouldn't be around as much.

"That's the problem." She lifted her cheeks into a fake smile. "It comes and goes."

Ray hollered from under the hood. "Hey, Paddy. Can you come here for a minute?"

He scowled, pushing away from the desk.

After Paddy went out the door, Drew gave it a nudge. The old wooden plank swung around but stopped just short of closing. "I don't buy it, Sam."

"You don't buy it?" She let out a short laugh. "Since when do you know anything about engines?"

"Since I've spent the last week leaning over your shoulder." Her gaze swept Sam's body. "Memorizing each and every move you've made."

Sam shifted uneasily. "I thought we were talking about the car."

Drew moved closer into Sam's space. "We are?"

"Don't." Sam gave her a pleading stare.

"Will you take a look at this?" Paddy came back through the door rolling a bead of black goo between his fingertips. "Somebody put gasket seal in the fuel line."

Sam widened her eyes, and she brushed by Drew. "What?"

"Luckily Ray found it before it made it to the engine."

She was concerned now. Someone had done something to the engine.

Paddy turned back to the garage. "Let's go check that injector, Samantha. You need to give it the once-over to make sure it wasn't damaged.

"Surprised Ray found it?" Drew said, stepping in front of her.

"I'm glad he did." She truly was surprised. "I don't care what you think, but I would never compromise these cars."

"I wonder who did?" Drew's stare burned so deep into her, Sam had trouble keeping eye contact, but she didn't flinch. She wasn't giving in on this one. She would never deliberately sabotage any race car and refused to let Drew think she had.

Drew shook her head and blew out a short breath through her nose. "I have a couple of things to do this afternoon. I should be back for dinner, if you want to talk."

"Talk about what?" Sam got the feeling Drew didn't believe her.

"About this." Drew pulled Sam to her and pressed her mouth hard to hers.

"Dinner…uh…sure." Sam's mind raced as her body flew into overdrive, and the words just rolled out. She stumbled back against the wall and didn't move until the office door clicked shut. *Damn. She did it again.* She whirled around and paced behind Paddy's desk. She'd meet her, but there would be nothing more than dinner. She took in a deep breath. That was a lie. Thinking about her crooked, cocky smile, Sam slumped down into the chair. She'd had a taste of her, and Drew was running hot in her system. She wouldn't be able to flush her out until she ran the full extended course.

CHAPTER TWENTY-FOUR

When Sam had brushed her off this morning, the feeling of loss rolled through Drew like a tidal wave. She'd felt the sting of rejection before, but it had never stung quite so deep.

Knowing Sam could barely think when she was around was the only thing keeping her sane right now. It confirmed that she meant something to her. Drew's biggest obstacle now was the way she felt about Sam. Drew knew exactly what helpless state she was talking about. It was an unmistakable sensation that crashed into her whenever Sam was around, and it was getting in the way of her job as well.

"Hey, Thompson."

Drew spun around and found Lieutenant Barnes standing right behind her. "Good morning, sir."

"How's everything going on that black-widow case of yours? I hear she's pretty good at sucking them in."

"Where'd you get that information?" Drew was suspicious. The lieutenant's transfer from Narcotics to Internal Affairs had happened so quickly, it led Drew to believe they had something on him. Now that he was in I.A., Barnes seemed to be in Drew's business all the time.

"I didn't get it from my daughter, if that's what you're insinuating."

Drew shook her head and gave him a cold, hard stare. "Jade's not a snitch. I would never imply that. I have too much respect for her."

"You just make sure you back her up. I've already lost one daughter because of you."

"I lost her too, Jack." She didn't want to get into this discussion again. Drew knew who was responsible. He couldn't blame her any more than she already blamed herself.

Jack raised an eyebrow. "Better be careful. I won't be there to cover your ass this time."

Drew creased her forehead "Were you there last time?" He hadn't backed her up at all. Jack had claimed he'd had car trouble and hadn't made it to the scene until after Drew and her partner were already down. She'd concluded that someone must have tipped them off. When she went in, things just didn't feel right, the old warehouse strangely still. It was supposed to be an easy meet, but everything went bad before the transaction even started. Drew hadn't seen the gun or the shooter. If she had, she couldn't remember.

Drew suspected Barnes had had her transferred. She could feel it in her gut. He'd wanted her off the case from the very beginning, said she was lucky she'd only gotten a shoulder shot. And he was right. If she went back undercover in Narcotics, she would've been dead in a week. Barnes had thrown her to the wolves and then switched sides to save his own hide.

"Maybe you'll be her next victim," Barnes said.

"You'd like that." Drew turned and continued down the hall to the lab.

Next victim, hmm…That was a definite possibility. Someone had rigged the injector line, but Drew couldn't find it in her heart to believe it was Sam. Yet she *was* acting way too cool, and Drew didn't know why.

As Sam waited for Drew in her room, the incessant buzzing edged her out of her drowsy state. The room was completely dark now, and she tried to focus on the analogue clock. She didn't know how long she'd been asleep, but her worn-out body was demanding more rest. She didn't want to move. She rolled over and pulled a pillow over her head, but the buzzing continued. Unclear about what she was hearing, Sam sat up and searched around the room, trying to locate the sound. As the room came into focus through the darkness, she swiped her fingers across her eyes. She moved to the side of the bed, and the buzzing got louder.

Opening the nightstand drawer, she found the phone creating the noise. The message displayed across the screen from the Bureau of Forensics Crime Lab said, "DNA 1 positive, DNA 2 negative." She stared at it as if that would make the message more comprehensible. After the screen went dark, she touched the button to make it visible again.

Crime lab. DNA. Sam suddenly felt sick. Who in the hell was this woman she'd been sleeping with for the past week? She bolted off the bed and pulled open every drawer in the place. Finding nothing, she flopped back down on the bed. Where would she put something she didn't want found?

She slid off the bed, fell to her knees, shoved her hands under the mattress, and felt the stiff edge of a file folder. As she scanned through the pages it contained, her nerves puddled. She'd never seen these pictures before—horrifically graphic ones of all the accidents that had occurred over the past year on the racing circuit. Some of them showed men with whom she'd been intimate and who were now dead. She closed the folder and sucked in a deep breath.

The folder also contained personal information about her and everyone else on Paddy's racing team. And it wasn't just the team. It was loaded with facts about everyone in her life.

She flipped it over and read the front cover. In small bold print on the front of the folder it said, California Bureau of Investigations. *She's a cop?* The emptiness crashed into Sam like a two-ton truck. She picked up Drew's phone and typed in something she knew she'd regret.

Drew opened the door and turned on the light. Sam was sitting on the floor propped up against the bed, and her mood perked. When Sam raised her gaze to meet hers and Drew saw her red swollen eyes, she rushed in and dropped to her knees beside her.

"What is it? Did something happen to Paddy?"

"Paddy's fine."

"Tommy?"

"He's fine."

"What's going on?"

"I came here tonight to tell you I was wrong about what I said this morning about not wanting to live without you." Drew moved toward her, and Sam threw her hand up between them. "But now I'm not even sure who you are." As Sam roughly wiped the tears from her cheeks, she shuddered and let out a ragged breath. "There's a text on your phone from someone at the crime lab."

Drew closed her eyes and shook her head. "I forgot it."

"I was here waiting for you when it started buzzing."

She spotted the case file on the bed and raked her hand through her hair. "You weren't supposed to see that." She reached over and picked it up.

"Not part of your plan?"

"I don't have a plan, Sam."

"You actually think I could've hurt those people?" Tears welled in her eyes. "I was—"

"I know. You were involved with them." Drew saw the pain in Sam's eyes, and her heart clenched. She wanted to hold her, touch her, take away all Sam's doubts about her. Sam wouldn't let her now, so the only other thing to do was to find out the truth. "But you were engaged to Brad."

"I've been engaged to Brad on and off again for five years now." The hurt in her voice turned to anger. "We're never getting married. He just doesn't want anyone else to have me." She rummaged through the drawers, pulled out a few of her shirts, and stuffed them into the plastic laundry bag she found hanging in the closet. "I was his in with Paddy." She shook her head and let out a short breath. "Brad thought keeping the boss's daughter happy would keep him in his good graces. I only accepted to piss off Paddy."

"You're not going to marry him?"

"Of course not." She stopped and stared, her red, bloodshot eyes burning into Drew's. "I don't love *him*."

There, she'd done it. Sam had finally told her what she wanted to hear, and now it was too late. She would never trust Drew again. "Sam, this all started as a job."

"And I'm sure it was a difficult one for you. Seducing this poor, lonely girl."

"It wasn't like that."

Her gaze snapped back to Drew's. "As I recall, you were going to take me to bed the first night we met."

"I didn't even know who you were then."

"And now?"

Drew swept her fingers through Sam's hair, catching them in her thick red curls. "I think you know how I feel about you."

"No, I really don't." Sam's voice softened. Maybe she understood her dilemma.

Drew brushed her lips across Sam's ear. "I've never met anyone like you, Sam. I think I'm falling in love with you."

Sam reared back, and her deep-green eyes darted anxiously. "I don't believe you." She tried to push past her, but Drew clamped her arms around Sam's waist and held her tight.

"God help me, I am." Drew let her mouth meld onto Sam's, and the salty taste of her tears burned her lips. Seeing Sam so vulnerable, so fragile, made Drew question who she really was. Sam had an effect on Drew like no one else ever had, and it scared the hell out of her. She knew what her mission was, but somehow it had become unclear as to who was her suspect. How she could hurt someone she loved?

"I have to go."

"Not until we get this straight." Still holding her tightly, Drew stared into Sam's eyes.

"I've got it straight." Sam's voice was steady. "You had a job to do, and I was one of the perks along the way." She broke away, and Drew spun her back around.

"Don't walk away from me." Drew's voice deepened. "That's not what happened, and you know it."

"Oh, now you want to fight, huh!" Sam came at her hot and slapped her across the face. Pain seared through Drew, and she fought to keep tears from welling in her eyes. "Come on. Give me all you got. That's the kind of love I'm used to anyway," Sam said.

Drew sucked in a slow, unsteady breath, burying the pain piercing her face and her heart. "No, I don't want to fight with you, Sam. Especially not like that." She saw something in Sam's eyes, a glimmer of hope, but Drew had to forge on. "Can you honestly tell me you didn't rig that car today?" Sam balked, and Drew thought for a moment that maybe she had, but it didn't matter. Drew tugged her back and pressed her mouth hard to Sam's. Instead of her soft, welcoming mouth, her lips quivered, and Drew broke away, remaining forehead to forehead. "I just want to keep you safe."

"I don't need you to protect me."

Drew released her and moved aside.

"I don't need anyone." Sam stuffed the rest of her clothes into the bag and went to the door. "That's the way it's always been. That's the way it's going to stay."

Drew didn't try to stop her this time. After the door closed, she turned to the cell phone on the night stand and read the text message. The message had been sent to her personal cell, to which only a few people had the number, and she hadn't given it to anyone at the crime lab. The man who'd blown her cover had to be Jack Barnes.

CHAPTER TWENTY-FIVE

Sam flew out the door as fast as she could. Drew was close, too close again. She loved her and hated her all at once. She wanted to run back inside and let Drew protect her. She swiped at the hot tears still streaming down her cheeks. She couldn't stand much more of this.

Drew was right about one thing. Someone needed protection around here, but it wasn't Sam. She needed to protect Drew from herself.

She headed straight to the track to see Paddy. Her anger reaching a boiling point along the way, Sam threw the office door open, and it cracked as it slammed against the wall.

Paddy pushed back in his chair and stood up. "What the hell's the matter with you, young lady?"

"Drew Thompson is a cop."

"Humph. You don't say." Paddy slid back down into his chair and focused back on his paperwork.

Sam clenched the edge of the desk with her hands. "You already knew!"

He rocked back in his chair and nodded. "I did."

"And you didn't tell me?" Her voice wavered.

"Someone is destroying my racing team, Samantha. I have to find out who it is."

"Did you know I'm Drew's prime suspect?"

He glanced up at her without responding.

"You did." Her voice was just a whisper now.

"You never let anyone else work on the cars."

"That's not true."

"Oh, but it is." His face reddened. "You might let Ray clean up after you once in a while, but you're always in control of them."

"Do you actually think I could do that to them? To you?" She sank into the chair across from him. "Do you know anything about me?"

"Samantha, I know you didn't do any of it." Paddy's voice slipped into the fatherly tone he always used when he was trying to appease her. "But the detective said she needed to keep total anonymity to gain everyone's trust, including whoever has been causing these accidents."

"Well, she got that. So much so that I've been sleeping with her for the past week."

"With Drew Thompson?" He scratched his head. "What about Brad?"

Sam let out a short breath. "You should really open your eyes around here a little more, Paddy." She plucked the framed trophy picture of Brad from the wall behind her and tossed it at him. "He's been bedding me and every other woman at the track for longer than I can remember."

"That bastard. I'll kill him."

"You can't do that." Her voice rose. "He's still your number-one driver." There was always another number-one driver besides her.

"I'll take care of this, Samantha. I promise."

"Do me a favor, Paddy. Don't attempt to be a father now. Save it for after the race. Just do what you do best. Make sure he wins." On her way out of the office, Sam slung the door closed and heard it bounce back open behind her. She swung back around and pulled the door closed until she heard it latch, then let her forehead drop against the weathered wood between the door frame and the window. Through the corner of her eye, she saw Paddy spring up and pace across the office.

Paddy had spent most of his life winning car races, not raising daughters. He'd had women in his life from time to time, but they didn't always take to her and Faith. They had learned most of life's facts on their own, and it hadn't always been a pleasant experience.

The racetrack might not have been the proper place to raise them, but it was Sam's home, and she loved it. She hated Paddy for it sometimes, but he'd done the best he could at the time.

Sam pushed away from the door and headed out of the garage. She couldn't watch Paddy pace. If she stayed much longer, she'd lose her resistance and end up back in there apologizing for something she'd had no control over.

❖

Drew gave the door a light knock and waited for Jade to open the door. "You alone?" she asked, glancing around the room.

"Yeah. Tommy went with Brad to the drivers' meeting. Why aren't you there?"

"She knows." Drew pushed through the doorway and closed the door behind her.

"Who? Sam?"

"Yep. She found my case file."

"Under your mattress?" She raised an eyebrow. "You should really find a better place for that."

"It wouldn't have mattered. Some idiot from the lab sent a text to my personal cell, and that started her searching."

"How'd they get that number?"

"Don't know. No one should be using it except Captain Jacobs." Drew knew who the culprit was, but she didn't want to alert Jade until she could prove it. Only a few people on the inside were privy to the information, and if the leak was who she thought, Jade wouldn't believe her anyway.

"Does she know about me?"

"Not yet, but it won't take her long. She's a smart girl."

"What are you gonna do?"

"What I came here to do. Find out who's rigging those cars."

"And if it turns out to be her?"

"It isn't her." She knew what Jade was thinking, yet she still trusted Sam with her life. "It can't be. My instincts have never been that far off."

"Why don't we go do another inspection?"

"Of the car?"

Jade shrugged her shoulders. "Couldn't hurt."

❖

Sam slid her hand across the smooth, cherry-red finish as she circled the number-fifteen car. Paddy had made one point. Sam was the only one who worked on the team's race-car engines. If she wasn't rigging them, who was? She dropped down and let her chin rest on top of the cold fiberglass door panel. These cars were her life. How could Paddy think she would ever do anything to destroy them?

She reached inside and traced the steering wheel with her fingertips. Her heart ached as she thought about all that had happened during the past week. These cars had always been her number-one priority. They were her passion, her livelihood, and now they seemed unimportant—because of Drew. *A lying, sneaking woman who thinks Sam's a cold-blooded killer.* The ache inside her suddenly morphed into anger, and she plunged through the window opening. She scanned the dash. Everything looked right on the outside, what she expected. Changes deep inside the engine were causing the problems. It had to be someone with access and knowledge of race cars. She slid back out of the car and headed to the bus. Kneading the back of her neck with her fingers, Sam knew this was only the beginning of a very long night.

As she rounded the outside corner of the garage, her eyes didn't adjust to the darkness fast enough, and she ran smack into someone coming the other way. She grabbed at whoever was tumbling into her, and they both flew up against the wall.

"Sorry," she said after realizing who it was. Jade! Then she shivered as fear for her brother tore through her mind. "You could've done it."

"Done what?"

"Rigged the cars."

Backing up, Jade seemed stunned as her gaze skittered across Sam's face. "That's crazy. Why would I do that?"

With her eyes adjusted to the darkness now, Sam moved closer demanding contact. "Or maybe you're crazy."

"What the hell, Sam?" Drew took her arm and spun her around, and Jade disappeared around the corner of the building.

Her heart sped wildly at the sound of Drew's voice. She hadn't seen Drew trailing her in the darkness.

"Let go of me."

"You need to settle down."

"Settle down?" She clenched her fists and pushed hard at her chest, but Drew stood firm. "You just told me I'm a suspect in a murder case, and you want me to settle down?" As Sam spun to leave, she grabbed Sam's wrists and pulled her around the back of the garage with such force that, for the first time, she was truly frightened of Drew. "Let me go," she demanded, forcing her voice to remain steady.

Drew released her and raised her hands in surrender. "I'm sorry, but I'm undercover here, Sam. You can't go spouting that fact off to everyone, or you're gonna get me killed."

"She's going to get away."

"Who?"

Drew wasn't getting it. Sam could see in her eyes that she thought she was crazy. "Jade! She's the one who's been sabotaging the cars."

Drew raked her hand down her face. "No, Sam, she isn't."

"She has access. She could've done it."

"She could've, but she didn't."

"What makes you so sure?"

"Wait here." Drew sucked in a deep breath and pinched her lips together before walking back around to the side of the building.

Sam didn't do as Drew demanded. As soon as Drew was out of sight she followed her to the corner and peeked around. She couldn't hear Drew and Jade whisper, but something was going on between them. Drew swept her hand down Jade's arm and squeezed her wrist as she turned to go.

"You can't just let her leave." Sam took off after her, pushing Jade into the side of the building.

In an instant, Sam found herself with her face forward, pushed up against the building. The sting from the metal scraping against her cheek began to match the pain shooting up the arm Jade had twisted up behind her back.

"Don't do that again." Jade released her and turned to Drew. "Now, tell her."

"What the hell is going on here? Are you sleeping with her too?"

Drew shook her head. "She's my partner."

Sam's mouth dropped open. This was unbelievable. "You're not even a therapist?" The fear gone now, and Sam's anger took over. "What about my brother? Does he know?"

"No. Tommy doesn't know."

"What are you going to do when you're finished here? Rip his heart out?"

"It's not like that and you know it," Jade said.

"I don't know anything about either one of you, except you both seem to find it very easy to lie about everything." She narrowed her eyes. "Just remember, I warned you."

Jade didn't respond, and at this point, nothing she could say or do would make Sam understand.

Drew jerked her around by the arm. "Sam, get a grip. Don't you want to stop this killer?"

"I want to be done with all of this." She jerked her arm out of Drew's grip. "To be done with you."

With her adrenaline on the verge of topping out, Sam rushed into the bus, yanked open the cabinet doors, and rummaged through the defective parts. The only thing she could do now was find out what the hell had happened with the cars that had issues, starting with the one she drove in the trials. Per standard procedure, Ray had changed out the fuel injector, but hopefully he hadn't torn the whole thing down yet. Sam needed to do that herself.

She found it right where she'd put it, still in one piece. After she pulled open a few drawers to check her tools, she went back to the door and locked it. She didn't want anyone walking in on her, especially Drew. Trusting anyone could be deadly at this point, even if she was a cop.

It didn't take Sam long to dismantle the injector, and she knew exactly where to look. The pop pressure-release valve was glued shut, altering the fuel mixture to make the car accelerate. She was damn lucky the engine hadn't blown.

Whoever was involved knew exactly what they were doing. Pop valves were an old-school way of turbo-charging engines, and not everyone, especially an amateur, knew how to deal with them. She squirted some solvent onto the valve and pried it loose with a screwdriver. She'd checked and double-checked all the moving parts the night before the race. Even with her head in a fog, she couldn't have missed this, and it certainly would've been caught at inspection. No one was allowed to touch the car after inspection, yet somehow, someone had gotten to it.

CHAPTER TWENTY-SIX

Drew's stomach churned as she sat at the darkened poolside watching Sam go into Brad's hotel room. Sam had laid it all out, plain and simple. She wanted Drew out of her life, and in just a few short days that would happen. She would never have to see her again. Drew had deceived her, taken her to bed, and worst of all, she'd let Sam fall as hard for her as Drew had fallen for her. She deserved Sam's anger, her hatred, and everything else she wanted to spew at her. And if that hadn't been enough today, Paddy had called her in for a meeting and told her the racing commission was investigating a Tweet sent from her account about Brad's drinking habits, which she hadn't sent. Someone had hacked into her account, and the whole incident could get her suspended from the race, something that couldn't happen at this point.

Drew took the cell phone from her pocket and punched in Captain Jacobs's number. "We've been made." She tried to disguise her relief. She was having a hard time keeping up with the lies.

"What the hell happened?"

"The lab sent a text to my personal cell. Sam saw the message." Drew should've told her. She might have reacted the same way, but she would've been coming clean instead of being exposed. She'd let her feelings for Sam get in the way and had let it go too long.

"How'd that happen?"

"You tell me. You're the only one that knows we're here, right?"

"I'll look into it." The hesitation in his voice led Drew to believe the captain wasn't the only one who knew.

"You need to have my back on this one."

"I said I'll look into it. How is this going to impact the investigation?"

"I don't know. From the expression on her face, I got the feeling she's more likely a victim than our guy." Drew let her feelings seep out, unable to hide the fact she was honestly relieved that Sam knew who she was. "I think you're barking up the wrong tree here, Boss. I've gotten to know this woman. She's not a killer."

"I should pull you off this case."

"Don't do that. I've almost got it cracked." Drew couldn't conceal the panic in her voice, and the captain paused. It was clear he knew Drew was in too deep.

"This is my fault." The captain let out a heavy breath, and it resonated through Drew's cell phone. "I saw it coming, and I pushed you into it."

"Give me a little more time. I swear I can catch this guy." Slipping back into her usual arrogant persona, Drew let her voice strengthen. "Besides, you can't get anyone else in deep enough to prevent anything from happening in the next race. If it is Sam, she won't try anything while I'm here."

"Don't make me regret this."

"I gotcha covered, Boss." Drew ended the call and headed around the building to her room. She had to find the killer and regain Sam's trust in the process. She wasn't about to make the kiss they'd shared this afternoon her last.

Jade followed the shadowed figure into the garage, careful not to let him see her. With her ankle-gun drawn, she worked her way around behind one of the oil drums. Baseball cap, coveralls, it was a man. She watched him take something out of the tool chest before opening the hood of the number-fifteen car and clicking on a small intense-beam flashlight. She heard something whirr but couldn't make out what it was. Slipping around to get a better view, she kicked a stray grease gun, sending it clanging across the floor. *Fuck!* The sound echoed, and the flashlight clicked off.

Jade dropped to her knees and shuffled into a darkened corner. She waited patiently in the darkness, listening for any type of movement. After a long silence, she heard the metal door click open and then close again. The man was gone. She slid back over behind the oil drums and peeked through the slight space between them. Feeling a whoosh of air from behind, she whipped around to face two coverall-clad legs. As panic rocketed her upward, she felt a severe pain in her head, and everything went black.

When Jade came to, the lights in the garage were on, and Drew was hovering over her. She shoved whatever awful-smelling substance she had in her hand aside and sprang up quickly, searching the garage.

"Damn. I almost had him."

"Who?"

"I don't know." Jade growled in frustration. "I saw someone come in here, but I guess he saw me first." She was too embarrassed to tell Drew she'd kicked the grease gun and given herself away.

"Can you describe him?"

"No. It was too dark." Feeling a little dizzy, she sank back against her elbows.

"Height, weight, anything?"

"Taller than me. I'd say about six feet. He could weigh anywhere from one-fifty to two hundred. He had coveralls on just like everyone else around here."

"Hair?"

"I think he had some." She pulled herself to her feet and headed for the car.

Drew raised her eyebrows. "What color?"

"I couldn't tell. He was wearing a hat."

"That description fits half the men at the track."

She lifted the hood. "Don't you think I know that?"

"What are you doing?"

"Before he saw me, he was doing something to the engine."

"From what I could hear, he was using some kind of drill." She pointed to the tool chest. "He took it out of the bottom drawer over there."

Drew pulled the drawer open. "This?" She held up a battery-powered Dremel and turned it on.

"Yeah. That sounds like it."

"He punctured something." Drew checked it over. "No bit. He took it with him."

"I don't see any leaks. Maybe he heard me and didn't get a chance to do any damage."

Drew pulled the cell phone from her pocket. "Maybe, but I'd better call Sam and have her take a look just to be safe."

The phone was on its third ring before the groggy male voice picked up. "What."

Hearing Brad's voice made Drew's throat tighten. "I need to talk to Sam."

"Go to hell." The phone went silent.

"I'll go get her." Drew slid the phone back into her pocket. "Are you all right?"

"Yeah." Jade rubbed the back of her neck. "I'm fine."

Drew squeezed her shoulder lightly. "I'll rattle Tommy while I'm there."

"Thanks."

Jolted out of her sleep by the incessant pounding, Sam shot up in bed. She thought her head was throbbing, but now it was clear some idiot was at the door. Snapping out of her drowsy state, she pulled on her robe and peeked out the peephole. *Not again. Will you ever get the message?* She'd had more than one too many glasses of wine at dinner, trying to block Drew and everything else that had happened during the day out of her mind. Now Drew was back to give her another dose.

"What the hell are you trying to do? Wake everyone in the hotel?" she said, opening the door and slipping out onto the landing.

Drew's eyes flickered up and down her, then focused on Sam's. She felt the night air whisk across her and realized it had made her nipples peak against her tank top. She clenched the top of her robe closed.

"Jade caught someone tampering with the number-fifteen car tonight."

"Who?"

Concern filled Drew's eyes. "She doesn't know. He popped her on the head and took off before she could get a good look at him."

"Is she okay?"

"She's got a little bump, but she's fine."

"Was Tommy with her?" She fired questions at her urgently.

"No. I thought I'd wake you first before I roused him."

"I'll get dressed."

"Jade thinks the guy was using a Dremel."

She turned quickly before going back inside. "He was puncturing something?"

"Probably. I was hoping you could figure out what."

"Give me a minute."

"Is Brad with you?"

She stopped, turned around, and narrowed her eyes. "No."

Drew peered around her. "He answered your phone when I tried to call."

"I guess I left it in his room." She'd been there earlier collecting her things.

Drew gave her a soft smile. "I'll get Tommy."

"Okay." She slipped back into the room. Stumbling in the darkness, she pulled on her jeans and flannel shirt.

When they got to the garage, Sam spotted Jade sitting on the stool holding an ice pack wrapped in a crimson-soaked shop rag to her head.

"My God, are you all right?"

"I found this in the freezer. I hope you don't mind."

"Of course not." She pulled the ice pack back and saw the gaping gash in Jade's scalp. "You left her here alone, like this?"

Drew shrugged. "She said she was all right."

"Tommy, take her to the hospital. This needs stitches."

Jade protested. "No. I'm fine,".

Tommy rolled over to her and lifted the pack. "Sam's right."

"Jesus, Jade. Why didn't you say something?" Drew said, checking the wound.

Sam couldn't tell if Drew was putting on a show or if she truly was unaware of how badly Jade was hurt.

"I didn't notice the blood until I put the ice pack on it."

"Come on. Let's go."

Jade winced as she shifted the pack. "You can take me after we finish here."

Sam clamped the spotlight to the hood and started probing the engine. "Was there a bit in the Dremel?"

"No. I think he took it."

She ran her fingers over a few different hoses before dragging them across the fuel line.

"Look here." She rubbed her fingers together, feeling the moisture before raising them to her nose. "Top and bottom of the fuel line. He must have used a small bit and drilled right through it."

Drew pulled her brows together. "Is that enough to cause the engine to quit?"

"In a race. No." She shook her head. "But in a test run with the constant increase and decrease in acceleration, fumes could gather in the chamber." She wiped the fuel from her hand and felt around the engine again. "All it would take is a spark to set it off." She fingered a strange shape under the injector. She stopped, went to the bench, and picked up a putty knife. After prying a small, radio-controlled transmitter loose, she handed it to Drew. "Something like this."

"Holy crap. I would've been toast."

"Yep." Sam took a piece of chalk and marked the area of fuel line that was punctured before retrieving a new stainless-steel braided line from the parts cabinet. She pulled the damaged hose free from the injector, plugged it with the stub end of a pencil, and then pushed the new hose onto the injector nipple. After snaking the other end through the engine and down to the pressure regulator, she pulled the bad hose off. Fuel spurted out, covering her hand and wrist as she pushed the new hose on. She had the line changed within minutes.

She slipped the damaged hose into a plastic bag. "Here. You might need this." After handing it to Drew, she walked over to the sink to wash her hands.

Drew held it up, scrutinizing it carefully. "This isn't rubber?"

"No." Sam shook her head at her inexperience. "We haven't used rubber hoses on race cars in years."

"What is it?"

"It's a stainless-steel braided, ultra-lightweight Teflon, silicone, Nomex composite hose with nickel-plated ends." Sam rattled the description off quickly as she pulled a few paper towels from the dispenser and dried her hands.

Drew frowned. "What the hell does that mean?"

Sam laughed abruptly at her baffled expression. "That means it's impervious to all automotive fluids and capable of much higher temperatures than the old-fashioned rubber hoses."

"Oh," Drew said, still looking confused.

"Nomex is the same material used to make your racing suit fire retardant."

Drew examined the hole, which was no bigger than a pin head. "So whoever drilled this tiny little hole knew what he was doing."

"Uh-huh, and it wasn't me. I was at the bar with Brad most of the night." She didn't have to throw that jab out there, but Drew had hurt her more than she'd wanted to admit. "As for my DNA, I'm sure it's on everything in this garage. I fix the car. And yes, I've had sex in here too." She turned and caught Drew's wounded expression, but continued anyway. "And just for the record, you're probably going to find it in some other places you really don't want to know about either." Her stomach knotted. She could see the pain clearly in Drew's eyes—no jealousy or rage, just plain hurt. She kneaded the paper towel between her hands, then tossed it into the trash barrel. "I'll check everything more thoroughly in the morning."

Tommy rolled his chair over with Jade on his lap. "Sam, I'm going to run her to the emergency room."

"You want me to come along?" she asked.

"No. I've got the van. I can manage if you can get a ride back to the hotel." Tommy's gaze darted to Drew and back to Sam again.

Sam nodded. "I can get one of the security guys to give me a lift."

"I'll make sure she gets back safely," Drew said. "Now go, you two. That cut needs attention."

Drew persuaded Sam to ride with her, and instead of pulling up in back by the motel pool, Drew drove her Jeep around to the side and parked in front of her room.

"Come in, so we can talk?" Drew didn't wait for an argument. She rounded the vehicle, opened the door, and waited for Sam to get out.

Drew took her hand, and Sam cursed herself as a tingle shot through her. It was still there, that crazy feeling she got whenever Drew touched her.

As Drew led Sam to her room, Sam stared at the clean-cut hairline she'd noticed the first night they'd met. Imagining the feel of her fingers running across it, she felt her willpower puddle. "This isn't a good idea."

Drew twisted the knob, pushed open the door, and waited for Sam to go in first.

This was a very dangerous situation. Sam couldn't find a middle ground anymore. It was all or nothing. She stared into Drew's eyes. If she entered she couldn't turn back. Then she took the final step.

"Acting like strangers isn't helping either one of us," Drew said.

"I don't know any other way to handle this situation." This was a mistake. Sam rushed back to the door and grabbed the knob. She didn't know how much longer she could contain the emotions coiled inside her.

Drew's hand covered Sam's, and her warm body pressed against her back. The warm pulse of Drew's breath hovering across her neck comforted her.

"Please don't walk out on me again. I've told you everything now. What more do you want from me?"

"Honestly?" She twisted around, and the soft flesh of Drew's breasts pressed against Sam's chest. She could feel the rapid pace of her heartbeat, and it made hers thump faster. "I want to feel you all over me." Sam curled her arms around Drew's neck. "Just for tonight." She could see the ambivalence in Drew's eyes and thought she might send her on her way. Then Drew's mouth covered hers, and she was locked in a steamy, urgent kiss, a kiss she'd longed for since she'd left her, a kiss more powerful than anything she'd ever felt. Even the euphoria of winning couldn't beat this feeling.

"And tomorrow?" Drew said breathlessly. "What are you going to want then?"

Sam wanted to make undying promises, an oath to never leave her side again, to be only hers forever, but she wasn't ready for that yet.

"I can't make any promises about tomorrow."

Drew stared for a just minute longer. "The way things are going, I could wind up dead tomorrow."

"What?" Fear flooded Sam, jolting her back to reality.

"I'm still a cop, remember?"

"How could I forget?" Sam's stomach knotted, and she let her arms drop from Drew's neck. She couldn't erase the feeling of betrayal that had devastated her when she'd found out. "And I'm your suspect."

"No, not anymore. You're the woman I love."

Love? She'd said it again. Sam stared into Drew's eyes, which were deep, dark, and serious. A rush of heat cursed her as she swept her hands up into Drew's hair, and her mouth met hers. Sam held on tight, never wanting this incredible feeling to end, but it had to. She pushed away.

"You can't love me. People who love me get hurt." Sam felt anxious and unsteady. "You said it yourself. You could wind up dead tomorrow." The tears spilled out. How could she have done this again? "If you do, I'll be all alone."

"I won't." Drew cupped Sam's face and ran her thumbs across her moist cheek.

Sam pressed her head to Drew's chest and listened to the rhythm of her heart. It was slower now, an almost indiscernible thump. She wasn't worried at all. How could she be so sure? Sam wished she could be so confident. She desperately wanted to trust this woman who seemed to make all her problems fade away. It would take a leap of faith. Sam would have to trust Drew if she wanted her to do the same in return. She had to give Drew her all—mind, body, *and* soul.

Sam let her hands roam Drew's back and heard the thump of her heart quicken. Drew lowered her chin and met Sam's mouth with hers. Sam didn't protest. She gave in to what she'd wanted all along—Drew's warmth, her compassion, and her strength.

Chapter Twenty-seven

Sam snuggled close into the crook of Drew's arm as she watched the numbers change on the digital clock. It was after three and she couldn't sleep. That was nothing new. She never could. Insomnia was a curse with which all the Kellehers were burdened. She didn't dare budge, or this fantasy of hers might come to an end. She gazed around the room. It was the same as the first night she'd seen it, only something was different. She pressed her lips to Drew's chest, and Drew tightened her arm around her. This place, here with Drew, was her sanctuary, and she was a permanent part of it now.

She heard the roar of an engine outside and tried to shift out of bed, but Drew slid closer, holding her tightly.

"I have to go."

"Uh-uh."

"Did you hear that engine?"

"Umm…Someone's coming in late"

"My sister." The sound of Faith's Porsche was unmistakable. "She probably went around back searching for me."

"She's not going to find you." Drew pulled her close with a tug and wedged her face into the crook of Sam's neck.

"Drew, it's really late. She must need something."

Drew opened one eye, glanced at the clock, and grumbled. "Okay, but I'm coming with you."

Sam pulled on her jeans and shirt before going to the window. She didn't see Faith's car. "Come on, hurry, and put some clothes on." She turned and caught the sight of Drew's incredibly tempting nakedness on the bed. "Nothing difficult to take back off, though."

Drew gave her a sexy smile as she dressed and then took her hand. It was a small gesture, but Sam wanted Drew to know tonight wasn't only about sex. Sam was letting her back into her life.

They headed up the stairs and rounded the corner just in time to see Faith slip into Brad's room.

"She must have already tried mine."

Drew didn't know what Sam was thinking, but something wasn't right. Faith had barely had enough time to make it up the steps, let alone stop at Sam's room first. She tried to get ahead of her, but Sam had already pushed the door open and jerked to a stop. Drew could see Sam's eyes following the trail of clothes left from the door to the two naked bodies in the bed.

"Faith?" Sam's voice sounded surprisingly vulnerable.

The woman was locked in a heated embrace with Brad. Sam's gaze darted back and forth between them.

"What the hell are you doing?" Brad tossed her to his side, and Drew was immediately aware that it wasn't Sam's sister in Brad's clutches. It was her own sister, Liza.

"You called me," Liza said, making no attempt at modesty until she made eye contact with Drew. "Oh, fuck." She pulled the sheet up around her.

"Oh my God," Sam said.

"Oh my God," Drew echoed as she stood frozen in place. She didn't know what to do. She hadn't been less prepared in her life than she was right now. "What the hell?"

Brad hopped out of bed and pulled on his boxers. "It was all her, Sammy. I swear."

"*You* shut up," Sam said, raising a finger before glancing back at Drew's sister. "Liza?"

Liza's eyes widened. "I'm sorry. I had no idea," she said as she pulled the sheet up tighter around herself.

Drew noticed the glare Sam gave Brad, and she couldn't read it. Did it express sadness, pain, or contempt? Brad's blatant infidelity alone would've provoked any or all of them, but with Drew's sister involved, it was so much worse.

"Put some clothes on, man." Drew swiped a pair of jeans from the chair, squeezed them into a tight wad, and threw them at Brad before pushing by him to sit on the edge of the bed next to Liza. "Did he force you?" she asked softly.

Liza avoided eye contact as she flopped back against the headboard. "No, Drew. He didn't force me. Not now, not ever."

"You've been here before?" Drew glanced back at Sam and saw her lip quiver. Sam wasn't just angry. She was hurt. Witnessing her in such turmoil made something tear deep inside Drew.

Sam went full force into Brad, pushing him against the wall. Drew bolted up and grabbed her from behind, holding her back."

"Listen, Sammy. She came to me," Brad said, rubbing his neck. "The first time was a mistake. I had a little too much to drink at the sponsor party. She has a nice place, so I crashed there. Thought she was just a rich girl looking for some fun." His voice lifted in simplistic irony. "I had no idea she was Drew's sister. That's just a perk."

"And I had no idea he was involved with you, Sam." Liza got up and dressed quickly. "I'm out. No man is worth this mess." She took off out the door.

"Let's go, Sam." Drew took her hand, but she pulled it away. She couldn't believe Sam was actually listening to this bastard.

"In the dark, a body's a body." Brad raised his eyebrows and shot Drew a smile. "Isn't that right, Thompson?"

"You're a miserable prick, Brad. You know that?" Drew grasped Brad's arm and twisted it up behind him before shoving him onto the bed. "Don't touch her again." It all made sense now, the reason Sam kept pushing Drew away. *She's never had a normal relationship with anyone. Her anger is the only way she can protect herself.*

Brad smiled and laughed as he slid back into bed. "She always comes back for more."

Sam lunged forward. Drew swung her arm around Sam's waist, holding her as she tried to break free.

"He's not worth it, Sam."

"You can bet I won't be back this time." She kicked her feet and pried at Drew's arms, but she didn't let her loose. She stopped fighting and collapsed back against Drew.

"Come on, Sam. Let's go." After moving her to the door, Drew loosened her grip and pushed her out the door before turning back to Brad. "I will pay you back for this. I promise."

Chapter Twenty-eight

Brad hopped out of the number forty-four car and threw his helmet off, letting it bounce across the concrete garage floor. "Are you trying to fry me? It's hotter than hell in there." He took a bottle of water out of the refrigerator, twisted the top off, and poured it over his head.

Sam opened the hood. "It'd serve you right. I'll check the firewall. It could have a crack in it," she shouted, trying to keep her temper at bay.

This wasn't all Brad's fault. She'd never cared who he slept with before. But this time was different. This was Drew's sister. She was supposed to protect her from men like him, abusers who damage a woman's mind as much as her body. Sam's anger was mild compared to the guilt that must be eating away at Drew.

"Whatever it is, you'd better get it fixed fast." He stormed across the garage to the main entrance. "And make sure your girlfriend tests it first next time."

Ray made a sniffing sound and slid his eyes from side to side. "Is it just me, or does it smell like bacon in here?"

Sam shook her head and laughed. "What would I do without you, Ray?"

"Don't know, but if I have my way, you'll never have to find out."

"Why don't you take a break?" She put her arm around his shoulder and squeezed. "It's going to take at least an hour for this engine to cool down enough to get inside it."

"You want to go over to the snack bar? I'll buy."

"That's okay. You go ahead. I'll get something later."

"Tell you what. I'll bring you back one of those vegetarian wraps you like."

"Thanks, Ray. That sounds good."

Sam smiled as she watched him go around the corner before she flopped down onto the stool. She thought she'd worked out all the kinks in that car. Now she was going to have to tear it down to repair, or maybe even replace, the firewall. She slid back off the stool to make a closer inspection.

Brackets secure, bolts tight. She wiggled the metal sheet covering the front of the driving compartment. When she examined it closer she could see someone had cut slits around the edges on both sides, just big enough to let the heat through. At first glance they were unnoticeable.

Sam popped up, hurried to the tool chest, and slid open a drawer. Last night, she'd fixed the fuel line on number fifteen but hadn't bothered to check number forty-four. *Who the hell is doing this?*

She slammed the drawer shut and scanned the garage. She didn't know where to start with all these distractions. Brad's temper was the least of her troubles. Drew's life was on the top of her list. She thought she could handle the pressure, but it was too much for her.

Sam had checked the number forty-four car while she waited for the number fifteen to cool. She'd just finished all her adjustments and had left Ray to work on the firewall while she stepped out to eat her wrap in the sunlight. She was checking in with him when she heard the side door clang open. Brad crossed the garage in his usual arrogant manner and took in a deep breath, clearly trying to suppress his anger.

"Did you get it fixed?"

"Workin' on it." Glancing up, Ray flipped the protective glasses up onto his head and turned the welding torch off.

"Is your girlfriend's car working?" Brad asked.

"Yeah, but I want her to take another test run to make sure."

"Where is she today?"

"I don't know." Sam lied. Drew had gone into the city to update her captain on the case. "Maybe Paddy's got her doing something else."

He raised an eyebrow. "Maybe she's gotten a glimpse of that frigid bitch you keep locked inside."

Sam didn't respond. He wanted a battle, and she refused to give it to him.

"Paddy can't find her. So I guess I'll have to take it out and break in the new car. Any problem with that?"

She walked over to the car, pulled the hood down, and let it slam shut. "It's all yours."

❖

Sam heard the sirens and rushed to the track. When she saw the mangled car frame, her vision tunneled, and she felt like she was going to pass out. "No. It can't be," she said, out of breath and stumbling. *She'd just checked the car a few hours ago.* There shouldn't have been an accident.

"What happened?" Sam sucked in a deep breath, trying to calm herself.

Ray scratched the back of his head. "He topped out. The car spun, slid back onto the track, and then another car hit him."

"Can you take me out there?" Sam knew she should just run out there, but she didn't feel the same urgency she did when her brother crashed. What was wrong with her? Was Brad right? Has she turned into a cold, unfeeling bitch?

"They'll be gone before we get there."

She whirled around and threw herself against Ray's chest. The car was out of commission, but Brad was hurt badly enough to be taken to the hospital. A sharp tingle of panic shot through her. That could've been Drew.

Ray's arms curled around her. "I'm sure he'll be okay. It's just a side hit."

Paddy pulled the headset from his ears. "He's probably got some bruised ribs, maybe a broken hip. We'll know more when he gets to the hospital."

He wasn't dead, but he'd come damn close to it. Sam let out a sigh of relief and took off out of the pit.

"Hang on there, Samantha," Paddy shouted after her.

"I need to go."

"I'll take you." Paddy tossed his headset to Ray. "Take care of the car."

Paddy slid into the driver's seat and fired the ignition. "You know this never would've happened if you hadn't been messin' around with that detective."

"You're right." What Paddy didn't know was just how right he was. "You should've told me who she was. I would've steered clear." That wasn't true. She would've fallen for Drew anyway.

"It wasn't my choice, Samantha. They're trying to catch a killer."

"You mean they're trying to catch me."

"I know you didn't have anything to do with those crashes." He narrowed his eyes. "You need to stay away from Drew Thompson and let her do her job."

"I said you're right, Paddy. Now just leave it alone." He didn't know just how right he was.

"What's gotten into you, Samantha?"

"There's something wrong with me because I'm agreeing with you?"

"It is a bit unusual."

She pressed her fingers to her forehead. "I'm just tired of fighting." *Maybe it's time I realized I'll never be happy.*

"You know what you have to do."

Her stomach knotted at the thought of what he expected of her. "I have to make things right."

"That's my girl." He reached over and gave her leg a light pat.

Drew was at the station house when she got word about the accident. She pulled up to the emergency-room entrance and left her Jeep in the red zone, knowing it would be probably be towed before she got back. After rushing through the double doors, she bypassed the desk and started pulling exam-room curtains back.

"Hey! You can't go back there," a nurse said, chasing her.

"Race-car driver. Is she here?" Drew asked, ignoring her order and continuing to the next curtain.

"He was brought in a few hours ago."

"He?"

"Yes. They took him to the fifth floor."

Relief washed through her. *Wilkerson was driving.*

She spun around, took off to the elevator, and punched the button repeatedly. The doors opened, and there stood Paddy in the middle of the elevator with a cup of coffee in each hand.

"Well, what would you be doing here, young lady? I thought you'd be checking out the wreckage by now."

"I thought…"

"You thought what? That it was Samantha."

"Yeah."

"She's safe and sound, upstairs."

She stepped on to the elevator. "Since I'm here, I need to see how Wilkerson's doing."

"I didn't think you and Brad were friends."

"We're not." She pushed the already lit number-five button. "Maybe he can tell me what happened."

Paddy rolled his lips together. "You want to see my daughter."

She nodded. "Is she okay?"

"When these accidents happen, she takes them pretty hard." Paddy took a swig of coffee. "Always thinking it's her fault."

"I'm afraid I haven't helped matters much in that area." Drew had only added more to her burden by telling her she was a suspect.

"Aye, but she knows who you are now. You don't really think she's the one causing these accidents, do you?" Paddy stepped off the elevator and Drew followed.

"No. I never did."

"Go on. I'll let you have a minute alone with her."

Drew cringed inside when she saw Sam hovering over an unconscious Brad. When Sam glanced up, Drew could see the guilt was tearing her up.

"How's he doing?"

"He'll be all right, but he's out of this race for good now."

"I'm sorry to hear that."

"This could've been you. He was driving your car." The tears welled at the bottom of her eyes, slowly spilling out one at a time.

"You shouldn't be here." Her expression was blank. "And I should have never…This is my fault." Sam swiped her sleeve across her face and sucked in a ragged breath.

"It's not your fault."

"Yes, it is."

Drew stopped short. Could she have been that wrong about her? Was she about to get a confession from a killer?

"I'm the crew chief and I've been distracted." Sam wouldn't make eye contact with her, and Drew knew she was talking about her. Her stomach churned. Drew thought she was much more than a distraction to Sam.

"I'm trying very hard to be understanding, Sam. But sooner or later you're gonna have to make a decision." Drew watched her stare at Brad, bruised and sedated, as she slid down into the chair next to the bed.

"Go home, Drew." She picked up Brad's hand and pressed it to her cheek.

From whatever warped sense of obligation Sam felt, it was clear she felt responsible for this accident and wasn't going to leave Brad here alone.

Paddy patted Drew on the back. "Go on back to the track. I'll stay here and keep an eye on her."

Drew sat staring into the half-empty water glass in front of her, Sam's words still ringing in her mind. She didn't believe it, but Sam had made her decision. It was clear as the crystal goblet she was holding. Sam was going back to Brad.

A sudden sense of loss washed through her. She shouldn't have pushed. She'd known she was being selfish when she gave her the ultimatum.

"Is everything all right, dear?"

"Everything's fine, Mom. I'm just not very hungry."

"Well then, we'll have the cook wrap it up and put it in the refrigerator for later."

"Thanks."

"Are you staying tonight?"

Drew gave her a thankful smile. Her mother knew something was bothering her, but she didn't pry. She knew she'd come to her when she was ready.

"I'd like to, if that's okay? I need to get a few good night's rest before the race." Hanging around the track, watching Sam cater to Brad was more than Drew could take. She would make herself available for all test runs and the race, but she needed some distance. It probably wouldn't help much, but a little time off-track couldn't hurt.

"Of course. Since your father's away on business, I'd love the company." Johanna got up from the table, opened the French doors, and stepped out onto the veranda. After slipping a utility apron around the waist of her white, blended-cotton slacks, she turned back momentarily. "I'm going into the garden to tend to my roses. You're welcome to join me if you'd like."

Drew slid out of her chair and followed her.

"How could she believe it was her fault?"

"What, darling?"

"The accident?"

Johanna sat down on a redwood bench and patted the space next to her.

Drew nodded. "Cars fail all the time. It's not always her fault."

"You're speaking of Samantha?"

She nodded again. "I've never had this much trouble with a woman before. I don't know what to do, Mom."

Johanna took a pair of scissors from her apron, clipped a rose from the bush, and held it up in front of her. "Women are like roses, Drew. We may be beautiful, but we all have our thorns."

Drew pulled her brows together. She knew her mother was offering her some wisdom but wasn't sure of her point.

"You have three choices." She twirled the stem between her fingers. "You either have to learn how to avoid those thorns, wear them down over time, or simply clip them off." She scraped a few thorns from the stem.

"She doesn't want me. She wants this guy who's a total asshole to her." Drew didn't understand it. She'd been given strict orders to keep her distance, yet she couldn't stay away. Drew had put her career on the line for Sam.

"My handsome girl." Johanna stroked her cheek and smiled. "You're very experienced at giving heartbreak, but I'm afraid you have a lot to learn about receiving it."

Drew lowered her eyes. Her mother was right. She'd broken a lot of women's hearts without ever giving them a second thought."

Johanna touched the bottom of Drew's chin and their gazes met. "If you're hurting this badly, she's hurting worse."

"What do I do now?"

"Give her a little time, but stay close. If this other man is as dreadful as you say, she's going to need you." A thoughtful smile warmed her face. "You want to be there when she does."

"That's the problem." Drew flew up off the bench. "She doesn't need me. She doesn't need anyone."

"Drew. Everyone needs someone." Johanna pulled her into an embrace. "That includes you."

❖

Sam had never intended for anyone to get hurt, but she hadn't done her job, and Brad had been. Her penance was taking care of him as he nursed his bruised ribs. He would be well soon. Then Sam would let him go and be free of her conscience, once again.

Brad had promised to steer clear of Drew's sister as well as other women for the time being, and Sam had agreed to stay until he was fully recuperated. Satisfying his every need wasn't in her plans. Was she this weak? Or was this some sort of punishment she was inflicting on herself for the way she'd treated Drew? She didn't have an answer. When Brad had tried to touch her, Sam's stomach had lurched. Promise or not, it became all too clear she couldn't live this way anymore.

"No. I swore I wouldn't do this." She pressed her hands hard against his chest and pushed him aside.

"Watch the ribs!" Brad's face twisted in pain.

Pulling the sheet up around her, she scooted up against the headboard. "Do you love me?"

He groaned, pulling a pillow under his chest, propping himself up on one elbow. "What kind of question is that?"

"An honest one." Sweeping her hand across the top of his head, her fingers caught in his gel-hardened hair.

He took her hand and flung it back at her. "Just give me a minute, will you?"

She sank back and hugged her knees to her chest. *Why am I back here again? Drew would've never pushed me away.* "I have to go." She swung her legs over the side of the bed.

"Why?" he asked, the sound of honest confusion ringing in his voice.

Tucking one leg up underneath her, she turned back to him. "Tell me you love me right now, and I'll stay." She stared into his eyes, hoping he couldn't say it.

He traced a finger down her arm and took her hand but didn't speak.

Relief washed over her. "I didn't think so. You're not the only one. I don't think about us in terms of love anymore either." She gave his hand a light squeeze, then got up and slipped on her flip-flops.

"What's so important about love?" He flopped back onto the pillow. "This has always been good enough."

"Things are different now." She shook her head. "I'm different." She spoke with sadness. "I want someone to want me the way I want to be wanted."

"I want you." His voice rang with an odd sense of sincerity.

"No, you don't. You don't want me any more than the dozens of other woman you've been with."

"I told you, I won't do that anymore."

"Don't you understand, Brad? I want someone to feel that burn of desire inside when I walk into the room. And I want them to know I'm feeling that too."

"And we don't have that?" His voice rose.

"No, not in a long time."

"So now you're going back to your second-string racer?" Anger filled his voice as he held a hand to his ribs, and he scrambled out of bed.

Sam squeezed her lips hard together, trying not to respond to his incitement. Brad loved to fight, and their battles always ended with sex.

"This isn't about you or Drew. This is about me." She opened the door a crack. "It took me a while to figure it out, but I finally realized I don't need anyone else to survive. If, and when, I want someone, I'll make that choice."

Brad caught the door halfway. He slammed it shut and pinned her against the wall. "I think you have something of mine." He fingered the ring dangling on the chain.

Sam clutched it. The stone had hung around her neck for so long she'd almost forgotten it was there. Giving it back would be easy because it was never truly hers. After she unfastened the clasp, she let the ring slide from the chain. "Take it. I don't want it anymore."

CHAPTER TWENTY-NINE

Drew sucked in a deep breath before heading into the garage. She'd avoided Sam all day, and it was time she made her presence known again. She'd done exactly as her mother had suggested. She hadn't made contact but was staying just close enough to Sam for her heart to squeeze.

Brad was out of the race, and now it was up to Drew to bring home the purse. Plus, a killer was still on the loose. Even if nothing else came from this, Drew was sure Sam was not a suspect. The roar of the engine echoed through the steel building, and Drew spotted Sam at the number-fifteen car with her head ducked under the hood. The body was shot, but the engine sounded good.

"You going to have that car finished by tomorrow?" Drew shouted.

Her voice must have rung through the noise, because Sam spun around to meet her gaze.

"Of course I will." She reached inside the car and cut the engine. "When I start something, I finish it." Just as she had finished with her.

"Let me know when you want me to test it."

"We don't have the new body ready yet. I probably won't run it until tomorrow. When I need you, I'll send Ray after you." She glanced over at Ray, who nodded.

"Sam." Drew hesitated, aching to tell her she didn't care about her job or anything else. She was afraid Sam wouldn't believe her, and that would only make things worse.

"What?" Sam said, her eyes softening a bit.

"Never mind. I'll see you tomorrow." Drew turned and went out the side door, sending it clanging closed behind her. She wanted to tell Sam so much, but for her to remain safe, Drew needed to keep her objectivity, which wasn't a difficult task at this point.

❖

Sam stared at the engine, her mind still cluttered with thoughts of the woman she'd just let walk out the door. She didn't tell her she'd left Brad. She wasn't ready to talk yet. She squeezed her eyes shut and tried to shake her feelings about Drew, but they were overwhelming. She'd never imagined such a perfect fit. No adjustment required. Two people melding as though they were one. Needs being satisfied completely—needs that she ached with now and wants that burned to her very core. Desires running so deep within her, they would never be forgotten. All these things, she'd never felt until Drew, the woman who'd opened the doors to her sexuality, a magical portal that would never be closed again, not as long as she was near. How could she have ever wanted this woman out of her life?

"Drew," she mumbled.

"She already took off. You want me to get her?" Ray asked.

"No." She fought to conceal the heat rising in her cheeks. "That woman drives me crazy." She snatched up a wrench and tossed it into the toolbox.

"You won't have to worry about her much longer anyway."

"Ray?" She hesitated. "What are you talking about?"

He pulled the tarp off the new car body. "It came early this morning. All we have to do is change it out." It was bright yellow instead of cherry red, with number thirty-six on the hood. "Now you can drive, and Drew can move on."

"I can't drive that car, Ray."

"Why not? She's in tip-top condition. You can be the first driver to win with the number thirty-six. No one's ever done it before."

"I appreciate everything you did, Ray, but after what happened the last time I went out on the track, I don't think I can do it."

"Sure you can. You can handle yourself. You proved that. You brought the car in without a scratch on it."

"I panicked. If Drew hadn't talked me through it, I would've gone straight into the wall."

Ray's gaze darted nervously from hers. "You give her too much credit. You would've handled it just as good without her."

"I'm not so sure about that."

"You're the only stable woman I know." Wandering closer, his expression changed. "Jenna left me." His voice was low and gruff.

"I'm sorry, Ray. I didn't know." She hadn't seen Jenna around the track at all lately, but when she'd asked him about it, he always had an excuse.

"She took everything I had."

"Ray, I wish you'd told me. Do you need any help financially?"

"No. I'll be okay after the race."

"What happened with Jenna?" Some friend she was. She didn't know he was having trouble.

"Guess she got tired of competing."

"Competing?"

"With my job." He moved closer. "I'm kind of like you. The track's my life. Now that I'm single, maybe we could have a drink sometime?"

Sam didn't know what to do. Ray was her best friend. She didn't have the slightest romantic interest in him, but she'd never seen excitement in his eyes like this before. Sam hedged. She couldn't break his heart. Not now. He'd probably never speak to her again. Losing her lover and best friend in one week would be too much.

"I guess it wouldn't hurt."

"When?" His response was quick and eager.

Sam shrugged, blowing out a short breath. "How about after the race tomorrow? We can celebrate."

"Awesome. I'll see you then," he said, giving her a broad smile. "If you're through with me here, I'm going to go get a bite to eat."

"Go ahead. I'll finish up."

"You want anything?"

"No thanks." Wondering if she'd done the right thing, Sam watched him sidestep the doorway, letting Jade come through before he went out.

"What's he so happy about?"

"He asked me to have a drink with him after the race." She shook her head. "Seems he's got a crush on me. Can you believe that?"

"And you said?" Jade tipped her head forward, obviously waiting for an answer.

"I said I would." Sam smiled uncomfortably.

"Seriously? What are you doing, Sam?" Jade's voice hissed with exasperation.

Sam avoided the question and swiped her hand across the hood of the car. "Did you see the new body? Ray thinks I should drive it."

"Are you gonna?"

"No. Paddy's got Drew set to drive tomorrow."

Jade pulled the screwdriver out of Sam's hand. "Go see her."

"Who?"

"Drew, you idiot." She tossed the flathead into the toolbox.

"I've already seen her today."

"And?"

"And I ripped her to shreds, as usual." Sam sank onto the stool.

"Well, then go glue her back together."

Sam sprang up and pulled the hydraulic jack across the garage. "I can't. I'm not wired like that."

Jade was right on her heels. "You're too tough to let yourself be happy?"

"Yeah. That's me. The tough one." She flipped the jack handle toward the wall, and it clanged against the metal panel.

"This isn't a race we're talking about, Sam." Jade took her by the arm and swung her around. "This is the rest of your life. It's not going to be over tomorrow."

"It might as well be."

Jade released her grip and let her arms drop to her sides. "If I were you, I'd be over there in a minute, taking everything that woman had to offer." She let the door clang as she left the garage.

Sam thought about what Ray had said earlier. She didn't want to go out with him, and she didn't want the track to be the only thing she had. She wanted more. She wanted Drew.

❖

Drew slid the six-pack of beer onto the table, pulled a can free, and popped it open. It was ice-cold now but would be warm soon. She never had bought a cooler. After drinking down a long, slow gulp, she dropped into the chair and pinched the bridge of her nose. Swiping the remote from the table, she punched the power button. The blue picture flickered to life, and the DVD she'd watched a thousand times played. It was the recording of Tommy Kelleher's accident.

He had to be crazy, Drew thought, dropping to her knees in front of the television screen. "Why didn't you just pit?" Zooming in closer, she hit the rewind button and played the tape again. Watching the number-thirteen car slam into the barrier, Drew tried to make sense of it, to find an obvious reason for the crash. Nothing was ever obvious in racing. Twisted metal ripped from the mangled machine and flew across the roadway after the first high-speed impact. Without slowing, Lucky Thirteen shot across the track and barreled into the side rail. After skidding back onto the asphalt, the car finally came to a complete stop before bursting into flames.

In all practicality, there was no hope for Tommy. Then, out of nowhere, Sam appeared from the side of the screen, yanking and pulling him from the car. A suicidal move. Suddenly, like metal to magnet, the flames attached themselves to her lower body, and she was engulfed in an instant bonfire. A vise gripped Drew's chest at the sight.

Catching a faint shadow in the fading sunlight beyond the window, she paused the DVD, glanced up, and sucked down the last of her beer.

She took a minute to deal with the unsettling reaction in her stomach, then slid back and leaned against the bed frame. She'd never been like this before. Drew didn't like being the vulnerable girl, the one who rethought every situation because of a woman. She hurled the empty can at the wastebasket and swiped her fingers across her mouth. She squeezed her eyes shut momentarily before she focused on the screen again.

The still picture showed the two flame-engulfed people lying motionless, hopefully unconscious, on the track. She hit the Play button and watched firemen crowd the screen, dousing them with fire extinguishing foam. She squinted and inched closer to the set again.

"Sam was still moving," she murmured, squinting at the TV screen, wishing the picture was clearer. She was unbelievable. With no concern for her own safety, she'd saved her brother from a slow, painful death and was still trying to move him out of danger. She loved her brother so much, she was willing to die saving him.

"Stupid move." Drew no longer believed in the myth of painless death. She'd hung on the edge, clinging to life for too long. It was an agonizing torture, and she would never forget it.

Glancing back at the screen, she watched another figure jet across the track. Throwing a blanket across her, he shielded Sam from flying debris. The red-hot flames claiming her torso had been extinguished, but that was only the beginning of her pain.

Drew remembered the scars covering Sam's backside. In one brief intimate moment, the question that had skidded through her mind so many times before had been answered. It was Sam who'd risked her life to pull an unconscious and flaming Tommy Kelleher out of that car.

She turned off the TV and flopped back onto the bed. In the past few weeks, Drew had risked her life, her job, and more importantly, her heart. What was she thinking, getting involved with her number-one suspect? Letting her head fall back, she stared up at the ceiling. Drew knew exactly what had gone through her mind—the scent of her hair, the smooth, silky feel of her skin, and most of all, the warmth of Sam when the two of them were coupled. She should've trusted Sam from the start.

Her mind had cleared of everything but Sam, and Drew was thoroughly primed and ready to go when a knock at the door jolted her back into the real world.

"Just a minute." She launched herself off the bed, stumbled to the door, and pulled it open. She stared for a minute and then squeezed her eyes closed. She had to make sure the woman standing in front of her wasn't just a fragment left from a lingering dream.

Chapter Thirty

Sam was caught off guard by the hazy look on Drew's face when she opened the door. "I'm sorry." She scrunched her cheeks. "You were asleep." Drew was exhausted. Sam saw it in her eyes.

"I was just dozing off." Drew raked her hand across her neck, kneading the base of her skull.

Sam stared for a long time. Drew held her gaze and she backed up. She shouldn't have come.

"Wait." The single word escaped Drew's lips in a whisper.

Wait. The word echoed through Sam's mind. She wanted her to stay.

Unable to remain strong any longer, Sam broke like a brittle dam overcome with a flood of raging rain. She threw herself against Drew and let her warmth wash across her.

"I'm stubborn, pigheaded, and not very smart, sometimes." She snaked her arms around Drew's waist and squeezed. "I'm sorry, Drew." The tears streamed down her face. "I've been such an idiot." She took in a ragged breath and held it, waiting for her reaction.

Drew held her arms in the air before letting them drop and twine around Sam. "You're not an idiot. A little neurotic, maybe, but not an idiot."

She pulled back and gave her a smile. "Neurotic. Yes, that fits." *Like a glove.* Sam tilted her head back and stared into Drew's eyes. "I want to be so close to you, but somehow I keep pushing you away."

"Not far enough." Drew cupped Sam's face in her hands before moving her thumb across her cheek to wipe away the moisture. "I've missed you." Drew's mouth came down against Sam's, hard, selfish, and insistent. Hot and demanding, her tongue engaged Sam's in a heated dance she would never forget. Sam couldn't think, didn't want to. All she wanted was to be with this woman. Now.

"Make love to me, Drew." Sam gazed up at her again. "Please." She sensed Drew's hesitation. "I haven't—I mean I didn't sleep with Brad. I wouldn't do that to you again."

With a nudge of Drew's hand, the door was closed, and Sam knew she wanted her too.

❖

Sam felt the tug as Drew twined a strand of red hair around her finger. "You awake?"

She pressed her lips to Drew's breast but didn't speak.

"What are you thinking about?" Drew asked, kissing the top of her head.

"Ray."

"Not exactly what I expected to hear." Drew rolled over on top of her.

Sam laughed drowsily. "I thought that might get your attention."

The warm, mischievous glow dancing in Sam's eyes made Drew tingle all over. She touched Sam's lips tentatively at first and then let her mouth melt onto hers. Sam responded completely, and Drew knew she was still hers.

"Did something strange happen today?" Drew grinned. "I mean, why else would you be thinking of Ray when you're in bed with me?"

"Something odd did happen today, but I'm not sure I should tell you." Sam let her fingers drag across the valley of Drew's collarbone. "You might not like it."

"He asked you out, didn't he?"

"How'd you know?"

Drew chuckled, and Sam felt it vibrate through her. She hadn't realized how much she cherished that sound.

"I'm surprised he hasn't asked you sooner." Drew slid to her side, and Sam rolled into her.

"Is it that obvious?"

"Mmm…Yeah."

"I guess his wife left him."

"He didn't tell you about it?"

"No. I had no idea. I thought he was happily married. I was totally blindsided." Sam traced her finger around Drew's belly button. "Now I'm going to have to turn him down."

"Guess I'm lucky he's a slow mover, or you wouldn't have given me a second look." Drew pressed her lips to Sam's neck.

"Right." Sam let out a haughty laugh. "That first night when you came around asking for Slick, *you* didn't give *me* a second look."

"Oh, I saw you all right, but I was working, remember?"

Sam caught her bottom lip between her teeth and let it slowly drag loose. "That didn't seem to bother you later."

"Thank God I didn't know who you were then. If I had, I would've had to resist."

"You could've resisted?"

Drew shook her head, let out a short breath, and smiled softly. "No. When you came into the bar with these loose, red curls flying…" She plucked a few strands of hair from Sam's shoulder and kneaded them between her fingers, "and these sweet hips swinging." She squirmed at the sensation as Drew slid down her body, letting her lips drag across her hips. "You were so hot. I had to have you."

"Hot?" The word escaped her lips in an involuntary squeak.

"Hot, sexy, sensual, seductive—absolutely all woman."

Sam had never had anyone describe her that way. Practical, smart, bossy—those were the usual tags with which she was marked. Not sexy or sensual, and certainly never seductive.

Drew's tongue tripped across Sam's stomach, and she jerked. The gap between her legs smoldered. She *was* hot *and* wet. Sam tried to spread her legs, but Drew kept them clamped together, teasing the small slit amid them with slow, weightless strokes. When she slipped her warm, silky tongue just inside, Sam shuddered. This was ecstasy and pure torture in the same moment.

"Stop. If you don't—" Her tongue swept deeper and harder, rocketing Sam into orgasm. "Omigod." She arched into Drew, and her mind spun into wild flashes of color, her body straining to contain the endless bow of pleasure as she rode it out. When the last tremor rolled through her, Drew slid up Sam's body and kissed her lightly. "Ready for the second heat?"

Second heat? How could she possibly do that again?

Drew pressed herself against Sam, who was energized. What the hell? She was willing to try. Letting her hand drift southward, she made contact, and Drew let out a groan. She was wet and slick, clearly ready to race.

"Just for your information. I would have definitely given you a second look."

"I'm glad to hear that." Drew trailed kisses across Sam's shoulder, her hand roaming the curve of Sam's waist. "'Cause I don't want anyone else touching you." Her mouth reached the base of her neck, and Sam's skin sizzled.

Drew's eyes turned a deeply wicked brown, and Sam shuddered. She didn't want anyone else touching her either. Not this way. Ever again.

Each swipe of Drew's tongue across her nipples, which were achingly sensitive, made her tingle. Her breaths grew shallow, and Drew continued to torture her, licking, sucking, devouring every inch of them. Sam let a low seductive groan roll from her mouth, and Drew plunged her finger deep inside. When Sam lifted her hips, Drew slid another finger into her.

"Wait." Sam shifted beneath her.

"Don't tell me you're sick again?"

Sam heard the desperation in her voice let out a low throaty chuckle, and spread her legs farther apart. "No."

Drew slid in still another finger, and Sam's pleasure reached new depths. She shuddered as her hot, slick wetness surrounded Drew's fingers. Waiting a moment longer than she thought she could, Sam pushed against her, driving her fingers deeper, and her body quaked against Drew's hand. She let out a gasping whimper and clasped her legs around Drew's, while she responded wildly, capturing her fingers in place. Drew pulled back slowly, and she savored the drag before Drew drove her fingers into her again. Sam let out a heavy-breathed squeal, and Drew thrust faster and harder. Sam was swallowed by the impact of her climax as she rolled over the edge. When Drew removed her hand and hovered above her, she seemed to be memorizing her face.

Sam didn't want to leave her just yet. "Please don't move. I want you right here." She dug trenches into Drew's back with her fingers, and Drew held her tight as they rolled. Never losing contact, Drew pulled her on top of her, blanketing her with her heat.

❖

Snuggled in right where she wanted to be, Sam circled her finger lazily around Drew's belly button. She didn't think she could be this happy. She had no doubt in her mind now—they fit together perfectly. How could she have ever wanted this woman out of her life?

Earlier, when Drew had opened the door, she was in a foul mood and had made no effort to hide it. Sam had harbored serious doubts they would ever be this close again.

She'd had it all planned—what she was going to say and how she was going to say it. But standing in the doorway, with those hard, brown eyes staring her down, her thoughts had scattered, and she'd lost it all.

She had to do it now. She had to come clean about the Tweet if she wanted this thing between her and Drew to last for longer than tonight.

"Drew, are you still awake?" She raised her head, waiting for her to open her eyes.

"Not again, woman." She smiled, letting out a throaty growl. "I need some rest."

Sam laughed at her feigned resistance. "It's not that." *Well, maybe. No, you have to tell her.* "I need to tell you something."

"What is it?"

"I'm responsible for the Tweet that may get you suspended for the race." She stared into Drew's deep, warm, brown eyes and balked.

"Sam, you can't always feel responsible when Brad does something stupid."

"But this time, I am responsible. I did it."

Drew stiffened immediately. "What?" Her voice rang with uncertainty. The warm, loving sparkle in her eyes vanished.

Sam dropped her gaze. The thought of Drew losing faith in her sliced straight through her. "Don't say another word." Drew bolted up and swung her legs to the floor.

Sam followed, plastering herself across her back. "I did it because of you."

"Because of me?"

"I didn't want you to get hurt." She pressed her cheek to Drew's shoulder.

"Now I could be suspended from the race." Drew jerked forward and dropped back down onto the bed, breaking the contact Sam desperately needed between them.

Drew made it perfectly clear she didn't want Sam touching her. "Please, let me explain." She sat down beside her, skimmed her fingers across Drew's shoulder blades, and felt her muscles tighten. "The last car shouldn't have crashed, but it did."

"I'm listening." Drew didn't move.

"Someone adjusted the inertia switch to cut the engine when the car hit the first turn, but it didn't die. It accelerated."

Drew turned around. "Did you do it?"

Sam couldn't read her. Drew's eyes were dark and void of any emotion. She straightened her shoulders. "No. Of course not. I would *never* put anyone in jeopardy."

"Then who did?"

She shook her head. "I don't know. I thought it was Brad at first, but he wouldn't have gotten in the car if he'd done it." Drew's gaze skittered across her face, and Sam knew she doubted her. "You don't believe me." She felt deflated.

"I want to believe you, Sam." Drew's eyes made contact, and she held firm. "But what am I supposed to think? Brad *was* hurt. *Badly.*"

"I wanted you out of here, so I sent a Tweet, Drew. I didn't want you injured." Sam clung to her like this was their last moment together. She didn't care if Drew knew how desperate she was. She needed Drew to believe her. She stared into Drew's eyes hoping for a glimmer of understanding but saw only anger. "I just wanted you out of the race. The only way to do that was to get you suspended."

"To get rid of me. You've been trying to do that since I got here."

"No. To keep you safe."

"And you did that for me?"

Sam nodded, dropping her head onto Drew's shoulder. Drew didn't move. Maybe she still had faith in her after all.

"You know you seem guilty as hell right now?" Drew popped up, sending Sam sailing back onto the bed. "Don't tell anyone else about this." She pulled on her jeans. "No one. Not Paddy, not Jade, not Ray. Understand?" Drew's words came out low and demanding.

Sam scrambled from the bed and threw her arms around Drew. "Please don't go."

Drew broke free and pulled on her shirt. "I need some air."

"I'll go with you." Sam couldn't believe this was happening. Drew was actually leaving.

"No." Drew spun around and put up a hand. "I need time to figure this out." She left without another word.

CHAPTER THIRTY-ONE

Drew pounded on Jade's door. No one answered. *Where the hell could she be?* She went to the railing and stared into the darkness.

When Drew and Sam had met, neither one of them had been monogamous, let alone truthful with one another. Sam was a case file, and Drew was just another driver. Drew didn't know when it had happened, but somehow, somewhere, they'd made an emotional connection, a bond that wasn't just about sex. And when Drew had opened the door earlier and found Sam standing there totally vulnerable and unguarded in front of her, begging Drew to make love to her, no way in hell could she send her away.

It had been only a few days since they'd been together, but each minute they were apart, Drew ached for her. When she'd kissed her, Drew's resistance had dissolved. Captain Jacobs had just told Drew—ordered her to keep her distance now—but when she'd stared into her simmering green eyes, laced with sincerity, Drew lost control. After they'd made love, Drew had felt the warm, steady heat of Sam's breath against her neck. Sam didn't sleep often, but she'd slept soundly. She was a proud woman, and she'd given Drew everything, including her dignity. Nothing that had just happened between them had been easy for Sam, including admitting she'd sent the Tweet about Brad's drinking.

She pounded again. "Stop," Jade growled as the door swung open. "You're going to wake everyone in the fucking hotel."

"I need to talk to you."

"Who is it?" Tommy's voice was groggy.

"It's Drew."

"What's up?"

"I think she's drunk. Go back to sleep." Jade pulled on a hoodie and slipped out the door.

"I'm not drunk." Drew wished she was, and then maybe, in the morning, she wouldn't remember any of what Sam had said.

"Then what's your excuse? It's three a.m."

"She did it?"

"Who did what?"

"Sam. She sent the Tweet that may get me suspended from the race." Reality stung Drew, and she threw her fist into the wall. Sam had wanted her gone. She'd played Drew well, she'd manipulated her, and Drew had fallen for her. Conflicting emotions tore at her. Nothing she'd ever endured had ever hurt this badly. "Said she was trying to protect me. Wanted me suspended, so I couldn't drive in the race tomorrow." She shook her throbbing hand and then checked her watch. "Scratch that. Today's race."

"Do you think she rigged the car?"

Drew rubbed her face wearily. "I don't know. I honestly don't think she could hurt anyone."

"If she'd been responsible for the other crashes, I think she would've told you."

"I'm not so sure about that. She's a very smart lady."

Just then, Sam rounded the corner and stopped. She gave Drew a gut-wrenching stare before she slipped into her room.

Drew had been sucker-punched. Sam had snuck in the back door and robbed her blind. The woman had taken everything she had and left her bleeding inside. "I fell right into her trap." She reared back to throw another fist into the wall.

Jade stepped in front of her. "Are you *trying* to break your hand before the race tomorrow? Then you won't race for sure."

"If they believe I Tweeted that crap about Wilkerson, it won't make a difference." She rubbed her eyes. "Everyone knows it's all true, but no one can put it in print."

Jade poked at her chest. "Stop feeling sorry for yourself and figure this out."

"That's the problem. I can't." Trying to clear her head, Drew leaned back against the building and closed her eyes. No matter what happened between her and Sam, she had to focus on the case.

"Of course you can. Who else are we looking at here? Brad, Paddy, Ray?"

She sprang forward. "Sam said Ray was acting strangely today. He asked her out."

"Yeah. She told me."

"I just don't get it. Sam's like his only friend. He didn't even tell her about his issues with his wife while they were happening."

"He probably didn't want to talk about it. You're a perfect example of that."

Drew grabbed the railing. "Not this guy. Something else is up with him."

"Did you see him do something to the car?"

"No, but he's been telling Sam all along that everything's fine with his wife."

Drew whirled around to face her. "Now all of sudden, she's gone, and they're divorced."

Jade's eyes widened. "What? She didn't tell me that. Let me see the case file." Jade pressed a palm to Drew's chest, and she let her pass.

When she and Jade entered Drew's room, her stomach knotted at the sight of the bed. Her life had been perfect only a few hours ago. She and Sam had made love, and Drew knew Sam loved her. Now all she felt was anger and betrayal. She pulled the rumpled sheets from the bed and tossed them into the corner. She didn't need any reminders of her night with Sam.

"That's it." Jade headed to the table in the corner and fumbled through the files. "All this time we've been trying to find some conspiracy surrounding the race. "But it isn't about the race. It's about Sam." Jade brought a file back to the newly stripped bed and opened it. "Check this out. Victim number one, Josh Jamison. Sam dated him from January to April of last year, right?"

"I really don't want to go over her past affairs." Drew let the papers drop to the mattress.

"Wait. This is important. She did date him, right?"

Drew sank down onto the bed. "Right."

"And Frank MacNamara." She flipped through a few more pages. "She dated him from May to September."

"Uh-huh. She's very touchy about that one."

"Josh was injured in May."

"Yes, but by then, she'd already stopped seeing him."

"From what I've heard around the track, he wanted her back. And wasn't she still seeing Frank when he was killed in September?"

Drew pulled her brows together. "That sounds right."

"She's the only link to all of these men."

"That's why she's our prime suspect."

"What about the trials?" She scooted around and tucked a leg underneath her. "The throttle stuck when she was driving."

"Ray didn't know she was going to drive that day. Brad was supposed to lead off, and Paddy slipped her in at the last minute."

She scratched at her chin. "What about Tommy? She certainly wasn't dating him."

"You're right. Something's wrong there."

Drew hit the power button on the remote, and the blue screen flickered on. "Got a question for you." She pressed the Play button, and a blazing car filled the screen. "Who is that, carrying her away from the car?"

"Is this footage of Tommy's crash?" Jade's voice cracked.

"Yep." Drew rewound the tape and let the scene run again. "Have you watched it?"

"Not recently."

"I found something you missed?"

"I didn't miss anything. Back it up again." Jade leaned forward, studying the screen. "Is it a fireman?"

"I don't think so. He doesn't have any gear."

"Stop right there." The screen filled with a blurry silhouette. "I think it might be Ray."

Drew flipped the folder closed and scooted closer to the screen. "Really."

"See the black racing suit?" She pointed at the screen. "Look at the patch on the shoulder. It's one of ours." She shrugged. "Why didn't he let the firemen get her out?"

"The same reason Sam didn't wait for them to get Tommy. In some freaked-out, puppy-dog sort of way, he loves her."

"From what I've seen, it's always been platonic." Jade let out a breath and smiled as though it all made sense. "Until yesterday. When he asked her out."

"His feelings for her must run pretty deep. A man doesn't risk danger like that for friendship." Drew spread the papers across the bed. "But why would he want to hurt Tommy? He wasn't a threat."

Jade rummaged through the papers and picked out the race schedule for the day of Tommy's accident. She read it and let her eyes slide closed. "He wasn't supposed to race that day. Brad was scheduled." She floated the paper across the bed to Drew. "He came down with the stomach flu, or more likely a hangover."

"There's our link." Drew smiled. "He either wants her, or in some perverted fashion he's trying to protect her." She pushed the papers to the side and propped herself up against the headboard. "Either way, the man's dangerous. Sam needs to stay away from him."

"Ray wouldn't hurt her."

"He may when he realizes she's not interested."

Jade fell back against the headboard and let out a heavy breath. "What about tomorrow's race?" Her sobering stare pierced Drew, and she knew in an instant what Jade was thinking.

"That means I'm next." She thought about how many engine parts and electrical components Ray could tamper with.

"The car is locked up in the garage, but Ray has a key. He's very good, Drew. He could do just about anything to that car tonight, and Sam would never find it before the race."

"I'll be ready for it."

"You can't seriously be thinking about driving that car tomorrow."

"I'm not just thinking about it. I *will* drive that car tomorrow."

"Are you crazy?"

"Don't worry. I can handle it." Drew got up and opened the door. "I'll walk you back."

❖

Drew spent the few remaining hours until sunrise staring at the ceiling, thinking of the warmth of Sam's arms clamped around her.

Emotions had been running high last night, and she hadn't gotten much sleep thinking about Sam's confession and her reasons for sending the Tweet. They were irrational but understandable. Who was Drew to talk? She'd deceived Sam too. On the way back to her room, she'd almost knocked on her door, but she couldn't have any contact with Sam until this race was over. It was too risky. Drew needed to stay as far away from her as possible.

She'd just started to get up when the door flew open, and there stood Sam in the doorway. Drew's misguided lover looked uncharacteristically weak and vulnerable.

"Sam, I can't do this today."

"You have to know I would *never* do anything to hurt you."

"I know that."

She sat on the bare mattress next to Drew. "I was so afraid I'd lost you." She pressed her mouth to Drew's, who felt the difference in her kiss. Sam's usually soft, delicate mouth had turned urgently insistent.

This can't happen. Breaking away, Drew let out a short breath and shook her head. "I should put you in jail for what you did."

"No need. I've talked to the commissioners and told them I was the one who sent the tweets." She blew out a breath and dropped her gaze to her hands. "You're clear, but the decision on me is up in the air." She stared up at Drew. "I never meant to hurt you."

Sam meant what she'd said. Drew saw it in her pleading eyes. But she had to keep her distance today. "Have you seen Ray this morning?"

"I just left him. He brought me coffee this morning. He wanted to confirm our date for drinks tonight."

Drew's nerves tightened. "Did you?"

"No. I told him I can't." She stared, her emerald-green eyes pooling with tears. "I'm in love with someone else."

Thumped in the heart again. Drew wanted to take her in her arms and never let go, but no matter how much she said they, Drew didn't know if they were true.

Drew got up and jerked the door open. "Go back and tell him you changed your mind."

"No. Whether you like it or not, Drew, I'm not giving up on us." Sam kicked the door out of her hand, sending it slamming closed.

"Damn it, Sam. You need to stay away from the track today." She couldn't tell her any more. She couldn't take a chance on her getting further involved.

"How am I supposed to do that? It's *race day.*"

"Just go away." Drew reached for her wallet and fumbled through it. "Here. Take my credit card." She took Sam's hand and pressed her fingers closed around the card. "Go back to the Goose Creek Inn."

"No." Sam threw the card at her. "I'm not going anywhere without you."

"I'll meet you later. I promise. Just stay out of that garage today."

Sam's shoulders sank as she turned and pressed her head to the door. "You think I rigged the car again."

"I don't know what to think."

Sam spun around and threw herself against Drew with such force the air in her lungs whooshed out. "Then don't race."

"I have to race. It's my job."

"I thought your job was to find a killer." Sam pushed her away. Putting up no resistance, Drew dropped onto the bed.

"Driving that car is part of it."

"I'll show you I didn't do it. I'll drive." Sam slid onto the bed next to Drew and rested her head on her shoulder.

"You're not going anywhere near that car." Drew shot up, and Sam squealed in pain as her jaw popped against Drew's shoulder blade. Drew turned, wanting to comfort her, but she didn't dare.

"Drew, I'm begging you. Please don't do this."

"This obsession you have with racing has gone too far, Sam." Drew left her on the bed. Keeping her mood distant was the hardest thing she'd ever had to do.

"You mean my obsession with you."

"You lost me when you sent those tweets."

"I know that was wrong. But—"

"But what? A killer's still on the loose. We don't know who we're dealing with." Drew went to the window and pulled one of the curtains back. "For all we know he could have been watching us last night."

She hopped off the bed, snatched the other curtain open, and stared out. "You know no one else was here last night. She glanced at the wad of sheets in the corner. "It was just you and me."

"I don't know anything right now." Drew sank into the chair and pulled on one boot, then the other. She yanked at the laces, and one of them snapped.

Sam dropped to her knees and gazed at Drew with clouded eyes. "You're not going to let me get in that car, are you?"

"Not on your life."

"Then let's get out of here. You and me, right now." Sam took Drew's hand and pulled her to the door.

A rush of heat filled Drew. Sam didn't have the slightest desire to drive. Racing wasn't the most important thing in her life anymore.

Drew pulled her around to face her, and Sam shuddered out a weeping gasp. Drew saw the fear in her eyes, torment she hadn't understood until now, deep-down desperation that forced her to do things she would've never done before. "You know I can't do that." Drew pulled her close and held her tight.

"We can leave here and never come back."

"This man has to be stopped, or he'll keep killing people."

"Let someone else do it. Please." Sam pressed her lips urgently to Drew's, and they trembled. "Drew, please come with me."

She didn't want to race any more than Sam wanted her to. But if she didn't get this guy, Ray's obsession would escalate, and Sam would be in more danger.

Sam took her face in her hands. "I love you."

"Don't waste your breath." She couldn't look at her "We had a good time, and now it's over." She pried her arms from her waist. "You lied to me, Sam. I can't trust you."

"And you lied to me." Her temper flared.

"I did, Sam. It was all a lie." It wasn't true, and it took everything she had to say it. The anger in Sam's eyes turned to hurt.

"I never lied about my feelings for you." Sam's voice shook with a level of anguish Drew hadn't expected.

"At this point, I don't know what to believe." She jutted her fingers through her hair. "But I have to race."

Sam's hands hit her chest hard, and she shoved Drew away. "Then you'll have to do it without me in the pit."

"Good. I don't want you anywhere near that track."

"I won't stand by and watch you die." She gave her a hard-cold look before her stare faltered. "I can't."

"I'm not going to die." Whether she would be alive at the end of the race was a toss-up, and they both knew it. In a moment of weakness, Drew moved toward her, but Sam rushed by her to the door.

"I've had it. You do what you have to, but I'm not going to stick around and watch."

She might never see Sam again, but at least she would be safe.

Drew checked her watch. One hour until race time. She'd wandered around the garage area for hours but hadn't been able to find Sam since she'd left her room this morning. She couldn't blame her for taking off and was glad she had. She'd been hurt when she'd rebuffed her. Drew could see it clearly in her eyes. In truth, she was more than tempted to do exactly as Sam said, to leave right then and never go back. But her experience told her something was going on here besides Ray's attraction to Sam, and nothing was more important to Drew than Sam's safety.

"Hey," she shouted, spotting Jade at the window of the snack shack. "You got a minute?"

"Sure." Glancing back over her shoulder, Jade smiled at Tommy and held up a finger. He nodded before picking up a section of the morning paper.

Drew checked her watch again. Nine o'clock, two hours 'til race time.

"Walk with me. I have to suit up."

"Give me a sec." She grabbed a cup of coffee and breakfast burritos from just inside the window and took them to Tommy. Jade said something to him, and he waved.

"What's up?"

"Sam came by my room this morning."

Jade raised her eyebrows. "Did you tell her?"

"No, but I think Ray's our guy for sure now," she said, barreling right into the case, hoping to waylay her curiosity.

"She had more information?"

"He showed up at her room this morning with coffee." She opened the bus door and motioned Jade in front of her.

"Are you sure it's not just a big-brother thing?"

"It's bad enough that he asked her out. Now he wants to make it exclusive."

"Oooh." She didn't say anything further. Drew could see the wheels turning in her head.

Pulling the door closed behind them, Drew thought she heard a noise inside. "Is Ray in the garage?"

"Uh-huh."

"You sure?" Drew pulled open the first two lockers. "You're getting a little paranoid, aren't you? Ray couldn't fit into one of those lockers if you cut him in half."

"Yeah. I guess maybe I am." She took her racing suit out of the locker and headed for the back of the bus. "Have you seen Sam?"

"She didn't come with you?"

She sank onto the couch. "She's not coming today."

Shifting her weight to one leg, Jade blew out a short breath and shook her head. "How'd you manage that?"

"I told her she's still a suspect."

"How'd she take it?"

"She said she'd drive." She shook her head. "The woman is willing to die just to prove something to me."

"She's remarkable."

"Yep." She could tell from Jade's pained expression that she wasn't convinced she'd be okay, either. "I need you to find her and keep her safe. She might do something stupid."

"What about you?"

"I can take care of myself. Now, if you don't mind, I could use a little time alone."

"Okay." Jade shrugged and headed back down the steps. "I'll be right outside."

She knew what Jade was thinking. Sam was smart to get the hell out of here. If she had any brains at all, she'd have gone with her.

Drew pulled on her fireproof suit and zipped it up. It was heavier than the usual racing suit because she'd had it lined with an extra Kevlar vest. It would stop any bullet shot at her, but she didn't know how much good it would do if the car blew up.

When she stepped off the bus, Jade was right there, watching her back. Drew had initially had major reservations about working with the sister of her deceased wife, but she had no questions now, and she held no grudges.

"Car's ready. Are you?"

"Ready as I'll ever be."

"I'm gonna take another look around for Sam." She stopped before entering the garage. "Just to make sure she left. I'll see you down at the track."

Jade headed up the stairs to the bus. "I'll be there as soon as I get my gear on."

Sitting in the driver's seat of the bus, Sam hunched over the large steering wheel. It wasn't easy, but she'd managed to evade Drew all morning. She'd even hid in one of the empty lockers when she'd come in to suit up. After listening to her, Sam knew what she'd said earlier wasn't true. She wanted to show herself, to beg her, once again, not to race. But Drew wouldn't comply.

After leaving her room this morning, she'd gone straight to the garage and checked every connection, every gasket, and every wire on the engine, anything she could think of that might be tampered with. She still couldn't wrap her mind around the fact that Drew thought she might be sabotaging the cars. She didn't find anything, but that didn't mean there wasn't something wrong. She'd failed to find the problems causing the previous crashes.

She heard the back door click open and shrank farther down into the high-back seat.

"You're not very good at this, you know."

Sam raised her chin and glanced back to find Jade peering over the seat at her.

"Yeah. Well, I don't want to be good at it. I don't like it."

"She'll be all right, Sam."

"You don't know that." Sam shot up and pushed by her to the back of the bus.

"I know she's good at what she does."

"So am I. People still got hurt." Stripping down, she plucked her long underwear out of the locker and pulled it on. "I'll be damned if I'm going to stand around and watch another person die because of me."

After tugging her racing suit on, Sam took her helmet from the top shelf and slammed the locker shut. She wasn't thinking straight, and Jade had to know she was going to do something stupid.

"Sam, I can't let you go down there."

"Try and stop me."

Jade pushed her up against the door. "Come on, Sam. I don't want to hurt you."

"I don't want to hurt you either." Sam flung her helmet up, crashing it into the side of Jade's head. "But that should take care of you for a while." Sam lugged her to the back of the bus, laying her out on one of the bunks.

Pulling the door closed, she spotted Drew in the garage and headed in after her. *One down, one to go.*

CHAPTER THIRTY-TWO

Jade slipped off the bus and held her position at the garage entrance. Rubbing her head, she didn't know how she could be so inept, letting Sam get the jump on her.

"Have you seen Sam?" she asked, stopping Ray as he came out.

"She's at the track." His gaze jumped to the side of her face that was radiating with pain. "What happened to you?"

"She knocked me out. I think she's planning to race today."

"She can't do that." Panic filled his eyes.

"You know what she can't do, Ray? She can't watch that car roll out and wonder if it's going to come back in one piece." She watched him pace the entrance. "It's not gonna come back today, is it, Ray?" She brushed by him and went into the garage. "If it doesn't come back today, neither will she. Where's the car?"

"The crew already took it down. I gotta stop her."

"What'd you do to it?"

"I never meant for anyone to get hurt." He sounded anxious, almost frantic. "Now she's gonna fuck it all up."

Drew took the last screw out of the doorknob and pulled it loose. The metal bar wedged under it clanked to the ground, and she pushed the door to the supply room open. She should've known better when Sam coaxed her inside, but when it came to her, Drew's instincts were useless. Sam wanted her out of the race, and now she was. She would never make it to the track in time.

Hearing voices, she stayed put and watched Jade take a few steps back. Something wasn't right. She could see she was in defensive mode. Then she spotted Ray. Sneaking around the inside perimeter of the garage, Drew hid behind the string of tool chests and waited for Ray to admit something.

"I've done everything to get them off my back, but they never stop. They keep adding interest."

"The debt never gets any smaller, Ray. That's the way it works. They're gonna keep you on that leash as long as you keep helping them. We can make that stop if you help us."

Ray took a few steps away and then whirled around, slapping Jade across the face with the back of his hand. "You have no idea what you're asking. They'll kill Jenna."

Jade fell back against the number forty-four race car, holding her cheek with her hand. Drew slipped the gun from her ankle holster and started out after him. "No!" Jade shouted, her gaze flashing from Ray to Drew and back again. "Ray, you don't want it to end like this. Let me help you. Then you can get your life back with Jenna." Her voice settled back into a soft, soothing tone.

"Jenna's gone."

"Ray." She tried to make eye contact with him. "You didn't hurt her. Did you?"

"Hurt *her*? No. I would never hurt her." He moved closer, but Jade didn't budge. "She left when she found out about the money I owed."

Drew scooted around the line of tool chests to get a glimpse of Ray. Sweat filled her palms, and she recalled the night she was shot. *Not now!* She clamped her eyes shut, purging the vision from her mind.

While Jade coaxed information out of Ray, Drew propped herself against the tool chests to get her bearings back. They needed a confession, and Jade was playing it perfectly.

"She's already got someone else."

"Ray, I had no idea."

"I was just trying to get out of this mess." His voice cracked, rising in desperation. "Then she might come back." He shrugged, reaching for her. She backed away. "Please don't be afraid of me." He touched Jade's swelling cheek. "I'm sorry about that. I didn't want to hurt you."

She rubbed her forehead nervously. "I'm not afraid, Ray, I—I just don't know what you want from me."

"I want you to forget this ever happened. Then I can get the hell out of here."

"What about Sam? She's driving the car you've sabotaged." This went much deeper than Jade thought. He was living in a fantasy world. She thought about what Drew had said. He wasn't stable and could turn against her at any moment.

"Ray, you can't let Sam drive the car. You have to pull it."

"I have to let her drive. I need her to lose to pay off my debt."

Where the hell are you, Drew? Jade glanced around the garage, then at the door. They were all alone, just the three of them. Everyone else was at the track. Her pulse jumped, and she took in a deep breath. She had to keep it together.

She saw Drew jump back, shifting behind another chest.

"I know that, Ray. But can't we find another way to fix this without hurting Sam?" Fear filling every part of her, she moved forward and touched him on the shoulder. "You know Sam will do whatever she can to help you." She hesitated, waiting for some kind of reaction, and she got it. His eyes skittered back and forth across the garage. "If you did something to the car, we have to stop her." She clasped his hand. "Come on. Let's get down to the track." He turned quickly, and she commanded herself to remain still. "Just fix the car, and I won't tell Paddy what you did." She forced a smile. "I promise."

"You stay here. I'll go to the track."

"Ray," she said softly, regaining eye contact. She put her hand to his cheek and stroked the weather-hardened skin with her thumb. "Please tell me what you did."

He brushed her hand away. "All I ever wanted was for Jenna to love me." His voice broke.

"I know, Ray, and I'm sure she does." She smiled again.

"The tires." He swiped his hand across his face. "I filled them with compressed air instead of nitrogen. They'll start to wobble when she reaches about a hundred."

"She'll hit that after the first turn." She headed for the door. "We have to stop her."

Ray took Jade by the arm and swung her back around. "I can't let you go. You'll spoil everything. I have to save her."

Drew sprang from behind the tool chest. "Hands where I can see them, Ray."

"Drew, we have to get to the track."

Seeming honestly confused, Ray raised his hands. "Is this some kind of joke? Where'd you get that gun?"

"It's no joke. State Police. You're under arrest."

"Police?" He dropped his hands and turned to Jade. "Everything you just said. That was all bullshit?"

She shook her head. "No, it's not bullshit, Ray. Sam doesn't want anyone else to get hurt."

"Do what I said." Drew's voice was deep and stern.

Ray closed in on Jade quickly, swinging her around in front of him.

"Is this really what you want, Ray?" She didn't struggle. "You want to hurt Sam?"

"No. I'd never hurt Sam."

"Then let's go to the track."

Jade felt him twist his head. He was looking for something on the bench. He moved backward, slowly taking her with him. Turning his head toward Drew, he let his hand search the surface. When he located the cordless drill, he pulled it from its base and pressed it to Jade's neck.

The cool steel of the drill bit scraped against her skin, and she fought to contain the fear that filled her.

"Don't do it, Ray." Drew took a few steps forward.

"Stay away," he shouted, pointing the drill up in the air and pulling the trigger.

Jade heard the motor whirr. Adrenaline filled her. Wrapping her hands around his arm, she raised her feet, letting her weight drop. His hand clamped like a vise to her shoulder, but he couldn't hold her dead weight with one arm, and she fell to the floor.

Drew fired, one—two—three shots into him, sending him flying back against the bench before slumping into a heap. His eyes opened wide, then fluttered closed.

Drew felt his neck for a pulse and shook her head.

The loudspeaker from the track echoed into the garage. Drew shot up, slid into the midnight-blue number forty-four race car, and squealed out of the garage.

Racing to the pit, she shouted to Paddy, but he couldn't hear her. Drew jumped the wall and ran full force into him.

"It's the tires. Ray filled them with air. They're gonna blow."

"Who in the hell is driving my car?" Paddy's face twisted in confusion.

"Sam." Panic filled her voice. "The tires are filled with compressed air. Once they heat up, they'll become unstable."

Seeing that Paddy still wasn't getting what she'd said, Drew pulled the headset from his ears.

"Sam, you need to pit. The tires are faulty." There was no response. "Sam, can you hear me? Damn it!" She pulled the headset off and threw it to the ground before jumping across the partition into the next pit area. "I need your headset," she said, pulling it off another person's head. Flipping the dial to the team's channel, she shouted into the microphone. "Sam, can you hear me?" Still no response. *Fuck!* She pulled it off and tossed it back. "He jammed the signal."

Hoisting herself back into the race car, Drew threw the car into gear and rammed through the pit wall. She could see the wrath in Paddy's face as she rolled onto the track. She'd blown the race for them now. They'd be disqualified, and she would face stiff sanctions. But none of that mattered anymore. She punched the pedal, and the number forty-four car soared into the lane.

Coming around the first turn, Sam hit the straight-away at 107. As she flew around the track toward turn number two, the car began to shake. She lightened up on the gas, and it shook more. A tire blew, and Sam couldn't hold it. Bracing for impact, she threw the car into neutral. It bounced off the wall, steam billowing from under the hood—the radiator was gone. She fought for control as it spun out, hitting over and over again.

Pieces of the car ripped from the frame surrounding her. The only thoughts flashing through her mind were of Drew. She didn't want to die. Not now. Not ever. She wanted to live with Drew for the rest of her days. If she survived this, she swore she would never put herself in this kind of danger again.

As the car came to a complete stop, Sam knew there was no hope. She'd been here before. The engine popped and smoldered, threatening to ignite at any moment, the fire trucks nowhere in sight. With heat surrounding her, Sam pulled back the window safety net and tried to move. The steering wheel had her pinned.

Then she heard Drew's voice. "Sam, get out!"

The engine popped. "Get away. It's gonna blow."

Drew knew now why Sam had risked running into a raging inferno to save her brother. Drew would rather die than leave her in that car to burn.

"I'm not leaving you."

"The steering wheel." She gripped the top, trying to move it. "I can't get it loose."

"Spread your legs and suck in your gut."

She popped the lever, and the wheel slid back. "More." She pushed the wheel farther, and Sam screamed.

"Shift as far to the right as you can." Drew tugged harder. "Just a little more." After she gave it one hard tug, the wheel popped off. Sam was finally free.

Drew crawled halfway in the window and tugged her up and out. The car exploded with such force they flew across the track like pieces of the fiberglass hull, thrown to the ground one on top of the other.

"Sam, are you all right?" Drew rolled her to his side, but her eyes didn't open.

"Sam?" She cradled her head in her hands. "Talk to me, baby."

"Do you believe me now?" Her voice was low and raspy.

Drew chuckled. "I guess I have to." She covered her face with little kisses.

"You don't have to."

"I do if I want to be part of your life."

"But you said…"

"I know what I said. Fuck that. It was the job talking."

"A job you're gonna keep."

"Not if there's still a slot open on this race team."

Using her as leverage, Sam put a hand on Drew's chest, and she winced. "If you do that, you're gonna have to suffer with my nasty moods and angry disposition." Her lips jerked up into a one-sided smile. "You won't always be on my good side."

"Nor you, on mine." Drew let her smile fade. "Sam, when I saw you trapped in that car…"

"I know." Sam pressed her mouth to hers, strangling her words. "From now on you drive, and I'll fix your gears."

"That sounds like one hell of a good deal to me."

The sirens from the fire truck whined, coming closer, but they barely heard them.

EPILOGUE

Sam caught sight of Drew stretched out on the chaise lounge, half dozing as she watched Sam swim back and forth in the pool. It had become a daily ritual for Drew to lie in sun while its heat warmed her aching bones. The combination of the blast plus the dead weight of Sam's body had taken her to the ground so hard that two of her ribs had been broken, along with a few minor cuts and bruises. Sam considered her extremely lucky.

She'd spent a few long days in the hospital, and when she'd confessed to Sam about her PTSD from the night she'd been shot, she'd suggested Drew seek help with hypnosis. She seemed to have begun to get past the paralyzing moments that cursed her. Sam had been annoyed at first, after Drew was released from the hospital and had directed her to the beautiful gated house that she'd taken her to after their night of mud racing. Apparently, it was one last secret she'd saved to surprise her. This was Drew's home, and Sam had been overwhelmed that she'd wanted to share it with her. Moving from hotel to hotel was no way to live, so having a place to come home to was wonderful. As Sam floated in the pool's crystal-blue water, she realized she was getting used to the idea of living here.

Swimming to the side of the pool, she slung her arms up onto the concrete. Drew was asleep again. She thought about the last time she'd been here and felt a little stupid for not realizing the house was hers. It had been pretty clear she knew the place inside and out.

After pulling herself out of the pool, she dried off and stood in front of Drew, blocking the afternoon sun. "Are you hungry?" she asked, watching her eyes flutter open. "I can fix you something."

"How about a nice, juicy T-bone?"

"How about egg salad?" She twisted her hair and flicked the excess water at her.

Drew winced and shifted in the lounger. "I'm fine."

"Are the bandages too tight? I can adjust them."

"I said, I'm fine," she snapped.

"Then what's wrong with you?"

Her brows drew together into a pained expression. "You're what's wrong. You come out of that pool dressed in that skimpy bikini, and I can't do a thing about it."

"Poor baby." She put her hand on her hip and gave Drew a sultry smile. "If you can make it to the cabana, I bet *I* can do something about it."

Drew's gaze darted from Sam to the cabana, measuring the distance. "Someday we're going to laugh when we tell our children about this." She slid out of the lounge chair slowly. "One boy," she said, standing up.

"And one tomboy." Sam smiled, taking her hand and leading her inside.

The End

About the Author

Dena Blake grew up in a small town just north of San Francisco where she learned to play softball, ride motorcycles, and grow vegetables. She eventually moved with her family to the Southwest, where she began creating vivid characters in her mind and bringing them to life on paper.

Dena currently lives in the Southwest with her partner and is constantly amazed at what she learns from her two children. She's a would-be chef, tech nerd, and occasional auto mechanic who has a weakness for dark chocolate and a good cup of coffee.

Books Available from Bold Strokes Books

A Fighting Chance by T. L. Hayes. Will Lou be able to come to terms with her past to give love a fighting chance? (978-1-163555-257-7)

Chosen by Brey Willows. When the choice is adapt or die, can love save us all? (978-1-163555-110-5)

Death Checks In by David S. Pederson. Despite Heath's promises to Alan to not get involved, Heath can't resist investigating a shopkeeper's murder in Chicago, which dashes their plans for a romantic weekend getaway. (978-1-163555-329-1)

Gnarled Hollow by Charlotte Greene. After they are invited to study a secluded nineteenth-century estate, a former English professor and a group of historians discover that they will have to fight against the unknown if they have any hope of staying alive. (978-1-163555-235-5)

Jacob's Grace by C.P. Rowlands. Captain Tag Becket wants to keep her head down and her past behind her, but her feelings for AJ's second-in-command, Grace Fields, makes keeping secrets next to impossible. (978-1-163555-187-7)

On the Fly by PJ Trebelhorn. Hockey player Courtney Abbott is content with her solitary life until visiting concert violinist Lana Caruso makes her second-guess everything she always thought she wanted. (978-1-163555-255-3)

Passionate Rivals by Radclyffe. Professional rivalry and long-simmering passions create a combustible combination when Emmett McCabe and Sydney Stevens are forced to work together, especially when past attractions won't stay buried. (978-1-163555-231-7)

Proxima Five by Missouri Vaun. When geologist Leah Warren crash-lands on a preindustrial planet and is claimed by its tyrant, Tiago, will clan warrior Keegan's love for Leah give her the strength to defeat him? (978-1-163555-122-8)

Racing Hearts by Dena Blake. When you cross a hot-tempered race car mechanic with a reckless cop, the result can only be spontaneous combustion. (978-1-163555-251-5)

Shadowboxer by Jessica L. Webb. Jordan McAddie is prepared to keep her street kids safe from a dangerous underground protest group, but she isn't prepared for her first love to walk back into her life. (978-1-163555-267-6)

The Tattered Lands by Barbara Ann Wright. As Vandra and Lilani strive to make peace, they slowly fall in love. With mistrust and murder surrounding them, only their faith in each other can keep their plan to save the world from falling apart. (978-1-163555-108-2)

Captive by Donna K. Ford. To escape a human trafficking ring, Greyson Cooper and Olivia Danner become players in a game of deceit and violence. Will their love stand a chance? (978-1-63555-215-7)

Crossing the Line by CF Frizzell. The Mob discovers a nemesis within its ranks, and in the ultimate retaliation, draws Stick McLaughlin from anonymity by threatening everything she holds dear. (978-1-63555-161-7)

Love's Verdict by Carsen Taite. Attorneys Landon Holt and Carly Pachett want the exact same thing: the only open partnership spot at their prestigious criminal defense firm. But will they compromise their careers for love? (978-1-63555-042-9)

Precipice of Doubt by Mardi Alexander & Laurie Eichler. Can Cole Jameson resist her attraction to her boss, veterinarian Jodi Bowman, or will she risk a workplace romance and her heart? (978-1-63555-128-0)

Savage Horizons by CJ Birch. Captain Jordan Kellow's feelings for Lt. Ali Ash have her past and future colliding, setting in motion a series of events that strands her crew in an unknown galaxy thousands of light years from home. (978-1-63555-250-8)

Secrets of the Last Castle by A. Rose Mathieu. When Elizabeth Campbell represents a young man accused of murdering an elderly woman, her investigation leads to an abandoned plantation that reveals many dark Southern secrets. (978-1-63555-240-9)

Take Your Time by VK Powell. A neurotic parrot brings police officer Grace Booker and temporary veterinarian Dr. Dani Wingate together in the tiny town of Pine Cone, but their unexpected attraction keeps the sparks flying. (978-1-63555-130-3)

The Last Seduction by Ronica Black. When you allow true love to elude you once and you desperately regret it, are you brave enough to grab it when it comes around again? (978-1-63555-211-9)

The Shape of You by Georgia Beers. Rebecca McCall doesn't play it safe, but when sexy Spencer Thompson joins her workout class, their non-stop sparring forces her to face her ultimate challenge—a chance at love. (978-1-63555-217-1)

Exposed by MJ Williamz. The closet is no place to live if you want to find true love. (978-1-62639-989-1)

Force of Fire: Toujours a Vous by Ali Vali. Immortals Kendal and Piper welcome their new child and celebrate the defeat of an old enemy, but another ancient evil is about to awaken deep in the jungles of Costa Rica. (978-1-63555-047-4)

Holding Their Place by Kelly A. Wacker. Together Dr. Helen Connery and ambulance driver Julia March, discover that goodness, love, and passion can be found in the most unlikely and even dangerous places during WWI. (978-1-63555-338-3)

Landing Zone by Erin Dutton. Can a career veteran finally discover a love stronger than even her pride? (978-1-63555-199-0)

Love at Last Call by M. Ullrich. Is balancing business, friendship, and love more than any willing woman can handle? (978-1-63555-197-6)

Pleasure Cruise by Yolanda Wallace. Spencer Collins and Amy Donovan have few things in common, but a Caribbean cruise offers both women an unexpected chance to face one of their greatest fears: falling in love. (978-1-63555-219-5)

Running Off Radar by MB Austin. Maji's plans to win Rose back are interrupted when work intrudes and duty calls her to help a SEAL team stop a Russian mobster from harvesting gold from the bottom of Sitka Sound. (978-1-63555-152-5)

Shadow of the Phoenix by Rebecca Harwell. In the final battle for the fate of Storm's Quarry, even Nadya's and Shay's powers may not be enough. (978-1-63555-181-5)

Take a Chance by D. Jackson Leigh. There's hardly a woman within fifty miles of Pine Cone that veterinarian Trip Beaumont can't charm, except for the irritating new cop, Jamie Grant, who keeps leaving parking tickets on her truck. (978-1-63555-118-1)

The Outcasts by Alexa Black. Spacebus driver Sue Jones is running from her past. When she crash-lands on a faraway world, the Outcast Kara might be her chance for redemption. (978-1-63555-242-3)

Alias by Cari Hunter. A car crash leaves a woman with no memory and no identity. Together with Detective Bronwen Pryce, she fights to uncover a truth that might just kill them both. (978-1-63555-221-8)

Death in Time by Robyn Nyx. Working in the past is hell on your future. (978-1-63555-053-5)

Hers to Protect by Nicole Disney. High school sweethearts Kaia and Adrienne will have to see past their differences and survive the vengeance of a brutal gang if they want to be together. (978-1-63555-229-4)

Of Echoes Born by 'Nathan Burgoine. A collection of queer fantasy short stories set in Canada from Lambda Literary Award finalist 'Nathan Burgoine. (978-1-63555-096-2)

Perfect Little Worlds by Clifford Mae Henderson. Lucy can't hold the secret any longer. Twenty-six years ago, her sister did the unthinkable. (978-1-63555-164-8)

Room Service by Fiona Riley. Interior designer Olivia likes stability, but when work brings footloose Savannah into her world and into a new city every month, Olivia must decide if what makes her comfortable is what makes her happy. (978-1-63555-120-4)

Sparks Like Ours by Melissa Brayden. Professional surfers Gia Malone and Elle Britton can't deny their chemistry on and off the beach. But only one can win... (978-1-63555-016-0)

Take My Hand by Missouri Vaun. River Hemsworth arrives in Georgia intent on escaping quickly, but when she crashes her Mercedes into the Clip 'n Curl, sexy Clay Cahill ends up rescuing more than her car. (978-1-63555-104-4)

The Last Time I Saw Her by Kathleen Knowles. Lane Hudson only has twelve days to win back Alison's heart. That is if she can gather the courage to try. (978-1-63555-067-2)

Wayworn Lovers by Gun Brooke. Will agoraphobic composer Giselle Bonnaire and Tierney Edwards, a wandering soul who can't remain in one place for long, trust in the passionate love destiny hands them? (978-1-62639-995-2)

Breakthrough by Kris Bryant. Falling for a sexy ranger is one thing, but is the possibility of love worth giving up the career Kennedy Wells has always dreamed of? (978-1-63555-179-2)

Certain Requirements by Elinor Zimmerman. Phoenix has always kept her love of kinky submission strictly behind the bedroom door and inside the bounds of romantic relationships, until she meets Kris Andersen. (978-1-63555-195-2)

Dark Euphoria by Ronica Black. When a high-profile case drops in Detective Maria Diaz's lap, she forges ahead only to discover this case, and her main suspect, aren't like any other. (978-1-63555-141-9)

Fore Play by Julie Cannon. Executive Leigh Marshall falls hard for Peyton Broader, her golf pro…and an ex-con. Will she risk sabotaging her career for love? (978-1-63555-102-0)

Love Came Calling by CA Popovich. Can a romantic looking for a long-term, committed relationship and a jaded cynic too busy for love conquer life's struggles and find their way to what matters most? (978-1-63555-205-8)

Outside the Law by Carsen Taite. Former sweethearts Tanner Cohen and Sydney Braswell must work together on a federal task force to see justice served, but will they choose to embrace their second chance at love? (978-1-63555-039-9)

The Princess Deception by Nell Stark. When journalist Missy Duke realizes Prince Sebastian is really his twin sister Viola in disguise, she plays along, but when sparks flare between them, will the double deception doom their fairy-tale romance? (978-1-62639-979-2)

The Smell of Rain by Cameron MacElvee. Reyha Arslan, a wise and elegant woman with a tragic past, shows Chrys that there's still beauty to embrace and reason to hope despite the world's cruelty. (978-1-63555-166-2)

The Talebearer by Sheri Lewis Wohl. Liz's visions show her the faces of the lost and the killers who took their lives. As one by one, the murdered are found, a stranger works to stop Liz before the serial killer is brought to justice. (978-1-635550-126-6)

White Wings Weeping by Lesley Davis. The world is full of discord and hatred, but how much of it is just human nature when an evil with sinister intent is invading people's hearts? (978-1-63555-191-4)